EVIL KNOWS NO BOUNDS

EVIL KNOWS NO BOUNDS

HARRY GILLER

T

Troubador Publishing Ltd
Unit E2 Airfield Business Park,
Harrison Road, Market Harborough,
Leicestershire LE16 7UL
Tel: 0116 279 2299
Email: books@troubador.co.uk
Web: www.troubador.co.uk

ISBN 978 1 80514 474 8

British Library Cataloguing in Publication Data.
A catalogue record for this book is available from the British Library.

Printed and bound by CPI Group (UK) Ltd, Croydon, CR0 4YY
Typeset in 11pt Minion Pro by Troubador Publishing Ltd, Leicester, UK

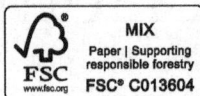

This book is dedicated to my wife, Linda, without whose love, support and never-ending patience it would never have been completed.

ACKNOWLEDGEMENTS

Thanks for their invaluable technical help to my former colleagues:

Tony Dickinson
John Dunn
Dave Holmes
Richard Smith
Stephen Watson

ONE

The gates of Leeds's Armley Prison closed behind him with a loud clang, but this time Miles Kingston was overjoyed that, for the first time in three years, he was on the outside of those forbidding walls. It was more than enough time for anyone to put up with in that stinking place. He didn't even care that it was a grey day and that a light drizzle was falling. Maybe it would wash away the clinging stench, from all those tightly packed unwashed bodies, the overused and rarely cleaned toilets, not to mention the seemingly never-ending smell of boiling cabbage. Probably not, he thought, convinced that whilst it may wash some of the smell from his clothing, it would take more than a little rain to totally eradicate those all-pervading odours entirely from his consciousness.

Miles had a lot to do and some important people to see if he was going to fulfil the promise he made to his cellmate, the man who had looked after him so well for the past eighteen months. Without that help, he may not have survived, especially the attentions of the cellblock hard men who had seen him as a potential 'boyfriend'.

First thing was to get home to his flat for the very long hot shower and clean clothes he had dreamt of for so long. It was amazing how prison, by denying those privileges, could make even the most basic pleasures seem like untold luxury. His mother had promised to look after the flat for him and, on her infrequent visits, she assured him it was exactly as he had left it. He would soon know.

Then his priorities were to get some of his hidden cash, quickly followed by a drink, some decent food and finally a woman. None of it seemed unreasonable to him or anything less than he deserved after paying his debt to society. He had to smile to himself at the thought that the powers that be might actually think he was a reformed character. No chance. Crime was his full-time occupation, and he intended to get back to it as soon as possible. With the help of his jailhouse friend, he had a big score planned, the biggest of his criminal career and one that would set him up for life, or at least for a very long time. In common with all criminals, he believed the plan they had concocted was pretty foolproof, but what really appealed to them was the thought that they were going to set someone else up to take the blame, gaining revenge on the mug whilst deflecting attention from themselves. It was a win-win. That could all wait for now, though; he had other priorities for today.

It wasn't the first time Miles Kingston had been locked up in his forty-three years, but it was his longest sentence yet and, without a doubt, the hardest so far. He definitely didn't want to go back anytime soon.

It was undoubtedly the strangest time he had spent in jail. Who could have expected to deal with the COVID-19 worldwide pandemic, causing huge numbers of deaths and serious illness? His incarceration, along with the so strictly applied rules, had largely protected him from the ravages of the disease, but a few inmates had still caught it in there. Some had died.

However, May 2022 was a good time to be released, just as things were returning to some sort of normal. Many businesses had reopened, including entertainment venues, which suited him down to the ground. Without them, the master plan would have failed before it started, not to mention that he had a three-year thirst to quench.

He was not surprised there wasn't anyone at the gate to meet him, but he didn't care. As the jail was one of those old Victorian edifices built within city limits, he found no trouble getting a taxi home. He wasn't sure that the pathetic few quid he got for his Prison Discharge Grant was intended for such use, but it worked for him. He didn't see himself as a public transport sort of person.

God, it was good to be out, back in his hometown.

TWO

The sunlight came through the open curtains as Miles smoked his first cigarette of the day. When he looked at the woman next to him in bed, he realised several things. Firstly, the bright morning light didn't really do her any favours, making it clear that she was older than he had first thought. She had certainly looked better in the dimly lit pub, but to be fair he was quite drunk by the time he picked her up. Lastly, he now knew that she wasn't a real blonde, something that, given his preference for blondes, made him feel a bit cheated. Still, he hadn't had to pay and she'd served her purpose willingly and enthusiastically, despite her initial objections to some of his more unpleasant proclivities. The resultant bruises and bite marks were now clearly visible on her, none of which he thought were that serious or anything to worry about. Okay, she might need some make-up till her cheek settled down a bit, but so what?

Now all he had to do was to get rid of her as soon as possible and get a shower. Getting out of bed, he rubbed his temples whilst searching the bathroom cabinet for painkillers to counteract the hangover headache he could feel coming on. He had a lot of work to do today.

It took him nearly an hour to get shut of her, but by the time she left they were definitely not on the best of terms. It was mainly because he couldn't remember her name, a problem he managed to make much worse by offering her money in thanks for her company. She screamed that she wasn't a tart and didn't deserve to be treated like one, nevertheless accepting £200 for her trouble. They didn't exchange phone numbers.

Once the woman had left, Miles sat down with his breakfast of coffee, painkillers and toast to plan his day. Following the instructions from his former cellmate, his first port of call would be to see a man whom he had highly recommended. Before he did that, he needed to get some money and make sure his best suit still looked okay. Appearances can be important, even in the criminal world. He was certain it would still fit; after all, nobody puts weight on from eating prison food.

As he sat there, he couldn't help but realise how poky and tatty his surroundings were, with stained and peeling wallpaper along with an odour of general decay. His flat was on the first floor of a house conversion, with his mother living in the ground-floor flat. That was why she was able to look after it and probably why it hadn't been broken into whilst he was away. He could tell things had been disturbed and had no doubt the old cow had searched high and low for his hidden cash. She hadn't found it. There again, neither had the useless bloody police.

One advantage to these flat conversions was that they usually retained some of the original building features, particularly large fireplaces. His flat was no exception. Miles made sure his door was locked before lifting the electric fire away from the boarded-up fireplace. Once the boarding was removed, he was able to reach into the chimney and, after removing a loose brick, retrieve his cash. After the money he had taken yesterday, there was only a bit less than three grand left, but it would have to do until he got things sorted. Two thousand pounds went back in the hole, with the remainder in his wallet. He then replaced the brick, boarding and electric fire, making sure there were no giveaway signs of what he had been doing. He was sure his mother wouldn't give up.

Now it was time to shower, shave and get dressed.

THREE

It was about 12.30pm when Miles Kingston found himself studying his appearance in the betting shop window. He looked smart and considered the money he'd just spent on a haircut to be a good investment. He told himself again that it was important to look the part.

It wasn't that warm, but Miles was sweating a little as he walked up and down trying to pluck up the courage to go in. He didn't have an appointment. You didn't make appointments with this man; you just hoped he would grant you an audience.

Whilst psyching himself up, Miles studied the rest of the street. It was only a short street with one side made up of terraced houses and the side he was on consisting of businesses. At one end was a pub and at the other end a very downmarket second-hand car dealer's. In between them there was a takeaway, the betting shop and a pawnbroker's with a sideline in unsecured loans at a murderous rate of interest. Along with those were a café and a tanning salon with some rooms above where a number of women were available to offer personal services to gentlemen.

He didn't know it, but all the businesses were owned by the man Miles was hoping to see. Had he known, he may have realised all of them were predominantly cash enterprises, which, whilst profitable in their own right, allowed their owner to channel money through them from his other illicit activities. Skilful bookkeepers and accountants ensured a steady flow of profits, concealing them from the taxman and police whilst making sure only minimum taxes were paid.

Miles finally controlled his nerves, took a deep breath and went into the premises, seeing one man behind the counter and two customers who were staring avidly at the horse racing on the wall-mounted TV screen. He approached the counter realising that his appearance was somewhat at odds with the premises and its clientele. The clerk never bothered to look up from his newspaper and only did so reluctantly when Miles coughed to attract his attention.

"Hello, I'd like to speak to Mr Harris, please."

The man shrugged and with a bored expression replied, "Don't know nobody called Harris."

Miles was not surprised by his response and, ignoring the clerk's assertion that he didn't know Harris, simply said, "Okay. Well, if he does come in, will you tell him I'm here and that Karl sent me. I'll study form for the next race while I'm waiting."

True to his word, over the next half-hour, Miles patiently looked at the runners and riders, placing two losing bets. At long last, a door at the rear of the room opened and one of the biggest men he had ever seen came into the room. He was about six foot three tall but looked about as wide as he was tall. His face was completely blank, but he carried an air of menace whilst his eyes were constantly on the move checking everyone in the room. He didn't speak, just beckoned Miles over and directed him to the open door.

He found himself in a corridor with an open office door at the end. Before he could move towards the office, Miles was thrown violently against the corridor wall by the huge man, who expertly searched him for weapons. He managed to gasp, "I'm clean," but only received a grunt in response. He was then shoved down the corridor towards the open door.

Once inside, he was confronted by a fairly nondescript man sitting behind a desk who, if anything, looked like a bank manager or accountant. He appeared to be in his fifties with a hard expressionless face, thinning hair and was wearing an obviously expensive three- piece suit. Most striking of all was the cold, penetrating pale blue eyes that seemed to look straight through him. If he didn't know it already, he was now certain that this was a man to be treated with respect, someone to be feared.

"Hello, I'm Frank Harris. Take your clothes off, all of them."

Miles was astounded by the instruction and was slow to move, not understanding why he should do that, when he felt a heavy hand on his shoulder and a gravelly voice in his ear. "Shall I do it, boss?"

Frank Harris shook his head and gestured impatiently for Miles to hurry up. Needing no second telling, he was stood completely naked in front of the desk within seconds. He noticed the big man examining the clothing, including his shoes, before throwing everything on the floor and shaking his head to the man behind the desk.

Harris, still expressionless, like this was an everyday occurrence, merely said, "Okay, get dressed. We just like to make sure no one else is listening to our conversation." His lips twitched in what might almost have been a smile, but if it was, it never got anywhere near his eyes.

Understanding that they were checking to see if he was wearing a wire, Miles said, "I'm not a grass, Mr Harris, and I don't work for the pigs. I hope Karl told you I can be trusted."

"Indeed he did, but in my line of work it pays to be careful. Now sit down and tell me why you're here. How is Karl, by the way?"

"He seems to be doing okay now that he's moved from the maximum security jail to a more normal regime. The plan he's hatched has given him something to keep him occupied. I understand he managed to get a message to you about it."

"Yes, he did, but only a broad outline. I want to hear all the details from you, and what exactly you want from me."

So Miles sat down and spent the next hour explaining, in some detail, the plan he and Karl had worked on over many long hours locked up in a cell together. When it was over, Harris stared at the younger man with a thoughtful expression on his face. He reached into his desk drawer, producing a bottle of whisky and two glasses, pouring both of them a hefty measure of the aromatic amber liquid. He touched glasses with Miles, almost in approval of what he had just heard.

"Okay, it sounds like a decent plan, and there is a reasonable chance that it could work, but it is complicated. As I understand it, not only do you want to make a lot of money, you also want to make sure someone else takes the blame. Am I correct?"

"Yes, Mr Harris, that sums it up perfectly. I want money and Karl wants revenge."

"As I said, it sounds good, but it's got a lot of moving parts, and the failure of any part could cause the whole plan to collapse. I'm sure you've heard that famous quote from Mike Tyson, 'Everyone has a plan until they get punched in the mouth'. Do you know what it means?"

Miles nodded. "Yes, I understand. Outside influences and unexpected events often affect what you're doing even if you don't want them to. However, we've spent a long time planning this, and I believe we've introduced plenty of obstacles for others as well as opportunities for us to halt the operation and walk away if necessary."

"I can see that. I take it you do know how Karl ended up doing forty years?"

"He told me all about it. I know he was unlucky, and we've tried, as much as we can, to guard against it happening this time."

Harris gave his almost-smile and nodded. "So what is it you need from me?"

"Well, sir, the first thing is money to fund the job."

"Don't call me sir. I'm not a screw or a copper. Call me Frank. How much money do you think you are going to need?"

Miles drew in a deep breath before saying, "I reckon fifty grand should do it."

11

"That's a lot of money. Do you understand how it works when I fund something like this? I expect to make a profit, so if I give you that much, I expect a hundred grand back."

"That is a bit more than I was expecting, but I'm sure I can manage it."

"Miles, I think I need to be crystal clear about this. If the job fails and you end up back in prison, I still expect my money back, and, believe me, I can easily get to you there. Even if you end up dead, I want my money. A hundred grand in cash, no discount for failure. Are we clear? So the question is, what security can you give me?"

He was caught a little on the hop, having failed to realise that whilst Frank Harris might operate in the back of a betting shop, he certainly was not prepared to gamble with his own money. Even though he thought he knew a lot about this man, Miles couldn't help a slight shudder as it started to dawn on him just how dangerous his new partner was.

"I understand, Frank. All I've got is a flat that I own outright. It's probably worth that much if it will do as security."

"We'll see. When you leave, give the details to Jimmy there and we'll check it out." He pointed to the thug standing like a statue in the doorway.

"So what else do you need?"

Miles Kingston retrieved a sheet of paper from his inside pocket and placed it on the desk. "I've jotted down a list of things you may be able to help me with."

Harris pushed himself back from the desk, recoiling almost in horror and shaking his head as he refused to touch the paper. "Listen, son. Never, ever put anything in writing, especially for me. Tell me what you want and I'll see what I can do. I'm sure me and Jimmy will be able to remember what you say."

So Miles picked up his paper and went through the items he had listed, as well as the help he was going to need from some other people. Whilst he was well aware of the old truism that nothing remained a secret once more than one person knew it, he had no choice but to get expert help if he was to successfully complete the job. However, everything was compartmentalised and he was sure no one would learn anything close to the full plan. Even if, somehow, they did, he was convinced there would be no loose talk, not when Frank Harris was involved.

When he'd finished, his new partner simply said, "Okay, hopefully, none of that should be too difficult. Give me a phone number and I'll be in touch in a few days. Don't forget to give that information to Jimmy on your way out."

Realising he was being dismissed, Miles simply nodded, before standing and getting out of the office as quickly as he could. Once out on the street, he breathed a huge sigh of relief before heading for the nearest pub, unknowingly putting more money into Frank Harris's pocket.

Whilst standing at the bar sipping his drink, the would-be master criminal wondered what Frank Harris would say if he found out that Miles had not been entirely truthful in his description of the job. He shuddered to think what his reaction might be. He definitely had to have an escape plan ready in case things went wrong, something to take him a long way from the gangster and his certain retribution.

FOUR

Kingston spent a couple of anxious days awaiting a summons from Frank Harris. Having already given the details of his flat to the man Jimmy before leaving the meeting, he had expected things would move more quickly, particularly since he had already had a surprise visit from an estate agent to value the flat. The man had refused to divulge any information to him.

However, Miles had not wasted his time, spending some of it studying the unsuspecting fool lined up to take the fall for the crime he was going to commit. Thanks to the internet, he was able to print off some very up-to-date pictures of him and, amazingly enough, was able to identify the village where he currently lived. Not the exact address, but that should be easy enough to find. He was also able to read the man's book and watch some television interviews he had given. That helped in practising his mannerisms and speech, much helped by the fact that they were both from the north of England. He noted that he was about three years younger than this man Wade, who was in his mid-forties and had no idea what hell was going to come down on him.

After three anxious days, Miles Kingston finally received a call from the thug Jimmy instructing him to see Frank Harris the next morning at 10am, and to bring a bag. He fervently hoped that it meant the job was a go.

Having arrived bang on time, Miles went through the same routine, once again being searched for weapons and then strip-searched for hidden bugs. It appeared that he was never going to be trusted by these men. At least he was allowed to sit down.

Harris did not beat about the bush. "Okay, Miles, this is the score. I am prepared to back you and I think you've got a reasonable chance of pulling the job off so long as you stay focused and are very careful. Most importantly of all, if you do anything, and I do mean anything, that leads back to me, you will have serious problems. Am I clear?"

Realising the job was now a definite go, Miles couldn't help smiling as he said, "All understood, Mr Harris, I mean Frank. Thanks a lot."

"Don't thank me too soon, not until you've heard the conditions. Firstly, the people I'm going to put you in touch with are all valuable to me, and, if you do anything to draw police attention to them, the consequences for you will not be good. Understand?"

"Yes, Frank, I've got it." As he acknowledged the not so subtle warnings from the unsmiling man facing him across the desk, Miles felt an icy finger running down his spine. He had been warned that people who displeased Frank Harris ended up very dead, and he was sure that would be his fate if anything did go wrong with the job. It was up to him to ensure that everything went off without a hitch, or make sure he made rapid use of his escape plan before Harris, or more likely Jimmy, got to him.

Harris nodded thoughtfully. "There is one small problem before we go any further. I'm afraid your flat is not worth enough to provide sufficient security for the loan you want from me. However, my people have looked into things, and it would appear your father left you the full house when he died. Is that correct?"

Miles just nodded, suspecting he knew what was coming next.

"Okay, I am prepared to advance the money on condition that the whole house is put up as security. Do you agree?"

He knew the two flats were worth more than the £100,000 repayment but knew he had little option if he wanted to proceed. What he had planned needed some money up front, and he couldn't imagine he would be successful if he submitted a loan application to a bank for the stated purpose of committing crime. Getting the money from Harris was his only option, but he did have one question before agreeing.

"Should things go wrong and you end up with the house, what happens to my mother?"

Harris gave his sort of smile before replying. "Miles, she'll be out on her ear, I'm not running a charity. She's your mother. If you want her to keep that flat, you better make sure this job goes exactly as planned and I get my money."

Miles almost smiled to himself. For a fleeting second, he thought it was worth everything going tits up just to see the bitch out on the street. She'd never been much of a mother, and he'd spent a lot of time avoiding all the 'uncles' she had brought home and shared her affections with over the years.

He quickly agreed to the deal, signing the documents prepared by Harris's solicitor, which were then witnessed by the ever-present Jimmy.

As he was leaving, Harris explained to Miles that he should contact Jimmy, on a mobile phone number they gave him, when he needed the details of those people with the specialist skills he required. He emphasised that all their future business dealings would be verbal, nothing on paper that could be connected to him.

Harris had one final thing to say. "Miles, I like you and I think you could pull this job off, but if it goes wrong, don't come back here. We'll find you. The only time I want to see you is when you bring me my money. Understand?"

Miles nodded and left with £10,000 in cash, which he put in the holdall he had brought with him as instructed. He would get the rest as and when needed.

Once outside, Miles Kingston shuddered as he wondered just what his former cellmate had got him into, but realised it was no longer of any importance. Frank Harris wanted his profit no matter what, and possibly the life of his new partner if he didn't get it. Things had gone too far to stop now.

FIVE

Badly shaken by his meeting with Harris, the full enormity of what he was about to do, and whom he was dealing with, hit Miles Kingston with all the force of a runaway train. It was no longer some theoretical discussion in a cell planning a crime, but the real thing, with a serious danger of him ending up injured, dead or back in prison for a very long time. Of course, it might just come off, in which case he would be rich and something of a celebrity within the circles in which he moved. In any event, he was too far down the road now; he had no choice but to continue.

He decided that he was entitled to have a few days off, to hit the bars and get some women before he began work in earnest. So for several days he was in a semi-permanent alcoholic haze, unable to remember how many women he had pleasured or any of their names. He knew it had cost him a fair few quid, though.

So by this bright Monday morning, he had been free for only two weeks but was ready to get back to work. He acknowledged that he needed to stay off the booze before he made a stupid mistake, or forgot something important. Following Frank Harris's lead, he made no written notes which might later incriminate him.

He mentally ran through the things he needed to do this week. Firstly, he needed to see the make-up artist, get some phones and find somewhere safe for the money Harris had advanced him. It was clear that he couldn't risk leaving that much money in his fireplace hidey hole for too long. He'd have to give some thought to that.

Using the number he had been given by Jimmy, only a few minutes earlier, he rang Justin Sinclair from a public telephone and arranged to see him at his city centre studio.

When, an hour later, he arrived at the address provided, Miles was a little surprised to see that it was actually a terraced house in a fairly run-down area. Sinclair turned out to be a small man of indeterminate age who was probably in his sixties but trying to look forty, and appeared to be wearing make-up himself. There was a distinct odour of fried food, booze and cigarettes permeating the whole house and definitely the man himself. Miles was shown into the studio, which was clearly the former dining room of the house and was just as tatty as the rest of the building.

It really was difficult to believe that this wreck of a man could help him, but Miles had no option but to trust Frank Harris.

He showed Sinclair the photos of the man he had printed from the internet, explaining that he wanted to be able to pass for him, even under fairly close scrutiny. After studying the photos for a few minutes, Sinclair nodded and said he thought it could be done, adding that he assumed Miles would want to be able to transform himself when required. If that was the case, the price would be £500 payable now.

Once Miles had agreed and handed the money over, Sinclair set to work. He made Miles sit down in something similar to a barber's chair and focused a desk lamp on his face. Having walked around the chair, studying him from all sides, the little man started to explain his conclusions.

"Okay, these are my initial thoughts. You don't want to be using any make-up, because it's not easy for an amateur to apply and can be easily detected when close up. You must remember theatrical make-up is applied heavily to emphasise features, and also to be seen from a distance. Close up, it can look hideous. Likewise, film and TV make-up is applied by experts and made to look better by subtle lighting. So definitely neither of those is any good for you."

Miles was unable to hide his frustration, blurting out, "So what am I supposed to do, and what exactly am I paying you for?"

Sinclair smiled. "You're paying for my years of experience and skill. You are trying to create the illusion that you are this man, and fortunately most people see what they expect to see, so whilst you will never be a perfect match, I think we can get you very close. You are lucky that you have a similar shape face and similar colouring, and the fact that he wears glasses will cover up that your nose is slightly wider across the bridge. He also has a moustache, which I see you have replicated. The downside is that your hair is a different colour and style."

"So what do we do?"

"Firstly, I don't believe we can get your hair cut in the same style, and changing the colour can be difficult to maintain, so I think the only alternative is a wig. I can get one in the right colour and style it as necessary."

Miles looked a little sceptical. "Will it be easy for me to take on and off, and, most importantly, how noticeable will it be?"

"Don't worry. I'll show you how to fit it. I've got to tell you that a decent wig properly fitted can be virtually undetectable, especially to the casual observer. Now, moving on, you need to let the moustache thicken out a little and we need to work on the colour a bit. We also have to get the same glasses and contacts to change your eye colour. All this means you can transform yourself in minutes, and remember, if the people you meet expect you to be this man, then that is what they'll see. Almost anyone you deal with in this new persona who is later shown a genuine photo of this man will, without hesitation, identify him as the person they met. You may also want to give some thought to deflection tactics as well."

"What's that?"

"Well, for instance, someone may casually remark, after looking at photos, that you've lost or gained weight, so have your answers ready. For example, you could say, 'Thank goodness that gym membership is paying off at last,' or 'Time to go steady on the Big Mac and fries.' Do you get it?"

Miles could only nod as it dawned on him that there was more to this than he had imagined.

"Are you happy with what I have said?"

"It's sounds okay, but if you don't mind, I'll reserve judgement until I've seen the results."

"Fair enough. Now go away and come back next Monday at the same time, when I should have assembled our props and be ready to have a trial run. There will be an extra charge for the stuff, of course, and also for any photos you may require."

Once again, Miles was caught off balance. "Why do you mention photos?"

"Isn't that obvious? Most people who come to see me for a change of appearance are doing it for a new identity, and, of course, they need the proper documents."

With their business concluded, Miles left, not at all sorry to leave the malodorous house and the odd little man.

He still had work to do.

First stop was a nearby large supermarket where, using cash, he bought a cheap pay-as-you-go mobile phone. Commonly called burner phones, they usually came with pre-paid time on them whilst the identity of the user was not known unless they wanted to pass the contact details on to others.

He then repeated the process in two small general stores, another supermarket and finally a petrol station shop. Cash was used every time to complete the transactions.

After purchasing the fifth phone, he decided enough was enough for one day and went for something to eat. Well aware more phones were needed, he thought he could leave that for another day. His intention was that, during his forthcoming operation, he would allocate a separate phone to maintain contact with only one person at a time before discarding them when that contact was terminated. He was really proud of the idea, believing that for a small outlay it would make him harder to trace and consequently much less likely to be caught.

To round off a hectic day, Miles took himself off to Fat Harry's music club in the city centre. It was about 10.30pm and fairly full for a Monday night, the clientele being a mixed bunch in appearance and of varying ages. This was work, not pleasure, so he allowed himself one small drink at the bar. He was carrying out his initial survey of the club and the people who used it. During this first visit, he noted all the exits, how many staff were on duty, and particularly how many security staff. Miles was pretty sure that no one even noticed him but was not bothered if they did because the next time he came here he would be coming as Wade. That is, if Sinclair got it right.

Having gone into the club by the front door, he left through a small exit that took him into a narrow side street. As he walked along the street, Miles was more than pleased that the only camera he could see was the one outside the premises

SIX

Kingston was now at a bit of a loss whilst he waited for Justin Sinclair to perform his magic by transforming him into the fall guy. Hopefully.

However, there were some jobs he could do, even if he wasn't in a position to complete most of them. For instance, he was able to purchase another five pay-as-you-go mobile phones, buying them one at a time from different outlets. One of the phones was a little different to the others and necessitated a visit to a specialist mobile phone store. Confident they would not be traced back to him, he didn't bother changing his appearance or hiding from cameras.

He trawled the local estate agents, managing to identify a remote farmhouse with outbuildings for rent and also a decent-looking flat that he could get on a short lease. However, he was not yet able to proceed.

Miles realised he was not achieving anything concrete so put on hold his plans to find a metal worker who could build him a large dog kennel to order or, indeed, someone who could fulfil his needs off the shelf.

Lastly, he contacted Jimmy to arrange a further £10,000 advance from Frank Harris, which he collected at the end of the week. It reminded him that he needed to sort a secure place to keep the money after the job. He was thinking that, as discussed with Karl, a safe deposit box may well be the best option, although the companies were very careful and there was a danger of later identification. It needed more thought.

Accepting that there was little he could do, Miles spent the rest of the week eating, sleeping and watching TV in his flat until it was time to visit Sinclair's 'studio' again. One thing he did manage to do, whilst idling his time away, was to ring Jimmy from one of the burner phones, telling him that it was his new phone and that it was the one he should be contacted on in the future. As planned, an added layer of security.

Once again, an anxious Miles Kingston found himself in Sinclair's dining room on a Monday morning, seated in the same barber's chair. The mirror had been covered over with a dirty towel, which Sinclair explained would be removed for the big reveal.

"Okay, the first thing we need to do is fit the plain brown contact lenses which are going to cover your quite noticeable blue eyes. Have you used these before?"

Following a shake of Miles's head, he continued. "No worries, it's very easy. I'll show you how."

He proceeded to put one lens in his customer's eye, before getting him to do the other eye himself. He then made him remove both lenses, before once again putting them in his eyes.

"Happy?"

"Yeah, seems easy enough."

"Okay, good. Now sit back and let me fix the rest. I've covered the mirror so that you see the finished article and get the full effect of the transformation. Now close your eyes and relax, no peeking."

Miles felt the little man pulling something over his head, which he assumed was the wig, but was then confused when something else was pulled on top of that. Next, he could feel his moustache being trimmed, before something wet was applied to it. Lastly, he felt a pair of glasses being fitted.

The process took a matter of minutes. When Miles was told to open his eyes, the towel had been removed from the mirror and he was astounded at just how closely he resembled the photo he had given Sinclair. It was a little unnerving, if he was honest.

"Have I delivered what you wanted?"

"Yes, you have, it's amazing. I look just like him."

The make-up artist spent the next half-hour schooling Kingston in how to make the transformation himself. The mystery of the two head coverings was quickly cleared up, and was quite obvious really. The first cover was something similar to a hair net, fitting closely to his head and holding his own hair out of the way. Next, of course, was the wig, which had been artfully styled and coloured to match the hair of the man he intended to impersonate.

The glasses were plain lenses set in a fairly narrow silver frame, which were identical to those worn by the man in the photo. Sinclair was right in that they helped to cover part of his nose, but they would also form a large part of what people remembered when giving statements or making identifications.

Miles soon mastered the techniques needed, including applying the dye, provided by Sinclair, to his moustache. Next came the photos, four passport style with him wearing glasses, four without and one portrait size for his reference when applying the disguise. He also needed some photos of himself without the disguise, but obviously now with the recently grown moustache.

He thought the final £500 payment was taking the piss a bit, but he had no other option than to pay.

They parted company with no pleasantries between them, but Miles had to admit the man had delivered on his promises. No doubt he had also kept copies of all the photos, much good they would do him. What Kingston didn't realise was that, along with his cut from the fee, copies of the photos were sent to Frank Harris. Sinclair didn't know what good they were to the man but complied without hesitation, not daring to do any other.

Miles had a busy week ahead but was determined to make time to practise donning his disguise so that he could do it quickly and perfectly.

After storing the props in his bedroom wardrobe next to the ten mobile phones, he again rang Jimmy, obtaining a contact number for the woman he needed to see in Wales. He then put her number into one of his 'burner' phones, using it to make an appointment to meet her the following day.

Thinking about the things in his wardrobe, Miles was pleased he'd had sufficient foresight to change the locks on his flat, especially as he was going to be away for a couple of days. No telling what the witch downstairs would get up to if she got in for a look round.

SEVEN

On the train to South Wales, Miles Kingston had much to ponder.

He thought back to his first meeting on the landing with Karl Smithson, when they had both been transferred to Armley from other institutions. He, of course, knew who Karl was. He had almost legendary status as the man who had kidnapped a millionaire's daughter, murdered one police officer and severely wounded another. The inmates blithely ignored the fact that he had been captured and was currently serving a forty-year sentence, making him a man to be reckoned with in their eyes. Maybe if they had known the rest of the story, including his later cooperation with the police, their opinion of him would not be quite so high.

Having spent over eight years in a maximum security prison, the new lodgings seemed very much like a holiday camp to Smithson.

After a few days' assessment and induction into the new regime, Miles found himself sharing a cell with Karl, something which, until now, he had always considered a lucky accident. He was now starting to think that maybe it wasn't by chance after all and that Smithson had engineered it in some way. He did seem to have the ear of one or two screws, some of whom could be bought or threatened into helping inmates. It was a relatively small number, so you had to be very careful which of them you approached for 'favours'.

When he first saw his own image alongside the photograph of Richard Wade in Sinclair's house, he had been amazed just how similar they were, and how little had been needed to make them almost identical. He couldn't believe how he, someone who looked so much like that man, had been put into a cell with someone who was determined to destroy that same man, no matter what it cost. It was just too much of a coincidence. He was becoming decidedly uncomfortable.

He remembered the long hours spent in the cell with nothing to do but talk and make fantastic plans. That was when Karl Smithson told his story and outlined his scheme for getting even with the ex-policeman Wade, amongst others.

Karl was a man obsessed, and it took him days to tell the story, often repeating himself and emphasising that it was only bad luck that everything had gone wrong. It started when, wrongfully, in his opinion, he had been sacked from a factory job he had been doing for only a few weeks. He decided to get even, and make the big score he had always dreamt of.

He kidnapped the ten-year-old daughter of the factory owner, John Ross, as is usual, demanding a cash ransom for her release. He had been stopped by two police officers whilst he had the girl tied up in the boot of a stolen car. He attacked them with a knife, eventually killing one and severely wounding the other, but they had managed to handcuff him to a car before the officer died. He continued to claim everything was just bad luck.

Smithson became almost incandescent with rage when he talked about the surviving officer, Richard Wade, who at the time was an Inspector. He described how the snivelling coward had been on his knees begging for his life, whilst leaving his fatally wounded colleague to fight to the very end. He was the one wholly responsible for Karl's arrest, not Wade.

Acknowledging that the dead officer had fought incredibly bravely despite his horrific injuries, Smithson insisted it was his own fault he'd died. Pc Steve Brown could have kept his nose out, and if he had just let the kidnapper go, would still be alive today.

It was everybody's fault but his, something Miles realised he truly believed.

After the trial, when Smithson was convicted, Wade was praised by the press and politicians, promoted and, unbelievably, given a medal. He had told a very good story indeed. What seemed to annoy Karl the most was that the gorgeous blonde nurse who looked after Wade in hospital had ended up as his girlfriend. He went on and on about the constant press coverage and the photos of them together.

Karl Smithson then took great delight in telling his enthralled listener how he had worked with a reporter to bring 'the hero' down. He explained how he had provided the real facts of what had happened, managing to ensure all the man's lies were exposed, despite official cover-ups. He was happy that Wade had lost his girlfriend, turned to drink and been forced to leave the police service, along with some others, and had learnt to be content with that. He failed to mention that his cooperation with the police was key to bringing about Wade's downfall.

Revenge had been so sweet.

Karl was, however, disappointed that he had not achieved his main objective of seeing the disgraced officer receive a long sentence, especially since he had committed perjury at his trial.

Smithson became visibly angry when he began to tell the next part of the story. How, a year earlier, he had seen Richard Wade being interviewed on television, looking fit and healthy, appearing to have drastically cut back on his drinking. It transpired that he had written a book giving his new account of events when he and his colleague had arrested Karl. Once again, he twisted the facts to show himself in the best possible light, explaining how some of his lapses of memory, when describing the arrest, were clearly down to post-traumatic stress disorder. Warming to his theme, he had conceded that the dead officer, Steve Brown, had acted heroically, but asserted that so had he. He claimed that a later investigation was carried out by officers determined to blame him for the inadequacies of their own initial inquiry.

That had been too much for Smithson, who had thrown his television to the floor. That cost him two days in solitary.

Later newspaper articles and internet searches showed that Wade's account had been largely accepted, or at least not challenged, and in the eyes of the chattering classes he was completely exonerated. He had even written another book and was picking up television work.

Some of the people who might have challenged his story had passed away, or moved on and didn't wish to endanger their careers or reputations by becoming involved. Others simply couldn't be bothered.

That was when Karl Smithson had decided that it was up to him to take Wade and maybe some others down again, but properly this time. He began working on his master plan to do so, the biggest problem being finding someone able to impersonate his enemy to such an extent that Wade would take all the blame for what would later transpire.

Miles now fully understood why he ended up sharing the cell with Smithson, and just why he had been befriended and protected. He hadn't known, during all their hours of planning and scheming, just how similar he was to Wade and how devious his cunning cellmate had been.

He had truly been played like a fiddle and, what's more, he was in far too deep to get out now. He couldn't see Frank Harris accepting that he'd changed his mind and calmly writing off the £20,000 Miles had already been advanced. He could run, but, deep down, he still thought it was a good, if very complicated, plan that had a good chance of success with potentially huge rewards. He had to carry on; he had no choice.

Karl might want revenge, but he wanted the money.

EIGHT

After getting off the train in Swansea, Miles walked to his budget hotel carrying an overnight bag containing the usual stuff along with his precious photos and papers. There was also a special present from Frank Harris for the lady he was here to meet.

That evening, as arranged, he met Brenda Thomas for the first time in the hotel bar. Just as she had described herself, she had mid-length dark hair and was wearing a white blouse and a red skirt. As she was the only woman there, it almost made a joke of their cloak-and-dagger meeting arrangements, but who was to know? Miles, for some reason, was surprised by just how attractive she was for a woman in her early forties, especially appreciating her shapely figure. It was a shame she wasn't a blonde.

After a quick introduction, they had a drink together, making small talk, whilst Miles studied her a little more closely. Brenda had dark rings and more creases around her eyes than she probably should have, both of which she had tried to cover up with a bit too much make-up. It was clear she was also tense and a bit twitchy, which could not be entirely put down to their business.

When the drinks were finished, Miles took Brenda's arm and led her to his room, earning himself a knowing smile and a wink from the barman.

Once in the room, before she could speak, Miles held up his hand and said, "Take your clothes off."

Brenda looked stunned and hissed, "Fuck off, you pervert. You're not getting a cheap thrill from me."

"A man of our mutual acquaintance taught me to ensure that when discussing business I should make sure the other party is not wearing a concealed police listening device. That is why I want you to strip, so don't flatter yourself, darling. Remember, you can forget the present I've got for you if you don't do as I say. It's up to you."

Miles saw that Brenda was licking her lips and fidgeting, before, with downcast eyes, she reluctantly started to unbutton her blouse, which she removed and dropped to the floor, quickly followed by her skirt. As she stood before him in only bra and pants, he was able to confirm that she did indeed have the good body he had expected.

Brenda looked at him in mute appeal, but he wanted to see what else she had to offer, not for one second thinking there may have been a wire concealed, if he ever had. He just nodded.

She removed the rest of her clothing and stood completely naked, trying, ineffectually, to hide herself with her hands. Miles reached into his bag and removed the small bottle of green pills, showing them to the thoroughly cowed and humiliated woman.

Revealing his real motives, he said in a hoarse voice, "If you want these, love, put your hands down and let me see what you've got."

Brenda was too far gone now and without further argument put her hands to her sides, giving him a clear view of her body. He stared appreciatively, before throwing her the pill bottle, deliberately a little too short for her to catch, at the same time telling her to get dressed. Tellingly, she was on her hands and knees, looking for the bottle without a thought to concealing her nakedness, presenting Miles with some extremely tempting views. He reluctantly restrained himself, deciding that business was more important at the moment, but there would be other opportunities, he was sure. It was only after she'd gone to the sink and swallowed one of the pills that Brenda dressed.

Whatever the pill was, it had a remarkable effect, calming the previously agitated woman and giving her a slightly dreamy expression almost immediately. She sat on the bed and said, "Okay, what do you want from me?"

Miles was certain that Brenda was an addict; he'd seen enough to know, especially whilst in the nick. It was clear she couldn't manage without the pills and would do anything, suffer any indignity, to get her hands on them. He filed that away for future reference; you never know when information like that might be useful. He was determined to make it his business to find out exactly what those little green pills were as well.

He remembered Frank's sly smile when he told him that he would need some forged driving licences and how they would form an integral part of the plot. It was only when he had finished that Frank told him there was no problem getting them, but not forgeries. He could get genuine ones from the DVLA at Swansea, the place where Brenda just happened to be a supervisor.

Whilst on the train, Miles had thought long and hard about exactly what licences he required. He swung back and forth between having one bearing both Wade's personal details and his photo or having one with his own photo on and Wade's details. How much difference would it make? After all, the photos were virtually alike. He eventually decided to get a copy of the licence currently held at the DVLA with both Wade's photo and details on it. He had two reasons; the first being that if anyone should photocopy the licence, when used as identification, it was important that, if compared later, both images matched beyond question. The second being that if anyone displayed concerns about his appearance differing to that on the licence, he could explain it away just as Sinclair had taught him.

Next, he required a fake licence with Wade's photo on it, his actual date of birth and a fictitious address not far from where the man currently lived but bearing the name James Adamson.

Lastly, he needed a fake licence for himself in the name of Peter Webb with his own new photo on it and, for ease, his own date of birth but bearing a fictitious address in Keighley.

Miles's only concern was that he had never seen Wade's real licence and if the photo on it was of him without glasses, his plans would need to change. He would have to risk having his photo, disguised as Wade with glasses, substituted for the original. The glasses were essential for enhancing his similarity to Wade, making it harder for witnesses to tell them apart and giving them something to focus on when giving descriptions to the police. When this was all explained to Brenda, she voiced no concerns, seeming to accept everything with complete equanimity. He hoped it was because she really did understand and not because of the drugs.

He gave her Richard Edward Wade's full details, including the picture of him he'd taken from the internet, to enable her to find the correct licence. Finally, he provided normal photos of himself and disguised as Wade in case they were needed. She made some brief notes on the back of the envelope containing the photos.

He hoped she was clear what was needed; he was starting to lose track himself. She assured him that everything was clear and that there should be no problems, confirming that each licence would cost £1,000 on delivery. Funny how everything seemed to cost a thousand pounds or multiples thereof. He showed her out after confirming that he would be back at the same hotel in a week's time. She had the number for his burner phone in the event that any problems arose.

His last remark as she left was "Hey, Brenda. Wear stockings next time." She left without further comment.

NINE

Having got home from Wales that afternoon, Miles decided he would take in the music night at Fat Harry's bar, which was held every Wednesday. They usually gave opportunities to up-and-coming bands or, occasionally, they put on a disco/karaoke night, all of which were well attended by a pretty disparate age group.

He got there about 10pm, wearing his full Richard Wade disguise, along with black jeans, a nondescript windbreaker and blue baseball cap. At first, he had been fairly self-conscious, sure everyone was looking at him, but pretty soon realised that nobody was taking the slightest notice of him. It was important to get used to wearing the wig and glasses in public, learning to feel comfortable and confident in doing so. He was greatly reassured that there was clearly nothing about his appearance to set off alarms with anyone.

Even though the club was reasonably busy, Miles found a seat at the bar and was quickly served. Once more, he had to remind himself that this was work, not pleasure, so he had to limit his alcohol intake and remain alert.

He had two reasons for being there, both of which were essential to the successful outcome of the job he and Karl had so carefully planned. Firstly, he was there to continue his observations of the club and the way it operated, but importantly to build his image as a non-threatening regular who never caused any problems.

There were a lot of women in the place, one or two quite young, some of whom Miles quite fancied, but he did no more than give them a friendly smile. He even nodded to one blonde girl, who looked about twenty, but paid her no more attention as he continued to watch the staff moving around.

The band was surprisingly good and, in different circumstances, he would probably have thought it was a good night out. He did catch a glimpse of the blonde girl leaving by the main entrance at midnight when the band had finished, but took no notice otherwise.

A short while later, Miles left as well, pleased and reassured that his appearance had drawn no attention. He felt confident now that he could carry it off, but to be absolutely sure would need to try it out in daylight.

Thursday morning found him, once again, in full disguise and wearing the same clothes as the night before, boarding a bus to the city centre. He thought it best to stay away from his own neighbourhood for fear of being recognised. There were some right fly bastards round there, he could tell you. Miles spent the day going in and out of shops, cafés and pubs, testing his appearance to destruction, as he saw it.

By the time he got home, the lowlife crook was completely confident in his ability to pass for Richard

Wade without question or comment, and certain he could carry out the crime he was planning that would take him into the big league.

By now, Friday, he was a little stuck as to what to do whilst waiting to see Brenda again in Swansea. So much depended on getting the driving licences he needed to prove the various identities he was intending to use. However, they weren't the only documents he needed so was back on the phone to Jimmy, once again using a burner phone. His plan was still to compartmentalise the whole operation by using individual burner phones for each person he dealt with. Up to now, he had one for Jimmy and one for Brenda, both of which he would dispose of when contact with that individual was at an end. He wanted to maintain security and, hopefully, prevent any of the calls being traced to him.

Not wishing to use up his burners unnecessarily, Miles again made use of the telephone kiosk to ring the number he had been given, making contact with the man he would only ever know as 'the forger'. It seemed this man also believed in security, as he refused to meet anywhere but a pub, certainly not at his home.

An hour later, Miles and the forger were seated at a small table in a backstreet boozer, both nursing pints. Miles thought he was careful, but this man was something else, with his eyes on swivels, constantly scanning the room, looking for anyone watching them. He outlined exactly what documents were needed and, surprise surprise, the price was £1,000. He should have known. Miles was beginning to suspect that Harris or his minder had told everyone he dealt with that he had money, so the price went up, probably meaning a kick-back to the big boss. That would make sense, lending Miles money that he had to pay back and all the while skimming off the money he paid out.

Ready on Sunday, same time, same pub, bring cash. A man of few words.

Miles met the forger for a second and, hopefully, final time, as instructed in the same pub, noting that he had to pay for the drinks once more. He was very cautious again, looking around non-stop whilst he passed an envelope under the table. Just as Miles was about to open it, the forger whispered urgently, "Not in here, son, take it away to look at. Give me my money and we'll go our separate ways. If there's any problems, you know how to get in touch."

He wasn't happy but, feeling he had no choice, passed his own package under the table, which the forger put in his pocket, then got up without a further word and left the pub in a hurry. Miles looked round, almost expecting the police to come bursting in at any minute. He did notice that the other man had not touched his drink.

Once back in his flat, he opened the envelope to examine the documents it contained. They were superb. Firstly, there were two utility bills, one electricity and the other council tax, for the address which would be on the fake driving licence in the name of James Adamson. In addition, there were two letters written in different hands on different paper in different ink and in different envelopes. One was an employee reference from a national company, on headed paper, attesting to his good character, his work performance and current salary. The second letter purported to be from a former landlord, who described his ex-tenant in glowing terms, expressing the wish that all his tenants were like him.

Next, there were exact replicas of the other documents, but this time for the false address in Keighley, which would be on the fake driving licence in the name of Peter Webb.

Finally, there was a replica of the council tax bill for Richard Wade's current address in a village outside Leeds. How he got those details God only knows.

All he needed now was for Brenda Thomas to deliver the forged driving licences and the copy of Richard Wade's licence. Once he had those, along with these documents, he could do almost anything he liked, convincing people that Wade was responsible. Things were coming together and, whilst he still had much to do, he was collecting the tools he needed to achieve his objective.

When discussing his needs with the forger, Miles had been unable to resist asking how he would manage to create the authentic-looking documents he needed. He was none the wiser, having been told to mind his own bloody business.

All he knew for sure was that with this number of driving licences and forged documents, he would need to be on the ball. It was certainly a complicated plan and, as Frank Harris had said, it did indeed have lots of moving parts, maybe too many.

TEN

Another depressing, wet Monday night in Swansea sitting in the same hotel bar. This time, he was there ahead of Brenda, but once she arrived, he just hoped it had been worth the wait. She was clearly a little edgy, but they had a quick drink, exchanging desultory small talk whilst the barman studiously took no notice of them. It was all somewhat forced; after all, this was business, not pleasure, and they were definitely not friends.

Twenty minutes later, they were in his room. She was about to say something when Miles held up his hand to stop her, saying, "You know the drill."

She looked at him with a mixture of embarrassment, anger, sadness and possibly even fear before nodding. Once more, she took her clothes off under his eager gaze.

"I'm glad to see you wore the stockings this time. Keep them on. They look good on you, very sexy."

"Can I get dressed now?"

He was enjoying her discomfort hugely. "I don't know. I like looking at you like that."

"Please," she whispered, almost inaudibly.

He was having a good time and really wanted to carry on, knowing that, as desperate as she was for the drugs, he could do whatever he wanted to, but he was here to collect his licences.

"Okay, use the hotel dressing gown on the bed there."

She never questioned why the dressing gown and not her clothes, but grabbed it gratefully and covered her nakedness. As a reward, Miles took a small bottle from his pocket, tipping one of the green pills into his hand before passing it to Brenda, who swallowed it at once. As before, she calmed down almost immediately and soon had a dreamy expression on her face.

He couldn't help but be reminded of the circuses he had been to as a child, when the man training the seals would get a piece of raw fish from his pocket as a reward for them if they had performed as he wished. Brenda was not so far gone that she didn't wonder why he had that nasty smirk on his face.

"Okay, Brenda, have you brought the licences?"

Without speaking, she reached into her handbag on the floor, removed a brown envelope and passed it to Miles, who emptied the contents onto the bed. There were three perfect official DVLA licences, including the paper copies, just as he had requested. He was relieved to see that the copy of Wade's did in fact have a photo of the man wearing glasses, and there was hardly any difference to how Miles looked when in disguise. The other two were spot on, although it was a little odd to see him as Peter Webb with a moustache, which was essential for him to pass as Wade. He was going to have that facial hair for a while yet so had better get used to it.

He stood up again. "Brenda, that's great work. Just as I wanted."

She nodded meekly as Miles took a package containing £3,000 from his overnight bag and passed it to her. She didn't bother to check it before putting it in her capacious bag.

"As a thank you, I've brought a small reward. I know it's OxyContin that you like, and I've brought your usual supply from Mr Harris, but I've got some powdered Oxy for you as well. I crushed it personally and it'll give you a super-quick hit, if you want it, that is."

"Oh, yes, please."

"Right, in that case, I think I'd like to see you without the dressing gown again."

Brenda never hesitated for a second, unfastening the belt and dropping the gown to the floor with some alacrity. She held out her hand for the white envelope he was holding, making no attempt to conceal her nudity. Once she had it, she emptied the powder onto the bedside table, bent over and took a large sniff of it into each of her nostrils. As promised, the hit was immediate as she became relaxed with a building feeling of euphoria. The pleasure was almost too much but was wonderful. She faced Miles once more with shining eyes and an almost rapturous expression on her face.

"It looks like you enjoyed that. Now kneel down."

She hesitated and opened her mouth as if about to speak when he punched her hard in the stomach. Brenda fell to the floor in pain, striving desperately to drag some air into her burning lungs. When she was finally able to breathe, albeit in a tortured fashion, she looked up at him with tears in her eyes. He just nodded.

Eventually, she managed to drag herself to her knees, tears still running down her face.

He liked that.

He started to unfasten his trousers and said, "Now open your mouth."

She was unable to speak and shook her head weakly before he slapped her, as hard as he could, across the side of her face. She fell to the floor once more, her head feeling as if it had exploded and the pain almost overwhelming. Even the Oxy she had swallowed and snorted didn't seem to make much difference.

"Come on, I haven't got all night. I won't tell you again. On your knees."

She dragged herself back to her knees in front of him with her head pounding and more tears coursing down her burning face. She knew what was coming and that she was powerless to resist. It wasn't the first time this had happened to her, and she was sure it wouldn't be the last.

Thoroughly crushed, Brenda opened her mouth without being told, allowing him to push his erect penis so deep into her mouth she almost gagged.

"Come on, you slag, you know what to do."

Indeed she did, and did the best she could, in fear of upsetting him anymore and risking a further beating. It didn't take that long. When she could feel he was about to finish, she started to pull away, but he was having none of that and locked both his hands into her hair. He pulled her head tighter towards him so that she could hardly breathe, finally shooting a copious quantity of liquid into her mouth. Involuntarily, she swallowed some of his filth before he pulled away, allowing her to fall to the floor once more.

She tried to spit some out before crawling to her bag, removing a tissue and using it to wipe her mouth as much as she could. Brenda made sure he wasn't looking as she surreptitiously put it back in her bag.

Miles waited until his breathing had returned to near normal before he looked at the woman on the floor. "Come on. Hurry up, get dressed quick and fuck off. I've got things to do."

She needed no second bidding, dressing as quickly as she could before heading towards the door.

Miles couldn't resist one final comment. "You've got your money and filthy drugs, so be grateful. Now clear off, you slag, and remember this stays between us."

She opened the door and left without another word, hoping to get home before anyone could see what he'd done to her.

Back in his room, Miles had a shower, remembering with some pleasure what he had done to Brenda. She was very attractive and well built, but, even though she was a druggie, he couldn't get rid of the feeling that she thought she was better than him. Or was it possible that it was he that thought she was better than him? She was definitely efficient and organised, delivering the licences he had requested without a hitch. Being totally honest, he had felt threatened by her, and that was why he had enjoyed brutalising her so much. He needed to bring her down a peg or two.

Miles liked women for sex, but not in any other way, certainly not as a friend. He took great pleasure in hurting them but wasn't sure why, other than he had a need to show them who was the boss. The other thing, of course, was that it excited him when he hurt women and made them cry.

He often wondered if it had anything to do with his upbringing. His father left when he was young and his mother entertained herself with a succession of boyfriends. She wasn't exactly a prostitute but did accept gifts from the men, often to prevent her telling the police about the numerous beatings she received. Having said that, she wasn't averse to giving him a good hiding on a regular basis, so maybe that was why he always liked it when her gentlemen callers gave her some of the same. He really hated her.

Maybe witnessing what went on at home persuaded him that behaviour of that nature was normal between men and women. He'd certainly never had a proper girlfriend, nor did he want one.

Studying him would be a psychiatrist's dream; they'd probably get a book out of him.

ELEVEN

Brenda Thomas was deeply ashamed. She couldn't believe that she had got herself into this position again. Would she never learn?

She had kept her head down on the way out of the hotel, managing to flag a taxi down in the street outside. Once in the back seat, she ignored the looks directed her way by the driver, turning her head to one side in a futile attempt to hide her bruised and swollen face.

It was a good job that it was such a miserable night because, once she was dropped off at the end of her street, it allowed her to dodge into her house without bumping into any of the neighbours.

Once inside, she began sobbing uncontrollably, helping herself to a large measure of neat vodka, both as a consolation and in an attempt to rid herself of the taste of him. It didn't help much in either case, but she already knew that it wouldn't. The only thing that would help was those little green pills. She resisted temptation as long as she could, which wasn't long at all, before giving in and swallowing two pills. She soon began to feel better, but she knew she had already taken too much, which, along with the drink, wasn't very sensible.

The next thing was to inspect her face in the mirror. It wasn't a pretty sight, swollen and red all down one side with the start of some bruising around her eye. Brenda took a packet of peas from her freezer and held the cold bag to the side of her face. She didn't really know if it worked, but they always seemed to believe it did in films and TV programmes. She had to try something or she would never get to work tomorrow. She couldn't afford any more time off; questions were already being asked.

Brenda refilled her glass and took a large drink before curling up on her sofa. She half smiled to herself; at least she wasn't reduced to drinking straight from the bottle, not yet anyway. She was a clever woman with plenty of self-awareness, conscious that she was going downhill fast as her dependency took a tighter and tighter grip. What could she do?

For at least the thousandth time, she wondered how it had come to this, but, more importantly, how she was going to get out of it. She could always go to the police, who would be overjoyed with the information she could give them, but perhaps not. It would certainly piss off an awful lot of bad people, and the police definitely would not be supplying her with pills, would they?

As always, when she felt sorry for herself, Brenda thought back to the stupid way this had all begun and the impact it had on her life and, crucially, the financial cost and damage to her self-esteem.

Just over two years earlier, she had accepted an invitation from an on/off boyfriend to play squash after work at the local sports centre. It sounded good, particularly as it was to be followed by a meal and drinks, with who knows what later. It had been a while, after all. She wasn't a great squash player but had played a bit in the past and was looking forward to it. If she had only known!

At the time, she had found it reassuring to know that, even having just turned forty, men still found her attractive enough to want to take her out and enjoy her company. Brenda was not married and never had been, not that she hadn't had offers. Maybe she had been too cautious, but she simply hadn't been sufficiently enamoured of any of the suitors to accept their proposals.

Brenda Thomas had no close relatives except for her mother, but had many friends and an active social life. She also enjoyed her job immensely, being deeply committed to achieving as much as she could. In short, she had been happy.

Brenda was having a great night. Okay, she was losing but not getting embarrassed, just having fun. They had been playing for about half an hour when, chasing a shot from her partner, she slipped and crashed into the side wall. Her left knee took the main impact, causing her to collapse, screaming in agony. Her leg was twisted at an unnatural angle, with the kneecap looking as if it had slipped to one side. She could hardly bear the pain and certainly couldn't stand to look at it.

She remembered it all so well, the trip to hospital by ambulance, the examinations and X-rays before the good news, bad news, worse news. Her leg wasn't broken, but the knee, including the kneecap, was severely dislocated and would require manipulation to return it to somewhere near its normal position. Specialist confirmation would be needed but the doctor was fairly sure she had the classic footballer's injury, an anterior cruciate ligament tear, also known as an ACL. The worse news was still to come. Her 'boyfriend' informed her that he would really have liked to stay, but his wife was expecting him home. She certainly hadn't seen that one coming.

A sleepless night followed despite the drowsiness caused by the heavy pain medication. The next day, her leg was manipulated back into the correct shape and position, followed by a repair to the torn ACL. Two days later, she was home, with her leg heavily bandaged and in some sort of orthopaedic brace, but not plastered. She also had crutches to get her about. The hospital had provided everything she needed but nothing that could deal effectively with the waves of overwhelming pain. For some reason, they seemed to think that paracetamol would do the trick. It didn't, not even anyway near. Despite her pleas to the hospital staff and her own doctor, all she was told was that things would settle down, but she made such a nuisance of herself that she was eventually prescribed ibuprofen to take as well. It helped a little, but not much.

Both the pain and resulting lack of sleep were wearing her down. Luckily, Brenda belonged to a private medical scheme and was able to arrange an appointment with a private orthopaedic consultant very quickly. He examined her knee and was pleased to tell her that the treatment had been spot on and everything would settle down nicely. She explained about the ongoing pain, pleading for some stronger painkillers.

She remembered how distinguished she thought

James Parker looked in his well-cut suit, with his swept-back grey hair and neatly trimmed moustache. She could see that he was clearly a man to trust as he studied her carefully, apparently in deep thought, before finally nodding. He'd gone on to explain that there was a very strong painkiller called OxyContin available which had been developed from opium and was stronger than morphine. He cautioned her that Oxy, as it was known, could be addictive and so could only be taken for a very short time. He questioned her carefully to ensure that she fully understood the risks.

Brenda knew that she was a smart woman with a responsible job and was convinced she would have no problems dealing with Oxy. She just wanted the pain to stop and to get some much-needed sleep. Mr Parker would only give her a prescription for a one-week supply of the drug.

She took the prescribed dose as soon as she got home. The effect was immediate, the pain eased and the initial feelings of pleasure began to turn into euphoria. It was so wonderful that after a couple of good nights' sleep she felt able to return to work. She felt human again.

She saw Mr Parker twice more, who wrote a prescription each time for a week's supply of Oxy, on the final occasion stressing there would be no more of the drug. She wasn't bothered. Everything was better, the pain had gone; no problem.

However, two days after she had taken her final dose, Brenda was climbing the walls. She didn't know it but she was displaying classic signs of addiction to OxyContin; lethargy, itchy skin, vomiting and, most damaging from a work viewpoint, moodiness and a lack of interest in personal appearance.

She quickly arranged to see Parker again, explaining her position and assuring him that she was certain another couple of weeks' prescriptions would do the job. At first, he was adamant that it was impossible, and even though he was sympathetic, there was nothing he could do. She remembered her embarrassment as she had cried and pleaded with him.

Eventually, he conceded there may be something he could do, but it was a little unconventional. A mystified Brenda was so pleased that she hardly noticed him go to his office door, lock it and return to his desk, where he took a small pill bottle from a drawer. He gave her a glass of water and emptied a green pill into her hand, which she swallowed gratefully. She began to feel more relaxed immediately, so when he instructed her to remove her clothes and get onto the examination couch she did so without argument. The pill must have been having a dramatic effect because she didn't even wonder what he was doing when he took his trousers off. He was a doctor; it would be fine. What she didn't realise was that the distinctive green pill he had given her was the stronger 80mg dose, much more powerful than she had previously been prescribed.

That was the first time Brenda sold herself to get Oxy, but it certainly wasn't going to be the last.

James Parker tired of their twice-a-week sessions after three months, or possibly his wife suspected that something was going on. When he told Brenda, she became distraught, begging him to carry on their arrangement. How else was she going to get her supplies of OxyContin?

Not wanting to have a desperate woman plaguing him, the consultant had arranged for her to see a Doctor Jack Reynolds, who specialised in pain relief and had agreed to continue supplying Brenda with the drug. However, he made it absolutely clear that Reynolds had only agreed to supply her on the condition she adopted the same arrangements as those she had with Mr Parker. She simply didn't care, so desperate was she for more of the little green pills.

So her descent continued, passed from one man to another like a second-hand book, in the insidious grip of her drug addiction, to be discarded when no longer needed. In her brief periods of clarity, she continued to believe she was not an addict, certain she could stop whenever she wanted to. Her leg was completely healed; she was no longer in pain and didn't actually need the drugs anymore. Women like her simply were not drug addicts, were they?

Jack Reynolds was almost the direct opposite to Parker, being black-haired, swarthy and pretty rough around the edges. Worst of all, he was very overweight and sweated profusely during their sexual encounters, which in turn created an unpleasant odour. Added to all that, his tastes were a little unconventional and at times he treated her quite violently. Another man who seemed to like hurting her and causing humiliation, but his one saving grace was his use of a condom. However, being the pig that he was, he had taken huge delight in making sure that she knew it was to prevent him catching anything from her.

At least Parker had been scrupulously clean and very gentle.

The only consolation was that her supply of Oxy continued unabated, at least for now.

Unfortunately, he soon tired of Brenda as, despite her best efforts, she had been unable to put on a convincing show of enthusiasm during sex. So, five weeks later, after a final bruising sex session, Reynolds told her he wasn't going to see her again. She was once more frantically wondering how she could continue to get her supply of OxyContin and begging Reynolds for help. Simply to get rid of her, Jack Reynolds told her that any evening she could go to the Woodhut café in the docklands area and ask for Marco, helpfully writing the name and address down for her on his headed notepaper. He would see her right, but it would cost.

What Reynolds didn't know was that Brenda had recovered one of his used condoms from the bin when he had gone into the office bathroom to clean up. At the time, she wasn't sure why but had a vague idea that at some time in the future it may come in useful.

That very night, she went to the café. It was a dark night and she had a lot of trouble finding it in the narrow streets. It was dirty-looking and, once she entered, she discovered it was even dirtier inside, full of steam and the smell of old fried food. There were only a couple of customers at one table and an immensely fat woman, wearing a dirty apron, behind a small counter.

She could remember how afraid she was and how strange these surroundings felt to her. At first, she told herself that she didn't belong there, but then realised that it was exactly where she did belong. She was a drug addict and needed her supply, no more trying to fool herself that she could stop if she wanted to. She couldn't. She couldn't forget how the conversation had gone and how things had eventually got worse, not better.

Brenda approached the woman nervously and said, "Is Marco in?"

"Maybe. Why do you want to know?"

"Jack Reynolds sent me."

The woman nodded. "You better buy something and I'll see if he's about."

Brenda took a cup of tea to one of the greasy tables, hardly daring to touch it. Five minutes later, she was joined by a small dark-haired man who, along with two earrings, had a multitude of tattoos.

"I'm Marco. My wife said you wanted to speak to me. What do you want?"

It was almost comical that this little man was actually married to the huge woman at the counter, but she didn't show her amusement.

"Jack Reynolds said you may be able to help me with a purchase."

"What exactly is it that you want?"

"80mg Oxy pills."

Marco looked carefully at her, taking in her nervous manner, pale, sweaty face and trembling hands. He smiled slyly. "We get a lot of women like you in here. Okay, I can do that, but it'll cost you. Two hundred pounds for ten pills."

Brenda gasped. "That's an awful lot of money."

"Take it or leave it, I don't care."

When she nodded, Marco got up and said, "Same time tomorrow night, and bring the money."

Thus began a relationship that, over a six-month period, drained her of all her savings, caused her to sell her car and to beg, steal or borrow money wherever she could. She fell behind with her rent and, as she became more and more desperate, sold everything of value that she had. Friends began to avoid her, and, to add to her problems, her appearance and work performance suffered badly, causing more questions to be asked resulting in unpleasant interviews with senior managers.

It was amazing how quickly the money disappeared as she needed more and more Oxy pills to maintain the yearned-for high. Eventually, she went to see Marco, explained her position and asked if there was any other way she could pay for the drugs. He nodded and beckoned her to follow him into the backyard.

With hopes of salvation rising, she followed him into the darkness whereupon he suddenly turned and punched her in the face, knocking her to the dirty ground. He then proceeded to kick her several times about the body and legs, causing agonising pain. He shouted that she was a stupid cow and that sex was not what he wanted, it was money. Didn't she realise he had people to pay as well?

Marco was pitiless as she lay in the dirt crying. "I don't care where you get the money. Steal it from work if you have to. Otherwise, no more pills."

She sobbed, "We don't deal with money in my job, and I've already sold everything I can. There's no one else I can borrow from."

"So where do you work then?" Not even bothering to pretend he was interested.

Still crying, she said, "At the DVLA."

After Brenda said that, Marco's attitude appeared to change as he helped her to her feet and apologised for what he'd done. He gave her some pills on account, as he put it, telling her they should keep her going until she could come back the following week, when he may have some good news for her.

Marco thought of himself as a businessman and, believing he had seen an opportunity, instructed one of the café hangers-on to follow Brenda and find out where she lived.

Once again, she had been a total mess and, unable to go to work, had been forced to take the rest of the week off. At least because of COVID she could work from home, borrowing a computer from work as she had already sold her own.

When Brenda's doorbell rang only two days later, she was amazed to see what looked like the biggest man she had ever seen in her life on the inbuilt camera. She reluctantly answered the door but, when he told her he was a friend of Marco, she let him in. He introduced himself as Jimmy, telling her that his boss, whom he did not name, had sent her some Oxy as a goodwill gesture and, just like music to her ears, suggested the supply could be continuous if things worked out.

After her initial excitement, she realised there was sure to be a heavy cost.

Once Brenda had confirmed that she was a departmental supervisor at the DVLA, dealing particularly with the issue and renewal of driving licences, Jimmy told her what his boss wanted. He didn't mess about, telling her bluntly that his boss wanted her to create driving licences as and when he asked her to, and for that service she would receive a regular supply of Oxy from Marco. However, first, she would need to prove she could deliver. He gave her some passport-style photos and the personal details that should appear on the licence, asking how long it would take. She was desperate to please and told him two weeks should be enough.

She knew security was tight and that she would be running tremendous risks, but the chance to get a constant supply of her drugs was irresistible. She was well aware that what she was about to do was against the law but did not hesitate for a second.

As instructed, she delivered the envelope containing the licence to Marco, who simply told her she would be contacted, which in due course she was. Evidently, she passed the test because once more Jimmy arrived to explain the arrangements. Every Monday night, she was to visit Marco, who would hand over her longed-for supply of the green pills. He would also give her any orders for driving licences, which she would complete and return two weeks later. Simple for them, but dangerous for her.

Occasionally, she may have to meet personal callers at local hotels who wanted licences, for which she was instructed to charge £1,000 a time. The money would then have to be given to Marco to pass back down the chain to whoever was in charge. No doubt it meant some people were paying more than once for the same service, ensuring profit all the way for little expense. Of course, that cash would also pay for Brenda's drug use.

What she didn't realise was that 'businessman' Marco had effectively sold her to Frank Harris, of course.

After about three months, she was surprised to see Jimmy when she went to her usual Monday evening meeting with Marco. She dutifully handed over the envelope containing the latest driving licences and, whilst he studied them, waited for her pills.

She remembered how he had looked at her with his expressionless face as he baldly told her that she needed to speed up supply, once a week, from now on. He handed her an envelope with a fresh order.

Brenda had started to protest, when the big man slapped her gently across the side of her face, which was similar to being hit with a sledgehammer by anyone else. She tried to explain but he would not listen, repeating that it was to be once a week or no more drugs and, just to drive the message home, no drugs this week either.

Once more, she had found herself pleading with them, crying, offering to do anything. Marco had stepped in, giving her the name of a street nearby where she may be able to find a dealer who might supply her. She remembered nodding and wandering off in a daze.

To cut a long story short, she found a dealer who, despite her having no money, offered to help, suggesting a way she could get the money to buy some Oxy from him. He showed her the pills, giving her a free sample to make what she had to do a little easier to cope with. Brenda knew she had finally reached rock bottom when she found herself laid on a thin dirty duvet in a nearby alley. The first man hoisted her dress up and, in his eagerness, ripped her knickers as he wrenched them off. The drug helped, but only a little, as he fucked her on the filthy bedding which gave her little protection from the broken ground. At least it didn't take long.

Over the next two hours, a further five men had their way with her. One group of three turned it into a spectator sport as they watched each other perform, shouting advice and encouragement whilst making lewd comments about her. One of the men was unable to perform but, as usual, blamed Brenda, slapping her across the face and screaming at her to show some interest. Why did they always have to hit her?

Bad as all the painful sex was, the almost unbearable smell of sour beer on the men's breath as they slobbered over her was nearly as bad. At last, it was over, with a last backhanded compliment from her final customer who told her that she wasn't so bad for an old tart.

Having got the OxyContin in payment from the pimp, she staggered away with his final words ringing in her ears: "You're welcome here anytime, love. The punters liked you, and there's always plenty of business for a looker like you."

Making her way home, she became aware of the grazes on her body. The scratches on her back and buttocks were sore, as were the scrapes on her knees and elbows from the rough ground where she'd been turned every which way. Brenda told herself that she would never go back to that alley but knew deep in her soul that she would have no choice if the drugs ever ran out again. She was all out of options, and it was only sex after all. So why was she crying?

When she went back to work, she found shortcuts to help her produce licences within the new timescale, helped by the fact that it was mid-2021 and the whole world was dealing with the COVID outbreak. Many of the staff were working from home, so she had access to numerous unused computers, and there were few, if any, prying eyes. The downside was that prior to the outbreak, waiting time for new licences was up to four weeks. Now there was no certainty of anyone answering the phone, let alone getting a licence. As fewer and fewer licences were being produced legitimately, her chances of being found out increased dramatically.

Brenda was fully aware that once the epidemic was over, and people returned to work, her chances of continuing to supply illegal driving licences undetected were slim indeed. She had no idea what she would do then.

The following Monday, on delivery of the licence, normal service was resumed with Marco, thank God. She would deal with what was sure to come her way in the future when she had to.

Brenda had risen to a fairly senior position within the DVLA and, despite her recent issues, was still a trusted employee, just about. Apart from her drug use, she was no fool, knowing full well that at some stage her production of illegal driving licences would be detected. She needed some sort of insurance policy, a bargaining chip, if you like, that she could use as and when needed.

She came to the conclusion that she needed evidence against these men who had taken advantage of her and so cruelly used her, deciding that her best option was to keep a record of events and, where possible, a copy of everything. She started with the original note given to her by Dr Jack Reynolds, containing the address of Marco's place of business, followed by the used condom from Reynolds' office, now carefully stored in a sealed plastic bag, which could be used to prove sex took place. Next, she managed to download and print a picture of Jimmy from her doorbell camera, quickly joined by copies of the test licence she had created for him. That was just a start as she kept a copy of every single licence she made and all the photos and personal details she was given to fulfil the jobs. She kept a record of every meeting with Marco from that time, and with any of the men and women she met in local hotels for the same purpose.

That was why, as well as copies of the driving licences she had made for him, Brenda had kept the tissue she had used to wipe her mouth after her encounter with Miles Kingston, which, after making sure it was dry, she had placed in a plastic bag. She had watched enough true crime stories on TV in her time to know that whilst she may not know his name, she had his DNA, if needed. At least she hoped so.

Finally, Brenda had taken photos of the injuries sustained after every beating or bout of rough sex, and there were many. She also kept details of when and where those beatings took place, who by, and if medical treatment was required.

The only man that she didn't really have any evidence on was the consultant Mr James Parker. Thinking back, all she could remember was that he had a mole in the centre of his right thigh and that on every occasion they had sex he was wearing white boxers with blue stripes. It was not much, but it may help.

The following morning, despite her battered condition, she took everything from her humiliation at the hotel to her mother's house, placing it in a cardboard box with everything else she had gathered. She knew it was too risky to keep the records at her house, particularly as she had a feeling her home had been searched at least once. These men were dangerous, and it was clear the police were not the only ones for whom she may need a bargaining chip.

There was undoubtedly a link between the monster Jimmy, his boss, the two doctors and Marco, but who was supplying whom and with what, she was not sure. She told herself that there was no way it could last, but there was no harm in hoping.

The only good news was that now she was getting an unbroken supply of her drugs, she was able to manage her life in general and work in particular much better. However, it was very much a balancing act, with her taking only a sufficient amount of the drug during the day to enable her to work effectively. Once home, it was a different story, where she drank vodka and hit the Oxy pretty hard, not always remembering to eat and usually falling into bed in the small hours. She was losing weight and her appearance was deteriorating. Brenda had no recollection of weekends at all.

Brenda had been supplying driving licences for over a year now and knew it couldn't last much longer, particularly as working from home was coming to an end. She sometimes thought about going to her bosses to own up and ask for help. The thought only lasted until the next pill.

TWELVE

On the Tuesday morning, Miles returned home by train, mightily pleased with his efforts but shuddering slightly as he considered what Frank Harris's reaction would be if he became aware of the way Miles had treated Brenda. Perhaps another reason to get away as quickly as possible once the job was done.

He no longer needed the burner phone he had used to communicate with Brenda so removed the SIM card and battery before putting them in a bin on Swansea station. The phone itself was broken up and thrown into a canal near his home. He was convinced that it was now no longer possible to prove a link between himself and Brenda Thomas. How wrong can you be?

Once back in his flat, Miles couldn't help studying the three driving licences, especially the photographs, which he thought were perfect. He had to laugh at himself, realising that of course they were perfect, having been produced by the DVLA itself.

Now he had the licences, it was time to stop hanging about and to get his arse in gear before it was too late.

Especially since Frank Harris was going to want his money back, and time had a habit of getting away from you. He really didn't fancy a visit from Jimmy.

He had to sort out some properties and cars but couldn't make his mind up which to do first. He eventually decided that getting the properties sorted was his priority, especially if they had parking for the vehicles.

He spent the afternoon touring a number of city centre estate agents, all of whom seemed to have a ready supply of flats for rent. He eventually saw one he liked the look of, described as a luxury apartment with two bedrooms on the third floor of a modern block overlooking a green space. He had to laugh at the agent's jargon, especially the final 'Only £2,300 per month'. Only!

On entering the office, he was greeted effusively by a woman wearing too much make-up with obviously dyed blonde hair. Still, she wasn't too bad-looking, and on another day, he might have tried his luck with her.

Once he had expressed his interest in the apartment, the woman, Jean Cook, offered to take Miles for a look as it was currently unoccupied and only just around the corner. Once there, he was quietly impressed, although he didn't say so, admitting to himself that it certainly was luxurious, at least to someone from his background. It had two bedrooms, one with a king size bed and en-suite, a further bathroom and a combined lounge/kitchen/dining area, with all the fittings and furnishings being of a high standard. The lift in the block had certainly been a bonus.

Further questioning confirmed that the apartment came with a private parking space and, more worryingly, security cameras. For what he had planned, Miles didn't want himself, or anyone else using the flat, appearing on film. He would need to give that some serious thought, acknowledging that he was unlikely to get a place matching his requirements that didn't have security of one form or another.

Back at the office, Jean went through the details of the lease with him and was a little concerned that he only required a six-month let on the property, which was a total lie anyway. However, he explained that he had recently moved to the city, having been promoted by his employer, and that he didn't want to commit to a longer lease until he saw how things worked out. She muttered that she understood, before asking for proof of ID and references.

A little apprehensively, he produced the fake driving licence in the name of Peter Webb with the false address in Keighley, which he had stipulated to Brenda. It passed muster with hardly a glance from Jean. Miles explained that, at the moment, he was staying with a friend, having recently split up from his wife, something that had been on the cards for a while. She was very sympathetic and hardly glanced at the references and utility bills, so skilfully created by the forger, but nevertheless photocopied them along with the driving licence. The bills were so recent that it was clear he had lived at the address in Keighley until very recently. As she had already made the deal, Miles doubted very much that she would even bother to check the references, but if she did, he expected to be long gone before she realised there was a problem.

Having noted that the estate agent appeared to work alone and that the office was small, with few properties on display in the windows, Miles decided to take a chance.

He offered to pay the first month's rent in cash, explaining that with his current marital difficulties he didn't want his wife to know anything about his financial affairs. He was probably talking absolute nonsense, but, after an initial show of reluctance, Jean eagerly accepted the offer. As he suspected, cash flow was an issue for the small business, and no doubt the flat owner would see less money than they were expecting. Because that was what he would have done, he just assumed that everyone else would do the same.

Miles wanted to move in as soon as possible, telling Jean how difficult it could be camping out in someone else's home. She agreed that Friday would be okay if he could return to her office the following day to sign the lease and pay the money.

Miles congratulated himself on a good day's work, still hardly believing how easy it had been.

He was very tired; it had been a long day. He went for a couple of pints and something to eat before going home for an early night, ready for another busy day on Wednesday.

THIRTEEN

Whilst renting the apartment had been very important to his and Karl's plan, it was undoubtedly true that the next property Miles was looking for was absolutely vital to a successful outcome. With that in mind, after taking Jean her cash and signing the lease for the apartment, he spent Wednesday morning trawling the city centre estate agents seeking a suitable property.

He was surprised to find that the farmhouse he had seen recently was still in the agent's window available for rent, assuming correctly that the slightly remote location was putting people off, not to mention the £3,000-a-month rent. It was exactly that isolation and the number of outbuildings that suited him down to the ground.

Before going in, Miles spent a few minutes checking himself in the estate agent's window. He was in his Richard Wade disguise and wanted to make sure everything was as perfect as could be.

Once inside, a young man, wearing a shiny suit that had fit him about two stones ago, jumped up from his desk and rushed forward to meet the man who he would come to believe was called James Adamson. Robert Grundy's eyes lit up when his visitor enquired about renting the property, which had so far proved very difficult for them to shift.

Miles explained that he was an author looking for somewhere quiet to write his next novel, joking that it was sure to win the Nobel Prize for literature. Robert nodded hesitantly, the remark having completely passed him by.

It was quickly agreed that Grundy would take Miles to view the property, which was about ten miles outside Leeds in a north easterly direction. The car journey took about half an hour but seemed much longer as he listened to the agent's incessant inane chatter.

Once there, Miles couldn't believe how perfectly the building met his needs, having several bedrooms including one downstairs complete with an en-suite bathroom. It was clear from the way the bathroom was fitted out that it had been for the use of an elderly or disabled person. Outside, there was a double garage and several outbuildings where he could store more vehicles than he would ever need.

Standing in the yard, he could only see one other building, which was several miles in the distance. Considering it was the first building of this type he had viewed, Miles was amazed at just how lucky he had been. This would do very nicely indeed.

When he told the agent that he was interested in the property, it was clear from the man's demeanour and nervous cough that there was something on his mind. Miles waited patiently, expecting bad news, until Robert decided it was time to come clean.

"There is one small issue, I'm afraid, Mr Adamson.

Unfortunately, it's absolutely impossible to get a mobile phone signal out here. I do hope that won't be a problem."

"Well, I know I said I wanted peace and quiet to write, but it is a bit awkward not being able to communicate with people."

Wearing his most hopeful expression, Robert responded. "There is a working landline, so you wouldn't be completely out of touch. I know it's not ideal, but it's better than nothing."

"Okay, I suppose it's not that bad. Exactly how far do I need to go before I actually do get a mobile signal?"

Embarrassed once more, he muttered that the previous tenant had said it was something like three miles before he got any sort of usable signal.

Miles thought about it for a minute or two, trying to think about his future plans, at the same time checking his phone to confirm there was indeed no signal. He eventually decided that it wasn't a big problem and that it could actually be beneficial for what he was intending.

"Okay, Robert, let's check the landline out and, if it's working, we'll see just how far I have to go for this phone signal."

Mostly for show, not intending ever to use it, he confirmed that the phone was connected and appeared to be in good order. Having locked the door, the agent drove Miles back down the road, where they discovered it was actually just over three miles before they got a good signal. Attempting to circle the property, they were unable to find a better signal anywhere nearer. Perhaps they would do better on foot, but neither man was interested in walking over the rough hills surrounding the farm.

Despite expressing his irritation at the phone situation, it was quickly agreed, much to Robert's delight, that Miles would take the property for six months at the full £3,000 rent per calendar month. On the way back to the estate agent's office, Miles went through his routine about having split from his wife, suggesting he would pay the first month's rent in cash up front to prevent her knowing anything about his financial affairs. Robert was very reluctant to accept the arrangement, fearing his boss would not be happy, but quickly came round to the idea when Miles offered him £200 compensation for his trouble. Just between them, of course. Once again, Miles Kingston's jaundiced view of his fellow beings proved accurate.

Back at the office, the driving licence in the name of James Adamson along with the utility bills and references were produced by Miles and photocopied by Grundy. Again, little attention was paid to the paperwork, and it seemed unlikely anyone would bother to check them. If they ever did, he wouldn't be around anyway. Arrangements were made for the lease to be signed, rent to be paid and keys collected on the Friday morning.

Definite progress was being made.

As it was late afternoon and Miles intended to visit Fat Harry's for a further recce of the Wednesday night music scene, he decided a drink and something to eat was in order. Once again, he was careful, especially as he was still disguised as Wade, making two pints last until it was time for his visit to the club. He needed to be Wade when he was there and couldn't afford any slip-ups, not this close to the job going off.

Wearing his usual windcheater and baseball cap, he arrived at Fat Harry's about 9.30pm but wished he hadn't. The DJ, a pimply-faced youth, was screeching into a microphone and playing music Miles had never heard before in his life. Things had started off okay with a friendly nod from the bouncer on the door, clearly recognising him as someone who had been to the club before, if not exactly a frequent visitor. That was good as he needed staff to be able to describe Wade and identify him later if necessary.

He found a seat at the corner of the bar where he was able to survey almost the whole expanse of the club whilst he lingered over his drink. He saw one or two faces he recognised, including that attractive young blonde girl. She really must be a regular.

Barely able to stand the dreadful row coming from the stage, Miles knew how important it was to stay if he wanted to study the comings and goings in the place, and to be seen as a regular. On his way back from a visit to the toilet, he stumbled into the back of the blonde girl, who was standing at the bar, spilling half her drink. Miles immediately apologised, insisting on buying her a replacement gin and tonic once she had told him what she was drinking.

As the barman prepared the drink, Miles smiled at the girl and said, "You'd better take your drink direct from him rather than me. You can't trust people these days, so play safe and stay safe." He paid in cash as usual, giving a big tip. He wanted to be remembered.

He nodded to her, brushing off her thanks as he returned to his seat.

Shortly before midnight, the girl walked past him, gave

him a wave and left the club alone by the front door. Her friends always seemed to leave earlier than her, whilst she hung about, perhaps having a final drink. He'd had enough himself and went home with a pounding headache. Did he really need to come here again?

FOURTEEN

M iles got up on the Thursday morning with his head spinning. He had already done a lot and still had much more to do, but felt like a juggler trying to keep all the balls in the air at the same time. Drop one and they would all fall, ensuring everything went horribly wrong. He just could not risk forgetting something or making a silly mistake, so made the difficult decision to keep a written record of what he had done so far and what he had still to do. It was certainly true that committing things to memory and not putting anything in writing was a simple and effective security precaution to make sure his plans were not accidentally revealed, and to prevent incriminating evidence falling into the hands of the police. Whilst Frank Harris was able to do it with ease, he was finding it increasingly difficult to keep everything in his head.

As Harris had previously observed, it was a complicated plan with a lot of moving parts, and the failure of any of those parts was liable to cause a total disaster, something he could ill afford.

He reasoned that as he was already in possession of illegal driving licences, forged documents and, very soon, property leases in false names, there was already plenty to keep the police busy. Would a few notes to keep him on track really make much difference in the long run?

Once he'd reached that conclusion, Miles soon made a very brief record of what he had done already and an outline of the tasks he had yet to complete. Of course, no mention was made of Harris, Jimmy or Brenda. If he hadn't realised it already, a quick study of his notes made Miles very aware of how audacious the complex plan was and just how crucial timing would be if it was to be carried off successfully.

He was not foolish enough to carry the notes about with him, so they went into his chimney hiding place, a reminder that finding a more secure place was a priority. It was not just to keep the plans from the police but from Harris as well who, not being fully aware of all the job's wrinkles, maybe wouldn't be too pleased to find out that he had been kept in the dark. Crossing that man, or, more accurately, being caught doing so, did not figure at all highly in any sane person's to-do list. As Miles had thought earlier, going back to jail was one thing, but ending up dead at the hands of an angry Frank Harris was a very different proposition indeed.

The ways he could bring the wrath of Harris down on himself were beginning to mount most uncomfortably, so he had better pull it off successfully if he wanted to survive.

Feeling much happier, and a little more clear-headed, Miles set off on his first task of the day, having decided he had two weeks to do this. It was definitely doable.

It was all getting close, scarily close. It was one thing to sit in a prison cell discussing plans for the big score with Karl Smithson, but it was an entirely different proposition when it came to pulling off such a massive job singlehandedly. He had to admit he was nervous, and not a little scared, but he had gone too far to stop now if for no other reason than that he now owed Harris a great deal of money. Besides which, it was the chance to change his life forever, the only question being would it be for better or worse?

A short time later, he was at Bargain Motors, the car dealer's on the street where Frank Harris's business empire was based, talking to Charlie, who claimed to be the owner. Not quite the archetypal used car salesman, he was still dressed in a smart suit and very colourful tie, with his dark hair neatly arranged to cover his thinning thatch. At least he wasn't wearing a sheepskin coat.

By this time, Miles was beginning to realise just how far the gangster's tentacles reached, certain that Harris was skimming money off every purchase he made, and that meant he would be repaying him the money he had borrowed more than once. Talk about money making money, for some anyway.

Introductions over, he got straight down to business. "I need two decent-condition saloon cars, and they must be reliable."

Charlie put on his most ingratiating smirk. "I've been expecting you. I've got to tell you that I only supply quality vehicles and at a fair price."

"Okay, but as you know who suggested that I come to you, I think we should cut the crap. I need two nondescript four-door saloons. Something common."

"Right, over the last couple of weeks I've been looking out for something suitable for your needs. A very large friend of our mutual acquaintance informed me of your requirements, shall I say. I've got a blue Ford Fiesta, not the fastest but nippy enough, and, as long as you don't get into any car chases, it won't let you down."

Miles nodded. "That sounds like the sort of thing I'm looking for. What else?"

Charlie smirked again. "What do you think about a 2-litre Ford Mondeo? Very common, you might say."

"Okay, they sound good. When will they be ready?"

"As I said, I've been expecting you, so they're ready now. It's just a matter of price."

Miles smiled ruefully. "Tell me the bad news."

"Well, as I've explained, these are high-quality, hand-picked cars that have been worked on by my team of highly trained, experienced mechanics. So obviously they're not cheap."

"Surely our mutual friends would expect a hefty discount. Tell me how much."

"Look, Miles, trust me, I'm not making a penny on them. Honest. I can do the pair of them for fifteen grand cash."

For form's sake, Miles knew he had to haggle. "I need to test drive them first and, if they're as good as you say, I'll give you thirteen. To top it off, I'll sell them back to you inside a month for eight grand. That'll be the easiest money you've ever made."

Charlie stopped smiling. "No deal, definitely not, no way. Do you really think I'm stupid enough to think of buying hot cars from you? God knows what you're going to use them for, and I don't want to know. No, I never want to see them again. It's fifteen grand or you can fuck right off now."

Miles knew he was beaten. What choice did he have? He nodded meekly. "Okay, it's a deal."

Charlie's smile returned to its full wattage. "Did you forget the motorbike?"

He was embarrassed to think that he had but refused to admit it. "What have you got for me?"

The dealer, knowing he had the upper hand, was now in a very good mood. "I've got a 125 trials bike. A bit tired-looking but mechanically spot on. Trust me, I've been told to look after you, and that's what I'm doing. That'll set you back another 2,500, but I'll throw in a helmet for free. Can't say fairer than that, can I?"

All Miles could do was nod in acceptance.

Charlie was very happy for a man who claimed not to be making a profit. All that was left now was to arrange payment – cash, of course – registration and collection of the vehicles. Miles showed him the James Adamson driving licence, suggesting he might like to photocopy it to help in completing the registration documents, and perhaps even keep the copy for his own records.

Having glanced at the licence, he wryly observed that Miles had changed somewhat, but agreed that if asked, this was the man he would identify as having bought the vehicles. The evidence was beginning to mount against the hapless Richard Wade.

Miles confirmed that he would return the following day for the Ford Fiesta and would collect the others sometime the following week. Charlie, not so delicately, reminded him not to forget the cash. Friday was shaping up to be yet another demanding day.

Before he left, Miles had a final request of the car dealer, wanting to know where he could find someone to make him new number plates, no questions asked. That was an easy one, and he was directed to a factory unit around the corner where the dealer got his own plates made. No comment was made or questions asked.

There was one more job to do that afternoon, very much related to his need for someone to make false registration plates for his newly acquired vehicles. Once again, he thought back to the hours of planning with Karl Smithson and their desperation to succeed, most of which would entail avoiding police attention whilst committing a major crime. Karl had been acutely aware that when stopped by the police, he had been forced to attack them in the hope of escaping before they discovered he was driving a stolen vehicle. He was convinced that any vehicles Miles used should avoid police scrutiny at all costs, hence the cars being legally purchased from Charlie, complete with registration documents.

However, the more they thought about the vehicles, the more they realised how, with the advent of modern technology, slipping under the radar was going to be difficult, if not impossible.

Things had moved on since Smithson had been arrested, with nearly every city centre street covered by cameras, as were many public and office buildings. Bus and even doorbell cameras had been used to arrest and convict criminals. They knew that it would be impossible to avoid being caught on camera, so needed something to throw the police off the scent, for a short time at least, until they pointed them in the direction of Richard Wade.

Fitting totally false number plates would ensure Miles was immediately spotted on the Automated Number Plate Recognition (ANPR) camera systems and quickly detained before he could put their plan into operation. In the past, criminals had stolen plates from similar vehicles and fitted them to their own, enabling them to survive cursory police checks. The downside to that was that the plates were invariably reported as stolen pretty quickly by the owners and, in this technological age, was not really a helpful option.

Their solution was to copy or clone the registration numbers of vehicles legitimately driving the streets of Leeds, and to fit them to the cars purchased from Bargain Motors. They fully realised that as soon as any serious crime was committed, the police would be immediately trawling through all available video footage to identify suspects and vehicles. The unfortunate owners of the real registrations would come in for some attention from the police, but why would Miles and Karl worry about that?

The trick was to find vehicles that matched his and to note their registration numbers, but Miles obviously didn't want to be filmed going round car parks noting number plates. His solution? Sit at a café in the city centre paying attention to passing cars until he spotted ones that suited his purposes. Who would take any notice of him as he enjoyed his afternoon pot of tea whilst waiting patiently for the right ones to pass by? He didn't expect it to be too difficult or to take too long, which was precisely why he had specified the need for two commonplace four-door saloons.

It only took about twenty minutes to identify a similar model blue Ford Fiesta of about the same vintage as the one he had bought. The Mondeo took a little longer, necessitating the purchase of a second pot of tea, but he found one after just over an hour's patient observation. Having noted both numbers, a tired Miles made his way home to spend a last night in his flat, satisfied that he had two cloned plates that would not trigger any alerts on police ANPR systems.

His last task of the day was ringing Jimmy to arrange for the handover of another £20,000 cash to be collected on the Friday morning.

FIFTEEN

Brenda Thomas's world finally collapsed around her at the same time that Miles Kingston was enjoying his afternoon tea in sunny Leeds.

Brenda's stony-faced boss entered her office at the DVLA unannounced, accompanied by a man and woman who introduced themselves as Detective Sergeant Lily Croft and Detective Constable Joe Morrell.

Without preamble, Ds Croft said, "Brenda Thomas, you are under arrest on suspicion of theft and illegally supplying driving licences. Stand up, please."

Unable to speak, she was on the edge of panic, barely hearing the words when she was cautioned. She desperately needed one of her pills. Brenda was allowed to put her coat on, before she was handcuffed and led from the office, past several of her colleagues who stared in disbelief at the scene unfolding before them.

Lily Croft carried Brenda's handbag, whilst her boss locked the office as they left.

Fifteen minutes later, a tearful Brenda was in the custody suite at Swansea Police Station, trying to understand what was being said as she was booked into custody.

When she heard theft mentioned again by the officers, she could only whisper, "But I haven't stolen anything." Her comment was ignored.

Having had the handcuffs removed, she endured the indignity of being searched and having her watch and jewellery removed, before the contents of her bag were emptied onto the counter. The purse, make-up and a comb generated little interest from the watching officers, but the small bottle of green pills certainly did.

The Custody Officer picked the bottle up. "What are these?"

Still unable to speak, Brenda started to cry.

"Are these pills yours?"

She nodded.

"What are they?"

Brenda just looked at the officer, tears running down her cheeks.

Joe Morrell, a former drug squad officer, took the bottle from the Sergeant and shook one of the pills into his palm for closer examination.

"Sarge, these look like OxyContin to me, a prohibited drug. You've probably noticed there's no label on the bottle, so I doubt they've been prescribed."

"Okay, Joe, you better arrest her for that as well."

Brenda could only look on in horror as Morrell cautioned and arrested her on suspicion of being in possession of controlled drugs. She was unable to reply.

The Custody Officer then asked her if she wanted a solicitor.

At last, Brenda found her voice. "Is that best?"

"I cannot advise you. It is your choice and will not cost you anything."

She nodded. "All right then."

"In a few minutes, you will be fingerprinted and a sample for DNA analysis will be taken. However, before that, I must ask if you have any more drugs in your possession."

"No."

"In the circumstances, for your safety and to secure evidence, I am authorising a strip search."

"No, no, please."

Minutes later, Brenda was taken to a cell and stripped naked in the presence of Ds Croft and a female detention officer. She was not searched intimately, but her hair and the soles of her feet were checked for concealed drugs. Crying hysterically, she was given a blanket to cover herself whilst the officers carefully checked her clothing, finding nothing of interest. The poor woman had lost count of the number of times she had been forced to take her clothes off in front of strangers since her addiction began. It never got any easier, nor was the humiliation any less.

The officers left the cell, closing the door behind them, whilst a thoroughly humiliated Brenda dressed herself, wondering what else was going to happen to her.

Unable to do anything until their prisoner had seen her solicitor, Croft and Morrell searched Brenda's office and, with an Inspector's authority, her home. They found nothing related to their ongoing DVLA investigation, which they found a little surprising, but did recover some more OxyContin in her bedside cabinet.

Somewhat disconcerted by their failure to find any incriminating evidence, the officers could only conclude that Brenda was either innocent or extremely clever.

By early evening, Brenda's solicitor, Alex Watson, had consulted with her and was ready to speak to the arresting officers. They met in an unoccupied interview room.

"Good evening. I'm Ds Croft and this is Dc Morrell from the TARIAN."

"Just a minute, as I understand it, you only deal with serious crime. This woman hasn't got any previous convictions and works as a supervisor at the DVLA. What on earth do you think she's done?"

"You're quite right. We are the Regional Organised Crime Unit dealing with serious offences across the whole of South Wales. For some time, the managers at the DVLA have been aware of discrepancies in the issue of driving licences and so they called us in. We've identified your client as the person we believe to be responsible."

"What sort of discrepancies?"

"Paperwork not matching the number of licences issued, payments not recorded for their issue and some containing addresses that do not exist. In short, we believe a number of fake driving licences have been created by your client."

Watson shook his head. "Surely we're talking petty fraud here. Why all the heavy stuff?"

Ds Croft sighed heavily. "Firstly, we are talking potentially dozens of bogus licences. As I am sure you are aware, driving licences are often used to prove identity, for instance, helping to open bank accounts and obtain other documents. They offer huge potential to organised crime, including operating fraudulent schemes and possibly people trafficking. I am sure you can see just how serious this could be."

"Yes, I understand. Let me have another word with my client."

Half an hour later, Croft and Morrell were seated opposite Brenda Thomas and her solicitor in an interview room. Their first impression was how ill the woman looked. She was visibly shivering and, even though the room was warm, had wrapped herself in a blanket. She was unkempt, her hair was a mess and she was grey-faced, with red and swollen eyes from her constant crying. However, most noticeably, she was shaking and twitching. It was clear that she was starting to withdraw from her drug use.

The recording machine was switched on. The officers introduced themselves again, with Dc Morrell cautioning Brenda once more.

At this point, Alex Watson interjected. "Officers, you can clearly see that my client is not well. I have advised her not to answer any of your questions at this stage. However, she has indicated that she is actually relieved to have been arrested, recognising that she needs urgent help. She agrees that she has been forced to create hundreds of fake licences, all of which she has copies of, including documents and photographs. In addition, she has proof of being raped and assaulted along with evidence against a number of men for trading in drugs. You are probably not surprised to hear there are at least two doctors involved. Finally, she believes she may be able to point you in the direction of the main men involved in the organised crime groups."

Even though they were both experienced officers, Croft and Morrell could not hide their surprise at these revelations.

Ds Croft recovered first. "What does Miss Thomas want from us?"

"She doesn't want to be prosecuted and in return she is prepared to give evidence when necessary. She is a respectable woman who has been used, abused and manipulated by these evil men. Her life has been made hell by them. However, her priority is urgent treatment for what is clearly her addiction to OxyContin."

Croft carefully considered the solicitor's words. "Brenda, just one question, if you will. Is what Mr Watson just told us true?"

She looked towards her solicitor, who nodded that it was okay to reply.

"Yes, it is. I want my life back. Please help me." Despite her best efforts, the desperate woman started to cry again.

Ds Croft looked at the solicitor thoughtfully before nodding. "Okay, Mr Watson, you have given us a great deal to think about, so we will conclude the interview for now."

They switched off the recorder, returning Brenda to her cell.

They told Alex Watson that what he was asking them to do was way above their pay grade so would necessitate consultations with higher authority. He was not surprised at that and was happy to accept their assurance that he would be contacted later or possibly in the morning with an answer. Of course, he stressed that his client should, in no circumstances, be interviewed further without him being present.

After updating the Custody Officer, Croft and Morrell followed the age-old police practice of adjourning to the canteen for a team talk. Once they had their coffee and were seated at a table, well away from eavesdroppers, Croft spoke first.

"Well, Joe, what do you think?"

"I've got to say, Lily, it came as a bit of a surprise, but there is a ring of truth about it. When you look at the woman, she's a total wreck, desperate for drugs and probably prepared to do anything to get them."

"I tend to agree, Joe. My view is that even though we haven't got the full story yet, it looks like the poor woman is a victim. It will be interesting to find out how she got into drugs in the first place."

"Well, in my experience, OxyContin is a strong painkiller and is usually prescribed to relieve pain after injury. It is not unknown for people to get hooked and, if that's how it happened, it would certainly help her case."

"Our next problem is what Watson told us. It moves this inquiry into the big leagues, what with hundreds of fake licences involved, sexual and physical assaults, drug dealers, bent doctors and a possible way in to the men at the top. We need to consult."

"Yeah, I think you're right. The other thing to consider is what exactly these licences have been used for. That's a major inquiry on its own. Lily, this could be a monster."

Whilst both were experienced officers, they could not possibly imagine where this job would lead and the impact it would have on many, many people.

Finding an empty office, Croft rang her immediate boss, DI Paul Davies, giving him a brief but precise summary of events. His predictable response was that whilst it sounded good, higher authority would need to be consulted, including, no doubt, the Crown Prosecution Service, one consideration being that if it was as big as it sounded, then more staff would definitely be needed. He instructed them to return to the office immediately.

Before they left, aware that time was moving on, the Custody Officer was informed of the situation, but not all of it, with a promise that they would be kept in the loop.

They were not surprised that Detective Superintendent Dai Williams was waiting for them when they got back. Croft and Morrell updated him and DI Davies, telling them that at this stage they had no concrete evidence to confirm her story, but that they believed Brenda Thomas. They explained that a large number of fake driving licences had been created at the DVLA and that it was almost certain she was responsible. Explaining the drugs that had been recovered and her clear desperation for help, they suggested that this was a golden opportunity to get some major criminals off the streets. Finally, they gave a brief antecedent history, as far as they knew it, of Brenda Thomas, emphasising her previous good character.

Both supervisors were silent as they considered what they had heard. Williams spoke first.

"She told you that she has created hundreds of fake licences, not the dozens we thought?"

Croft answered. "That's right, sir, and she says she has the proof."

"Well, that certainly makes it a major job in itself, never mind all the other possible offences. Right, Lily, you've had longer to think about this than us. How would you suggest we handle this? Feel free to say what you think."

Taking a deep breath, Croft went straight in at the deep end. "Sir, clearly, I have spent only a short time with Brenda, but I am satisfied that she is a victim in all this and that we should treat her as such. At the moment, she is a wreck, withdrawing from the drugs, and frankly we couldn't interview her if we wanted to. We may have sufficient evidence already to charge her, but I feel strongly that by doing so we risk alienating her and losing any cooperation. I also believe we have a duty to help her, as we would with any person who fell into the clutches of these bastards."

Williams smiled at her passion. "Yes, I tend to agree with what you say. The question is how to proceed. Joe, do you agree with what Lily has said?"

"Totally, sir. If her masters don't already know she's in custody, they very soon will. Her arrest was pretty public and we don't know who else is involved at the DVLA, so we need to move pretty quickly. Like Lily, I believe we should treat her as a victim and do our best to protect her. She may be in great danger from these people, especially if she were to end up on remand in prison."

"Yes, I get all that. My question remains, how do we move forward?"

Speaking for the first time, DI Davies put his opinion forward. "It seems likely that charging her is not a reasonable or sensible option. Nor can we realistically consider interviewing her, so I suggest we release her on bail."

He held his hand up as both Croft and Morrell started to object.

"Hear me out. I agree, we need to look after this lady and help her as much as we can, which in turn can only benefit our investigation. What I'm proposing is that we liaise with her solicitor and the CPS with a suggestion that she be released under investigation. As part of her release, we will insist she receives treatment to get her off drugs, not exactly a bail condition, you understand. We would need to find a place where that treatment is available, hopefully on the NHS. I'm not sure our budget would stretch to a private clinic."

The Superintendent smiled. "Well, it's a little unorthodox, but it may work. Joe, you're the drug squad man. What do you think?"

"Obviously, there are places where she can get the treatment she needs. The good thing with OxyContin is that medication can be given to greatly reduce the symptoms of withdrawal, making it much easier for people to stay the course."

A slightly exasperated Williams asked a further question. "Joe, how soon do you think we will be able to interview her? The credibility of anyone on drugs and the evidence they may give in court would be destroyed in minutes by any half-competent barrister."

"Sorry, sir. The symptoms of withdrawal reduce significantly within two to three weeks, although there is still some way to go before drug users are in the clear."

"Okay, I like it. Paul, you get on to the Chief Crown Prosecutor and get his opinion. It needs to come from the very top. Lily, you speak to the solicitor to see what he thinks of our proposal, and don't be afraid to let him know what may happen to his client if we just release her.

Hopefully, you won't need to play bad cop, and, before anybody objects, that is definitely not a course of action we will follow. Joe, you find a suitable facility for the lady. She is very important to us. It's now 7.30pm. Let's all meet back here at 9pm. Get this done, people, there's a lot at stake."

The three junior officers left the office to go about their allocated tasks, none of which would be easy.

However, reconvening back in the Superintendent's office at 9pm, the reports were generally positive. First to speak was DI Davies, who was able to tell the others that he had been able to make contact with a slightly disgruntled Chief Crown Prosecutor for the area who, whilst cautious, believed their plan was legally and morally justifiable, if a little unusual. He stressed that his main concern was for the safety of Brenda Thomas, who, on the facts he had been given, was undoubtedly a victim and should be dealt with as such, unless and until more incriminating evidence came to light. The chance to close down major criminal networks was, in his opinion, too good to miss. So pretty much a thumbs-up, with the proviso that he would appoint one of his prosecutors to liaise throughout with the police.

Paul Davies added that his impression was that the prosecutor was quite eager, probably seeing it as a possible career-defining moment, especially as it would be the police who took the flak if it all went wrong. So situation normal then.

Lily Croft's report was much shorter. Alex Watson, after a brief consultation with his client, wholeheartedly approved the plan, once again stressing Brenda's deep fear of her criminal masters and her desire to make all the men who had used and abused her pay. Most of all, she was desperate to overcome her addiction to OxyContin.

Last to speak was Joe Morrell. "Sorry to rain on everyone's parade, but I am unable to find an NHS facility that can take Brenda at such short notice. They are all pretty much overwhelmed."

Supt. Williams was unable to hide his irritation. "I wish you'd told us this sooner, Joe. Looks like we're buggered, unless anyone has any other bright ideas."

Morrell jumped straight in again. "I may have, sir. I have spoken to the owner of a private clinic who is prepared to admit and treat Brenda at half their normal price. It's still £2,000, mind you."

"And why would he do that?"

Morrell looked a little embarrassed as he fidgeted in his chair. "Because of his work, he has a visceral hatred of drug dealers and the misery they cause."

"Come on, man, out with the rest."

"He owes me a favour. I helped him and his son out with an awkward problem some time ago."

DI Davies spoke as the Superintendent looked like he was about to blow a fuse. "Joe, do we need to know about this favour, and will it come back to bite us? Lastly, how exactly do you propose that we pay £2,000 to this clinic?"

"The favour was nothing illegal or underhand and led to the successful prosecution of a number of dealers. Trust me, sir, it won't be a problem. As far as payment goes, perhaps we could just register Brenda as a CHIS, and instead of paying her, we pay it directly to the clinic for her treatment."

The other three officers were stunned into silence by Morrell's suggestion.

Eventually, Williams spoke. "It's quite a creative solution, but, I have to say, I'm not sure we can do it. As you know, Covert Human Intelligence Sources or informants, as we used to call them in my early days, are usually paid on results, not in advance. In addition, that's quite a lot of cash."

"Yes, I realise that, sir. However, in my own experience, we have paid out larger amounts than that in the past and often for much less reward than we stand to gain from Brenda Thomas."

"I take your point, but what proof do we have that she has the information we need to take these evil bastards out?"

Lily Croft stepped in. "She was quick to correct us that we were looking at hundreds of fake driving licences rather than dozens, claiming to have proof. It's also absolutely obvious that she gets her drugs from somewhere, so at least we should get sufficient info to roll up her dealers. That alone could be worth the money. My final thought is that maybe Joe could prevail on his friend to take half his fee up front and the other half in four weeks' time when, hopefully, she gets released."

Williams nodded. "What do you think, Joe? Will he go for that?"

"Possibly, sir."

"Okay, we'll go for it. Paul, you will be in day-to-day command of this operation, but keep me in the loop at all times. Lily, you and Joe will be her handlers. Get the paperwork done and I'll sign it off. Remember, this is on my authority and if, as it probably will, the shit hits the fan, I'll try to protect you, but we may all end up damaged. This is potentially a huge job, so I believe it's worth the risk, but if any of you want to abandon ship, now's the time."

Nobody moved.

"Good, let's get to work. Please remember that she will be in danger from the people she has been supplying with licences. They will try to find her and her evidence. Can we come up with a cover story at the DVLA for her arrest?"

Davies answered. "We'll come up with something. In the meantime, if this job turns out to be as big as we believe, we need to maintain absolute security by giving it a code name and from this moment on referring to it only by that name. The next code name on the operation name list is Dingo."

Williams laughed out loud. "God knows where they get these names from, but Operation Dingo it is. We'll need to refer to Brenda Thomas by something else as well, both in conversation and paperwork, to protect her as much as we can."

"They're using dogs for the list this month, sir. I suggest we just call her Witness Bravo. It's easy to use in conversation."

Everyone readily agreed with Davies, confirming he would take care of the necessary confidential registration of the operation.

Williams smiled as he said, "Lily, Joe, I want you to move Bravo immediately and keep close contact with her and the clinic. I would suggest you visit her every couple of days. In the meantime, Paul, I want you to liaise closely with the DVLA to get us moving forward, but I'm afraid we're a bit in limbo until our source gives us the full story. We'll draft in more staff if and when we need them. Okay, everybody?"

After confirming their agreement, the other three officers left the Detective Superintendent's office to carry out the designated tasks, before heading home for some much-needed rest.

Within two hours, a pretty ill Brenda Thomas had been released and driven to the private clinic by Croft and Morrell. It was stressed that she was in grave danger and that, under no circumstances, should she contact anyone.

SIXTEEN

The following day, a story began to circulate at the DVLA that Brenda Thomas had been arrested for serial shoplifting and would not be returning to work. It was the best they could do in the time available.

Later that same afternoon, Croft and Morrell met Brenda and Alex Watson at the clinic by pre-arrangement and with the consent of medical staff. When arranging for the solicitor to attend, Lily Croft had stressed that there would be no interview but merely a discussion to plan the way forward.

Wearing something resembling a tracksuit provided by the clinic, Brenda still looked pretty rough, but had at least stopped shaking. Informing them that she had slept well following her first doses of the drugs to assist with her medical detox, the woman appeared much calmer. In simple terms, she had started the process of weaning herself off the OxyContin.

After confirming that Brenda understood this was not an interview, Lily Croft explained to her that she had been registered as a CHIS and what this entailed. The solicitor assured the officers that, having already spoken to Brenda, she was fully aware of her obligations. She understood that monies paid for the information she furnished were to be used for the clinic's fees. Also, her cooperation may prevent her being prosecuted for any offences she had committed. She knew that this was not guaranteed, but, if what she had said so far was true, and led to the arrest and conviction of others, it was likely.

Croft looked closely at the woman, who appeared to be listening intently. "Brenda, are you clear about all this?"

She answered in a calm and clear voice. "Yes, I am. Thank you for this."

"First things first. Are the documents and other evidence you claim to have safe?"

"Yes, they are."

"Can we get them yet?"

Watson intervened. "At the moment, no. Everything is safe and will be produced when my client is able to explain it all to you."

Morrell looked at the solicitor with some annoyance. "Don't you trust us? I think we've proved both our understanding of your client's position and desire to help her. We, and our senior officers, believe Brenda is a victim, and until there is evidence to the contrary we will treat her as such."

"Of course I trust you. Otherwise, I wouldn't be advising her to go along with it. I consider it to be her best option."

Slightly mollified, Morrell nodded. "Okay. Does your client need to explain her absence to any family or friends whilst she is in the clinic?"

Brenda answered quietly whilst her eyes began to fill with tears once more. "Just my mother. I don't have any friends left that might be interested or care where I am. I'm going to ring her later."

"Do you have a story prepared?"

"Yes, Mr Watson is going to stay with me whilst I ring, and I'm going to tell her a place on a course has come available at short notice. She'll understand."

Ds Croft spoke next. "Would you like us to go to your house and get some clothes?"

"Oh, yes, please."

After taking possession of her keys, the officers set off to fulfil that small task, planning to use the opportunity to have a further search of Brenda's home, which, of course, would prove fruitless.

They had arranged for the clinic staff and the solicitor to inform them as soon as she was fit enough to be interviewed properly. That wasn't going to stop them checking on her frequently themselves, having been told she should be ready in seven to ten days, even if she was expected to stay in the clinic for a month.

She had a very difficult road ahead. A month of medication, counselling and group therapy was only the start. The real test would be when she was released back out into the world.

SEVENTEEN

That same Friday morning, Miles realised that it was now just under a fortnight until he made the big score that was going to change his life and, although he had achieved a lot already, there was still much more to be done. He was nervous, but very excited. He constantly thought about the timing issues, particularly as everything was to be done by one man: himself. He dare not involve anyone else because once more than one person knew a secret, it was no longer a secret. That thought made him shiver nervously as it reminded him again that some of the crucial details had been kept from Frank Harris, a man not used to being kept in the dark.

Putting his worries to one side, Miles Kingston completed his first task of the day, collecting £20,000 from an ever-unsmiling Jimmy at the betting shop, which he deposited in the usual holdall.

As it was at the end of the same street, it made sense to visit the car dealer's next, where Charlie greeted him like a long-lost brother and, unlike Jimmy, had a broad smile on his face. In the office, away from prying eyes, Miles handed over £17,500 cash in full payment for both cars and the motorbike, which perhaps explained why the man was so pleased to see him. He took the keys for the Fiesta and registration documents for all three vehicles, confirming he would collect the Mondeo and the bike the following week.

He'd already decided that the car would have to do and there was little point in test driving it. After all, where else could he go to get something that matched his needs so perfectly? Included in the purchase price was the car dealer's promise that, as agreed, he would produce the copy of Wade's false driving licence in the name of James Adamson to identify him as the purchaser of all three vehicles when the police eventually got there.

As he drove away, Miles was reassured by the sweet sound the engine made and the smooth gear changes. Perhaps it would be okay.

He found the factory unit where the number plate maker was based easily enough, and was pleased to find that he was the only customer of the foreign looking man behind the counter.

"Hi, Charlie said you may be able to help me."

Miles was completely thrown when Tom Muscat replied in about the broadest Yorkshire accent he had ever heard. "What is it you want?"

He placed a piece of paper on the counter. "I want two sets of plates, please. These are the numbers."

Muscat looked at them quietly. "I assume that since these numbers are on a piece of paper, you do not have the registration documents that match them."

Miles just smiled as if they were two mates sharing a massive secret.

"Okay, I can do that. It'll take half an hour and I'll want two hundred and fifty quid."

"You must be joking. I can get them done at Halfords for about fifty quid."

Muscat laughed quietly as he shook his head ruefully. "Listen, mate, we both know why you've come to me and not to Halfords. These plates are bent and there's no way they would touch them with a bargepole. So let's stop pissing about, do you want them or not? Don't forget you're paying for discretion as well."

Yet again, he had no option but to pay the price demanded. Having previously put some cash from the bag into his wallet, he was able to pay the man without letting him know how much he was carrying.

Less than an hour later, Kingston was driving away with a set of cloned plates for the Mondeo and another set fitted to the blue Fiesta, with the originals in the boot. They would be needed again. He just hoped the owner of the cloned plates was not of any interest to the police; that would be beyond unlucky.

Driving to see the estate agent, Jean, he felt much happier, confident progress was being made and that he was getting nearer to his and Smithson's twin objectives.

When he eventually got parked near to the office, it was near to lunchtime and, as he entered, he could see that Jean was looking a little frazzled, to say the least. They quickly completed their business and she handed over his new apartment keys.

He still quite fancied his chances with her so took the opportunity to lay some groundwork. "Do you fancy joining me for a quick bite? My treat to thank you for your help."

"I haven't got long, but that would be great, thanks. There's a pub round the corner that's not too bad."

"Okay, let's go."

Miles was entertaining company, with a fund of risqué stories and jokes, none of which gave any indication of his murky past. Jean was no fool and had been round the block more than once, so she was not completely taken in by him but liked him nevertheless.

After a convivial lunch, he walked her back to the office, confident that he had made a good impression. He thought about a kiss but decided against it, simply taking her hand.

"I've got a lot of work on over the next couple of weeks, but perhaps I could give you a ring after that"

She had enjoyed the lunch and nodded. "I'd like that."

He left her at the door, wondering what she would think if she knew exactly what his business was over the coming weeks. He didn't know if he would even still be in the country, but if he did hook up with her, he must remember that she knew him as Peter Webb.

Returning to his car, he drove to the apartment, parking in the allocated space in the underground car park before taking the lift to the fourth floor, all the while keeping his head down to avoid being caught too clearly on any security cameras. Once inside, he was reminded how comfortable the apartment was, in stark contrast to the grotty place he currently called home.

Home was exactly where he headed next, leaving the car behind to prevent any mishaps with police or cameras and not wanting any more connections between it, him and either of the two flats than he could help. It may be risky leaving it there with the cloned plates, but it would cause more problems later if he left the original plates on, especially when it came to fitting Wade up properly. The apartment was to form an integral part of Richard Wade's downfall, and there could be nothing which suggested a prior connection between him and the property. If those plates were left in place, that may well happen, which would never do. He also had to make it as straightforward as he possibly could so even the idiot police couldn't make a mess of it.

Thank goodness for a decent bus service. He was home within twenty minutes and quickly began to pack a large holdall with everything he thought he might need for the coming fortnight. As well as clothes and toiletries, he added the cash, his notes and, most importantly, the bent driving licences and forged documents from the fireplace store. He definitely needed them for the next stages of the plan.

Amazingly enough, Miles almost forgot his stock of mobile phones, only remembering to take them from the wardrobe when he was retrieving the props that allowed him to become Richard Wade. He chided himself mentally for his carelessness, remembering once more that only perfect planning and execution would see the plan succeed. If he slipped up at any stage, he would be back in prison before his feet could touch the ground.

After a final check round, he donned his Richard Wade disguise for the next part of his day. He left the building quietly, careful to make sure there was no chance of bumping into his mother, especially looking like this. In any event, she should have been in either the pub or at the bingo, places where she spent almost every afternoon with the old crones she called her friends.

His one consolation was that if everything did go wrong, he might end up back inside, but Frank Harris wouldn't get his money back, so his mother, the old cow, would be out on the streets. It just proved that if you looked hard enough, there was always some good to be found in every situation.

Another short bus trip took him to the city centre where he met the other estate agent, Robert Grundy, in his office, hurriedly apologising for not having managed to get there in the morning.

"No problem, thank you for coming in, Mr Adamson. I've got the lease along with the terms and conditions all ready for your signature."

"What do you mean terms and conditions?"

Robert gave his most ingratiating smile. "It's just restrictions on what you can do whilst renting, you know, alterations, businesses, that sort of thing. I don't think there's anything that will prevent you writing your book."

Miles only just stopped himself from asking what the idiot was going on about, belatedly recalling that was the reason he had given for wanting such an isolated place.

"Okay, thanks, that fine."

He quickly signed the documents in the places indicated by Robert, before handing over the £3,000 cash to a very relieved estate agent who, when Miles hadn't shown up that morning, feared they would be stuck with the almost unlettable property for even longer.

Having left the office, with the property's keys in his pocket, Miles put his baseball cap on and headed to the railway station, intending to remove the Wade disguise in the toilets. Thank goodness it was only a couple of streets away, his holdall was getting heavy, but even so there would be a number of cameras covering the streets and then in the station itself. Well aware the police would examine the camera footage at great length, and go back as far as necessary, he did his best to cover his face by pulling the cap low and looking down as much as he could.

On reaching the station, he went into the toilets, quickly finding an empty cubicle. He took off the cap and jacket before removing the glasses, wig and contact lenses, all of which he put in the holdall. It was a fairly warm day so he left the toilets wearing jeans and a shirt.

Satisfied he'd changed his appearance as much as possible, he walked to the rented apartment, well aware that there was nothing he could do to conceal the holdall. However, it was pretty nondescript and, for goodness' sake, any number of people carried bags of some description as they left the station. Hopefully, that was good enough. What more could he do?

Just before he got to the street where the apartment block was, he once more put on a baseball cap, using the same measures to thwart any cameras in the street, and keeping it on inside the building until he got to his new, if temporary, home. Once inside, he breathed a sigh of relief, wishing he'd thought to get some beers in. Miles was tired. It had been a long day, but for all his meticulous planning he realised that not only had he failed to buy any beer but he had not got any groceries at all. He couldn't even make a cup of tea.

Sometime later, having been shopping, he was sat

watching football on the big-screen TV, drinking beer and eating the recently delivered pizza. Life was not too bad, was it? Soon, he would use one of the luxurious showers then try to get a good night's sleep in the king size bed. Just a pity he didn't have some company.

He had a big job to do the next day, Saturday, one that had been preying on his mind ever since this all started, and one he was certainly not looking forward to.

EIGHTEEN

There were at least half a dozen football pitches in the park, all of which were occupied on that Saturday morning by boys and girls of all ages playing organised matches. Quite a few men and women were watching from the sidelines, presumably parents of the players.

It didn't take Miles long to find the right pitch, in the corner near to the changing rooms. Just to be sure, he'd been told the colours of the home team: red and black striped shirts and red socks. The man he was looking for was easy to spot, wearing the same shirt as the boys, although it was stretched tight over his not inconsiderable beer belly. He was over six feet tall with a shaven head, several tattoos on his arms, and could be clearly heard shouting instructions to the boys in his role as coach. Of course, Miles recognised him easily anyway, having spent over eighteen months in Armley with him, the difference being that Officer Collier got to go home at the end of every shift.

Miles had timed his arrival to coincide with the last ten minutes of the match, and no one took any notice of an extra spectator. Once the final whistle went, he watched as his former custodian collected the players together for an after-match pep talk, followed by the usual man of the match presentation and photographs. As the players and their parents started to wander off, the coach busied himself collecting the footballs and other equipment together.

Constantly on the lookout for anyone paying too much attention, Miles approached Collier, nervously clearing his throat several times before he spoke.

"Hello, Mr Collier, nice to see you again."

Instantly recognising the speaker, Collier sighed heavily, totally taken aback to see an ex-con at the football match but knowing instinctively that no good could come of it. He had occasionally bumped into former inmates before, but fortunately he'd never had any problems with them and didn't want any now. It was obvious this was no accidental meeting and had been carefully engineered to catch him off guard.

"I know you, don't I? What do you want?"

"Mr Harris suggested you might welcome a donation for the football team. I wonder if we might discuss it."

Not for the first time, Collier wondered why he had allowed himself to get involved with Harris and his people. He knew the answer well enough; an expensive divorce along with a gambling habit leading to a desperate need for money meant he was an easy target for them. They owned him.

All he could do was give a resigned nod.

"I don't want much, just a package taking onto B wing when you go to work this evening. And there'll be five hundred quid in it for you."

Collier shook his head. "I thought I recognised your face. Kingston, isn't it? There's no way, I don't do that anymore. I won't do it."

"Look, I'm just the messenger. You know how Frank Harris works, and if you cross him, there will be consequences."

"I won't take drugs in, definitely not."

Miles smiled at the other man's tacit acceptance of the task, merely placing limits on what he was prepared to do. "You don't have to, it's only a phone. One more in there won't make much difference, will it?"

"Who's it for?"

"Karl Smithson. It should be easy for a senior officer like you."

Acknowledging that he had no real option, Collier said, "Where is it?"

Miles looked over his shoulder, before handing over a brown paper bag containing £500 in cash and the smallest mobile phone he had been able to find. There was also a charger, although how Karl was going to keep it charged in the future was up to him. Maybe Collier would help.

"Tell him the contact number has been put into the phone."

With a final scowl, Collier turned and started walking towards the changing rooms.

Enjoying his dominance over a screw, Miles couldn't resist calling out, "Remember what will happen if you let us down."

There was no response from Collier.

Half an hour later, Miles was back in the apartment checking the phone bearing the handwritten label 'Karl', making sure it was fully charged, as was the one being delivered to his friend. He remembered how long it had taken him to find a phone small enough to just about fit into the palm of your hand, making it easier to hide when cells were searched.

It seemed mad that he had loads still to do, but, at the moment, he was not able to do much more than some research. He set to work on his fifth different mobile phone, checking the cost and availability of lock-up garages, followed by train and, most importantly, ferry schedules. He did wonder, not for the first time, if it was absolutely necessary to use so many phones in the name of security. He supposed it was a sensible precaution, just as long as he kept them all labelled so that he didn't forget which was which. Keeping all nine phones fully charged was a nuisance, and he did have concerns that the five unused ones may not be enough. It would become easier as he disposed of them once they were no longer needed, as he had done with the one he had used to contact Brenda.

After much thought, Miles had decided that if he needed to make a run for it, especially from Frank Harris, his best option would be a trip to Rotterdam using P&O Ferries from Hull. His reasoning being that the port of Hull was only a short distance away and easy to get to, with less security than airports. Obviously, there would be some security and passport checks, but he hoped that by using his own passport he would have no trouble boarding, especially as he would be carrying a bag full of money. After calling the ferry terminal, he discovered that P&O Ferries sailed at eight-thirty every night, bound for Rotterdam. The good news was that he could just turn up on the day, buy a ticket and board the ferry as a foot passenger. The bad news was that the ferry was sometimes fully booked, so he could be turned away. If that happened, he would just have to book for the following day's sailing. At least that way, if all went as planned, he could drop everything and go when ready, with no need for too much future planning. Once in Rotterdam, his plan was to disappear and then, probably, make his way to France or Spain if he could, where it should be easy to mingle with the tourists and expats.

It would seem that getting a lock-up garage would not be a problem but, as usual, was not going to be cheap. So as not to arouse suspicion, he always had to agree to extended rental periods for properties when in reality he only needed them for a few days or weeks at the most.

For his final call, Miles had to use the phone marked 'Jimmy', with the man answering after two rings.

"What?"

"Hello, Jimmy. It's Miles."

"That's nice for you. What do you want?"

"Remember we spoke about a girl I would need to make use of. I'm ready to see her now, tomorrow if possible."

"I'll see what I can do." The phone went dead.

Fifteen minutes later, Jimmy rang back. "Two o'clock tomorrow in the bar at the Queens Hotel. Natasha, she's got blonde hair, will be wearing a black dress and carrying a red handbag."

Once again, he ended the call before Miles could reply. A man of very few words, our Jimmy.

One of the things Miles Kingston and Karl Smithson

had discussed at great length was how they could frame Richard Wade in such a way that he had no chance of avoiding being convicted for a crime he didn't commit. Their plan included posing as him, being seen by witnesses, being caught on cameras and making sure he had no alibi, but they didn't have one piece of solid indisputable evidence. Something like fingerprints or DNA perhaps, but how to get it?

Whilst he was reluctant to use the Ford Fiesta too often, not wanting to establish any connection with the apartment block, Miles decided he had no option but to use it for what he was planning. He was going to the village where Wade lived. Having studied the idiot's Facebook page, he had realised the background picture of a pretty cottage may well be where he lived, something easily confirmed with the details from the forged council tax bill.

It was only ten minutes' drive, and sure enough there it was on the main street, just opposite a pub. It all looked very peaceful, with a number of shirt-sleeved customers sat in a beer garden in the warm afternoon sun. Idly scanning the bucolic scene as he drove slowly through the village, Miles almost crashed the car when he saw Richard Wade seated alone at one of the tables. He drove into a side street, parking the car as he considered his next move. Not truly believing his luck, he made up his mind to act, knowing the chances of another such lucky break were slim to none.

Walking through the beer garden, he could see that Wade was smoking and had a good three quarters of his drink left; perfect. It was something with lemon in it, probably a gin and tonic. Purchasing his own pint, he returned to the garden and was unable to see any empty tables, the only space being at the table occupied by Wade. Oh well.

He approached the table and, with what he considered to be a friendly smile, said, "Do you mind if I sit here?"

Wade merely nodded.

It was a shock for Miles to see the man he had spent so much time impersonating in the flesh, and he realised just how good a job the make-up artist, Justin, had done on him. It was uncanny.

"It's a lovely day, isn't it?"

Looking surprised to have been spoken to, Wade replied, "Okay."

He turned slightly away from Miles, making it abundantly clear that he wasn't there for the conversation, especially with a complete stranger. Miles took the hint, keeping a surreptitious eye on the man as he stubbed his cigarette out in the empty ashtray, lighting another almost immediately.

Wade looked at his watch, giving an audible sigh before shaking his head as he looked around, apparently having been stood up by someone. He stubbed his second cigarette out, finishing his drink before slamming the glass down on the table. He stood and left without even a glance in the direction of his table companion, stalking off towards his cottage.

Quick as a flash, Miles picked up the backpack he'd so thoughtfully brought with him from the car, holding it down at the side of the table. Looking furtively around, he was pleased to see some of the afternoon drinkers had left, and those that remained were paying no attention to him whatsoever. Having come prepared, he took two plastic bags from his pocket before placing the backpack on the table, shielding the glass and ashtray from any casual observers. Placing one of the bags over the glass, he quickly put it into the backpack followed by the other plastic bag containing the contents of the ashtray he'd swiftly emptied into it. Putting the bag onto the floor, he casually finished his drink, all the time looking around, fearful his actions had been seen. None of the few people left were paying him any attention at all.

He finished his drink and returned to the car. Still unable to believe his luck, Miles started the car and headed back to the apartment. Okay, he'd gone to the village prepared, but he thought it was to rummage in Wade's dustbins, not to take the fingerprint and DNA evidence he wanted from a pub table. How lucky can you get?

Having returned the car to its parking space, he spent the rest of his afternoon and evening waiting for the call he was sure would come from Armley. Whilst having a few beers and an Indian takeaway, Miles did some thinking about tomorrow's meeting with the girl. One conclusion he came to was that, unless he wanted to start laundering sheets, he'd better stay out of the master bedroom with its king size bed, saving it for his guest. It didn't matter; the second bedroom was not too shoddy.

His only other worry was the number of fingerprints and DNA he was leaving in the apartment by living there for a couple of weeks. No matter, he thought; if the police ever came to this place, the game would have long been over.

Shortly after 11pm, he received the call he had been expecting from his old cellmate, Karl Smithson.

"Hi, Karl. I expected you sooner."

"So did I. There was some kerfuffle with one of the new boys trying to hang himself. It's all quiet now, though. How are things going at your end?"

"Good so far, but that Frank Harris is a scary bastard, and so is his fixer, Jimmy."

"Come on now, you know better than that, no names."

Miles had to laugh at Smithson's paranoia. If anyone was listening, or if they got hold of these phones, it wouldn't matter much what names they used anyway, but it was best to humour him.

"Yeah, you're right, sorry."

"So exactly how are things going? I haven't got long."

"Up to now, everything is going just as we planned. Things are starting to come together, but I've got to tell you, it's going to be bloody difficult for me to do on my own."

"Think about the rewards. Revenge for me and lots of money for you. Some people are certainly going to regret crossing me. So what else are you bothered about?"

Miles thought for a couple of seconds before replying. "I'm concerned about what Harris will do when he finds out that he hasn't been told the full story. The other thing is, I've decided to forget the dog kennel. I don't think I am going to need it, not with the property I've managed to find. It's perfect for the job."

"Don't worry about Harris. As long as he gets his money, he won't care, but you better have your escape plan ready just in case. The kennel thing is up to you, it's your decision. Anything else?"

"Just to let you know that I think I'm going to be ready to move in about ten days."

"Good, I'll try to ring you every two or three days, but if you need to contact me urgently, I'm sure our friend will get a message in."

Kingston was sure Collier would do exactly that if needed.

After bidding Smithson goodbye, he cut the connection. It was certainly hard to have a conversation without using names, and they had both soon lapsed back into doing so.

NINETEEN

He'd drunk too much beer after finishing the conversation with Karl so had slept like the proverbial log, waking late with yet another hangover. He had a pounding headache and saw that his hands were trembling slightly. Good job he had plenty of time to sort himself out in time for his meeting.

After a long shower and some paracetamol, he started to feel a bit more human, but definitely couldn't face any breakfast apart from black coffee.

Miles followed his usual routine, wearing a baseball cap and keeping his head lowered as he left the apartment, not removing it until he had cleared the street.

He got to the bar in the Queens Hotel by ten to two, ordering a soft drink, not able to face anything stronger, plus this was a business meeting. Idly watching the bartender, he saw him suddenly stop speaking in mid-conversation with another customer and stare at the entrance. Curious as to what he was looking at, and wary that it may be danger, Miles looked round, joining nearly every man in the bar as he stared at one of the most stunning women he had ever seen.

Natasha did indeed have blonde hair and, as described, was wearing a black dress and carrying a red bag. He had specified to Jimmy that she should be attractive, but she exceeded all his expectations by far. There was no mistake; it was the woman he was waiting for.

She was about five feet nine inches tall, made even taller by her high heels, and, boy, was she built, with long legs displayed to spectacular effect by her short tight dress.

She looked around the bar before unhesitatingly gliding across the floor to join Miles at the bar, earning him, in equal measures, the instant envy and hatred of every other man in the room. The women present viewed her entrance with obvious disdain, clearly deciding just what sort of woman Natasha was, even if they didn't exactly realise she was a high-class prostitute.

The lady obviously knew just how to make an entrance.

Having regained the power of speech, Miles ordered the vodka and lime Natasha had requested from the transfixed barman, who seemed in no mood to leave. Close up, he saw she was just as gorgeous as she first appeared, probably in her early thirties, with some small lines around her grey eyes which were minimised with the help of very skilfully applied make-up. However, if you looked closely enough, there was a certain hardness in the set of her luscious mouth. She would more than do.

Once she had her drink, they moved to a small table in the corner of the room where they could speak more privately, on the way giving all the men in the bar a show of something most of them would never get anywhere near.

"Natasha, I'm Peter. Nice to meet you. Jimmy must

have given you a good description for you to pick me out so easily."

"Not really, darlin', he gave me a photograph."

Feeling rather foolish, he just nodded, slightly concerned that his picture was being passed around. He assumed they must have cameras at the betting shop but, on second thoughts, realised it was more likely the make-up artist, Justin Sinclair, had passed it on.

"Have you been told why I need your help?"

"Not really, only that you need me to keep someone engaged for a couple of days. They said you would give me all the details."

Natasha, if that was her real name, was quite well spoken with a southern accent, ideal for what he had planned, but was she intelligent enough for the key role he had in mind for her? He was sure that, being a member of the oldest profession, she would be ruthless enough for his needs, as anyone connected to Frank Harris surely would be. No doubt she would also not come cheap.

"Okay. First thing, do you live round here?"

"Come on, does it sound like it?"

"No, but I have to be sure. I need you to come in for the job and leave as soon as it's finished. Any problems with that?"

"None at all, it suits me perfectly. I don't want to stay in this shithole any longer than I have to, believe me. So what do you want me to do?"

"I've got a job coming up where I need to keep somebody out of the way while I do it. I want you to pretend to be a reporter interested in doing a feature on him and a book he's written. You'll meet up with him and then get him back to an apartment I've organised. I don't want him going out or making contact with anyone else. Should probably take two nights and two days in all. Can you do that?"

"Wow. I'm good, but even I might have trouble entertaining him for that long."

"Don't worry. First thing is, he's a mug who has an inflated opinion of himself, and, as well as women, he likes a drink. It was a big problem for him once upon a time, but I understand he has it under control now. I can also provide some chemical assistance as well, if you know what I mean."

"I get you. That should be all right."

"Any questions so far?"

"Yes. When? And I hope there's no typing involved."

"I'm looking at a week on Wednesday. You get into Leeds during the afternoon. I'll meet you and take you to the apartment to get you settled in, but please wear something a little less noticeable. You'll meet him for dinner that evening, get him back to the apartment, then you do your business. You should be out of Leeds by mid-afternoon on the Friday."

"What about the typing?"

He laughed, fully realising she was taking the piss. "No typing, but you are pretending to be a reporter, don't forget, so when you go for dinner, dress nice but not too dramatic, shall we say. There are a couple of other things. I've got some brief notes and a picture of this guy so you can make conversation as if you are interested, and finally I may ring you at the apartment on the Thursday night just to check there are no problems. I'm not sure, though. All okay?"

"Sure. How much?"

"I'll get to that in a minute. It's essential that this guy cannot account for his time while he is with you, so you need to be in and out of Leeds as quickly as possible so nobody can trace you. Also, when you leave the restaurant with him, you must walk to the apartment by a roundabout route, which I'll show you. No taxis. Same when leaving. I don't want him to find this apartment again."

"How much?"

"Last thing. You will need to ring him a few days before to make the appointment to meet up with him. I've prepared a script with all the details. Don't let him say no, not that I expect the vain bastard will. Sell it big style, okay?"

She was starting to get angry. "How much?"

"Five grand."

A look of disdain crossed her beautiful face. "You are joking, of course. I could make that much in here before the end of the day. I want 10,000."

Miles laughed but was acutely aware that he was getting through Frank's 50,000 at a fair old rate. "I'll meet you halfway, seven and a half."

"Fair enough, but I've got expenses. Travel, clothes, hairdresser and make-up. Plus you expect me to study as well. I think another two and a half will cover that."

He couldn't help smiling and, recognising he had no choice, gave in. "Okay, ten grand it is."

He once again wondered if Frank Harris would be skimming some off the top of the money.

Miles passed her four pages of notes, which she folded up and placed in her bag. He then took her phone number, promising to ring with the final arrangements but, with his particular leanings, couldn't resist one final question.

"Are you a real blonde? I'd love to know."

"Fuck off, Miles. That will cost you a grand to find out. I don't do freebies."

With that, she got up and stalked out of the bar. He had seriously considered paying but very regretfully decided that maintaining a distance was more important.

It was only after she had left did he realise that she had called him Miles and not Peter, as he had so carefully introduced himself. Of course, he blamed Jimmy, who must have given the tart his real name, totally forgetting that he had never told the oaf that he was using a false name. He also found it a little unsettling but reassuring at the same time that Natasha never gave any indication that she knew he was lying when he welcomed her. Unsettling that someone else knew his name but reassuring that she had kept up her act; something he was now more certain she would be able to do with Wade.

So one small ball dropped from all those he was juggling. It didn't look as if it would be significant on this occasion, but who can be sure, and it was a reminder that he had to be at the top of his game all the time.

TWENTY

Miles Kingston was feeling the strain. He had been running around for several weeks now, putting things in place for his and Karl's master plan, with the added pressure of having to masquerade as different people. He was constantly worried that he would trip himself up or forget to do something. To add to his worries, Miles knew that, whilst not a problem yet, he was spending the money pretty quickly, but, thankfully, most of his major purchases had been made.

He was finding it difficult to sleep, unable to stop thinking through all the tasks he had completed and those yet to be done. The one thing he was most reluctant to face was his own fear. The crime he was planning to commit was, to say the least, very dangerous, with serious consequences for failure, the least of which would be a long time incarcerated.

Miles was aware he was drinking too much, especially to help him sleep, meaning he awoke almost every morning sluggishly, with a hangover. He resolved to cut back at once. Today was no exception as he splashed cold water on his face in an attempt to get his eyes to focus and took more painkillers to combat the pounding headache.

Thankfully, the jobs-done list was now longer than the jobs-to-do list, but he still had some major ones to complete.

After his usual coffee, Miles was back on the phone, firstly to Jimmy to ask for his final £10,000 and some more specialist equipment. Having prepared his explanation for the request, he was a little disappointed that there was no argument, just the usual grunt.

Next, it was the hunt for a lock-up garage in Pickering, a place he could remember visiting only once before in his life. The second estate agent he rang, Adam Walker, confirmed that he did have some garages to let at, what he believed to be, a very reasonable rent for the area.

"I see. Could you tell me what that rent would be?"

"£650 per annum."

"I see. Is it possible to rent it for a shorter period, perhaps six months?"

"No, I'm sorry. They are very much in demand, especially situated so close to the town centre."

Miles realised that once more he didn't have a choice. "I don't know Pickering at all well. Could you give me some idea where the garage is?"

"No problem. It's pretty central, part of a block of six garages in a small yard, off a side street near to the Co-op supermarket. May I ask what you intend to use the garage for as there are some restrictions on use, such as no chemicals to be stored, that sort of thing."

Surprised to be asked why he wanted it, Miles recovered quickly, giving his usual account when dealing with estate agents. "Oh no, nothing like that. To tell the truth, I've just split up from my wife and I want to store some personal belongings as far from the greedy bitch as I can. I'm sure you understand."

Adam laughed. "Indeed I do, sir."

"Okay, that sounds okay, but can you tell me about security?"

"It's a double door secured by your own padlock. No alarms, I'm afraid."

"What about security cameras?"

"No, nothing that sophisticated."

Miles was ecstatic; the last thing he wanted was cameras at the garage, and he hoped there were few of them in Pickering itself. "That's a little disappointing, but I'll make sure I have a good padlock. Can I meet you at the garage tomorrow lunchtime to finalise the details?"

"That should be okay. Give me a ring when you're near and I'll meet you. I'm not far away. Lastly, could you give me your name, please, and bring some proof of identity and address."

"No problem. I'm James Adamson, by the way."

Business completed, the call ended with the usual pleasantries.

Miles concluded that people would believe anything, or pretend to, as long as they could do the deal and make some money, as once again the low opinion of his fellow man surfaced.

One final call and he could pack it in for the day.

Charlie answered after only four or five rings. "Bargain Motors, how can I help?"

"It's Miles. Can I collect the motorbike tomorrow morning?"

"No probs, it's all fuelled up and ready to go."

"Good. Final thing, can you deliver the Mondeo to Pickering tomorrow for me?"

"Well, I can, but it will cost you. Will you be bringing the driver back?"

"Wasn't planning to."

"Well, that means two cars and two drivers. Even for a friend, I couldn't do it for less than two-fifty. How's that?"

"A bit steep. Haven't you got a trailer or something?"

"It's in use tomorrow. That's the best I can do."

"Okay. Will 3pm be okay?"

"Can do. I'll get them to ring you when they're close to arrange a meet."

Charlie cut the connection without another word.

That was it for today; he deserved some time off. First off, he was going to have a nice meal and a good drink, totally forgetting his earlier resolve to steady down. After that, he knew the address of a nice brothel, where the girls were clean and didn't charge anything like the delectable Natasha.

Tuesday found Miles in a much happier frame of mind. Despite his indulgencies of the previous afternoon and early evening, or maybe because of them, he got to bed early and had a good night's sleep. It was one of his few hangover-free mornings.

Determined to get moving, he quickly washed and dressed before going to a local café for a full English. Luckily, before doing so, he had remembered to retrieve the false number plates for the Mondeo from the boot of the Ford Fiesta still in its underground parking space. He put them in his backpack, along with the cash and some other items he was going to need today, especially the glass and cigarette ends he had recovered from Wade in the beer garden.

Jimmy was his first call of the day to collect the final 10,000 from Frank Harris. He was more than surprised when Jimmy spoke.

"Okay, dipshit, I'll ask. What do you want two pairs of handcuffs for?"

Trying to hide his shock, Miles did his best to come up with an explanation. "You know what the job is. There shouldn't be any interference, but if anyone does get in my way, I might need to stop them causing me any problems. Just trying to cover all the angles, that's all."

Looking far from convinced, Jimmy just nodded, quickly returning to his normal stone-faced self. Without further comment, he handed over the cash, handcuffs and remaining specialist equipment, several vials of Rohypnol. Miles was considerably surprised that the date rape drug elicited no comments from Jimmy at all.

With a little help from the AA, Miles knew that the journey from Leeds to Pickering took just over an hour by car, but as he was travelling on a 125cc motorbike he was going to allow himself two hours for the trip. With that in mind, and knowing he wanted to be in Pickering for lunchtime, he was at the Bargain Motors dealership by 10am. He took the cash from his backpack, careful not to let Charlie see the rest of the contents, particularly the other money he was carrying. He didn't think the man would try anything that might provoke Frank Harris's anger and certain retribution, but you never know. He handed over the £250 for the Mondeo delivery to an ever-beaming car dealer before taking possession of the bike and the – allegedly free – helmet.

Miles had a quiet word with the man before he started the motorcycle, informing him that when the car was delivered to Pickering, he would look like the photo on the driving licence Charlie had copied. So whoever delivered the car would need to see the photo to enable them to recognise Miles in his Wade disguise.

Miles had never thought to ask if the motorbike had electric ignition but was glad to find that it did. Kick-starting any bike could be problematic, not something he dared think about considering what he wanted the machine for. He couldn't afford for it to let him down, no way.

The watching car dealer and some of his mechanics, who were on a tea break, laughed uproariously, shouting not very helpful advice when an apprehensive and inexperienced Miles stalled the bike at his first attempt. He managed to get away at his second attempt, wobbling a little uncertainly off the forecourt and down the road, leading to more raucous comments from the watching men. However, he was soon enjoying himself but wished he had put on something a little warmer than his windcheater and jeans as, even though it was nearly summer, there was a bit of a chill in the air. He hadn't thought to bring gloves either. It may only be a small thing but, once again, he had fallen short in some of the detailed planning.

As he rode through the city, Miles stopped at the first hardware shop he saw to purchase a padlock and chain for the bike and a heavy duty padlock for the garage door, as usual, paying in cash.

His next problem was finding somewhere to put

on his Richard Wade disguise. Obviously, a mirror was needed, especially when fitting the wig, but where could he go? He had wing mirrors on the motorcycle but was a little concerned about doing it in the open, where he could easily be seen. He decided that he had no other option as the dangers were much the same if he risked using a public toilet or those in a pub.

As he rode along, he scoured the roadside for any lay-bys, field entrances and other likely places he could utilise. About ten miles from Pickering, an increasingly anxious Miles saw a narrow track leading into a small copse of trees, which he immediately turned into. He stopped after about thirty yards, confident he was out of sight of the road and, as far as he could tell, all other directions. Quickly dismounting, he removed his helmet before taking the items he needed from his backpack. He was now so practised that it took only a couple of minutes to put on the small hair net, quickly followed by the wig, the contact lenses and the glasses. Studying himself in a wing mirror, he was satisfied that he was once more transformed into Richard Wade, and a perfect match for James Adamson's false driving licence. A final look in the mirror confirmed he had done the right thing in fitting in another haircut and recolouring his moustache. Perfect.

Miles took the opportunity to ring the estate agent, Adam, who gave him directions to the garage, where they would meet in about twenty minutes. Easily finding the place and, as he had planned, arriving a few minutes before Adam, he slowly removed the crash helmet, careful not to disturb his disguise. A wonky wig would have been something of a disaster.

Only minutes later, about 11.45am, Adam arrived, introduced himself and shook hands with the man he believed to be James Adamson, expressing no surprise that he was using a motorbike. The agent did have to admit that the dirty orange trials bike was an odd choice for a man of his age, especially as it appeared to have some sort of lightning flash design on the petrol tank. It was a bike for a teenager was his guess, but it takes all sorts, and he'd met most of them in his line of work.

"Good morning, Mr Adamson. Number four is the one for us."

He took a small bunch of keys from his pocket and used one of them to remove a flimsy padlock from the sturdy double garage doors. It was empty, clean and dry, perfect for what Miles wanted, but lacking a power supply. That was no problem as he had no plans to be here in the dark.

"Adam, this is perfect. I'm happy to take it, please."

"Super. Would you like to come back to the office to complete the formalities? It's only a two-minute walk."

"Yes, no problem. I'll put the bike in the garage and put my own lock on the door. It's a bit more sturdy than the one you just took off."

With that, he pushed the bike inside, securing it with the lock and chain, then hung his helmet on a mirror before closing the door and locking it with the recently purchased padlock. He took the opportunity to have a quick look at his surroundings, not expecting to be back over the next few days. He was pleased to see that the yard did not appear to be overlooked, making it ideal for his needs.

Minutes later, at Adam's office, Miles went through the familiar routine, this time producing the James Adamson false driving licence and the farm lease as proof of identity and address.

"I'm sorry the lease is only recent, but, as I explained, I've only just split up from my wife and I had to get somewhere in a hurry."

"No problem, Mr Adamson, it's absolutely fine." With that, as usual, he photocopied both documents before placing the copies in a file.

The estate agent coughed delicately. "How would you like to pay? Cheque or bank transfer?"

Miles smiled. "Cash, if that's okay with you, Adam?"

"Well, it is a little unusual."

"I understand but if my soon-to-be ex-wife sees any transfers from the bank account, she'll want to know what it's about. Between us, you understand."

"Okay."

With that, Miles reached into his backpack, removed an envelope containing £650 and passed it over the desk to Adam, who counted it quickly. Satisfied the amount was correct, he stood, offering his hand to indicate their business was concluded.

He left the office, pleased that another box was mentally ticked off on the jobs-to-do list.

Realising it was still only 12.30pm, he rang Charlie, arranging for the delivery of the Mondeo as soon as possible to the Co-op car park. The dealer readily agreed, suggesting they would probably be there in just over an hour.

Plenty of time for lunch, he thought. He even found

time to wander across to the North Yorkshire Moors Railway station to collect a copy of the heritage railway's summer timetable.

Back at the Co-op store car park by 1.30pm, he waited impatiently until he finally saw the Mondeo turn in a quarter of an hour later. Clearly recognising the disguised Miles, the driver pulled into a parking space near him, got out and handed the keys over without a word. With that, he turned and got into the late-model BMW saloon which had followed him into the car park and sped away. Miles swiftly got into the car and drove off in a more sedate manner for the journey back to Leeds.

Pc Simon Johnson yawned, not for the first time, bored stiff as he sat in his patrol car parked at the side of the A169 just outside Pickering on the lookout for speeders. Why his Sergeant had given him this job an hour ago, he had no idea. As far as he was concerned, speeders weren't a problem along here.

He was about to get on his radio for permission to resume his normal patrol when a grey Mondeo saloon drove by, heading out of Pickering. There was no way that it was exceeding the speed limit, but, as policemen do, he decided to pull it over anyway just to relieve the monotony.

Miles was feeling very pleased with how well things had gone so far today when he heard a siren and, on looking in his rear-view mirror, was alarmed to see a police car behind him. The driver of the car tucked in behind him with lights flashing but had turned off the siren, a clear indication that Miles was to pull over. He felt sick but turned into an empty lay-by, followed by the police car, as he did his best to compose himself. Whilst he waited for the Police officer to approach him, he couldn't help thinking that this was exactly how Karl Smithson had ended up in prison. At least he wasn't carrying a knife, nor did he have a young girl tied up in the boot.

Miles lowered the window as the officer drew level with the door.

"Hello, Officer. I don't think I was speeding, was I?"

"No, sir, it's just a routine check. Does this car belong to you?"

"Yes, it does. I only bought it a few days ago."

"I see. Do you have proof of that, please?"

"I've got the part of the registration document given to me by the dealer. He's sending the rest of it to the DVLA. That's right, isn't it?"

Looking at the slip of paper handed over by Miles, the officer said, "Is this you, sir, James Adamson?"

Miles nodded.

"Have you anything to prove your identity?"

"I've got my driving licence."

Taking a wallet from his trouser pocket, Miles removed the driving licence and handed it over, concerned about the fake address on it. Everything else about the licence was perfectly genuine, as it should be, having been created and produced at the DVLA by Brenda.

"It's a good likeness, sir. I'll just jot down a few details, do a computer check as well, and then you can be on your way."

He watched as Simon Johnson wrote something in his notebook and then listened as he heard him do a check on the car and his name, or at least the one he had given.

Returning to the car, he handed back the licence and registration document.

"Everything seems fine, Mr Adamson. Last thing to do is to confirm your address. Is it where you live currently?"

Miles felt sick as he realised that a simple thing like a false address was going to put an end to all his and Karl's scheming. However, he must have been born under a lucky star because at the exact moment the officer raised the radio to his mouth he must have received some sort of message, as he said, "Go ahead."

He couldn't hear what the message was because Johnson was wearing an earpiece, but whatever it was, he simply waved to Miles, ran back to his car and sped off.

The lay-by was suddenly quiet, apart from the noise of a very relieved man's heart pounding loudly in his chest. Once he had settled down, Miles resumed his journey, more careful than ever not to do anything that could attract police attention. However, the more he thought about it, the more he realised that his careful planning and preparation for the trip to Pickering had allowed him to allay the suspicions of the police officer. He was wearing his Wade disguise, which meant he matched the picture on the James Adamson licence he had produced, which in turn matched the name on the vehicle registration document. Of course, he could also have shown the officer the lease for the farmhouse to show where he lived now and told him the usual tale about splitting from his wife, probably earning nothing more than a warning to update his licence.

Maybe keeping so many balls in the air at once was easier than he thought.

Back in Leeds, he thought he'd had enough for one day but then decided he could do one more job before he called it a day. It entailed him driving to B&Q to make several essential purchases, all of which were paid for in cash and stored in the boot of the car. He made sure to look directly at the security cameras, still disguised as Richard Wade.

On leaving the B&Q store, Miles went to a nearby pet shop where he was able to make one more important purchase.

He had intended to go to the farmhouse today but, this time, really had had enough. He found a parking space in a quiet street about half a mile away from the apartment, where he was able to duck down below the dashboard and quickly remove the disguise. He didn't need a mirror for that.

Still shaken by his encounter with the police, Miles stopped off at a pub as he walked back to the apartment where, once again, he overindulged himself before going home alone.

TWENTY-ONE

Another morning, another breakfast of black coffee and painkillers. He wasn't drinking his coffee black from choice but, once again, had failed to do any shopping. That was definitely something he would have to sort out next week.

It took an hour for the headache to settle down sufficiently so that he could dress and get on his way, with his first job being to collect the Mondeo. The half-mile walk to the street where he had parked the car helped clear his head, and, on entering the street, he was relieved to see the car was still where he had left it and appeared to be intact.

As he had one more shop to visit, Miles reluctantly decided he needed to adopt the Wade persona once more. Looking around, he decided to take a chance and do it in the car as the street was very quiet and he had no intention of ever coming here again.

First stop was a camping store, where he purchased something to sleep on and a stove, along with a kettle and mugs. He'd seen on his visit to the farmhouse that there was no furniture, certainly none that he was prepared to use. He wasn't going to be there long in any event.

Miles had also purchased a map of the local area, which he studied intently, planning his route from the city to the farm carefully. This was one part of their scheme that Karl and his cellmate had agonised over for some time. It was imperative that the car Miles used when he committed the crime was clearly captured on the city centre security cameras to establish a definite link to Richard Wade. However, he did not want the vehicle tracked all the way to the farmhouse too soon so had to find a more circuitous route.

As the farm building was to the northeast of Leeds, he decided the best way to confuse the police was to leave the city by the south, cutting through residential areas. He was sure they would still find a way to track him but hoped to make their job harder and to slow them down. He tried to avoid places such as shops and garages which may have cameras until he reached the countryside outside the city. Checking his map frequently, he plotted his way, avoiding buildings as much as he could, twice having to find ways round 24-hour garages. It took him about an hour in all, which was on the limit of what was acceptable but would have to do. Now satisfied that he could get from the outskirts of Leeds to the farm without being recorded on camera, Miles resolved to familiarise himself with the route a couple of times at night to make sure he could manage it without getting lost in the dark.

On reaching the house, his first task was to remove his disguise, quickly followed by fitting the cloned number plates onto the car, ensuring, no doubt, that a poor innocent motorist would receive an unwelcome visit from the police in the not-too-distant future. The vehicle's original plates were left in the boot.

Before entering the house, he put on a pair of latex gloves and, once inside, did a further inspection, confirming his decision to use the ground-floor bedroom only. He did his best to clean the room, using a sweeping brush he'd found whilst having a look round. He confirmed the electricity was on and that the toilet and wash basin in the en-suite worked properly.

He didn't expect to stay there long and, even though the building was fairly remote, Miles wanted to ensure his privacy so nailed some black plastic sheeting, courtesy of B&Q, over the only window. He wasn't much of a handyman but used his newly acquired electric drill to complete some simple but necessary tasks. He sorted out the sleeping arrangements and set up the camp stove and kettle, wishing he had just bought an electric kettle. Maybe he still would. He was careful to leave the receipts for his purchases in a discarded carrier bag in the corner of the bedroom, before placing the glass bearing Wade's fingerprints on a rickety table left by the previous owner. He couldn't decide what to do with the cigarette ends until he saw a tin lid, which would make an ideal ashtray, next to the glass. Possibly a bit too easy, but, with all the other evidence, he hoped the police would view it as the icing on the cake.

After securing the house, Miles was halfway to Leeds Bradford Airport when he realised that, once again, he had forgotten something of significance, meaning a stop in the city centre for more shopping. An hour later, he resumed the journey to the airport, the possessor of two new suitcases, one of which was black and fitted inside a larger red one. The black case contained his new set of nondescript holiday clothes and a pair of trainers. How could he have forgotten them?

He did have suitable clothes in the apartment but didn't want to take this car, with its cloned plates, anywhere near to it.

Getting to the mid-stay car park at the airport was easy, although not having pre-booked was a little risky in that there may not be a parking space available. If he had booked, he would have had to pay by card, something he definitely did not want to do, mainly because he didn't have a bank account in any of his various identities. Besides, in the long hours of planning and scheming with Karl, their mantra had been cash at all times, leave no trail that could get back to Miles. Happily for him, there was a ticket entry system which would enable him to pay for his stay in cash at the machine in the terminal before retrieving the car, not that he ever intended to.

He took a ticket on entry and easily found a space, details of which he actually wrote on the back of the ticket before putting it in his pocket. He reasoned that he could not afford to forget it. Besides, if the police got hold of it before he got back to the car, the job would be blown already. He had plans for that ticket.

He was about to put on his baseball cap and the Richard Wade glasses, which he believed to be enough of a disguise for the car park cameras, when he remembered that he needed to wipe the car interior down. He'd have been happier if he could have worn latex gloves in the car as he had done each time he was at the farmhouse, but imagine if he had been stopped by police. That would have taken some explaining. He spent ten minutes wiping every surface he believed he may have touched in the car, making sure, as far as he could, that no fingerprints were left. It would be more than stupid to spend all this time framing Wade and then leave his own fingerprints behind for the police to find.

After donning his disguise, Miles secured the car, having left the cases and clothes in the boot, before walking to the airport terminal, where he took a bus back to the city centre.

Later that same evening, Miles, wearing his usual clothes and Richard Wade disguise, went to Fat Harry's for what he hoped would be his final reconnaissance. On leaving the apartment, he had followed his normal procedure of wearing a baseball cap and keeping his head down to prevent recognition by any of the cameras in the apartment block or the street outside. It was tedious but had to be done, although he had nearly forgotten. He took the cap off before entering the bar, making sure the cameras got a good look at him once he was inside.

The club was not very busy, making it easy for him to look round, spotting regular faces, including security, before he found his usual spot at the end of the bar. He had only been there a few minutes when the blonde girl smiled as she walked past him with a couple of her friends. As far as he could recollect, the girl had been in the club every time he'd been there; she was more than a regular.

Half an hour later, the blonde was next to him at the bar ordering a round of drinks, nodding at him whilst she waited. It was clear that she considered him, if not exactly a friend, certainly someone she was happy to pass the time of day with.

Miles took his chance to get the info he needed. "Hi, how are you doing?"

"Great, thanks." She was quite well spoken with a soft voice.

Although blondes were normally his thing, the girl was far too young for him and a bit on the skinny side as well.

"This group that's on next week, are they any good?"

Her face lit up as she excitedly said, "Oh yes! Angry Dogs are fantastic."

Miles shook his head slowly. "Doesn't sound like my sort of thing."

"Trust me, you'll like them, but if you do come, best get here early or you won't get in. I'll definitely be here. I'm Mary, by the way."

Not seeing his slightly confused expression, the girl picked up her drinks order from the bar and returned to her friends before he could say anything more.

He only stayed another half-hour before heading back to the apartment, unable to cope with the noise and rubbish music being played by the witless DJ. An early night beckoned.

So the club would be busy next Wednesday, just as he wanted. His final thought before sleep engulfed him was that the plan was definitely a go.

TWENTY-TWO

The strident ringing of one of his mobile phones awoke a very surprised and groggy Miles Kingston at 8am the following morning. He was even more surprised to see that Jimmy was the caller. He shook his head in an effort to clear his befuddled senses before answering, fully aware that this call was not going to be good news. He almost never answered but quickly realised that crossing Frank Harris was not an option he wished to take.

When he did answer, Jimmy's rasping voice seemed to fill his head, ensuring any last traces of sleep vanished.

"What took you so long, arsehole?"

"I was asleep, what did you expect?"

"Don't get lippy with me, son, or you'll get a slap. Okay?"

"Okay, okay. What do you want?"

"Mr Harris wants to see you."

"When?"

"Now."

In a pathetic show of bravado, Miles said, "I'll just get a shower and some breakfast, should be there in a couple of hours."

There was a loud sigh down the phone followed by a voice even more menacing than normal. "Twenty minutes or I'll fetch you."

The phone went dead.

Miles scrambled to get ready and raced to the betting shop headquarters of Harris's criminal empire, fearful that there may be some reprisals for having taken half an hour to get there. He was very nervous, frightened of what Harris wanted him for, especially when he remembered that he had been told not to go there again.

Acutely aware that he was unshaven and, having dressed in such a hurry, looked like a bag of shit, he tentatively knocked on the door, which was immediately opened by Jimmy. Just how a man wearing a light grey suit and a red tie could look like a thundercloud defied understanding, but the man managed it with ease. Having let Miles in, he quickly scanned the street and, obviously seeing nothing to alarm him, closed the door before spinning round and, none too gently, punching the unsuspecting man in the stomach.

"I said twenty minutes, you prick. You don't keep Mr Harris waiting, now get in there."

Still gasping for breath, a shit-scared Miles stumbled down the corridor and into the office, where an unsmiling Harris pointed to the chair in front of the desk. He sat down, ever-mindful of the brooding presence of Jimmy behind him.

Looking and sounding more like a provincial bank manager than ever, Harris spoke in a quiet voice.

"I'm not going to search you for bugs today because we're partners and I trust you. Besides, I think you already know that if you ever cross me, you'll be a dead man. Isn't that right, Jimmy?"

Miles didn't turn round when he heard the loud grunt of affirmation from behind him but shifted nervously in his chair, expecting more violence from the huge thug. When it didn't immediately come, he relaxed a little in his seat with his most ingratiating smile.

"You can rely on me, Mr Harris, you know that."

"I hope so, Miles, I really do hope so. To tell you the truth, I'm getting a little concerned about this project that you and Karl have come up with. Jimmy keeps me up to date with what's going on, and I've got to say, some of your requests are causing me some concern."

Miles noted that his 'partner' no longer suggested he call him Frank, confirming his belief that it was very much an unequal partnership and making it clear who exactly was the senior partner.

"No problem, Mr Harris. I'll tell you anything you want to know."

As at their previous meeting, a slight curling of the lips, which, even if you were generous, could never be described as anything approaching a smile, preceded Harris's next question. "I know you will. From the plan you first told me about, I get why you wanted driving licences and sorting out with a make-up man, but not the rest. So when is this job happening? Why do you need Rohypnol and handcuffs? You've also got three vehicles and two properties, one of which is out in the country. You better run through things again."

The sinister expression was almost enough to scare Miles witless, causing him to pause, trying to collect his thoughts before he answered, anxious to get the story just right. The hesitation cost him dearly as a slight nod from an impatient Harris made Jimmy spring into action. A huge blow to the side of his head knocked Miles to the floor, leaving him completely stunned, with a throbbing head.

"Get up, son, and be quick about it or Jimmy may get angry. I haven't got all day."

Miles got back into his chair as quickly as he could, shaking his head in an attempt to clear his senses.

"It's like this, Mr Harris. The bloke I'm after is a Premier League footballer, and I can tell you he earns an absolute bloody fortune. He has some particularly unpleasant habits concerning young children and, unfortunately for him, I have in my possession some photographs that, if they became public, would certainly finish his career and probably get him sent to prison. I'm going to get him to pay me a lot of money for those pictures."

"Okay, Miles, so how did you get these pictures?"

"They were posted to me. It was something Karl Smithson arranged. I don't know where they came from."

"Two questions. Are you satisfied they're not fakes? Why did someone post them to you?"

"Sure as I can be. According to Karl, he convinced whoever sent the photographs to me that I'm a reporter who will expose this dirty bastard. I don't know why he's doing that when he could have at least made some money selling them to the papers."

Harris laughed. "Believe it or not, there are some poor buggers in the world with scruples and a conscience. So how are you going to put the bite on him?"

"Well, he's a regular at that club I've been checking out, always sniffing round the younger customers. I'm going to brace him there, probably let him see a sample photo to convince him I'm serious and then tell him how much I want. If he's as much of a fool as I hope, this could be a regular earner for me."

"Why the club?"

"I'm pretty sure he won't cause any trouble in public, plus I will be caught on film looking like Wade. The plan is to push him so hard that he does eventually go to the police and if he doesn't I'll tell them myself. One way or another, I'll make sure Wade takes a fall."

Harris looked thoughtfully at Miles Kingston. "I wish I had your confidence. As I told you a while ago, there are lots of moving parts to this plan and something could easily go wrong. People don't always act the way you expect or would like them to. So what about all the stuff you've asked for?"

"The Rohypnol is easy. The tart who's going to look after Wade for me tells me that she is very good at what she does, but keeping him occupied for two and a half days won't be easy, even for her. If she needs to, she'll give him some of the drug to make sure he stays compliant, shall we say. Same with the handcuffs. A bit of bondage will keep him occupied and prevent him from running off before I'm ready."

"Go on."

It was proving very difficult to think clearly, especially as the story he had just told to these two very violent and dangerous men was total bollocks.

"The flat is for Natasha, that's the pro, to entertain

Wade in, so he has no alibi. I've been living there while things get set up, but I'm going to be using the farmhouse for a few days. I'm making sure that it will look like Wade has been keeping out of the way there while he does the job, something I'll be making certain the pigs find out about."

"What about Pickering and the cars?"

"The footballer lives near there, so that's where I'm planning the cash handover. The first one anyway. I'm using the cars to move about a lot, trying to be fairly inconspicuous except where I'm using them to set Wade up. I think that's about it, Mr Harris."

It is always surprising how someone like Miles, who couldn't remember the last time he had seen the inside of a church, suddenly found religion, saying a silent prayer for his survival and, as backup, crossing his fingers as well. You could never be too careful.

Harris stared at him intently, clearly deep in thought as he considered what he had just heard.

For once, Miles kept quiet.

"Okay, son, I'm not at all sure about this plan you and Karl have cooked up, especially as it doesn't sound exactly like what you told me when you first came here."

Miles started to speak but was promptly told to be quiet by a very irate crime boss.

"Don't interrupt me again when I'm speaking. Understand? I have my concerns about this scheme, but it's your neck on the line. I want my hundred grand back, of course, but if you get nicked, I've got the house as security so that will be okay. However, if you do get nicked or anything else happens, it better not come back to me in any way whatsoever. If it does, you will be a dead man. Understand?"

Miles understood very clearly, shaken to his core by the calm and very convincing way the chilling ultimatum was delivered. He just nodded numbly.

"Right, son, moving on. Our Welsh lady seems to have gone missing. You were one of the last people to deal with her. What the fuck did you do?"

Miles nearly wet himself when he thought back to his last meeting with Brenda and what he had done. Shaking his head, he could only mumble, "Nothing, Mr Harris, it was just business. Honest."

Whilst Harris stared at him, Miles realised the man had actually said he was one of the last to deal with Brenda, not the last. So others had done business after him. Besides, if Harris knew what he had done to such an obviously valuable contact, then he would be dead already. Feeling more confident, he looked directly back at him.

"Did she say anything to you about packing it in?"

"Not that I can remember."

"What about the police?"

"God, no. All she was interested in was getting her money and drugs. If she'd mentioned the police, I'd have been out of there in a flash, I can tell you."

Harris stared at him with those intense blue eyes. "Listen very carefully, Miles. If I find out you're lying to me, then we'll have a big problem, a very big problem. Understand?"

"Yes, sir, Mr Harris."

"Right. Jimmy has been snooping around and there are some rumours circulating that she has been arrested."

"Shit, where does that leave me?"

"I think you mean us, don't you? Anyway, the stories suggest she has been arrested for shoplifting, which may be true. After all, she probably wanted to get money for more drugs. Who knows? Up to now, there is no sign that the police are investigating the licences, but be careful."

"I will, Mr Harris, I will."

The truth was that Harris was not at all concerned on a personal level as he had never met Brenda; all her dealings had been with Jimmy. He had not told her who his boss was and would never talk, so with him as a buffer between them there was no way the police would get anywhere near him. However, he was disappointed to have potentially lost his valuable source at the DVLA and a really good money-making scheme. How his partners would view things, he had no idea.

"Just like you, Miles, she knows better than to cross me. Now get out."

Not having seen the signal, he was caught off guard when Jimmy's huge hand grabbed him by the collar and hoisted him effortlessly to his feet. Miles found himself on the pavement seconds later, but it was some time before his breathing returned to normal, still unsure how he had got away with it, if indeed he had.

He'd warned Karl that it was a dangerous game telling a man like Frank Harris such a load of bullshit.

Smithson had insisted they had to do it because they needed his backing, and there was no way he would have got involved in what they were really planning. It wasn't anything to do with moral objections on his part, more the intense police activity and attention it was sure to bring his way. Harris saw himself principally as a businessman, and nothing was allowed to get in the way of his money-making operations, especially the illegal ones.

As well as everything else, Miles was now worried the police might come in his direction looking for forged driving licences. It was time to get things moving.

It was still early in the day and Miles had more things to do. He certainly could have done with a drink, but the pubs weren't even open yet. He made do with several cigarettes, smoked in quick succession.

Returning to the rented apartment, he decided that coffee was a better option, having to drink it black as, once more, he'd forgotten to get any groceries. He supposed it proved exactly how preoccupied he was with planning that he couldn't even organise some milk. It did have the benefit of focusing his mind on the fact that he needed to get food and drink in for Natasha and Wade when they arrived. He didn't want anyone having to go out, did he?

Miles saw it was 11am, hopefully not too early for Natasha. He allocated his sixth mobile phone to her and labelled it accordingly before inputting her number. As with his other mobiles, it was the only one it contained.

Calling the number, he was just about to hang up after a considerable number of rings when a sleepy voice answered.

"Hello, who the fuck is this?"

"Natasha, it's Miles."

"Who?"

He obviously hadn't made as big an impression on her as she had on him. "It's Miles in Leeds."

"Oh yeah. I remember. What do you want ringing this fucking early? I've been up all night."

On hearing that, Miles was unable to contain his laughter at the thought of her entertaining clients. Surely she meant to say 'it had been up her all night'. Believing he had just made an unbelievably funny joke, he was unable to stop laughing. He heard the phone click off.

Oops! He decided it might be wise to ring her back later in the afternoon. His laughter certainly helped to ease some of the tension from his meeting with Harris. Just a pity that he didn't have someone to share the joke with.

He went shopping for groceries, as always, aware of surveillance cameras.

Miles rang her back about four that afternoon, hoping she had had enough beauty sleep, trying very hard not to start laughing again at what he continued to think was such a clever joke. This time, she was much more amenable, meaning that their business could be discussed at once as, thankfully, she was in a much more pleasant mood.

When Natasha asked what he'd thought so funny earlier, he resisted the temptation to tell the truth, claiming it was something he'd heard on the radio.

Getting quickly down to the job in hand, he stressed that she needed to ring Wade either that evening or the following morning, using the script he had provided to set up their meeting for the following Wednesday. If she was not in a position to keep him occupied, then everything would need to be delayed or maybe even cancelled. All the work so far had been centred on making sure that Wade took the blame for a heinous crime. It was agreed that, if she successfully made the arrangements, she would arrive in Leeds by train the following Wednesday, leaving no later than the Friday afternoon. He confirmed what exactly was required of her, agreeing to pay £5,000 on arrival with the balance paid before she left. He reminded her that she would also need to contact him with her arrival time so he could meet her at the train station.

His final question before ending the call concerned what food and drink she required so he could stock up the apartment for his two guests.

Another job ticked off his list.

He thought briefly of all the things he had put in place to make sure the noose tightened inescapably around Wade's neck when the time came. Masquerading as Wade in his disguise when renting the farmhouse and the lock-up in Pickering, obtaining forged documents and buying cars. He was particularly proud of the cloned plates that he used when pretending to be Wade, ensuring that it made the man look like he was trying to keep his identity secret when driving round to make his essential purchases.

He waited in all night but did not hear from Natasha. He just hoped she would get on with things reasonably early the next day, no doubt after a long night's work. What he didn't know was that she had made two attempts to contact Wade that evening without success. She was almost as eager as Miles to get things into operation. After all, ten grand was a decent payday even for a high earner like her, but of course Frank Harris would be taking his cut.

She had no idea what Miles Kingston found so funny, but she had nothing but contempt for the man when she remembered how easily he had given in when negotiating her fee. He wouldn't be laughing if he'd known she would have been happy to accept £5,000 and had only tried it on when she asked for £10,000. A cold-hearted bitch, Natasha inhabited a dark world where she had learnt many hard lessons in her life, especially from the men who owned her and those she entertained.

She considered Miles a lightweight, someone to be taken advantage of at every opportunity, using all the weapons she had at her disposal. In her considerable experience, men would do anything for a pretty face and a nice pair of tits. They were such fools.

She finally managed to make contact with Richard Wade on the Saturday lunchtime, using the number he had so conveniently put on his Facebook page.

"Hello, Richard Wade."

Speaking in her soft well-spoken accent, Natasha launched into her rehearsed patter. "Hello, Mr Wade, I'm sorry to bother you on a Saturday, but I've been trying so hard to get in touch with you. Have you got a few minutes?"

"Not long, I'm afraid, but what can I do for you?"

"I'll try to be quick. My name is Sophie Young and I'm a freelance journalist. I've been commissioned to write a series of articles for the *Mail on Sunday* about people who have recovered from adversity and gone on to lead successful lives. I think, with everything you have been through, that you would be a great subject for the first article. Would you be interested?"

"Would there be a fee?"

Quickly realising he was already hooked, Natasha responded from her notes. "I'm afraid not, but it would be a wonderful opportunity to publicise yourself and your work. I understand you are currently working on a new book."

"Yes, I am indeed, and exposure in a national newspaper would certainly help to publicise it. What exactly is involved?"

"I'm on a fairly tight deadline. Would you be free next Wednesday? I'm thinking I could come through to Leeds and perhaps meet over a meal, my treat of course. How does that sound?"

Despite all his trials and tribulations, Richard Wade had managed to regain his old bravado and confidence, having convinced himself that he had been very badly treated. Typically, he had no thoughts for the others who had not been so lucky following the murder of his colleague Steve Brown.

"Well, I'm not promising anything yet, but a meeting can't do any harm, can it? Send me the details of the restaurant booking and a photo so I will be able to recognise you, please."

After agreeing to his requests, Natasha cut the connection.

She immediately rang Miles on the dedicated number she had been given.

Without preamble, she said, "He's hooked."

"For Wednesday?"

"Of course."

"I'll make the booking and text you the details. I'll book a taxi to pick him up as well. We don't want him to do it himself, because if he knows the taxi company, he may have the start of an alibi. We definitely don't want that."

"What about cameras in the restaurant?

"It hasn't got any. It's only a small place. There aren't any on the street either."

"Okay. He asked for a photo of me. Will that cause any problems?"

"No problem at all. Text him the photo, but don't send the restaurant and taxi details. Ring him back. I don't want him to have that information on his phone."

Miles almost started laughing again but restrained himself. It was better than he could have hoped.

Twenty minutes later, Natasha rang Wade, telling him that a booking had been made for 8pm at an Italian restaurant and that a taxi had also been laid on to collect him from his home at 7.30pm. Natasha wasn't aware that, after careful consideration, Miles had decided to collect Wade himself using the blue Ford. If, as planned, Wade was arrested and interviewed by the police, he didn't want him to give any information that may lead to a taxi being traced. It would surely further link the idiot to the car and, following his no doubt vehement denials, may even suggest he had an accomplice, further confusing the issue.

Minutes later, she texted him her professionally taken photograph. On seeing her beautiful face, Richard Wade couldn't believe how much she resembled his former girlfriend, Julie, whom he had loved and lost. Memories flooded into his brain, the good times and the bad times, including the pain of losing her, entirely due to his own actions. Suddenly he was very much looking forward to the meeting with the woman he believed to be Sophie Young.

Neither he nor Natasha knew she had been carefully

chosen by Jimmy for her resemblance to Julie, as specified by Miles, to make sure Wade would be unable to resist a meeting. Always a vain man, he was already thinking of his chances with the girl, especially if she wanted the story badly enough.

If only he knew.

Miles gave himself the weekend off, apart from one small task he had to complete on the Saturday morning. The job was getting close and he needed to relax, if he could. He was well aware of the consequences for failure and couldn't help worrying as all his self-doubts began to surface. He especially remembered the pack of lies he had told Frank Harris and wondered how he would react when the truth came out. Not well, he suspected. He'd better be prepared to use his escape plan at short notice if needed.

Of course, the rewards were potentially huge, making it all worthwhile, or so he believed.

TWENTY-THREE

After a weekend of considerable debauchery, Miles was ready to put the final elements of the master plan into place. Somehow, on the Saturday morning, he'd managed to confront the corrupt prison officer at the park where his team were playing another match. It cost him £250 for Collier to deliver a message to Karl Smithson when he started his night shift on Monday.

If he had felt unwell on the Saturday and Sunday mornings, then the Monday was considerably worse, so much so that he couldn't immediately recall where he had actually been for most of the Sunday night. Despite two cups of black coffee, from choice this time, and God knows how many paracetamol, he couldn't seem to shift the fearsome headache. Half an hour in the shower seemed to help, making him feel at least halfway human. Needing to create a good impression today, he was, by lunchtime, at last able to shave carefully and dress in his best suit.

Expecting to make a great deal of money in the next few days, Miles had spent much time calculating how much various denominations of notes would weigh and how much space they would occupy. He was very aware of the limits on what he would be able to carry and what size bag or bags it would fit in. Following these calculations, he was able to decide how much money, and in what denominations, he could reasonably expect to move about and, most importantly, where he could secrete it.

During his interminable conversations with Smithson, they had considered using a safe deposit box to keep the money they hoped to make safe and well away from prying eyes. Whilst the deposit box companies have no interest in what personal property is kept in their boxes, they are adamant that nothing illegal or dangerous is stored. Nor will they countenance items obtained through crime or which are the proceeds of crime. To assist them in this, they operate stringent security checks on those who wish to rent their boxes, including photo identification and residence checks.

Having finally made his mind up, Miles approached the safe deposit box company offices believing he was well prepared for his two o'clock meeting, but still nervous.

It couldn't have gone more smoothly. He was welcomed warmly and given a quick rundown on the services offered, including the rules and restrictions operated by the totally legitimate company. For some reason, Miles failed to mention that the money he intended to store would be wholly the proceeds of crime, explaining instead that there would be some family valuables and documents. He selected one of the larger boxes on a six-month rental at a fixed fee, with some additional costs for a key.

To complete the arrangements, he produced his driving licence in the name of Peter Webb, so carefully manufactured by Brenda at the DVLA, meaning that it appeared to be a totally genuine licence. Adopting his, by now well-practised, ingratiating manner, Miles confided to the assistant that the Keighly address on his driving licence was not where he lived at the moment. Once more telling the sad tale of his marital breakdown, he explained that was one of the reasons he needed a box to stop that grasping bitch getting her hands on everything. As proof of his current address, Miles furnished the rental agreement for the apartment and some utility bills he had found at the property. The sympathetic assistant confirmed they would be perfectly adequate, quickly photocopying the documents before returning them to him. Miles had to be aware that the deposit box company may send mail to the address, so it needed to exist and be a place where he could collect any letters. He was sure that enquiries by the forces of law and order would establish the link between Miles, Webb and the safe deposit box eventually. He consoled himself with the usual thought that if they got that close, he was already fucked, but anyway he hoped to be long gone by then.

Lastly, he was scanned into the company's fingerprint and facial recognition system as an extra layer of security when customers entered the vaults. Having jokingly told the operator that he may have to shave off the moustache, as his new girlfriend didn't like it, he questioned whether it would affect the facial recognition system. As expected, the man smiled at the weak joke, confirming that there would not be a problem.

It could not have gone better, ensuring that he was in and out within the hour. He was even more confident that the next time he did this it would be even easier now he knew how things worked.

Back at the apartment, he still felt incredibly fragile but very hungry. He made himself a cheese sandwich but, after one bite, started to feel sick and, unable to face any more, threw it in the bin.

Realising how badly the booze was affecting him, Miles resolved to stop drinking completely for a few days until the job was over. With that thought, he threw himself onto the settee and was instantly asleep.

Having awoken feeling slightly better, he spent the evening watching TV until the phone marked Karl rang about 10.30pm.

"Hi, Karl, good to hear from you. I see our 'friend' passed you the message."

"No problem. How are things going?"

"Everything's going just as we planned. No problems so far."

Smithson paused before speaking. "You sound a little doubtful. What's bothering you, Miles?"

"Firstly, I don't like lying to Harris. He's not the sort of man to stand for that, is he?"

"Look, don't worry about Harris. I've told you before, he won't give a shit as long as he gets his money back."

Keeping his escape plans to himself, Miles went on. "The other problem I've got is the job itself. Because I'm doing it all on my own, I don't think the timings are going to work."

"What do you mean?"

"There are too many journeys I have to make in a short space of time. I don't think I will be able to fit them all in."

"Probably not."

Almost hysterically, he said, "You knew that all along?"

Smithson laughed unpleasantly. "Of course. Don't forget I've been thinking about this a lot longer than you."

"So you're saying it won't work?"

"I'm definitely not saying that, you idiot. I think you already know what needs to be done so that it will all go as planned. You've got to cut at least one of the journeys out, haven't you?"

Feeling sick again, Miles replied. "There is only one journey I can cut out, and you know what that means. If you're suggesting what I think you are, I won't do it. I just won't."

"It's entirely up to you, but think about it for a while. You've spent a lot of time planning and preparing. Do you want that all to be wasted? You owe Harris a lot of money, which I'm sure he'd rather have than that poxy house of yours. Lastly, you'll be passing up the biggest payday you'll ever have in your life. It's your choice."

Miles was fully aware that Karl Smithson was trying to convince him to do the job very much for his own reasons, that being the final downfall of Richard Wade. It was clear that he didn't give a toss about his partner in crime.

"Look, Karl, I don't think I can do it. I'm not like you."

"I'm telling you straight, you've got to do it. It's the only way it can work. If you don't, it will cost you very dearly, trust me. A word in the wrong ear and you'll be in a lot of trouble."

"You wouldn't grass me up, surely."

"Don't be stupid, Miles. Harris would have a much

more permanent and unpleasant solution than the fucking police."

The connection was abruptly broken.

An almost tearful Miles sat on the sofa with his head in his hands. He knew he was trapped. He didn't know if he could do what Karl wanted, but didn't know how he could not. Even for him, it was too horrible to think about. He must have been really stupid to get involved in the first place.

He didn't get much sleep that night, whilst Karl Smithson, without a care in the world, slept like a baby.

TWENTY-FOUR

Miles Kingston reached an unhappy mental compromise with himself; he would carry on with the plan until he reached the moment when he had to make his final choice. It wasn't brilliant, but it was the best he could do whilst he tried to find a solution to his dilemma.

One consideration was abandoning the attempt to frame Richard Wade, but, whilst it was Smithson's most earnest desire, it also helped deflect suspicion from him as well, sending the police in entirely the wrong direction. Loyalty was a somewhat alien principle to Kingston, but he did have to admit that Karl had helped him get through his time in prison. Even though he now knew that it was largely for his own reasons, Miles supposed it was still a debt he had to pay, no matter how reluctantly.

Once again, he made himself presentable before heading off for his appointment at a second safe deposit box company. However, on the way, he stopped at a public toilet where he donned his Richard Wade disguise in one of the cubicles. He'd done it so many times he could almost do it in his sleep; nevertheless, he carefully checked his appearance in the mirror as he washed his hands. It was perfect.

This company operated to exactly the same high standards as the previous one, with the same strictures on usage and insisting on photo identification along with a utility bill as proof of residence. On this occasion, he produced the copy of Wade's own driving licence bearing his true photograph and current address, accompanied by the forged council tax bill, all of which were photocopied. They used the same biometric security systems, which again presented no problems. They would if Richard Wade ever tried to access the deposit box, though.

This time, he had no concerns about any confirmatory documents being sent from the company to Wade's home address; in fact, he welcomed it. One more strand to entangle Richard Wade in the carefully constructed web of deceit.

On the way back to the apartment, he used the same public toilets to remove the disguise, hoping that he was only going to need it a couple more times. His second stop was at a supermarket to shop for the booze and groceries the tart had insisted were necessary. The cheeky cow even had the nerve to specify the brand and quantity of cigarettes she wanted him to get.

Once at the apartment, he soon packed his purchases away before spending the rest of the day cleaning the place as thoroughly as he could manage. He spent what he expected to be his final night there, still plagued by his doubts and fears, so tired he eventually slept.

TWENTY-FIVE

It had finally arrived; the day he had spent so much time planning and scheming for was here.

He knew the plan was good and, with reasonable luck, would work if only he had the nerve, skill and, most of all, the ruthlessness to carry it through. Remembering his last conversation with Karl, all his doubts and fears rose to the surface as he considered his limited options. Do as he knew he must for the plan to succeed or abandon it altogether and run for his life, with no money and not much future.

He was too sick with anxiety to manage any breakfast, other than a cup of coffee, before he set about preparing for his first task of the day. Firstly, he dressed in his black jeans and windcheater before packing the rest of his clothing into a holdall. All the forged documents he packed into a carrier bag before placing it into his backpack along with some of his mobile phones, all of which were fully charged. He put his personal phone and Natasha's in his pockets for the moment. He didn't forget his Wade disguise either, which also went into the bag along with the remaining money advanced by Harris.

He couldn't afford to leave anything in the apartment for Natasha to find which she could, and probably would, try to use to her advantage.

After putting the holdall in the boot of the Ford Fiesta, his first call was to the safe deposit box building where he produced his Peter Webb driving licence, sailing through the biometric identification process. Once in the vault, he placed all the forged documents, some of which he may never need again, into his personal deposit box. He added several thousand pounds he had left, but kept some walking-around cash along with the money he needed to pay Natasha. He had considered keeping his notes in the box but, having decided he no longer needed them, had torn the papers into the smallest pieces he could and flushed them down the toilet before leaving the apartment.

He decided to hang on to the various driving licences, not quite sure what exactly he would need them for but better to be prepared. Miles realised the licences would take some explaining if the police got hold of him, but why would they?

He had considered leaving his own passport in his holdall in case he had to make his run to Hull quickly, but after much deliberation decided it was safer in the vault.

Returning to the apartment, whilst waiting for Natasha's call, he spent some time checking his appearance, which needed to be spot on tonight. His hair was still short enough so that fitting the wig would not be a problem, but he decided that, even though he'd been doing it regularly, he should add some more colour to his moustache to ensure it was just right. It didn't take long.

As time passed, Miles looked anxiously at his watch

every two minutes, worried that the prostitute had changed her mind. Even though he knew it was unlikely that she would pass up her £10,000 payday or, more pertinently, risk annoying Frank Harris, he still worried.

Finally, at three o'clock, the Natasha phone rang.

Half an hour later, Miles was waiting patiently, not without some anticipation, on the station concourse for the woman whose presence was essential if the plot to frame Richard Wade was to succeed.

Having suggested to Natasha that perhaps she should dress down a little, he did wonder if he would recognise her immediately. He needn't have worried as her idea of dressing down and his were somewhat different. She was wearing a pair of faded blue jeans and a red vest, both of which looked as if they had been sprayed on, emphasising her spectacular figure. Her one concession was to cover her blonde hair with a vivid red baseball cap. Obviously, her appearance had had an impact on one poor dope, who followed in her wake carrying an apparently heavy holdall.

As at their first meeting, it appeared all the men in the station were transfixed by her as she passed by, earning appreciative glances from them but scowls of disapproval from the women, some of whom, not too quietly, whispered, "Tart." Adding to his sense of unreality, she threw her arms around Miles's neck before plonking a big kiss on his cheek, whispering loudly, "Hello, darlin', great to see you."

Retrieving the holdall from the smitten admirer, he escorted Natasha from the station, concluding there was no point in asking her to tone it down. All he managed was to ask if she was going to dress down a little more tonight, receiving only a throaty laugh in response.

Walking her to the apartment, he did ask himself what on earth she had packed to make the holdall so bloody heavy, and why she hadn't brought one with wheels on. Once at the property, he showed her round, earning only grudging approval, which did make him wonder just what her home looked like.

"Okay. First, I want my money before anything else."

Miles silently handed over an envelope containing her initial £5,000 payment, which she placed in her handbag without bothering to count it.

"Glad to see you trust me."

He noted her earlier playful voice had disappeared as she replied. "If it's not right, somebody will be around to collect the rest. Trust me."

It was said in such a matter-of-fact way that it seemed even more menacing than an out-and-out threat.

She expressed her satisfaction when he showed her where everything was, including the booze and food, laughing uproariously when she saw the drawer in the bedroom containing her cigarettes, the handcuffs and several vials of Rohypnol.

Natasha smiled as she produced a bag from her holdall. "I've brought some weed as well to keep the party going."

"Good. If you're happy, let me show you where the restaurant is."

On leaving the apartment, Miles handed over a set of keys. The Al Dente was only a few streets away and easily reached in ten minutes on foot. He then showed her two different ways back, carefully explaining why.

"It's very important that Wade can't find his way back to the apartment on his own in the future. Remember, we are making sure he doesn't have any sort of alibi. I want you to get so much drink down his neck and have him become so infatuated with you that he doesn't pay any attention to where he's going. I don't want him to find his way back here even if he's following a trail of bloody breadcrumbs. Do you understand?"

"Of course I do, and don't worry. I'll make sure he's only paying attention to one thing, or should I say one person?"

"Are you happy about the restaurant?"

"Yeah, no probs. It seems quite nice and I'll find my way there and back okay. I like Italian food anyway."

"Please remember you're supposed to be a journalist, so dress nice, but not too flashy. By the way, are you happy with your story, and do you know the questions to ask him?"

"Come on, Miles, I'm a big girl, I know the score. Can I go for a shower now, for God's sake?"

"Yeah, yeah. Last thing, here's two hundred quid for the bill, and please ring me when you get settled at your table. I don't want him getting there too early."

With an amused look on her beautiful face Natasha nodded before walking the last few hundred yards to the apartment building on her own. He supposed you could call it walking, but it didn't really describe the way she sashayed down the street. He couldn't take his eyes off her and, from all he had learnt about their gullible target, felt sure he would react in exactly the same way, or hoped he would.

As the woman entered the building, a random thought crossed Miles's mind. What was to prevent her taking his £5,000 and just clearing off for no work on her part whatsoever? If that did happen, he would be really screwed, with no chance at all of setting this job up again. Totally screwed. After a brief moment of panic, he realised that she was highly unlikely to do that, firstly because she was too greedy to pass up the final instalment of her fee and secondly because, like everyone else, she was scared to death of Frank Harris and Jimmy.

The clock was moving quickly on if he was to be ready in time to collect Wade. He'd totally forgotten that he would need to eat and drink whilst he stayed at the farm, and if he didn't do the shopping now, he certainly wouldn't have chance later. Another small mistake, and whilst not a showstopper, it would have made things more difficult later on. It was further confirmation, if it was needed, that he was only one man trying to perform numerous tasks without attracting any attention. It was getting real, frighteningly so.

Still carrying his backpack, he used the rear entrance to get into the underground car park, heading straight to the Ford Fiesta. As he drove out, Miles reflected that it was unlikely he would be back there ever again, certainly not with this car.

In a side street just around the corner from the nearest supermarket, he put on as much of his Wade disguise as he could, namely the baseball cap and glasses. Without the wig, his hair was too light coloured really, but as most CCTV systems were black and white, he hoped it wouldn't matter. Anyway, he would try not to look too directly at the cameras in the shop.

Miles loaded the boot with water, soft drinks and convenience foods, such as crisps, energy bars and pre-packed sandwiches. Not forgetting the coffee and milk this time.

He was ready, or at least as ready as he could be, but still had time to kill. He considered taking the supplies to the farm but decided that getting there and back may be cutting it too fine. Having sworn off drink, for the moment at least, he decided he would go to the pictures. Why not?

Understandably obsessive about not wanting to draw any unnecessary attention to either the car or himself, he parked on a nearby street, paying at the meter for his ticket. It would have been beyond stupid if the enterprise failed so near to the finishing line, particularly after all these weeks of what he considered to be hard work, stress and fear, simply by not paying for a parking ticket.

TWENTY-SIX

By quarter past seven, Miles was back at the car, not really remembering what film he had been watching. There were too many things running through his head. The time had arrived to find out if all the planning and preparation had been worthwhile and if it would actually work as anticipated. Nervousness, or was it fear, was also playing a part as he constantly ran through what he had to do. It was still not too late to stop, but he knew that wasn't a realistic option.

He drove to Wade's cottage, wearing a different baseball cap in an attempt to hide his appearance. Even without the cap, he was fairly sure Wade wouldn't recognise him from their brief meeting in the beer garden, but better not to risk it. He also wanted to make sure that if and when he was picked up on the traffic cameras, his face would not show.

Pulling into the cottage's drive fifteen minutes later, he blew the horn twice to let Wade know he was there. He must have been waiting by the door because the man himself came out almost immediately, dressed in a smart suit. He obviously didn't do casual.

Climbing into the front seat of the Ford Fiesta, he looked around with his distaste evident.

"This isn't a taxi, is it?"

"No. I'm a friend of Sophie, so I offered to collect you. Taxis can be so unreliable. It's no trouble."

"That's true. Thank you."

Conversation over, Miles set off to the Al Dente restaurant, wondering when Natasha would ring. He took his time, making sure that he took a fairly roundabout route, driving up and down some side streets as he got closer to the restaurant, both to confuse Wade and to kill time.

Eventually, his phone pinged, signifying the receipt of a text, which, when he looked, was a thumbs-up from Natasha. Satisfied that he had done all he could and that things were in place, he dropped Wade at the front door of Al Dente. He got out without a word. Miles drove off without waiting for him to go inside.

Even in the dimly lit restaurant, Wade had no trouble spotting his dinner date's lustrous blonde hair and, as he drew closer, could see that the photo she had sent him was a good likeness but no way did it do her justice. He approached the corner table near the window with a confidence he didn't feel. It was a long time since he had had dinner with such a beauty.

The woman he only knew as Sophie stood to greet him, offering her hand in welcome. He almost stopped when he saw just how stunning she truly was, but managed to shake her hand.

She was wearing a short, close-fitting black cocktail dress that emphasised her not inconsiderable assets without, in any way, giving a clue to her real profession. It was almost demure, but not quite.

"Hello, Mr Wade, I saw you arrive. It's so nice to meet you. I'm Sophie."

"It's lovely to meet you too, Sophie, and please call me Richard." He gave her what he thought was his most winning smile.

"Thank you, Richard. I hope you don't mind but I took the liberty of ordering a bottle of wine. I hope you like it."

As she poured him a glass, she continued with the small talk typical of people meeting for the first time, something she was very practised at.

"What do you think of the restaurant? It was recommended by a friend of mine."

He looked around as if he hadn't noticed where he was. He only had eyes for her and she knew it.

It was a typical mom and pop-style place with low lighting, checked tablecloths with candles in empty wine bottles on each table and the usual fake grape vines and a couple of Italian flags. He actually quite liked it and said so.

"Richard, shall we order first and then we can discuss the article, if that's all right with you?"

He couldn't manage more than a nod, totally transfixed by her smile and husky voice.

Skilfully playing to his ego, she went on. "I'm not really used to places like this. Perhaps I could rely on you to order for us both."

"Of course, I would be glad to."

As he went through the menu making suggestions, which she happily agreed to, Wade was really happy to take charge, feeling his confidence returning. It was the way it should be. As she topped up his wine glass, Sophie almost laughed. It was so easy; men were so easy.

As the evening wore on, another bottle of wine accompanied the – admittedly delicious – food, with Wade becoming more flushed and voluble, chatting away as if they had known each other for years. He never noticed that it was Sophie who always topped up the glasses and that hers was always more than half full when she did so. She was working, and it was essential she remained in charge.

They only briefly touched on the subject of the proposed magazine article before moving on from small talk to more interesting and enjoyable stuff. He did notice that her hand brushed against his a couple of times. Was that an accident? he wondered.

On one occasion, when she went to the ladies' room, her hip 'accidentally' brushed against his arm, causing him to almost fall from his chair. Surely that was intentional. He was feeling very optimistic.

Once the wine and food was cleared away, they each had a brandy. In fact, Wade had two and didn't realise that when he went to the toilet she poured some of hers into his glass. He was getting fairly drunk, whilst she was still completely sober.

Eventually, having removed a shoe, Sophie rubbed her foot against Wade's inner thigh. Even in his befuddled state, an excited Richard Wade realised there was no way that could be an accident.

"Richard, I've had a lovely time, but we haven't really sorted this article out, have we? Perhaps you could walk me back to my apartment so we could have a drink and continue."

Confused as to exactly what she wanted to continue, he nodded happily, muttering his agreement. She paid the bill and as they stood up, he staggered slightly so that she held on to his arm, pretending it was her who needed the help.

Once outside the restaurant, Sophie steered an unresisting Wade into a nearby passage, where she pushed him against a wall, pressing the full length of her body against him whilst she kissed him deeply. He tried to grab on to her and put his hand up her dress, but her days of doing it in alleys were long past.

"Come on, Richard, we'll be more comfortable at the apartment. It's not far."

As instructed by Miles, she took him on a meandering route to the apartment, doing her best to distract him as they finally entered the block. She was confident he would never find his way there again.

Immediately they were inside the apartment, he tried to grab her again, but she pushed him away, pointing to the master bedroom.

"Wait in there while I get ready, darlin'." With that, she went into the bathroom.

Ten minutes later, Sophie entered the bedroom and, as expected, found the drunken man fast asleep in the king size bed, with his clothes scattered all over the floor. This was going to be easy money. If only he knew what he had missed, but she was fully aware that it would be necessary to deliver at some stage over the next couple of days if he was to be kept fully occupied. After locking the front door, she hid the keys so that Wade couldn't sneak out without her knowing.

Searching through his clothes, she soon located the man's mobile phone, whereupon she found and deleted her photo. Although she would be far away when whatever it was Miles was doing came to a head, a girl couldn't be too careful. If she had known, Natasha would have been on her toes immediately.

Getting into bed next to him, she promptly went to sleep.

TWENTY-SEVEN

After dropping Wade off at the restaurant, Miles Kingston drove round the corner, parking up whilst he thought about what to do next. After all these weeks of planning, it was finally underway, the only question being whether or not he had the balls to see it through.

Following the last conversation with Smithson and the realisation of exactly what he must do to make the plan work, he seriously had his doubts, but what alternative did he have? He was still angry at the way his erstwhile partner had manipulated him, totally ignoring the fact that he was doing exactly the same to a considerable number of other, largely innocent, people himself.

His mind drifted as he thought about the set-up that he had prepared so carefully to ensure Wade took the blame for the crimes he was going to commit. He couldn't help smiling to himself as he thought about the couple of nights and days the man would have in the company of the delectable Natasha, being shagged silly, no doubt. At least he would have something to remember for the rest of his ruined life.

Once again, Miles didn't make a decision, resolving to proceed as planned for the moment until he saw how things were going. Who was he kidding? He wanted that money so badly it hurt.

Reaching into the backpack, he retrieved the props necessary to transform him into Richard Wade, realising as he did so that he hadn't actually planned where exactly he was going to fit the disguise. Another small mistake that unnerved him slightly as he wondered if he'd missed anything else. All right, it wasn't perfect, but he decided to do it in the car. It was a quiet street with no passers-by that he could see. He quickly fitted the wig and contact lenses but left the glasses on the passenger seat for the moment before realising he needed to wear them at once as he was sure to be picked up on the numerous cameras. Chiding himself for his carelessness, he drove off looking for somewhere to check his appearance.

By half-past eight, he was parked up in the small street down the side of Fat Harry's, having confirmed his disguise was perfect in the toilet of a backstreet pub. He was ready; it was now or never. He got out of the car and walked round to the front of the club, where a small crowd were milling about. On this occasion, he was not wearing his baseball cap. As with the street cameras when driving here, he wanted the club cameras to show that it was definitely Richard Wade entering.

One benefit of frequenting the place so much recently was that one of the 'bouncers' recognised him and ushered him into the club. Miles voiced his thanks, slipping the man a tenner to show his appreciation. He wanted Richard Wade to be remembered by as many people as possible.

Once inside, the club was quite busy, but not heaving. However, it was still noisy, with the lunatic DJ playing music totally unknown to Miles. He hoped Angry Dogs were going to be on soon and silently prayed they would be an improvement on the current row. He was not optimistic.

He was able to find a seat at the corner of the bar where he could survey the interior of the premises. It was clearly not a popular seat as you couldn't see the stage very well, probably explaining why he often got to sit there. Ordering a large Coke, he made sure the barman got a large tip, ensuring he would get priority service in the future and be remembered. He was pretty sure he had already been picked up on the entrance door cameras. So far, so good.

After observing the crowd for a few minutes, he realised there was no sign of that girl Mary. A bit rich, he thought, considering she was the one who had sold tonight's featured group to him, but maybe a bit early. No sooner had he turned back to the bar than he heard a girly voice behind him.

"Glad you made it. Hope you enjoy the band."

Turning round quickly, Miles was just in time to see Mary's blonde head disappearing into the crowd in front of the stage with a group of friends. He assumed that was the prime position to see the band from and, as far as he was concerned, they were welcome to it. The noise from the DJ was starting to wear him down.

Half an hour later, he was beyond thankful when the five members of Angry Dogs took to the stage, all long hair, beards and scruffy clothing. He supposed it made them cool. In fairness, Miles had to admit that the group were not too bad, with a decent lead singer, even if they were still a bit loud for his taste. Still, they were a big improvement on the previous occupant of the stage.

As he had some driving to do later, Miles deemed it prudent to stick to soft drinks, especially considering the task he had set himself with the aid of Karl Smithson. If he did it.

The band wrapped up just after eleven and were replaced by canned background music, thankfully not the obnoxious DJ. The crowd in the club began to thin out, but there were still plenty of people milling about, some of whom were doing something that he supposed was similar to dancing.

Mary appeared through the throng, approaching him at the bar.

"Well, did you like Angry Dogs?"

"Yeah, they weren't too bad, I suppose. Better than the DJ anyway."

"Come on, he's not that bad."

"Okay, okay. Where are your friends?"

"Oh, they've gone. They're all lightweights, no stamina."

"I see. In that case, would you like a drink? G and T, isn't it? I suppose I owe you for convincing me to see the group."

Mary looked at her watch before replying. "Yes, all right, thanks. My lift won't be here for another half-hour."

That was a surprise; he should have known about the lift. Why didn't he?

Miles looked towards the barman, who was there almost instantly, taking the order for Mary's drink. Whilst waiting, he put a hand in his jacket, feeling the smooth surface of the small glass vial. Time to make a decision.

Another generous tip followed delivery of the drink, earning an appreciative nod from the barman. Picking up the glass in his left hand, Miles used his right hand to flick the top from the vial whilst still in his pocket. Concealing it in the palm of his hand, he emptied the colourless liquid contents into Mary's drink whilst holding it just below the bar top. It was done so quickly that he was certain no one could have seen him, especially in the dim lighting. Besides which, he'd practised doing it so many times that it took only two or three seconds.

Passing the drink to the girl, she immediately took a large swallow. No turning back now; he was committed.

After about ten minutes of desultory conversation, Mary leant against him, a little unsteadily.

She slurred, "It's really hot. I don't feel very well."

"No probs. Let's get some fresh air."

The barman responded with a conspiratorial smile when Miles explained that Mary was feeling a bit unwell so he was taking her outside for some air. What was it with barmen? Holding on to her arm, he walked the girl to the side exit and into the street, leading her to where his car was parked. He opened the Fiesta's front passenger door, helping her into the seat. By this time, she was almost unconscious and made no objection. He had nearly been caught on the hop by the speed at which the Rohypnol worked; it was certainly good stuff. Getting into the driver's seat, he quickly searched the girl, finding the mobile phone he was looking for in the back pocket of her jeans. He switched it off and, having fastened his and

Mary's seat belts, started the engine and drove away for his hour-long trip. Confident that her phone could not now be tracked, he used his carefully pre-planned route to the farmhouse, driving initially in the opposite direction until he left the city and the all-seeing cameras.

She was breathing deeply, almost snoring, he thought, as if she was asleep. This was a dangerous time; he couldn't afford to be stopped by the police.

Listening to the radio whilst waiting patiently in the sleek Mercedes saloon, it was Dan Richardson's usual Wednesday night job, as the family chauffeur, to pick Mary up from Fat Harry's. He'd seen a number of people leave the club already, with the door staff taking the barriers back inside. Checking his watch, he saw it was only five minutes until midnight.

By five past midnight, Richardson was becoming concerned at Mary's failure to appear, she was usually so prompt. In addition, he had not seen anyone leave the club in the last couple of minutes. He considered ringing his boss but decided he had better check inside the club first.

Locking the car and crossing the road, Dan was barred from entering Fat Harry's by a hand in his chest from a surly 'bouncer'. Quickly explaining he was here to collect Mary, he asked if the club was empty yet, receiving a nod from the man at the door. He asked about the toilets, to be told that they had been checked, as they were at closing time every night.

Somehow, he managed to persuade the man to let him see the manager. When she came to the door, the woman confirmed everything Dan had already been told, but recognising his obvious concern invited him into the club for one final check. It took minutes only to confirm that there were indeed no customers left in the club.

Returning to the car, an increasingly anxious Dan Richardson rang his boss.

Sir John Ross was watching the late-night news in his study, once more marvelling at the never-ending stupidity of politicians, when he took Richardson's call. A man used to taking charge, he immediately instructed the chauffeur drive round the side streets near the club in an effort to trace his daughter. In the meantime, he rang his daughter's mobile phone to be told the number he was calling was not available.

Fifteen minutes later, an ashen-faced Richardson returned to the house with only bad news, reporting that there had been no sign of Mary.

John Ross waited no longer, dialling 999 and requesting the police.

"Police emergency, how may I help?"

"I want to report my daughter missing."

"How old is she?"

"She's twenty."

"When did she go missing and where from?"

"My driver went to pick her up from Fat Harry's bar at midnight. There was no sign of her."

"Can I say, sir, that twenty-year-olds are late home from clubs all the time, and she has been missing for less than an hour."

Raising his voice in emphasis and anxiety, Ross almost shouted down the phone. "You don't understand. She is always on time and wouldn't go anywhere without letting me know. That's why I'm so worried."

Realising his obvious worry, the female officer replied, "I'm sorry, sir, but at the moment we cannot attend. If your daughter has not returned by the morning, you should ring us back. Goodbye."

A frantic and angry John Ross was left holding a dead phone.

Pouring himself and Dan Richardson a very strong drink, he considered his next steps, knowing with complete certainty that something untoward had happened to his cherished daughter. Making his mind up, he sent his driver to bed, explaining they may have a lot to do tomorrow and at least one of them should be fresh.

Once he had left, Ross rang the number of an old friend. Unsurprisingly, as it was now around one in the morning, it took several rings before the phone was answered.

"Hammond."

"George. It's John Ross. I need help."

After many years of late-night emergency calls, the former senior civil servant Lord George Hammond quickly cleared the fog of sleep. "Looking at the time, I am guessing this is serious."

"George, Mary has gone missing."

"Who?"

"Mary, my daughter."

Regretting his error, Hammond quickly recollected that up until three years ago the girl had been known as Linda and that Mary was actually her middle name. She had started using Mary for two reasons, firstly in an attempt to escape the publicity from earlier in her life and also in tribute to her late mother, Mary, who had died of cancer.

"Sorry, John. I must still be half asleep. What has happened exactly?"

Ross related the facts as he knew them, just as he had to the police. Not surprisingly, Hammond expressed similar doubts.

"George, ever since she was kidnapped by that maniac, Smithson, we have been super cautious, with lots of precautions in place. She would never go off with anyone without telling me first. Secondly, she loves Dan Richardson and his wife. They've worked for me all Mary's life and she would never leave him sat outside waiting. I think somebody's got her."

"Yes, I see what you mean. I assume you have been in touch with the police."

"They didn't want to know."

"Okay. Give me fifteen minutes while I contact a former associate."

Proving that the old boys' network was still functioning efficiently, Hammond was speaking to a former colleague from his time in the Home Office and Ministry of Defence within minutes. Explaining the situation to a sympathetic friend, he was told to await a call back.

Following the return call, George Hammond was back on the phone with Ross inside ten minutes.

"John, a man called Cooper and some associates will be with you within three hours."

"George, who is he? Police?"

"No, the police have rules about missing person reports and I'm afraid they will not be interested, not yet anyway. I think the best way to describe Cooper is that he's a specialist, and a very effective one at that. Believe me. Now try to get a couple of hours sleep and I'll ring you tomorrow."

Overwhelmed with fear for his missing daughter, sleep was impossible.

Whilst all this was happening, the still unconscious subject of all the concern had been laid on one of the camp beds in the farmhouse bedroom, having been carried in by Kingston. She would wake to find herself handcuffed to a length of chain, the other end of which was wrapped twice around the bathroom handrail and then padlocked to a bracket the kidnapper had fixed to the wall. His original plan had been to install a large dog kennel or run in the room, perhaps build a cage, but he had decided the chain was an easy and effective option, with the added attraction that no one else needed to be involved.

There would be no escape.

Whilst unloading the supplies from the car, he began to understand why Rohypnol was called the 'date rape' drug. He could have done anything he wanted to the girl without any resistance from her and, if what he heard was true, she wouldn't remember it either.

Fortunately for her, she was spared that indignity. He couldn't imagine having sex with an unconscious woman, wanting them to show some life, especially when he was rough with them. It wouldn't happen anyway; this was work, and besides, she was far too young for his tastes.

Before settling down on the other camp bed, he stood over Mary looking at her, a little sad at what he had done and what he had yet to do. Still, the money he expected to get would be a great comfort.

The last task was to remove his Richard Wade disguise,

placing it in his ever-present backpack. He found it a little awkward to do whilst wearing the latex gloves he had put on as soon as he arrived at the building, but he would need to get used to it as he would wear them for the entirety of his stay. Only Wade's prints should be found and, with that in mind, he must not leave any discarded gloves behind for police to get DNA or possibly prints.

Thinking about fingerprints reminded him that he had one more piece of evidence to help the police catch and convict Wade. He took the airport car park ticket from his backpack and placed it in the carrier bag with the shopping receipts, having copied the parking space number on another piece of paper for his own use.

He knew the bag of receipts was a bit obvious, but the police were very good with obvious.

TWENTY-EIGHT

Just after 5am, four men arrived by car at Sir John Ross's home. They were admitted to the imposing house by a bleary-eyed and deeply concerned father.

"My name's Cooper and these are my associates. We're here to help if we can, sir."

"Thank you very much, Mr Cooper. I know you aren't police, so where do you come from?"

"Firstly, it's just Cooper, and secondly, me and my team are employed by various people to fix problems. That's as much as I can say."

"Do you work for government?"

"I've told you as much as I can, Sir John. Shall we get on? Time's wasting."

"Fair enough. Let me arrange some food and hot drinks for everyone, then I'll fill you in."

Using an internal phone, he contacted Dan Richardson and his wife, who lived in an annex to the house, requesting the food and drink. Dan was his driver and gardener, whilst his wife, Ann, was his housekeeper, both of whom had been with him for over twenty-five years. Neither of them had been asleep, spending the whole night worrying about a girl they had known and loved all her life.

Ross resumed his seat and, as best he could, answered the questions put to him by Cooper.

He quickly established that Mary was twenty years old and that she was a regular visitor to Fat Harry's club on a Wednesday for the music night, no doubt meaning that many people would be familiar with her and her movements. As far as her father was concerned, Mary's visit to the club last night was perfectly normal, and he understood she would be meeting some friends.

Dan was to pick her up at midnight, as he did every time the girl went to the club.

Cooper couldn't help thinking that routine was always the killer in these jobs. Having been given a quick briefing about the family's history, he was a little surprised that better security measures were not in place.

"What do you think has happened to your daughter?"

"I'm very much afraid that she has been kidnapped."

"Why do you think that?"

"Mary was kidnapped about ten years ago and we were very lucky to get her back. Ever since then, we have been careful, making sure she is safe. She has never left Dan waiting in the car, and if there was a problem, she would ring one of us. She definitely wouldn't just wander off."

"Have you tried Mary's phone?"

"It's switched off."

"Have there been any demands yet?"

"Nothing."

"Has Mary got a boyfriend?"

"No, I'm pretty sure she hasn't. I'm certain Mrs Richardson would know. They spend a lot of time together."

Cooper was blunt. "Do you trust the Richardsons?"

For the first time, the millionaire displayed some anger. "They are like family to me and Mary. I would trust them with mine and my daughter's life, completely. Why are you wasting time with questions like this?"

"I don't know you, Mary or the Richardsons, so I have to get up to speed pretty quickly. Statistically, abductions are, in most cases, committed by people close to them. You must trust that I and my colleagues know our business."

The man just nodded dumbly.

Cooper beckoned one of his men over and whispered some instructions in his ear.

Five minutes later, he returned, accompanied by the Richardsons carrying plates of sandwiches and hot drinks. He reported to Cooper that the couple were heartbroken and had both broken down whilst he briefly questioned them. He was satisfied they were in the clear. He added that Mrs Richardson had confirmed that, as far as she knew, Mary did not have a boyfriend, and if she had, she would certainly have confided in the housekeeper.

"Nearly finished for now, Sir John. I understand you tried to report your daughter missing to the police, but they were not interested. Is that correct?"

"Yes. They said she was an adult and that young girls often slope off with friends when they've been out to a club. They wouldn't listen to me. That's why I reached out to Lord Hammond for help."

"That's why we're here, sir. I promise you we will do everything we can to get your girl back safely."

With that, Cooper turned back to his men, who were making big inroads into the coffee and sandwiches. They hadn't eaten on their journey and had learnt many years ago that in their particular form of employment you ate when you could, never knowing when there would be another chance.

Cooper drew them to one side of the room as he briefed them. "Mark, you set up here. Get all the phones wired for recording and be ready for the call when it comes. Tony, Andy, get down to that club and get access to the internal and external videos. I want to see where Mary went ASAP. If you can't get into the system from outside, call me and I'll find the club manager."

After telling Ross what his men would be doing, Cooper asked some further questions.

"Do you know anyone in the police who may be prepared to help us?"

"Yes, I think so. Amy Clark was brilliant the last time Linda was kidnapped. I haven't spoken to her for a while, but I believe she's a Superintendent now."

"That's good. Why did you call your daughter Linda?"

"Oh, sorry. Yes, up to three years ago, she was always known as Linda but was fed up of being known by a lot of people as the kidnap girl. Then when my wife, Mary, died, she decided she would use her own middle name. So she became Mary, but I still slip up sometimes."

"What happened to the kidnappers last time?"

Wise enough to know the direction the questioning was heading, Ross replied. "It was only one man and you don't need to worry about him. It was a man who used to work for me, called Karl Smithson, who is still serving a lot of years in prison."

"Nicely illustrates my point about kidnappers often being people you know. We'll get to that later if we have to."

Ross was lost in thought, probably thinking of the anguish he and his late wife had gone through at the hands of that maniac, and the subsequent events. His wife had never recovered.

"It was an awful time."

"Okay, I understand. Finally, what is your attitude to paying a ransom?"

Raising his voice, he said, "I don't want to give anything to these bastards, whoever they are, but I will. My daughter means everything to me, and I will give them everything I've got to get her back."

Cooper replied quietly. "Let's hope it won't come to that. Now we wait for contact."

Sir John Ross was reassured by Cooper's air of quiet confidence and natural authority, allied with the obvious competence and skills of the group as a whole. All four men were wearing dark clothing, appeared to be in their thirties and looked extremely fit. If he had to guess, he would have said Special Forces, but he didn't know and didn't really care, just desperately wanting their help.

TWENTY-NINE

Miles Kingston awoke abruptly to the harsh sound of his phone's alarm at 6am, unable to think where he was. He looked round the gloomy room in the weak early-morning sun finding a way in around the plastic sheets he'd put over the window.

He saw the blonde girl sitting on the edge of the bed, her large eyes staring fixedly at him, whilst trembling and crying.

He shouted at her to be quiet, but she couldn't or wouldn't. He tried a more soothing voice.

"Look, Mary, you'll be okay. You know me, I won't hurt you."

"Who are you?" she cried.

Miles belatedly remembered that he was no longer wearing his Richard Wade disguise, so how would she recognise him? Idiot.

"You don't need to know who I am. I'll let you go as soon as your father pays me the money I want. In the meantime, you stay chained to the bed. You can't reach the window or door, but you can get to the bathroom. I've left a few things in there for you. Any shouting or attempt to escape and it'll be the worse for you. Do you want anything to eat or drink?"

She shook her head forlornly.

He made himself a coffee, eating an energy bar, whilst he considered his next course of action.

"All right, Mary, I'm going to fasten this around your neck for a couple of minutes and then take a quick photograph."

He walked over to the bed and, despite her struggles, roughly fastened a leather dog collar around the girl's neck. Another result of his and Karl's constant scheming and planning, the collar had been made to look like an explosive device. It had two small black plastic boxes glued onto it, connected by a number of coloured electrical wires. No one would be fooled by a close examination but, viewed from a distance, it would do. Besides, who would be prepared to take the chance?

Taking her own phone, he switched it on, anxiously confirming that it was not receiving a signal. He made the girl stand up, before quickly taking a full-length picture, showing the chain fastened to her wrist and the collar around her neck. Once done, he removed the collar and brought her some bottled water and food across to her bed, thinking, *She can please herself.*

Whilst drinking his coffee, Miles composed a careful message to accompany the picture and, once satisfied, switched the phone off. He had spent a lot of time, over the previous few weeks, considering exactly what he needed to say in the ransom demand. He considered that keeping the message brief was essential, and he was particularly pleased with the way he had been able to suggest more than one person was involved in the kidnap.

Kingston's big regret was that he had been unable to ask for more money from such a rich bastard as Sir John effing Ross. However, he had been forced to face reality when he realised how heavy money was and how bulky a load it made. He had spent a lot of time researching and calculating exactly how much the different Bank of England notes weighed and, depending on the notes he selected, the exact dimensions of the bag he would need to fit the load into.

It had not been easy, and, more than once, he had almost given up in despair. On the face of it, five and ten-pound notes were the smallest and lightest, so it seemed they were the obvious denominations to demand. However, whilst twenty and fifty-pound notes were larger and heavier, you needed fewer of them so could manage a bigger total amount. Whichever way he looked at it, and however he did the sums, there was still, unfortunately to his mind, a limit on what he could carry and so what he could demand for the girl's return.

After using the toilet, he addressed the girl once more. "Look, I'm going out for no more than half an hour, so behave yourself and remember what I said. This room is wired so I can hear you on my phone if you make any noise at all. Do you understand?"

The girl nodded meekly.

If he was honest, her weeping and wailing was starting to get on his nerves already, hardening his resolve to see things through. The sooner, the better.

Once outside, knowing he had about three miles to go

before he could get a phone signal, the kidnapper jumped into the Fiesta and started the engine, before realising he couldn't set off immediately. It took him about ten minutes to put the car's original plates back on, careful to put the cloned ones back in the boot. One more problem for Wade to explain away.

Driving down the farm track to where it joined the main road, he turned left towards Leeds, stopping in a lay-by he had already spotted about 200 yards along. He switched on Mary's phone, quickly sending the photo and message he had composed to John Ross, whose number was, of course, already in the contacts list. Switching it off immediately, he had been on the phone less than a minute. He then opened the phone, removing both the SIM card and battery, making sure not to replace the back.

As he drove back to the farm, Miles threw both the SIM card and battery out of the window at half-mile intervals. Why the battery, he had no idea, but Karl had thought it was a sensible thing to do. A little further on, he stopped beside a small muddy stream where he stamped on the phone several times, breaking it into several pieces, before throwing them into the water. The back cover followed.

Returning to the farm, he put the car in a shed for the moment. Better to be safe.

He was especially proud of turning towards Leeds when he sent the message, hoping a phone mast covering part of the city would pick up his brief transmission. Karl had assured him that phone towers covered a large circular area and that whilst one would certainly pick up his transmission, it would not be able to identify a specific location. The further he got from the farm, the better for now, hopefully confusing any attempts to trace his location. He hoped that Karl was right.

Now he just had to wait with Mary. He really hoped she was going to settle down a little; otherwise, it would be a really long day and night.

THIRTY

Shortly before 7am, John Ross jumped to his feet, roused from a fitful sleep by the loud beeping of his mobile phone. For a man so used to taking charge of pressure situations, he was totally out of his depth and, surprised to get a text rather than the phone call he was waiting for, could only look to Cooper for guidance.

"Could this be them?"

"It's possible. Let's have a look, shall we?"

As he switched the phone on and viewed the text, the man gasped, and, if it was possible, his face turned several shades paler than it already was before. With a trembling hand, he passed the phone mutely to Cooper. He and Mark looked carefully at the picture and accompanying text, not at all surprised at its impact on Ross.

"What do you think, Coops?"

"Well, firstly, it's been sent from the girl's phone. The photo is definitely her and designed to have the maximum impact. She's got a chain fixed to her wrist and some sort of collar around her neck The demands seem pretty standard, but the amount they're asking for is a little unusual. Get it all printed out for me and then see if there's anything you can do to trace where it was sent from."

"I'll give it a try, but I'm not confident. Before I do, though, what do you think about that collar she's wearing?"

"Clearly, it's supposed to look like an explosive device of some sort, but I'm not sure. It could be a mock-up to fool us."

"Can we afford to take a risk, Coops?"

"No, we can't. Until we know different, we treat it as real."

Once Mark had produced a printed copy of the ransom demands, Cooper spent some minutes studying it carefully.

Mary is unharmed and will remain so if you do as we say.
She will be released on the payment of £400,000, half in £50 notes and half in £20 notes. Place the money in a holdall and await further instructions tomorrow.
NO POLICE. NO BUGS.
NO MARKED MONEY. NO DRONES.
NO ATTEMPT TO FOLLOW US.
If you deviate in any way from these instructions, we will remotely activate the explosive device.
SHE WILL DIE.
IT WILL BE ON YOUR HEAD.

His first question was to John Ross. "Can you get that amount of money?"

"I have the money, but getting that amount from the banks at short notice may prove problematical."

"I may be able to help with that. What are your thoughts about the instructions, specifically trying to track them and the money?"

"Let them have it, I don't care. I'm not going to risk Mary's life for money."

Cooper thought carefully about his next question. "What would you like us to do once Mary has been returned safely?"

After a few seconds' consideration, Ross replied in quiet, measured tones. "Find the bastards and kill them all." The thought of his daughter being in the hands of kidnappers once again was almost too much to bear.

Mark interrupted the conversation when he reported on his phone-tracking efforts. Basically, the phone had been on less than a minute and was not now available; probably disposed of, was his opinion. At least that was what he would have done. It had been picked up in the radius of a phone mast somewhere to the northeast of Leeds, but at the moment the exact location could not be pinpointed. He may be able to do better later.

Cooper looked at Ross, who appeared to be ageing by the hour. "Right, Sir John, this is where we're at. We now have confirmation, if it was needed, that your daughter has been kidnapped, but, on the bright side, Mary appears to be alive and well. The kidnappers seem to be pretty clever, certainly when it comes to phones. My men are trying to access videos at the club to identify them. We know their demands now, and you have authorised the payment of the cash. My advice at this stage would be to involve the police and to make an attempt to pursue the kidnappers when they collect the money. To be clear, do you want the police involved at this stage?"

"I don't think so. Not yet anyway. Maybe when we get her back. Will that be a problem?"

"Not for me. I work for you and will act on your instructions. However, I will offer advice based on my experience of similar events. What about attempting to mark or bug the money?"

"No. I've told you I don't care, they can have the money. I can't do anything to risk Mary's life by ignoring the instructions."

"Right, I'll get on the phone to get the money authorised once you give me the bank details. Okay?"

"Of course. You've not told me your fee yet, but you better add that to the total."

Cooper, surprisingly, was a little embarrassed. "Our normal fee is £50,000 for all of us, plus possibly some expenses. If that is agreeable to you, pay us when it's all over."

John Ross was a millionaire many times over and considered the ransom and the specialist's fee to be of little importance, especially if his daughter was returned safely.

They got to work.

THIRTY-ONE

Natasha woke with a start when she felt a weight across her breasts. Looking to one side, she saw that the still-sleeping Richard Wade had thrown his arm across her chest. What with his snoring and the sunlight streaming through the bedroom window, she knew more sleep was impossible. Besides, she needed the toilet. The bedside clock showed 10.15, much earlier than she was used to rising, but needs must.

The woman slid from under Wade's arm, trying not to disturb him but failing dismally. As she stood at the side of the bed in all her naked glory, Natasha knew she was giving him the show of his life, before she quickly realised this was not the behaviour of a hardworking journalist. Much to Wade's disappointment, she grabbed a short robe and held it in front of her to regain some semblance of modesty.

He looked at her eagerly before asking in a husky voice, "Did we…?"

"We certainly did, Richard, you naughty man."

His face lit up with a proud smile, whilst Natasha could only think how gullible men were.

"I'm going to the loo, then I'm getting in the shower. Do you want to join me?" She giggled as she added, "In the shower, I mean."

With that, she turned and headed off towards the toilet, treating Wade to another enticing view as she left the room.

He wasted no time in joining her, completely unable to keep his hands to himself. She allowed him to amuse himself for a while, assisting where necessary before putting an end to proceedings by telling him she was hungry and wanted some breakfast.

Wade sat at the table watching whilst Natasha utilised some of her other talents for keeping men happy by whipping up a delicious omelette and fresh coffee for them both. However, she made sure that, whilst wearing nothing but the short robe, some apparently accidental wardrobe malfunctions meant the man was kept interested in the other goods still on offer. He was mesmerised.

Whilst they were eating, Wade started to mutter about having to leave, claiming to have things to do. She was unfazed, being used to handling men, so to speak. Firstly, she expressed her disappointment then pointed out that they hadn't really had chance to sort out the article for the magazine yet. She was amazed when he still seemed to be wavering so played her trump card, standing up before letting the robe fall to the floor. Once more, his eyes nearly popped out of his head when he feasted his eyes on her amazing body.

"I know it's early but I've got some champagne in the fridge. Now we've eaten, I thought we could drink it afterwards in bed."

He actually asked after what before she took hold of his hand and led him into the bedroom. An hour later, Wade was back asleep after an exhaustive display of the prostitute's much practised and refined skills, followed by several glasses of the champagne.

Natasha dozed off whilst she waited for the dupe to wake up once more. She still had many tricks up her sleeve including, obviously, shagging his brains out, plying him with drink and making use of the drugs in her possession. The handcuffs were a last resort, but might be fun.

THIRTY-TWO

It proved a frustrating morning for Cooper and his team, who had managed only partial access to Fat Harry's camera system, or should that be systems? For some reason, part of the club was covered by modern state-of-the-art digital cameras, complete with recording system, whilst the remainder was covered by the oldest set of cameras Tony and Andy could ever remember seeing. They had simply been unable to get into the old camera recordings, if they existed.

They had seen Mary in the club, but only with her friends. The digital cameras seemed to focus mainly on the stage but did not cover the bar area or the various doors. There was no sign of whom her kidnapper might be, or anything at all suspicious.

One of Cooper's extensive network of contacts managed to access the local licensing records, identifying the club's manager and her contact details. Woken from a deep sleep, she was initially unwilling to turn out, but got to the club just after noon, having been given a cock-and-bull story about fire hazards and how seriously it may impact on the licence along with the possible attendant bad publicity for the club and its owners.

She must have still been half asleep, because she never asked why they wanted to examine the security system.

Within minutes of accessing the recording, they were able to find poor-quality pictures of a man helping a still-identifiable Mary Ross from the club through a side door. Working backwards, they found several images of the same man talking to Mary at various times during the evening, including him clearly buying the girl a drink. What they found odd was that the unknown man had made no attempt to hide his face and, on more than one occasion, appeared to deliberately look directly at a camera. Once they had spotted him, they found clearer images of him on the more modern digital system.

Finally, now aware what they were looking for, they found grainy images on the external door camera of the man helping Mary into the front passenger seat of a blue car before he got into the driver's seat. Minutes later, the car drove off. The pictures were so poor that the make and model of the car could not be identified, and there was definitely no chance of getting a registration number. Maybe they would get lucky with street cameras.

Both men thanked the still-grumpy manageress, before returning to the Ross house with numerous printed images from the club security system.

During the time Tony and Andy had been at the club, Sir John had set aside the dining room for Cooper to use as his ops room, with the added benefit that it had a settee and easy chair for the men to snatch some sleep when they could.

The four operatives were left alone after Cooper suggested to Ross that he might like to take a break, with a promise that any fresh developments would be relayed to him immediately. The truth of the matter was that it made it much easier for the men to speak frankly, giving honest opinions that perhaps the father of the kidnapped girl might not appreciate hearing.

The first order of business was to study the photographs retrieved from Fat Harry's. There were several very clear full-face shots of the man who could later be seen helping an unsteady Mary from the club, followed by the grainy ones of him getting her into the blue car.

Cooper looked around the group. "Any observations?"

Andy was the first to speak. "When we were at the club and first found the clear pictures of this man, we were immediately struck by the way he appeared to deliberately look at the cameras. It was as if he almost wanted to be identified."

"Anybody else?"

Mark was next. "When we got the ransom text, there were several mentions of we, clearly suggesting more than one person was involved. If that's the case, why does it appear only one person is involved in the actual snatch? Surely if more than one person was there, they would have found it easier to subdue Mary if necessary."

"Any thoughts, Tony?"

"Yeah, Coops. I'm worried about the money."

"In what way?"

"Do you remember that silly bugger who tried to extort money from the electronics firm and then, when it was handed over, couldn't pick it up because he had asked for so much? I've been thinking about it and while four hundred grand is obviously a lot of money, it's not so much when you start divvying it up between several people, and it's even less if you take away any expenses. I did some calculations about weight and bulk of that amount of cash and it's about at the limit of what you'd want to comfortably carry. If more than one person was involved, then each person could carry similar amounts, giving them a bigger reward for risking a lot of time in prison. I honestly think this bastard may be working on his own."

"Good analysis, fellas. I think you could well be right that this is a single-person operation. Like you, I'm worried about his apparent desire to be identified. It's odd, to say the least."

After a brief period of silence whilst he considered their next moves, Cooper once more addressed the group.

"Right. Mark and Tony, I want you to get into the street cameras, see if you can get a clearer look at this car and hopefully a reg. number. Then we need to find out where it went. Secondly, we need to get back into the club videos to find out if our suspect has been there previously. He must have scoped the place out before. He wouldn't just turn up and hope for the best, surely. Later on, we'll go and interview the staff at the club. Obviously, if we get that car number, we may be able to take more positive action. Everybody okay with that?"

The two men nodded, leaving Andy to say, "What do you want me to do, Coops?"

"Firstly, we show Ross the photos to see if he can identify the man. You know as well as I do, there is often a connection between the kidnapper and their victim or family. Then me and you will go with him to the bank to collect the ransom money so that we are prepared when the drop instructions come in."

Andy had further questions. "Are we really not going to bug the bag or mark the cash, not even try to follow them when they collect it?"

"This is between us. Ross does not need to know. I have been on the phone all morning making arrangements for the Bank of England to authorise the movement of that much cash and getting it delivered to a major bank in Leeds. Sir John Ross is our employer and the father of the victim, so we follow his instructions to the letter, so no bugs in the bag or marked money. However, I have arranged that £100,000 of the ransom will be in forged fifty-pound notes. It was not easy, I can tell you. The bank was not exactly keen to have that much forged money floating around the system, and I had to get some pretty high-level support. The idea is that when the money starts to get spent, we will be able to identify areas where it is turning up, hopefully pointing us in the right direction. It's not perfect and it will probably take several weeks to filter through, but it may give us a chance. Of course, it may not matter if we find Mary and our mystery man before then."

"That's a bit of a long shot, boss, but I guess it's all we've got."

"Come on, Andy, let's show Ross the photos and hope he can give us a name, then, as I said, we're off to the bank. By the way, make sure you all carry side arms until this is over. We don't know who we're up against yet."

If anyone had been listening, that instruction may

have given a clue to the current or former occupation of the four men.

Mark and Tony remained in the dining room, now able to access all the club camera systems remotely following their earlier visit. Accessing the street cameras was something they had done many times previously and, once again, did not present any major problems. Both men were confident that they would be able to identify the blue car and find out where it had gone.

Even Cooper, a man who had seen and done most things, the majority of which he would never speak about, was surprised by Sir John's reaction on being shown the picture of the man believed to have kidnapped his daughter.

He almost shouted. "Jesus Christ, I don't believe it. That looks like Richard Wade."

"Sir, who is Richard Wade?"

"I'll tell you, but, before I do, you better start calling me John. Otherwise, we'll drive each other up the bloody wall."

"Okay, John, who is he?"

"First thing to say is that I haven't seen the man for a number of years, but I'm pretty sure it's him. When my daughter was kidnapped the first time, she was freed as a result of two police officers stopping the car being driven by Karl Smithson. At the time, they didn't know she was tied up in the boot, but one of them, Pc Steve Brown, was acting on some scant information and instinct. The other officer was Inspector Richard Wade."

Andy was unable to prevent himself interrupting. "You're telling us he is a police officer?"

"Not now. Both officers were attacked with a knife by Smithson, who wounded Wade and killed Steve Brown. Wade was believed to be a hero, promoted and awarded a medal, whilst Smithson went to prison. A subsequent covert enquiry by the original investigating team established that Brown was the true hero and that Wade was far from such. He was, in fact, proven to be a coward and a liar. He was ruined but allowed to retire on a pension."

"John, why was he allowed to retire?"

"Politics. Too many people would look bad. Simple as that."

Wise in the ways of the world, Cooper smiled grimly. "So why would he do this?"

"I don't know. I threw him out of my office when he approached me for a job. Maybe revenge, maybe he just needs the money."

"Finally, how sure are you it's him, and would Mary know him?"

"I'm pretty sure she wouldn't know him, and I'm fairly certain it's him."

More confirmation that kidnappers were usually close to or actually known by the victim or their family.

Back in the ops room, the other two men had not been wasting their time. They had accessed the club's videos from the previous fortnight, all they had, and identified the same man in the club on the two previous Wednesday nights. It was clear that he had also passed the time with Mary on occasion.

Getting into the street cameras had, as usual, proved relatively simple, making it easy, with the improved images, to establish that the car was one of the most common vehicles on the road, a blue Ford Fiesta. Not knowing that the registration number they had identified was cloned, Mark and Tony believed they were onto a winner.

They had managed to track the car to the south of the city, before, due to a lack of cameras, losing it in the countryside. By their own secretive means, they had found the owner's address, which threw them slightly as it was nowhere near the area where they had last seen the vehicle on the cameras.

When Cooper returned to the room, they updated him on the results of their efforts, whilst he updated them on the bombshell delivered by Ross.

"We've got a lot to do. Myself and Andy have still got to go with Sir John to get the money from the bank. We don't know how this is going to pan out yet, so we need to be ready to do a cash exchange for the girl if necessary. In the meantime, find Wade's address and get yourselves down there. Make the usual discreet enquiries, and, if you need to, get in and have a look round. Take our car, we'll go in Sir John's, and don't forget to take a photo with you."

Mark chipped in. "What about this address for the Fiesta owner?"

"We're a bit thin on the ground so we'll do that later. It may be better after dark anyway."

They all knew what Cooper meant: a possible and potentially dangerous rescue operation.

It wouldn't be the first time, but they remembered that not all the operations had been successful.

Two hours later, they met for a further briefing back in the dining room, appropriately enough, eating some more of Mrs Richardson's sandwiches whilst drinking copious amounts of coffee.

The money had been collected and locked in a safe by Sir John, who was totally unaware that so much of it was forged. Fortunately, the notes were so good that even if he had inspected them, he would have been hard-pressed to identify them as such.

Mark and Tony reported on their visit to Wade's house, where they had posed as journalists, unaware of the irony that Natasha was also posing as a journalist to entrap the subject of everyone's attention.

Wade, of course, was not there, and some elderly neighbours erroneously stated that they thought he hadn't been about for a couple of days. The pair spun the story that they were doing an article about Wade and showed the couple one of the photos from the club, which they readily identified as him. Whilst Tony spoke to the neighbours some more, Mark had a prowl round, satisfying himself that Wade was not home. He did manage to look through the garage window, establishing that Wade's red Nissan Juke was inside.

Rejoining his colleague, Mark was able to ask the neighbours about Wade's car, confirming that he only had the red one and definitely did not have a blue car. It obviously jolted one man's memory, who had a vague recollection of his neighbour being picked up by someone in a small blue car. He couldn't remember when it was or the maker of the vehicle, and definitely hadn't seen the driver at all.

Cooper's only comment was that, in view of Wade being collected from his home, in possibly the suspect vehicle, there may well be more than one person involved in the kidnap. None of the others argued.

Having considered mounting a surveillance operation on Wade's home, Cooper explained to his men that he had decided against it because there were too few of them to do it properly. More to the point, he didn't believe the man would return as he must have stashed Mary Ross somewhere else. Clearly, neither of them, or any partners in crime, was in the house at the moment. It just didn't make any sense for Wade to come back until everything was over.

Realising the team had gone as far as they could for the moment, Cooper instructed them to get some rest as he was intending they should all go to the address of the Fiesta's registered keeper once it was dark.

Outside the address at 9pm, Cooper decided it was dark enough for their purposes. He and Andy were at the front of the small new-build house, whilst the other two were covering the back. The first surprise was that the Blue Fiesta, with the registration number picked up from the street cameras, was parked on the drive, which didn't necessarily mean anything, of course. Through the open lounge curtains they could clearly see a man and woman watching television with two children. Not exactly a hotbed of criminals, it would appear.

After that, things just went downhill. Knocking on the front door, Cooper produced something which may or may not have been a Police Warrant Card to the woman who answered. Spinning his rehearsed story to her, he explained that they were investigating an incident in which a car similar to theirs had been involved. Clearly shocked, she invited him and Andy into the house where she introduced them to her husband, offering them tea and shooing the children out of the lounge. The man bore no resemblance to Wade in any way whatsoever. Furthermore, his leg was resting on a pouffe, clearly encased in a plaster cast.

When asked about the car in the drive, he became a little heated, suggesting they could take it away with his blessing. He went on to explain that the car had been running poorly so a couple of days ago he had removed the engine to carry out some repairs. He'd got the engine into the garage before promptly dropping it onto his leg, hence the plaster cast.

Completely satisfied this family had nothing to do with Mary's kidnap, they hastily made their exit, confirming as they left that the car had indeed had its engine removed. Nevertheless, they would check at the hospital to verify the story.

They were disappointed, but not surprised, to find themselves back at square one when it became clear that the kidnapper had fitted cloned registration plates on the vehicle used to transport Mary from Fat Harry's. Cooper and the team had got as far as they could and would have to await the next set of instructions on the following day.

In the meantime, having updated Sir John Ross, the team settled down for as good a night's sleep as they could manage. Tomorrow was going to be a big day.

THIRTY-THREE

As he looked at his watch for what seemed like the hundredth time, Kingston began to think he was losing his mind. He had spent most of the day sleeping fitfully, constantly disturbed by the girl's incessant crying. Finally, reaching the point where he could stand it no more, he persuaded Mary to drink a glass of water that he had already laced with one of his remaining doses of Rohypnol.

Now she was asleep, it was the quiet that was getting on his nerves. Why hadn't he brought a radio? He chain-smoked for most of the day, having to be careful to put his cigarette butts in a jar he'd brought specially for the purpose. Having to be constantly aware of what he was doing at all times, trying not to leave any evidence for the pigs, was definitely putting him under even more strain.

Everything was preying on his mind all the time as he ran through what he still had to do if he was going to succeed in collecting the money and avoiding capture. Making sure Wade got the blame was becoming less and less of a priority for him, but he supposed he had gone too far to stop now, and he still had a deal with Karl Smithson.

However, amongst all his other thoughts and concerns, Miles was unable to stop thinking about what Natasha was up to with Wade. For God's sake, she was a tart, so why could he not stop thinking about her? She was a magnificent woman with whom he had become obsessed about having sex, something he knew he would be able to pay handsomely for very soon. Even though he knew she was a hard-hearted bitch and that it would be incredibly stupid to have any unnecessary contact with her after the job, he was finding the temptation almost irresistible.

He had no idea why he was so attracted to her, but he couldn't deny that he was, perhaps because he was unable to have her. Nevertheless, the thoughts wouldn't go away. Maybe he might be able to arrange something later.

Looking at his watch once more, Miles realised it was ten o'clock, time to check in. Taking the car, he drove to the lay-by he had previously used to get a phone signal before dialling the preset number.

Natasha answered on the second ring. "What do you want?"

For a moment, he revelled in hearing her voice, before he got a grip of himself. "Just checking to see if everything is okay?"

"All's fine. He's asleep now, partly because I've worn him out and partly because of all the booze and cannabis he's had. I suppose it might even have something to do with the Rohypnol I slipped him."

Miles felt a twinge of envy, imagining what it would be like to be worn out by Natasha.

"Good. Hopefully, I'll ring you after lunch tomorrow, so you can let him go as we arranged."

"Don't forget to meet me at the train station with the rest of my money. If I don't hear from you by four o'clock, I'm offski."

She broke the connection without giving him a chance to reply. She really was a bitch, but what a woman!

He was tempted to go straight back to the farm, but having previously promised Karl he would be available between 10 and 10.30 each night during the kidnap, he waited. Miles was amazed he even remembered the arrangement they had made all those weeks ago in their cell. With luck, the twat wouldn't be able to ring.

He'd actually started the car engine and was about to pull away when he was surprised by the loud ringing of the phone marked Karl.

"How are things going?"

Miles tried to hide his annoyance. "All good. I wasn't sure I would hear from you."

"So you managed to pull it off then?"

"Of course I did. I'm not a moron."

"I always had faith in you, Miles, but it's good to find out how things are going. How is my friend doing?"

"If that's who I think you mean, I can tell you he's fast asleep, absolutely shagged silly."

That was a cruel image to conjure up for a man who had not seen any women, other than female warders, for years and who might never see one again. Still, he did ask.

"Great to hear. Have you thought any more about what you need to do?"

"I've thought of little else."

"You know it needs to be done. I won't ring again unless something comes up. Good luck tomorrow."

Short and sweet, he was gone.

Back at the farm, Miles stood over Mary as he drank another coffee whilst trying to eat one of the – almost indigestible – pre-packed sandwiches he'd brought. She was a really pretty girl and, with thoughts of Natasha swirling round his mind, he was really tempted, but it just wouldn't be the same.

He threw the half-eaten sandwich into his bag of rubbish, which he intended to take away with him, and went outside for a cigarette whilst he finished his coffee. Deep in thought, he studied his problem from all angles before concluding, as he knew he would, that there was no option but for him to do it. Karl was right, the bastard.

Going back inside, he was proud of himself because, distracted as he was, he still managed to maintain his evidential security precautions by putting the cigarette butt in his jar. He didn't really know why but he decided to put some fresh latex gloves on.

Steeling himself for what must be done, he walked over to Mary's bed, bent over and grasped her tightly round the neck with both hands, pressing his thumbs into her throat. At first, there was no reaction from the girl, but she soon began to gurgle and struggle a little when she was unable to breathe. He squeezed harder and harder until the gurgling and struggling stopped. At the last second, just as he was about to let go, her eyes opened and a single tear ran down her cheek. He almost dropped her but continued to squeeze until she was as limp as a ragdoll and he was certain she was dead.

Miles was relieved it was over. He hadn't really wanted to kill her, but now he had, he was surprised by just how easy it had been. Of course, he knew that he'd not really had a choice and in his own mind he was easily able to rationalise what he'd done. It was simple really; if he hadn't killed her, the plan would not have worked. When he went to collect the ransom money, because of the length of time he would be away, he could not have risked leaving the girl alone in the farmhouse. Implausible as it was, she might have managed to escape or some unexpected visitor may have found her. In addition, there simply may not have been sufficient time to complete all his other tasks that day had he needed to return to the farm to release the girl. Now it could be weeks before she was found, and he would be well away by then.

Miles had to admit to himself that he actually experienced a frisson of excitement as he squeezed the life from Mary, although it might have been more enjoyable still if she had been able to put up a fight. He was well aware that he didn't much care for women and only used them for his own sexual gratification, enjoying rough sex and inflicting pain. For some peculiar reason, he liked to see them cry and was not the least bit interested in their enjoyment of the sex.

He knew it was probably something to do with his upbringing, his hatred of his mother and absent father. All of which made his yearning for Natasha more puzzling to him, although he did admit he would have enjoyed putting the bossy tart in her place.

Totally happy that he'd done the right thing, he lay down and was quickly lost in a dreamless sleep.

THIRTY-FOUR

Miles Kingston woke early full of beans, long before the alarm on his mobile went off. In a few hours, he was going to be rich, and, with the eternal confidence of most criminals, he was sure everything was going to be a walk in the park.

After showering, shaving and cleaning his teeth, he drank yet more coffee. About to leave, he did a final check of the room, attempting to make sure that he had left no trace of his presence. Satisfied, he collected his rubbish bag before making sure the glass bearing Wade's fingerprints was where it should be, next to the tin containing the cigarette butts collected from the beer garden. The bag with receipts and the airport parking ticket was under the table.

Even the police couldn't fail to find all that rather convenient evidence and use it to prove Wade's involvement in the crime.

Finally, he looked at the pale body of the dead girl. He hadn't really taken much notice of her whilst he'd been busy. She looked about fourteen. He considered covering her up, but hadn't so far, so why bother now? She certainly didn't need to be kept warm, not anymore, he thought with grim humour. As Miles stared at her, he realised that he didn't feel an ounce of remorse or regret; it had been necessary. Perhaps he was more like Karl Smithson than he thought.

He did consider taking Mary's body outside and burying it but couldn't be bothered or be sure the police would find it if he did. Even though it had not formed part of his initial plan, the girl's murder would, hopefully, ensure Richard Wade never, ever got out of prison.

He remembered, just in time, to put on his Richard Wade disguise before leaving the building for the final time as he set out for Pickering. Partway there, he stopped at a roadside bin to get rid of the rubbish bag, especially pleased with himself that he had remembered to include the toothbrush he had used whilst there.

The money drop was definitely the most dangerous part of the whole operation. If Ross had got the police involved, he needed to minimise their chances of setting up any sort of operation to capture him. To that end, he intended to send instructions, by text, at the last possible moment so needed to be in Pickering before doing so. His reasoning being that if he made them aware where the drop was to take place any sooner, it was possible an attempt may be made to stop him before he even got there. He was still driving the blue Fiesta, but now with the proper number plates on, which hopefully they would not recognise anyway. The cloned plates were in the boot just to help the police with their enquiries. If they got it right, along with the other clues, they should have ample evidence to tie Wade to the car and so the kidnap. Easy.

Whilst driving to Pickering, he thought about his conversations with Harris and how he had been forced to mislead him, a very dangerous game indeed. Whilst the story about the footballer was complete nonsense, parts of it had been true. He remembered being told, sometime in the past, that the best lie was the one which was the nearest to the truth as possible. One huge benefit being that it helped in remembering what you had said. So it was true the job took place at Fat Harry's and true that he intended to lie low at the farmhouse whilst Wade was entertained at the apartment by Natasha. His final truth was that the drop was to take place in Pickering.

It still worried him how Harris would react when he finally found out what Miles had done, fervently hoping that his hundred grand payment would placate the man.

Once more, he reassured himself that he still had his escape plan if not exactly in place then certainly in mind.

Reaching Pickering just after 7am, and not wanting to draw unnecessary attention to himself, he parked a couple of streets away from the rented lock-up. Removing one of his unused phones from his backpack, Miles switched it on, hoping there would be a good service. Once it was up and running, he carefully prepared a text message which he then sent to Ross's mobile phone, having already entered the number. When it had gone, he immediately switched off and, as previously, removed the SIM card and battery, before using his heel to stamp on the phone in the car's footwell, breaking it into several pieces.

As he had time to kill, Miles headed to the café he had used on his previous visit, having decided that he deserved a Full English and some hot tea. On the way, he dropped the SIM card and battery into one waste bin and the broken phone parts into another, believing he had safely covered his tracks.

Still wearing his Wade disguise, he was unconcerned about being picked up on any cameras or later identified by the café staff. In fact, he would very much welcome any further nails in Wade's coffin.

He really had to smile; it was so easy. Or so he thought.

THIRTY-FIVE

The seven people waiting in the Ross household dining room were startled by the beep of the owner's phone, even though they were all waiting for it. Knowing it was the instructions they had been waiting for, they all looked anxiously at the millionaire as he opened the message. He quickly read it before passing the phone, without comment, to Cooper.

Get to Pickering with the money by 9.30am today.
You will receive further instructions on arrival.
Your daughter is unharmed and will remain so as
long as you remember to do exactly as we say.
    NO POLICE. NO BUGS.
    NO MARKED MONEY. NO DRONES.
    NO ATTEMPT TO FOLLOW US.
If you deviate in any way from these instructions,
we will remotely activate the explosive device.
    SHE WILL DIE.
    IT WILL BE ON YOUR HEAD.

Cooper immediately took charge, asking Mark to make an attempt at tracing the origin of the text message, convinced it would be a waste of time once more.

He continued. "Dan, do you know how long it will take to get to Pickering?"

The chauffeur replied, "About an hour to an hour and fifteen minutes, I should think."

"Right, I want you to drive Sir John to Pickering in the Mercedes in case we are being watched. I'm sure that's what they'll expect. We'll follow in our car ten minutes later. Okay?"

Everybody nodded.

"Let's give ourselves an hour and a half. We can't afford to be late. So you leave at 8am. Do you know Pickering very well? I'm thinking of somewhere to park."

"Yes, not too bad. I'll park in the Co-op car park, it's pretty central."

Cooper smiled. "Sounds ideal."

Of course, none of them had any idea that it was the same location where Kingston had met Charlie's men for the Ford Mondeo handover.

Whilst Mrs Richardson busied herself with more tea and coffee before the men departed, Mark quietly reported to Cooper that the text message had been sent from the centre of Pickering, but that he could not be more accurate than that. He added that the phone now appeared to have been switched off.

Sir John and his driver left on time, with Cooper and his team leaving ten minutes later. When clear of Leeds, Dan Richardson pulled into a lay-by when instructed to do so by Cooper, once he had been as sure as he could be that they were not being followed. Minutes later, he joined Ross in the rear of the car. As agreed, the Mercedes parked in the Co-op car park to wait for the next message, with Cooper's men around the corner.

Ten minutes later, having had a very enjoyable breakfast, Miles Kingston almost fainted when he saw the parked Mercedes, recognising both Sir John Ross and his driver, although he didn't know the other man. Fortunately, as he was still some distance away, he managed to change the planned route back to his car, because, wearing the Wade disguise, he was sure to have been recognised.

Back in his car, Miles considered what to do about the mystery man. Concerned that he may betray how close he was, he decided not to tell Ross to get rid of him in his next message. Concluding that the man's presence was not a threat to what he still considered to be a perfect plan, he decided to say nothing.

Time was moving on. He quickly prepared another text message, sending it to Ross before immediately turning the phone off. Miles was feeling really proud of himself, confident that this was all going to work out, especially with the problems he had just set potential pursuers. He may have felt less sure had he realised that on his way to the lock-up he had driven past the car containing Cooper's team. In fact, he probably would have wet himself.

Ross was beginning to dread the sound that told him yet another text message had been received but reassured himself that it brought him nearer to Mary's release. Or so he fervently hoped.

He and Cooper studied the new message together.

Catch the 9.55am North Yorkshire Moors Railway train from Pickering to Grosmont. Sit in the last carriage. When you receive the command 'Now', you will have 10 seconds to throw the holdall from the nearside carriage door. Your daughter is unharmed and will remain so as long as you remember to do exactly as we say.

If anyone gets off the train, the girl will die.
NO POLICE. NO BUGS.
NO MARKED MONEY. NO DRONES.
NO ATTEMPT TO FOLLOW US
If you deviate in any way from these instructions, we will remotely activate the explosive device.
SHE WILL DIE.
IT WILL BE ON YOUR HEAD.

Dan, following instructions from Cooper, drove to the station. Before they alighted from the car, Cooper updated his team by phone on the current situation, instructing them to follow the train as best they could, reminding them that no attempt should be made to pursue the kidnappers. He also passed the mobile number that the last message had been sent from to Mark, who quickly confirmed that it was different to the previous one and probably already disposed of as well.

Cooper thought about their options, deciding they were very limited. The kidnappers had thought this through very carefully, ensuring they could not be contacted or traced immediately, but possibly could be later. They had no proof of life for Mary since the first message, although he thought it best not to mention that to Ross. Furthermore, the drop from the train was particularly clever, meaning, as they did not know about it until the last second, that no contingency plans could be put in place nor could they stake out any specific area. Even had they known it was to be from the train before now, they could not have watched the full line.

It seemed to him they would almost certainly get away today with the money, unless they made some really silly mistake, which they had so far avoided. He was sure there would be a protracted inquiry involving the police, who, no doubt, wouldn't be at all pleased to have been left out. The nature of any enquiries and the end result would very much hinge on Mary's safe return, and if that didn't happen, he already had very clear instructions from his employer as to what should happen. The police certainly would not be in favour of that.

As they had been instructed, Sir John Ross and Cooper bought tickets before boarding the last carriage attached to the waiting steam train. They had fifteen minutes before departure, not knowing how long the journey would take or how soon they would get further instructions.

THIRTY-SIX

Kingston was at his lock-up garage exchanging the Ford Fiesta for the motorcycle, which was warming up in the yard as he locked the car inside. He checked his watch at the same time Ross and Cooper boarded the train, realising it was time to move. He obviously needed to be in position before the train arrived at the place he had decided was the perfect drop point.

He thought back to the evening a few days ago when he had taken the bike out for a spin and to scout out the best location. It had been remarkably easy to find a good spot. What Ross and his colleague didn't know was just how close it was, but it had to be to allow Miles to make a swift return to Pickering and an even quicker departure. Having tied an empty holdall across the passenger seat and rear carrier with some bungee cords, he set off on the road to riches or prison.

Twenty minutes later, he was sat in a small copse about fifty yards from the railway, having ridden down a narrow farm track and over some rough land to get there. He was sure that he had not been seen by anyone and that both he and the bike were well concealed from the line and the train when it passed.

Bang on schedule at 10.15am, the train huffed and puffed into Levisham station with a squeal of brakes and a hissing of steam. Whilst some passengers got off, Miles activated his latest phone, quickly preparing his next message for Ross. He was ready.

Minutes later, the train set off, heading towards him, gathering speed. When he judged that it was halfway past him, he pressed send on the phone, immediately switching it off when done.

John Ross was holding his phone awaiting the message when it beeped once more. He and Cooper looked at the one-word message together.

NOW!

Cooper leapt to his feet, carrying the holdall to the carriage door and, having previously made sure it was unlocked, quickly opened it before throwing the bag well clear of the track. The bag was heavy but he managed. He just hoped they liked his choice of bag, probably not. Looking out carefully, he saw no movement whatsoever. He was sorely tempted to jump from the train on the other side but quickly discarded the idea as the risk of being seen was far too great. It also went against his employer's explicit instructions.

Returning to his seat, he contacted Mark by phone, instructing his team to return to the Ross house, whilst Ross rang Dan Richardson to request they be collected at the next station, whatever it was.

The man was grey-faced with fatigue and worry and, looking for reassurance, said to Cooper, "They'll release Mary now, won't they?"

"In my experience, that is what usually happens, John. They have got their money, and there is no need to hang on to her any longer than they have to. I expect they will want to get as far away as they possibly can, as quickly as they can."

Both men lapsed into silence, each preoccupied with their own thoughts. The father worried about his daughter, wishing only that she be returned unharmed; the operative concerned that the way this whole thing had gone so far, it would not end well. After all, why would the kidnappers want to release a potential witness?

Miles watched the train until it was almost out of sight and, having made sure no one had got off, broke cover to retrieve the bag. He had to smile at the fluorescent yellow holdall, supposing it was a clumsy attempt to track him despite his instructions, wondering why they thought he would risk carrying such an easily identifiable bag. It took him only minutes to transfer all the money from the colourful bag to his own holdall, which he then fastened onto the back of the bike. Good things, bungee cords. To be honest, his plan all along had been to transfer the money, not because he was expecting the lurid bag but because a bug on the bag was entirely possible.

He made the return journey to the garage even quicker than the outward trip, swapped vehicles and was driving out of Pickering ten minutes later, having followed his usual method to dispose of the last phone he had used.

Miles was euphoric, laughing and singing bits of pop

songs out loud in celebration as he drove. He'd done it; everything had been so easy when it actually came down to it. Why had he worried so much? For a moment, he thought about Mary and what he had done to her, knowing that at some stage her body would be found and that the hunt for him would become even more intense. He didn't care that the girl was dead, having completely satisfied himself that she had to die, his only regret being that his escape from justice would be made even more difficult. He was sure anyone would have done the same in his position.

The next part of his plan, and one he was particularly proud of, was to go to the same mid-stay car park where he had left the Ford Mondeo at Leeds Bradford Airport. During their long nights planning this job, Miles and Smithson had been especially worried about the possibility of being followed after collecting the ransom money. Because, in this modern age, they feared drones may be used to watch from high above, they had decided to go to one place that you were definitely not allowed to fly drones, even if you were the police. An airport. Other benefits included the massive car parks, where Kingston could abandon the vehicles plus, of course, the numerous cameras where he would ensure the case against Richard Wade continued to be built.

Just under two hours since he had collected the money, Miles was parking the Fiesta two rows from the Mondeo, not able to believe his luck that he had managed to get so close. This time, he remembered to wipe the car down before getting out, hoping that he had managed to eradicate all of his fingerprints from the vehicle. He was well aware how good police forensic teams were, having been caught that way before as a result of the evidence they collected. It was certainly a risk; one he would have preferred to minimise by setting fire to both cars, but that was hardly an option.

After taking the holdall and his trusty backpack from the Fiesta, he locked the car and went over to the Mondeo, glad that there was little activity in the car park. When he opened the car's boot, he was pleased at just how roomy it was, because this was a tricky part of the operation and had to be done quickly, with no mistakes. Placing the holdall alongside the suitcases, on top of the original number plates, he opened the red case, quickly followed by the black one, removing the newly purchased clothing from inside and placing it on the floor of the boot. All the time, Miles was continually looking around, happy to see there was no one around to see what he was up to.

Next, he transferred the money from the bag into the black suitcase. Already a tight fit, it was made even more so when he added the backpack and clothing. He fastened both cases before lifting the red case, still containing the black one, from the boot. The holdall was left where it was. After locking the car, he walked off towards the terminal, pulling his very noticeable case behind him, remembering to look at any cameras he passed both in the car park and when he reached the terminal building.

Richard Wade, or at least his doppelganger, was rapidly becoming one of the most photographed people in the area.

Kingston went into the first toilets he came to, selecting an empty cubicle where he lifted his case onto the toilet seat. Opening both cases, he changed, with some difficulty in the confined space, into the unremarkable holiday clothing, putting the clothing he removed back into the black case. He then removed the Wade disguise, which he put in the backpack.

Satisfied, he left the empty red case in the cubicle and walked out of the toilets, carrying his backpack over his shoulder whilst pulling the innocuous black case behind him. This time, with a baseball cap pulled low on his head, he made it a point not to look at any cameras.

He was quite happy that the suitcase would be found in the toilet and removed as found property or possibly blown up as a suspect object. Weren't they always telling you not to leave unattended items in airports? Either way, he didn't really care. Well aware that the clothing and case would probably yield DNA evidence, he considered it a risk he had to take, so confident was he that they would never be linked to the kidnapping of Mary Ross.

Richard Wade walked in, whilst a hopefully unidentifiable Miles Kingston, masquerading as a returning holidaymaker, walked out with the money.

Ten minutes later, he was on a bus to Leeds city centre, keeping his head down in case there was a camera on the vehicle. He was fully aware that his actions at the airport would not stand up to too much scrutiny, but it was all designed to confuse his pursuers and give him time to put distance between them and him.

Obviously, if they studied the terminal videos, they would quickly realise that Richard Wade had not come out of the toilets, nor had the holidaymaker gone in. Of course, it could well be some time before anyone even realised he had gone to the airport. All in all, he believed it had gone well, having, he thought, successfully broken any link between him and Pickering.

The cold-hearted killer was very pleased with himself, but time was getting tight and he still had much to do this day.

Once in the city centre, Miles put the keys for the Mondeo and Fiesta into separate rubbish bins, followed by the Fiesta parking ticket into yet another bin.

He then headed directly to the safe deposit box company where he had rented a large box under his own alias, Peter Webb. As usual, he passed through the various security checks without difficulty, quickly gaining access to the large box, where he was left alone. Looking anxiously round, he quickly opened the box, removing £2,000 from the cash he had previously left there, putting it in his backpack. This was to be his walking-around and celebration money. He was sure he deserved that. For the moment, he left the passport where it was. With a further look round, he opened his suitcase and quickly put £295,000 of the kidnap money into the box before locking it up once more. He was then forced to reopen the box as he had forgotten to get the envelope containing the second instalment of Natasha's fee.

Now that would have caused some trouble, reminding him that he was still juggling balls and to drop them now would be fatal, literally. He locked the box again before it was returned to storage.

On leaving the premises, he took a chance by going into a cubicle in a public toilet to don, what he hoped would be for the final time, his Richard Wade disguise. Having checked his appearance in a mirror, he went to the other safe deposit box company where he had rented a box under Richard Wade's alias, James Adamson. Explaining to staff that he had just had a couple of days away, he passed quickly through security with no problems and was soon alone with the rented box, which, after a furtive glance round, he opened. He then placed £5,000 of the kidnap money, in fifty-pound notes, from his suitcase into the box before locking it once more. Business completed, he left with a cheerful wave to staff.

Miles, who was reluctant to leave more of what he considered to be his hard-earned money in the box, wanted to pile on some more proof of Wade's involvement in the crimes. The police should be able to discover the deposit box registered in a false name, particularly if they found correspondence from the company at Wade's home. That would be the first thing for the man to explain, quickly followed by the secreted money, especially if it was identified as being from the kidnap ransom.

Returning to the same toilets, he removed the Wade wig, glasses and contacts for the final time before happily throwing them into the toilet waste bin.

Kingston's next task was one he was greatly looking forward to. He wanted to prove to his doubters that whilst it may have been a complicated plan with many moving parts, it had worked like a well-oiled machine.

Twenty minutes later, he was sat in front of Frank Harris, who, as ever, looked like an accountant sitting behind his desk. That is unless you looked into his eyes, or wondered why such a man would need a hulking brute like Jimmy to be present.

Noting the suitcase, Harris spoke first.

"Going on holiday, Miles?"

"No, Mr Harris, but I have brought you a present."

"Okay, funny man. I told you not to come back here, so why are you here?"

Opening the suitcase, he replied, "I've brought you a hundred grand as promised."

Harris nodded to Jimmy, who quickly examined the contents before saying, "It looks about right, boss. All in fifty-pound notes."

Harris frowned. "That's good, Miles, but I would have preferred smaller denomination notes. Fifties can be difficult to move."

"I'm sorry, Mr Harris, but smaller notes would have been much bulkier and difficult for me to move about."

"Okay. One last thing. I'm still not completely sure what you've done, so I'll ask you one more time. Will whatever you did come back to bite me?"

"No, honest, Mr Harris. Only me and Karl know about you, and we won't tell. Not ever."

"All right, Miles. Now piss off, I'm busy."

He cleared his throat anxiously. "Can I remind you about the deeds for my house?"

Harris smirked, recognising Kingston's discomfort. "Oh yeah, I forgot about them."

Reaching into his desk drawer, he passed an envelope across to his visitor.

Miles stood up, tentatively offering his hand to Harris, who ignored it completely.

Seconds later, he was relieved to find himself on the pavement outside the betting office, having been told by Jimmy not to come back. Whilst he was glad to have got

243

the gangster off his back by leaving the suitcase and its contents behind, he couldn't really say the meeting had been much fun. In fact, it had been terrifying.

If Miles Kingston had not been so complacent, with an inflated opinion of his own abilities, he would have been heading to Hull just as quickly as he could to catch that ferry to Europe.

He was desperate for a drink, but he still had Natasha and Wade to sort out. She answered on the second ring when he rang her on the phone marked Natasha, which he had retrieved from his pack.

In her usual charming fashion, she almost shouted down the phone. "Where the fuck have you been? It's nearly half past two."

"Calm down, it's all sorted. How is our man doing?"

"Pissed and worn out. He was starting to get fidgety, but I managed to distract him, if you know what I mean."

Once more, Miles's imagination was running riot as he thought about how she had managed to distract him.

"Right, we need to get him out of there and you on the train. Can you get packed and walk him out? Try and lead him round the houses a bit so he can't find his way back to the apartment. Is that okay?"

"Yeah, I suppose. What about my money?"

"I'll see you at the station with it, as arranged." He broke the connection without giving her a chance to answer.

Miles saw no reason to hang about so went straight to the railway station, particularly as he had no real idea how long she was going to be.

Less than an hour later, sitting on a bench with his second coffee, he saw the blonde epitome of sexiness sashaying into the station, dressed pretty much as she had been on her arrival in Leeds. Was it only a couple of days ago? She really didn't know how to do low key, did she?

He stood as she approached, hoping for a kiss that never came. She held out her hand and he passed her the envelope containing the money without a word, whilst she returned the apartment keys. Natasha turned on her heel, and the last thing he saw was her delectable rear end as she walked to the platform.

He watched until the prostitute was out of sight, wondering if perhaps he should have made an approach for her professional services. Reluctantly, he decided against it, realising he had to get her, a potential witness, out of the city as soon as possible. Still, it had been more than tempting, especially as money was no longer an object. Well, there were plenty of other women available and all of them much cheaper than Natasha, but maybe not so desirable.

That was it for Miles. Leaving the station, he hit the first pub he came to, quickly downing two pints before heading to a nearby restaurant for a slap-up meal. Didn't he deserve it? It had been a long hard day.

Walking back to the apartment, he took the opportunity to get rid of some more of his burner phones, namely the one on which he communicated with Natasha and the other one that he used when talking to Jimmy. He certainly didn't want to speak to him or his boss again, not ever.

Miles followed his usual pattern by disassembling both phones and dropping the constituent parts in various bins, actually dropping the SIM cards in roadside drains.

Nobody was going to trace him from any of the phones he'd used.

Returning to the apartment, he was pleased to see that Natasha and Wade had left plenty of booze behind. He was soon fast asleep on the settee in a drunken stupor.

In fact, he was so far gone that he didn't even hear the phone marked Karl ringing.

THIRTY-SEVEN

After escorting Kingston from the premises, Jimmy returned to the office, waiting patiently for instructions from his boss, who was deep in thought.

"Right, Jimmy, get George down here straight away."

Within minutes, a small scruffily dressed man, who looked like he hadn't been in the sun for years, entered the office with an anxious look on his thin face. He normally only ventured from his upstairs office to see Harris when something was wrong or when he had made a mistake, for which he usually paid a heavy price.

George was a disgraced accountant who had spent time in prison for indecently assaulting a number of women in cinemas across the city over a period of several months. Just the sort of man Harris liked to employ, weak with unsavoury tendencies. By allowing him reasonable access to the tarts in the brothel down the road, he was able to pay him a pittance whilst demanding absolute loyalty. Harris would never let him know just how valuable he was to him, keeping track of all his illicit earnings, moving the money about and, wherever possible, making sure it was clean. On top of all that, the man was a wizard when it came to tax, saving Harris considerable sums of money every year.

George hated Harris with a vengeance but feared him and Jimmy even more, realising he was stuck with his lot in life. On his visits to the brothel, he usually ended up with the oldest and ugliest prostitutes, but it was free and kept him happy.

He had a dream of diverting some of the money he managed for Harris and taking one of the women he particularly liked to some remote island where nobody would ever find him. Part of his fantasy was to leave enough evidence for the police to put Harris and Jimmy away forever. He knew all their dirty secrets but was certain he would never get away with it and was too afraid to try. This wasn't some rerun of *The Shawshank Redemption*: this was real life.

George stood anxiously in front of the desk waiting for his employer to speak, dreading what he might say. Significantly, he wasn't offered a seat. "There's a hundred grand in that suitcase, all in fifty-pound notes. How do you suggest we put that amount through the books?"

After breathing a hefty sigh of relief, a reassured George replied confidently. Handling money was his business and he knew how to manage it.

"I don't need to tell you, sir, that fifty-pound notes are not easy to deal with as they can draw unwanted attention. Obviously, I can pay some into the bank, but only small amounts so no one will notice. We could put some in the betting shop and use it to pay any winners.

"One good way to pass on larger amounts might be to use Bargain Motors. Mr Newton is always buying cars from punters and other dealers for, sometimes, reasonably large sums in cash. Fifty-pound notes would not appear so amiss there. Finally, there's always the pawnbroker's. I know we mostly get low-value or suspect items for which we don't pay much, but we should be able to introduce some of the notes and definitely where the loans business is concerned. They won't argue."

"Good, George. I like it. What about the books, though?"

"Well, sir, I'll need to be careful, but I'm sure I can manipulate the takings and expenses to gradually account for the extra income. May I ask; was this anything to do with that £50,000 investment a few weeks ago?"

Harris nodded cautiously, wondering how the bookkeeper had picked up on that. Still, he supposed that was why he employed him, but he would need to keep more of an eye on the clever bastard in the future.

"In that case, I can use some of this income to counterbalance that outgoing. The books will stand up to any audit, not that anyone, except you, will see the real ones, of course."

"All right, George, I like it, get on with it. By the way, get yourself down the street and have a bonus girl tonight on me."

"Thank you, Mr Harris. I have one final suggestion, though. I think we should tell all your businesses not to accept any fifty-pound notes for the moment unless absolutely necessary. It would be silly to take more in when we're trying to get rid of these."

"Good thinking. All right, off you go, and take the case with you."

"If it's okay with you, Mr Harris, I'll make a start this afternoon. I usually bank on a Friday, so I'll move some of the notes then and start spreading it out to your other businesses as well."

"The sooner, the better, as far as I'm concerned."

As he left, George wondered if he should just walk out of the front door with the case and its contents to start the new life he dreamt of. One look at Jimmy as he passed convinced him what a stupid idea that was. He wanted to live a little bit longer, even if it was a pretty miserable existence.

THIRTY-EIGHT

About the time that Miles Kingston was drifting into unconsciousness, an increasingly anxious John Ross finally asked the question that Cooper had known, for much of the day, would eventually come.

Ever since they had returned from Pickering, the whole group had been waiting for contact from either the kidnappers or Mary. As the day wore on and none came, they realised that it was unlikely they would hear anything, although Ross continued to believe in silent desperation. What else could a father do?

"She's not coming home, is she, Mr Cooper?"

Everyone else looked away as Cooper considered his answer, reluctantly deciding he had no option but to follow his normal policy of being totally honest with his clients, at least when they asked him a direct question.

"It's been nearly ten hours since the money drop was made, giving the kidnappers plenty of time to make their getaway. We followed their instructions to the letter, especially when it came to making no attempt to follow them. There is no situation I can conceive of where they would hang on to Mary any longer than they needed to. For instance, if they came back for more money, why would they expect us to follow their instructions, having been cheated on the first occasion? Lastly, keeping Mary captive can only be a burden to them, and the easiest way to remove that burden would be to release her unharmed. So in my experience, John, while I cannot be certain, I believe Mary will not come back."

That might have been hard to say, but it was even harder for Ross to hear, along with the other two people closest to Mary, Mr and Mrs Richardson. Whilst Ross somehow kept his composure, the driver and his wife could not as they sank into each other's arms in floods of tears. Andy approached the couple, helping them to their feet and out of the room.

Cooper was expecting the next question. "So what do we do now?"

"I believe we have no option but to inform the police. Obviously, if you wish us to, me and my men will continue our own investigations alongside the police. We will cooperate with them fully, but, I have got to say, we are not always welcome even though we may have sources they do not."

Ross nodded. "I agree we must tell the police and, yes, I do want you to continue, whether the police are happy or not. You no doubt remember our previous conversation about what should happen to these criminals when they are identified. I feel sure the police would not welcome such a suggestion from me. So when should we contact them?"

"I remember your instructions very well. I suggest we

do it now, but rather than report the kidnap via normal methods, I suggest we try to contact that police officer you mentioned, Amy Clark, direct. Do you by any chance have her number?"

"Sorry, no."

Cooper turned to Mark. "Get that number for me, please."

Five minutes later, Mark put his own phone down, having written something on a piece of paper which he handed to Cooper.

"Coops, that's her home phone, private mobile, work mobile and email address."

An incredulous Ross couldn't help himself. "How did you get all that, and so quickly?"

Cooper smiled enigmatically. "Police systems are not as secure as they may think, particularly if you have the right equipment and know-how."

Deciding she was more likely to answer her work phone, Cooper dialled the number. It was answered after only four rings.

"Clark."

"Good evening. My name is Cooper and I am employed by Sir John Ross. We wonder if you could come round to his house regarding a very serious matter."

A clearly irate voice came down the phone. "Who the hell are you, and, more to the point, how did you get this number?"

Remaining patient as always, he replied. "A very serious crime has been committed, one that could not, and should not, be reported through the normal channels. I cannot stress how urgent this matter is, but I'm confident you will appreciate my discretion later."

"Put Sir John on."

Cooper handed the phone over, whispering to the man that he should not give her any details of what had been going on.

"Hello, Amy, it's John Ross speaking. Please come at once, I desperately need your help."

Having no knowledge of the current situation, it was impossible for Clark to know how inappropriate her next question was, or the impact it was certain to have on Ross.

"Okay, but first I need to check you are safe and not acting under duress. Tell me your wife's correct name if you are safe and the wrong name if you are not."

Almost choking, as the tears started to flow, he said, "Mary."

"I'll be there in half an hour."

True to her word, she arrived at the house just before 9pm, wearing jeans and a cardigan, clear evidence that she was not on duty. She was met at the door by Cooper, who introduced himself to the slightly bewildered and clearly unhappy police officer, who gave the slightest of nods in response. As he led her through to the study, she was shocked to see the state Ross was in, looking about a hundred years old and clearly having been crying recently. No one else was present.

Attempting to take the initiative, Clark spoke first. "Will somebody please tell me what is going on?"

Having already agreed that Cooper would do the talking, Sir John nodded tiredly in his direction.

"Just before midnight on Wednesday night, Sir John's daughter, Mary, who you may know as Linda, was kidnapped from Fat Harry's club in the city centre."

Clark stared at Cooper, struggling to remain calm and composed. "So why am I only finding out about this now?"

"Well, Sir John did try to report this on Wednesday night, but, how shall I put this, your colleagues were singularly unhelpful. That is when we were contacted to offer some assistance."

Realising that there was little point in alienating the man, at least for now, she simply said, "So tell me the story."

Quickly and concisely, Cooper outlined the circumstances of the kidnap and its aftermath as they knew them, not mentioning the enquiries that had already been carried out and were still underway.

Contempt dripping from every word, Clark responded. "So you're telling me that you geniuses have handed over £400,000 to person or persons unknown and have still not managed to get Mary back. That's what happens when you get fucking amateurs involved."

"I'm not sure that's exactly true, but never mind. Sir John is very tired and his doctor is on the way here as we speak. My colleagues and I have been working from the dining room if you'd like to join us there, and I'll get Sir John's housekeeper and driver, Mr and Mrs Richardson, to stay with him. Is that okay with you, sir?"

Ross just nodded sadly.

Once in the dining room, Cooper asked Andy to get the Richardsons to join their employer in his study to await the doctor. When Andy returned, Cooper spoke once more to a clearly agitated Amy Clark.

"Whatever you may think, we are not amateurs and have probably had more experience of dealing with kidnappers than, I suspect, you yourself have. However, that is irrelevant, as we need to work together. I can assure you my advice to Sir John was to pursue the kidnappers with everything we had, but he didn't want to and the money was of no consequence at all to him."

"Why should I work with you? I don't even know who you are."

"As to who we are, I'm afraid you will just have to trust me and my associates. As to why you should work with us is more easily explained. Simply put, we have nearly forty-eight hours' head start on you, during which time we have begun to work on tracing phones, identified a suspect vehicle and finally we have managed to identify a suspect."

Clark realised she was in a difficult position. If she ignored the offer of cooperation, she would always be behind Cooper and may never get the information they possessed, possibly endangering the girl's life.

She strongly suspected that the group of men were, in some way, connected to some shadowy government agencies, but how Ross had been able to get their help was something of a mystery at the moment.

"Okay, Mr Cooper, I'll listen to what you have to tell me, but first tell me who exactly you work for and how you became involved."

"It's just Cooper. Can I just say we are contractors who have, at various times, done work for the government. I cannot say more than that, only that having done so we have gained useful connections to obtain information and other assistance where necessary. For example, I was able to assist Sir John in getting authorisation for the movement of the ransom money and, of course, in obtaining your contact details. We are here because high-ranking friends of Sir John requested our assistance. Now shall we get on?"

She nodded.

Cooper briefly outlined Dan Richardson's concern for Mary after she failed to appear for her lift home when Fat Harry's closed. Family history and a strictly-adhered-to routine convinced Sir John to contact the police in an abortive attempt to report his daughter missing.

At Cooper's instruction, Mark updated Clark on the phone situation, telling her that the initial ransom demand had been made by text on Mary's own mobile phone, suggesting the kidnap was genuine. He provided her with a copy of the actual message as well as showing her the picture of Mary that had accompanied it. He then told her that the following three text messages had all been made on separate pay-as-you-go or burner phones or whatever else you wished to call them, again supplying copies of the texts. He was convinced that Mary's phone and the other three had all been disposed of, having been used only once each. He finished by telling her that he was attempting to trace the origin of the three burners and who had purchased them. After the police officer expressed her scepticism, Mark told her that whilst it was difficult, there may be a way to do it. No promises. Apparently, when purchased, the phones come in a box bearing a serial number, and he was hopeful that by contacting the phone manufacturers, he may be able to match the boxes with the individual phone numbers. It would then be a case of identifying which shops had sold those particular items, and then hopefully studying in-store videos to find the purchaser.

Cooper took over, admitting that tracing the phone

purchaser was yet another long shot but one he believed worth taking. He told her their reasoning for thinking that they may be dealing with a single kidnapper based on the amount of money demanded and its dimensions. He then gave a brief description of the money drop, which earned him a shake of the head from Amy Clark.

"Okay, Cooper, let's get to it. You said you had a suspect and a vehicle, didn't you?"

"Yes, I did. We have examined the club videos and those from the street outside. They show a man helping an unsteady Mary from the club by a side exit. He then puts her in a blue car before driving off in a southerly direction. Incidentally, the ransom demand made on Mary's phone was picked up by a tower to the northeast of Leeds, making us believe he was trying to misdirect us. All of this man's actions suggest a well-thought-out plan, which may be explained by what we now know of his background. When you see the photo, you may well agree with us."

At her surprised look, he passed the photo across. If her expression prior to viewing the photo was surprised, it could only be described as dumbstruck when she looked at it.

"Is this for real?"

"Yes, it is. We can show you a copy of the video if necessary. Do you recognise him?"

Clark looked even more intently at the picture. "Yes. It looks like a former colleague and lying bastard Richard Wade."

Cooper nodded. "Sir John said the same thing when he told us Wade's story."

"Wade may be a rat, but I never thought he would sink

this low. He did blame everyone else for his problems, though. Let's have a look at the car and then I'll get enquiries underway."

He showed her the picture of the blue Ford Fiesta with the clearly visible registration number, causing her to reach for her own phone.

Cooper spoke again. "Before you do anything, I should tell you a couple of things. We've been to Wade's house and he's not home but his own car is. A neighbour told us he was picked up by someone on Wednesday evening driving a blue car, so maybe more than one person is involved after all. We traced the registration to a young family and are satisfied their plate has been cloned. We don't know the true registration number yet."

"You don't mind if I check these things out myself, do you?"

"I would expect that you would, but if I could make a suggestion. If he used the same car to travel to and from Pickering, hopefully the cameras should show the vehicle, even though it may have a different plate. We have a rough time frame, so while it may be a common vehicle, there can't have been that many blue Ford Fiestas in that area around that time."

In the most sarcastic voice she could muster, Clark said, "Thank you for the advice. I'm sure we would never have thought of that ourselves."

Ignoring her sarcasm, Cooper made one last statement. "I should tell you that in our considered opinion Mary is already dead, and, because he asked me directly, Sir John is aware of our thoughts, although he probably hasn't given up hope yet."

Clark nodded thoughtfully before leaving for a long night's work, having obtained Cooper's contact details, not that she was sure she would use them. Mark provided her with copies of the evidence they had gathered, although she knew the police would need to make their own enquiries at the club to obtain the same evidence, thus ensuring its integrity for court proceedings. She was pretty sure Cooper and his team would not be available to appear as witnesses.

Driving to the Police Station, she considered her next move, concluding that she would need to work with Cooper for a time at least. No matter how much it galled her, they simply had too much information that she needed.

Cooper had not shared the information about the forged notes being part of the ransom money with Clark. He reasoned that if she left his team out of the inquiry, this would be his way back in. If the forged notes began to circulate, he may need the police to inform him when they came to their notice, but if they didn't, he did have other sources.

Meanwhile, they would continue with their own enquiries, hoping a working relationship could be established with the police, although there was no way it would ever happen if they became aware of the instructions Ross had given to Cooper about how to deal with the perpetrators when they were found.

THIRTY-NINE

On her arrival at the station, Amy Clark's first job, after she had got some coffee, was to ring her immediate boss, Detective Chief Superintendent Adrian Gregson, at home. It was getting late and at first he was not at all happy to be bothered, suspecting it was going to ruin what was supposed to be his weekend off.

Having been given a quick rundown of events, during which she confirmed the positive identification of Richard Wade, his initial response was typically blunt: "Shit."

She had worked with this man over a number of years and wisely kept quiet.

Gregson took a moment to collect his thoughts. "Right, Amy, this is what I want you to do. Get your team in at once and while you're doing that, I'll arrange for some uniforms to be on standby. We need to hit Wade's house as soon as possible. As you know, I would normally spend some time confirming the information these men have gathered, but there simply isn't the time. I know it's unlikely but the girl could still be alive, so we need to move quickly. If Wade is there, he is to be arrested and the place searched from top to bottom. If he's not, we need to find him without delay. I know we don't normally jump in like this, but time is not our friend and a young girl's life may be at stake. Any questions?"

"No, sir, I would have suggested the same thing. However, the secrecy we normally maintain with kidnappings will go out of the window, but I don't suppose it matters now."

"Not at all, I'm afraid, Amy. I don't believe we have a choice. Do you think we can trust these men working for Ross?"

"Probably, at least up to a point. They look pretty dangerous to me, so if we do work with them, we need to keep them on a pretty tight leash."

"Right, Amy, you've got a long night ahead of you. I'm going to have to inform the duty Chief Officer, who will no doubt have a fit of the vapours, and I'll see you in the morning now that you've buggered up my weekend."

Clark found a Detective Constable doing paperwork in the office whilst it was quiet. She gave him the names of a dozen officers for him to contact, with instructions for them to come in at once, no excuses and no explanations. She then told him that he was to be her gofer, keeping a written record of events, starting now with the callout. He did wonder what explanations he could give to people when she had not told him what it was about anyway. That's bosses for you.

Over the next two hours, ten officers turned up for duty, some looking a little the worse for wear and some more than disgruntled, but they all knew it was part of the job. The remaining two were unable to be contacted.

Superintendent Clark briefed the officers, who included the Duty Uniform Inspector, in the CID general office at 1am. She outlined the circumstances of Mary Ross's kidnap and the evidence gathered by Cooper and his team, emphasising that they were civilian operatives but probably with some sort of military background. The group were then shown the videos from the club, which clearly showed Richard Wade and the blue Ford Fiesta.

Ds Ted Trace, who, with the usual police imagination, was universally known as TT, spoke first.

"Jesus, that looks like that bastard Richard Wade."

Clark replied, "That is exactly who we believe it to be."

Silencing the ensuing hubbub with a raised hand, she gave a brief potted history of Wade's career and subsequent downfall to ensure everyone present knew exactly who they were dealing with. Pointing out his connections to the Ross family and possible motives.

"Ted, you and five more of the team are to go to Wade's house and arrest him, leaving four officers there to search the property with a fine-tooth comb. A number of uniformed officers will attend for support and security. Be aware that we will need to get a forensic team in there first thing in the morning, so try to preserve as much as you can. This is initially a search for the girl or signs that she has been there recently."

Both Trace and the Duty Inspector nodded in affirmation.

"I know I don't need to tell you, Ted, but don't tell him anything other than the grounds for his arrest. We'll save our info for the interviews, which you'll be doing anyway."

After a brief pause, Clark continued. "As you now

know, the ransom money was handed over shortly after 10am yesterday, almost fifteen hours ago. There has been no further contact from the kidnappers or Mary herself, so, unfortunately, it is reasonable to believe that the girl may be dead. However, because there is still a chance, no matter how slim, that she may be alive, we must move quickly in the hope of releasing her unharmed. That is why we are acting before we have confirmed the accuracy of the information we have been given, although having met these civilian contractors, I am reasonably happy. Lastly, if Wade is not there, bloody well find him."

TT and his selected team organised radios and transport before heading off to Wade's cottage, determined to get him and, if at all possible, to save the girl.

The remainder of the team were allocated various tasks, including tracing any video images of the blue Fiesta from street cameras and starting to examine phone records. When morning came, the owners of the Fiesta whose plates had been cloned would be interviewed, as would Fat Harry's staff. Ross and the Richardsons would also be visited for statements. It was a lot to do in a short space of time, made all the more urgent as, if they had got Wade into custody, they would be working to the limits of time they could keep him detained.

On the dot of 2am, Richard Wade was awoken from a deep drink-induced sleep by loud knocking at his front door. Confused, he stumbled downstairs, somewhat unsteadily, where, as the knocking continued, he could see a number of shadowy figures through the front-door glass.

"Who is it? What do you want?"

"Police. Open up."

He opened the door, keeping the chain on. In the porch light, he could see a group of men and women, some in civilian clothing and some in uniform. Even more confused, he couldn't imagine why the police were at his door, particularly in such numbers. What the hell was going on?

In his usual bombastic manner, Wade tried to take control. "Who are you and what do you want?"

Holding up his warrant card, Trace said, "I am Detective Sergeant Trace. Please let me in, I have some questions for you."

"Look, what's this all about?"

Losing his patience, Trace responded angrily. "Look, sir, I am investigating a serious matter and I am not prepared to speak to you through the door where we can be heard and seen by your neighbours. Now open the door or we will force entry."

Knowing the police did not normally attend a house in such numbers, particularly at this time of night, it eventually dawned on a mystified Wade that something serious was happening. He reluctantly removed the chain, allowing Trace and another CID officer to enter the hallway.

"Are you Richard Wade?"

"Yes, of course I am, who else would I be?"

"In that case, I am arresting you on suspicion of kidnap and assault."

Trace then cautioned a bewildered Wade who, for once in his life, was totally speechless.

Trace told the other officer to take him upstairs for him to get dressed, stressing that he was not to touch or remove anything else.

Back in the hallway five minutes later, Wade was regaining some of his old bravado. "This is obviously a serious mistake on your part and I intend to make you pay for it. Why you would think I've assaulted anyone, let alone been involved in a kidnap, is simply beyond me. I want a solicitor at once."

"As you wish. One will be organised for you when we reach the custody suite." Then to the Dc: "Cuff him."

An outraged Wade was almost in tears as he protested, but was handcuffed anyway and placed in the rear of a police van for the short trip to the station.

A few minutes later, as he was taken into the custody suite, he was surprised to see Amy Clark waiting. He knew she was a Superintendent now and was amazed to see someone of her rank there at this time in the morning. He certainly wouldn't have been there when he was a senior officer.

He couldn't help himself. "I know what's happening now. You've always had it in for me, you bitch. Well, I haven't done anything, and this stitch-up won't work."

She looked at him with some disdain but did not respond to his comments in any way.

He was quickly processed, including taking his fingerprints and DNA, before, having made his request for a solicitor, he was placed in a cell.

An hour later, the detectives who had done a cursory search of Wade's house returned, having left a couple of uniformed officers to secure the property. Mary Ross, unsurprisingly, had not been found, nor were there any obvious signs that she had ever been there.

One of the returning officers handed over an evidence bag containing Wade's mobile phone and another containing a letter. He explained that the letter, with no sign of an envelope, was on the hall table and was from a safe deposit box company addressed to Richard Wade. He didn't know if it was significant but, never having seen one before, thought it could be relevant. When asked by Clark, the officer confirmed that they had not recovered any clothing matching that worn by Wade on the video of the kidnap.

Clark told him that she wanted to know everything that was on the phone and instructed him to make sure that it was examined as soon as possible by specialist officers. She was also extremely interested in the letter and made a note to ensure Trace asked Wade about it in interview.

In further more detailed searches by forensic teams over the following days, nothing of any evidential value would be found, especially nothing to establish that the kidnapped girl had ever been there.

With that, she sent everyone home to get as much sleep as they could, with instructions to be back by 9am and to be prepared for a very long day. After updating the Custody Officer and Duty Inspector, she went home herself, reflecting on another fucked-up weekend.

FORTY

Even Cooper and his men were beginning to flag; however, they were somewhat buoyed by progress they were making in identifying the phones and finding the kidnapper's Ford Fiesta.

Mark had spent some time identifying which companies had made the various phones used by the kidnappers, along with the networks used. There were three different companies involved and they had all promised to try to match each phone number with the relevant phone serial number, hopefully then being able to identify the distributors who had stocked them. It may still take a few days, but, with a lot of luck, if they could find the places where the phones were sold, a video may reveal the identity of the purchaser. If you didn't try, you certainly wouldn't succeed.

Tony had been busy hacking into the traffic cameras in and around Pickering in order to find the blue Fiesta if it had been used, either with the genuine plates or cloned ones. Having established that the final two texts had been sent from phones in the Pickering area, the first of them just after 7am, and believing the kidnappers had spent time in Leeds, he concluded that they would allow themselves at least an hour to get to Pickering. The cash drop had been about 10.15am, so, expecting them to leave Pickering immediately, he believed they would take a little more than an hour to get back to Leeds due to increasing traffic.

As he explained to Cooper, Tony intended to check the cameras for blue Fiestas covering the A169 into Pickering for the period between 5am and 7am when he believed they had entered the town. Next, he would then check the same cameras for the period between 10.15am and 11am hoping to catch sight of them as they left Pickering. He admitted that he had made several assumptions including that they had travelled from Leeds and were returning there, his estimation of the time windows and finally that they would use the A169 as it was the most direct route. Cooper agreed that it was a good starting point and they could easily extend the search parameters if needed.

Either by good fortune or the application of skills and judgement, developed over several years, he was back to see Cooper not much more than an hour later, with a broad smile on his face.

"We might just have got lucky, Coops. Working backwards from 7am, I found only three blue Ford Fiestas entering Pickering on that road. The good news is that only one of them left in the second time window. It did not have the cloned plates but I have managed to get a picture of the registration number."

"Great work, Tony. Now we're making progress."

"It gets better. I've done some checks on the vehicle

and, would you believe, it was sold about two weeks ago to a bloke called James Adamson at a backstreet car dealer's in Leeds."

"It's looking good. Right, get some rest and I think we'll pay this place a visit in the morning. I can't believe they would be stupid enough to use the same car, but you never know. By the way, do we know who owns the car dealer's?"

"Not yet. It's called Bargain Motors, but I'm still working on who actually owns it."

Before Cooper nodded off, he debated with himself as to whether he should tell Amy Clark what they had discovered. He decided that they did not have any hard facts yet so he would wait, not to mention that it was good to get there before the police. Any information they got could prove to be a good bargaining chip later, if one were needed.

By 10am, the slightly more refreshed team were parked down the road from Bargain Motors discussing strategy. It was agreed that Cooper and Andy would make the enquiries at the dealership whilst the other two waited nearby in the unlikely event that backup was needed. Before they entered the premises, both men checked their concealed radio links to Mark and Tony, who would record any conversation.

They had hardly set foot on the forecourt before Charlie was out of the office to greet them.

"Good morning, gentlemen. How can I help you today?"

As usual, Cooper took the lead. "Are you the owner?"

Somewhat surprised, the car dealer's smile was quickly wiped from his face. "Who's asking?"

"If you are the owner, we'd like a quiet word in your office."

"Not before I know who you are."

"Look, mate, you either talk to us or the police. It's up to you."

There was no need to tell him that the police would be along at some stage anyway.

"Okay, okay, but just remember I've got some handy lads here if you try anything funny."

Once in the office, all signs of the usual false bonhomie had disappeared from Charlie.

"So what do you want?"

Andy passed over a piece of paper with the registration number from the captured camera image of the Fiesta outside Pickering.

He said, "You sold a blue Ford Fiesta with that reg. plate about two weeks ago to someone called James Adamson. We'd like to know how he paid and where we can find him. Simple as that."

"Never heard of him or the car."

Cooper spoke quietly. "They call you Charlie, don't they?"

"I never said."

"Well, Charlie, we do our research, so I think that is you, and we also know you did sell that car to Adamson, and, if you like, I can tell you where and when you bought it. So stop pissing us about. This is heavier than you can possibly imagine, and a whole world of pain is about to descend on you. The police will be the least of your problems once tax inspectors and VAT examiners have finished with you, so let's just have the truth and part as friends, shall we?"

Totally defeated by these quietly spoken but dangerous-looking men, he could only nod.

"How did he pay for the car?"

"Cash."

"What address did he give?"

"I'll get the paperwork."

Whilst Charlie rummaged in his filing cabinet, Andy attached a very small electronic listening device to the underside of the desk. Eventually finding the documents relating to the sale of the Fiesta and the Mondeo, Charlie handed them over to Cooper. His expression never changed when he saw that a second car had been purchased, nor did it when he saw the photocopy of the driving licence in the name of James Adamson. There was no doubt that the picture was of Richard Wade. He would check out the address on the licence and paperwork but assumed it was fake.

The two men left a few minutes later with very clear photocopies of the relevant documents. Wade was starting to look totally fucked. Once again, Cooper thought how carefully some aspects of the crime had been planned, especially the single use of each of the burner phones and the organisation of the ransom drop. Even if they had known in advance that a train was to be used, it would still have been very difficult to mount any sort of operation which would have allowed them to trap the kidnappers. Yet, with all that planning and forethought, Wade had still allowed himself to be captured on film with the girl in the club, then using the Fiesta, and, to top it off, he'd used a false driving licence with his own photo on it. All very strange and not a little disconcerting; oddly, it was almost as if he wanted to be caught.

Back at the car, Cooper was interested to hear that as soon as he had left the car dealer's office, the man had spoken on the phone to someone called Jimmy and a second man whom he had addressed as Mr Harris. He was heard updating Harris on their visit and the information he had passed on, receiving only a grunt in response before the connection was broken.

Interesting. Who was this man Harris, and why was Charlie in such a hurry to contact him?

Deciding that he really ought to speak to Amy Clark, he rang her work mobile, which she answered immediately. At first, she was reluctant to speak but eventually confirmed that Wade was in custody and that Mary had not been found. She was initially even more reluctant to meet with him but relented when he explained that he had information that would be of great importance, especially when interviewing Wade. Neither of them wanted the meeting to be at the Police Station, agreeing that a nearby café would suit their purposes.

Cooper had to smile as he thought about Amy's unwillingness to see him at the station. She was a senior officer running a major inquiry and, understandably, did not want her authority undermined by an outsider. It suited him perfectly anyway; the fewer people that knew about his involvement, the better.

FORTY-ONE

Shortly after 10am, Detective Chief Superintendent Adrian Gregson faced the assembled officers, some of whom looked as if they needed much more sleep than they'd already had or were likely to get.

"Listen up, everybody. You already know that we are investigating a kidnapping, one of the nastiest crimes possible. Unfortunately, as a considerable time has elapsed since the ransom was paid without any contact from the kidnappers, it has all the appearances of turning into a murder inquiry. Every one of you is here as a member of the Regional Organised Crime Unit because you are experienced officers who have proved good at your job over many years. This type of offence is exactly why we were formed, to fight professional criminals who commit serious crimes with little regard for the lives of their victims or the rules the rest of us live by. We are able to cross into different police areas when required, obtaining their support as necessary, in pursuit of evidence to prevent and detect major crimes. Remember, at all times our main focus is to find Mary Ross and, if at all possible, return her safely to those who love her. Speed is of the essence. Superintendent Clark will be the Officer in Charge – OIC – of the investigation, and Inspector Connor will be her deputy. Up to now, the press have no inkling of this and hopefully that will remain the case. Once they become aware, there will no doubt be some frenzied activity, considering the family history and connections. I will deal, via the press office, with any and all media enquiries, doing my best to keep the heat off you so you can do your job to the best of your ability. Don't forget for one minute that an innocent twenty-year-old girl desperately needs our help. Get to it and good luck."

Gregson nodded to Amy Clark, before sitting down and drinking from his mug of rapidly cooling coffee.

By 10.30am, Amy Clark had finished briefing her team.

Ds Trace and Dc Karen Lee were nominated as the interviewing officers, who would carry out initial interviews with Wade as soon as his solicitor arrived, their main task being to put the allegations to him and, as far as possible, to ascertain his movements and any potential alibi. The officers had been given a copy of the photos of Wade, both at the club and with the blue Ford Fiesta, for which they would need to obtain his explanation. Hopefully, the officer sent to Wade's address would soon return with a statement from the neighbour who had seen Wade leave in a blue car on the evening of the crime. Depending on how the interview went, they may also ask him about the letter from the safe deposit box company. Was that where they would find the ransom money?

Clark did not go into too much detail about Cooper's

team but had obviously needed to mention where the initial photos had come from. She was unhappy about using the images because they were not from police sources, but felt she had no choice as speed was necessary whilst there was still any chance of finding Mary Ross alive.

Wade seemed to have a problem with women, especially those in authority, which was why Clark had designated Karen to be in on the interview with TT. Anything that may disturb his equilibrium was worth a try, not to mention that she was an experienced detective and very good at her job.

After her unwelcome telephone conversation with Cooper, she informed her deputy, Detective Inspector Ben Connor, that she was going out for half an hour but could be contacted on her mobile if there were any developments. She wasn't quite sure why she didn't tell him where she was going and whom she was to meet.

When she got to the backstreet café, Cooper was already seated at a small table in the corner, with his back to the wall and facing the door. She noticed one of his other men sat at a nearby table.

Helping herself to tea from the pot already on the table, she spoke first.

"Okay, Mr Cooper, what have you got for me?"

"It's just Cooper. May I call you Amy? I think it would probably be easier if we are to work together, don't you?"

"By all means, call me Amy, but I'm not at all sure about the working together bit."

"Well, you're here, so maybe we are already. Never mind. My team have been busy during the night and I believe we may have information that will be of great interest to you. As you know, four phones were used to contact John Ross, one of which was Mary's own appearing to show the user was to the northeast of Leeds. We believe it has long gone. The other three were burner phones and have probably also been disposed of. However, we have identified the manufacturers, who are cooperating in attempting to identify where they were sold. If we can do that, we may be able to identify the purchaser."

Clark shook her head. "Surely you don't think they will have paid with anything other than cash?"

"I'm sure you are right, but we may get lucky with people's memory or more likely surveillance cameras in and around the shops."

"Fair enough, but it's a bit optimistic, don't you think? If that's all you've got, I'll be on my way."

"Not quite. I did say we were busy. We managed to identify the blue Ford Fiesta as it went into and out of Pickering, and, luckily for us, they had got rid of the cloned plates. Anyway, we visited the car dealer who sold it a couple of weeks ago and had an interesting chat with him. Bloke called Charlie at Bargain Motors. Do you know him?"

"I've come across him a couple of times. I've seen straighter corkscrews."

"After some persuasion, he gave us the documentation relating to the sale of the Fiesta and also a second vehicle, a grey Ford Mondeo. Happily, he took a copy of the buyer's driving licence in the name of James Adamson."

"So who exactly is James Adamson?"

"I think you may recognise the picture on the licence."

As he slid the paper across the table, Amy was

expecting to see a picture of Wade's accomplice so was completely surprised to see a clear image of Richard Wade himself.

"I take it you and your men will not be available to give statements about all this or to give evidence in court."

Cooper smiled. "I'm afraid not, Amy. I know you will want to verify everything I've told you, but I'm sure you can see we are doing our level best to help even though I suspect it's too late for Mary. I've written the times when your people will find the car entering and leaving Pickering on the photocopy."

"What about the Mondeo?"

"No joy yet."

"Cooper, let me ask you a couple of questions. Firstly, how did you get into the cameras to find the Fiesta? Secondly, when you say you persuaded Charlie, I hope there was no violence."

"No. Violence was not necessary. With regard to accessing the various cameras, we have some expertise in that field and much experience, if I can just leave it at that."

Clark couldn't help noticing that he had said violence was not necessary, clearly indicating, to her at least, that it was an option that could well have been used. She was making as if to leave when Cooper held his hand up to stop her.

"Amy, how are things going from your end?"

She shook her head. "I'm sorry but I can't reveal details of any police enquiries. It could compromise the case, not to mention getting me in a ton of trouble."

"Look, I've already given you valuable information. We are a resource which may be able to go where you cannot and gain information where you may not. Use us. We are on the same side."

Again, she shook her head.

"As a result of my team's efforts, you now have the name James Adamson, details of a false driving licence, apparently used by Wade, and you also know that a second car was purchased. So, by sharing our information, it is clear that we are being of some help to you. Please return the favour."

Carefully looking around, she leant closer to Cooper before speaking. "All right, when we searched Wade's house, we found a letter addressed to him at his home from a safe deposit box company confirming a box has been rented. We have yet to ask him about that, but it seems a little odd to leave it out in plain sight if there is anything untoward about it. We will be seeking a court order to see what's inside the box on Monday."

"Right, I see. I assume you are hoping the ransom money may be there. If you do find cash, I may be able to identify if it is from the ransom."

"How exactly would you be able to do that?"

"I can't tell you, I'm afraid, but, if I can get the necessary authority, it may be possible to use it as evidence."

She stood to leave. "I guess I'll just have to trust you."

"By the way, after we left his office, Charlie spoke on the phone to someone called Jimmy and then a second man he called Mr Harris. Do you know them?"

She sat down again. "That would be Frank Harris, the local Mr Big. He owns everything in that street, including Bargain Motors, and Jimmy is his minder-cum-enforcer. It might be better if you stayed clear of them. Harris is an evil bastard and Jimmy is just a thug, but a big one."

"Thanks for the warning. Oh, one final thing to think about. Don't you think this is all a bit too easy?"

She didn't reply and, with a promise to stay in touch, left, not having touched her tea. It had been a useful meeting, but Amy Clark was more certain than ever that she was playing with fire and needed to be very careful when dealing with these men. Already Cooper had just told her that they had bugged the car dealer's office without any legal authority. How else would they have known about his phone call to Harris? Maybe she should update her boss, Adrian Gregson, to give her some degree of protection.

Cooper's last remark had certainly given her some food for thought, before she eventually dismissed it. From long experience, she knew that criminals were not as clever as they thought and invariably made mistakes leading to their capture. Even, or maybe especially, if you were an ex-Police Superintendent.

Had she heard the conversation in the café after she left, Clark would have been even less happy.

"Did you get all that, Andy?"

"Yeah, Coops. Clear as a bell, both audio and video. Some good full-face shots."

"Thanks. I hope we don't need to use it, I like her. Still, if needs must, we will have to."

FORTY-TWO

Back in the office, Amy got DI Ben Connor to join her. She quickly showed him the photocopy relating to the sale of the Fiesta and the second vehicle, eliciting a whistle of surprise as he saw the picture of Richard Wade. Clark told him that she had obtained the information from a source who, she explained, had identified the car from roadside cameras and traced it back to Bargain Motors.

"This wouldn't be the men working for Ross, would it?"

Not surprised by his rapid grasp of the situation, she smiled before replying. "Best you leave that side of things to me, Ben. If the shit hits the fan, and it probably will, it will be better if you can deny all knowledge. The trouble is, we can't use this stuff in evidence as we are not able to verify it. You've got the times the car was picked up on cameras, so I want you to get our people on it at once so we can obtain the same information from the cameras and use it in evidence. I also want them to follow the car as far as they can to see if we can find where it ended up. As well as that, get someone down to see that prat Charlie Newton and get the same info as this off him. Okay?"

He nodded grimly and left the office to set about the tasks he had been given. He wasn't happy. In his experience, it never ended well when working with these secret squirrel types as they usually disappeared into the distance leaving other people to clear up the mess they left behind. Still, she was in charge and had given him his orders, which didn't mean that he wouldn't try to cover his own back by keeping a record of what had been said.

Shortly after noon, Amy Clark was informed that the first interview with Wade had been completed and the interviewing officers, Trace and Lee, were ready to brief the team.

Ten minutes later in the main office, Ds Trace began his update on the interview.

He began by telling them that Ken Wilkinson, a local solicitor, was representing Wade. Given Wade's background as a police officer, and a senior one at that, he had been somewhat sceptical that his client could have committed such a crime. That was until he saw the evidence accumulated so far, which resulted in a lengthy solicitor/client consultation.

Wade had been cautioned and, on the advice of Wilkinson, initially no commented in response to the questions he was asked. However, typical of the man, he couldn't resist talking. Basically, he denied everything and claimed to have a watertight alibi.

When shown the pictures of him in the club, he claimed that it bore absolutely no resemblance to him at all and, in any event, he had never been in Fat Harry's club, nor had he ever heard of it. He certainly didn't have any clothes like that either. He went on to deny that it was him pictured putting the girl into the blue Fiesta, claiming to have never driven one in his life. He did admit to having been picked up in a blue car on Wednesday night at his home by a friend of the girl he was meeting. He denied knowing the make and couldn't identify the driver.

Karen Lee took over telling those present that the interview took a strange turn with Wade anxious, almost proud, to detail his alibi. After leaving his home, he was taken by the driver of the blue car to a restaurant in Leeds where he had a very convivial night with a girl called Sophie Young. He said she was a reporter doing a feature on him for the *Mail on Sunday* and that it was the first time he had met her. He was very pleased to tell them they had got on so well that he ended up going back to the flat where she was staying. In fact, things went so well that he stayed with her until the Friday afternoon, when she had to return home, somewhere down south. He said that he had not left the flat during that period.

There were some knowing smirks from the male officers at the thought of what the two of them must have been up to. Well used to the ways of her colleagues, Karen let them get it out of their system before she continued.

She said things had started to get a little weird as Wade continued to answer questions despite entreaties from Wilkinson. He was unable to name the restaurant or to say where it was. Nor could he give them any idea as to the flat's location. All he could say was that he had been very drunk and did admit some drugs had been taken as well.

TT stepped in again. He told them that Wade had claimed all the arrangements for the meeting had been made over the phone and that the girl had even sent him a photo. He was very confident that she would confirm his account.

Lastly, when shown the letter from the safe deposit box company found at his address, he denied having a safe deposit box and had no idea why the company would write to him confirming the rental. Maybe all would be revealed on Monday as denying its existence was strange indeed, making everyone wonder what it contained.

For the whole interview, he denied having any contact with Mary Ross or her father other than his professional dealings with them ten years earlier.

At that, Clark stood to address the group. "Obviously, we have some more enquiries to make and further evidence to put to this pillock. We need to find this girl Sophie, so get on to the newspaper and, if she exists, we can get the restaurant and flat details from her. We are seeking a court order to open the safe deposit box and to obtain the details of the renter. We have ongoing enquiries at the club and into the car, particularly where it may show up on cameras. Finally, it is absolutely essential that we get the information in Wade's phone. Anyone else want to say anything?"

Ben Connor put his tuppence worth in. "I'm sure it's not escaped anyone's notice that Wade's time with this girl neatly covers the period from just before the kidnap to shortly after the collection of the ransom and the sighting of the car leaving Pickering. Seems a little convenient to me."

TT was the one to answer. "I agree, boss, but he really seemed confident that he was in the clear."

Clark had heard enough. "Okay, thanks and well done,

both of you. Let's get to work, people. Ted, you and Karen have a break and then get together with me and DI Connor so we can prepare for the next interview. I think we need to go in a little harder with him while it remains an outside possibility that Mary is still alive."

With that, everyone set off on their various enquiries.

FORTY-THREE

Andy and Cooper rejoined the others in the car following their meeting with Amy Clark.

Mark spoke first. "What next, boss?"

"We'll drop you and Tony back at the house. I want you to get back on the cameras and find the Mondeo that Wade or Adamson bought from Charlie Newton. I don't know why he needed a second car or what he was doing with it, but I want to find out. It might mean there is more than one person involved, I just don't know. It's possible you may be able to track it from the car dealer's. If that's no good, try around the northeast of Leeds or maybe even Pickering. It all seems to happen around there."

"Where will you and Andy be?"

"We're going back to Pickering, to where the cash was dropped. We should beat the police there, I hope. They've got a lot on and we're still a bit in front of them. When I think of it, I'm not sure we actually told them where the drop was, other than it was from the train."

Tony chipped in. "Just a thought, Coops. We might get lucky and get a hit if we hack into ANPR and PNC if the car has been picked up by cameras on a journey or, if we're really lucky, even been stopped by police."

"I see what you mean, Tony, and it's worth a try, but I've got to say I think it's a bit of a stretch. Give it a go by all means, but please don't get caught."

Tony laughed. "As if."

Cooper had to smile but recognised there were still some dangers in hacking the computer systems, which were to some degree, but not totally, secure. Both the Automated Number Plate Recognition System and the Police National Computer contained sensitive information which could be of great value to criminal organisations. Whilst Tony may be dismissive of their levels of security, it would take someone of extraordinary skill to gain access to them. Perhaps someone of Tony's skill level, but to be fair he had the great advantage of inside knowledge and very high-level contacts if required.

It was only mid-afternoon when, after dropping the other two off at the house, Cooper and Andy drove into Levisham a little over an hour later. They parked their car at the railway station and set off on foot along the side of the track to where Cooper believed the money had been thrown from the carriage. Was it still only yesterday?

He hadn't been able to mark the exact spot, but it was a relatively small strip of land to search. They soon found the brightly coloured bag which had originally contained the ransom money, clearly having been dumped by the kidnapper. It had been worth a try using the bag, hoping it would be picked up on cameras or even by a witness, but whoever they were, they had been on the ball. Cooper assumed they had believed the bag may have been bugged so had taken a few minutes to transfer the money into their own bag. Clever indeed, but foolish to leave the other bag behind to mark the collection point.

The two men knew they were at a crime scene that the police would want to forensically examine in great detail so proceeded with some care. The ground was dry and dusty with only a sparse covering of grass, making it easy for Andy to discover a small pool of oil, obviously deposited by some sort of vehicle. Further examination revealed faint tyre tracks, easily identified as belonging to a fairly small motorcycle. That explained how they had got in and out over the surrounding farmland and scrub near to the railway line so quickly. The two men had seen enough and, rather than risk further contamination of the scene, returned to their parked vehicle.

Cooper was immediately on his phone. "Mark, I want you and Tony to stop what you're doing for the moment. We know the kidnapper used some sort of small motorcycle to get to and from the cash drop. It probably had an empty bag on it on the way in and a full one on the way out. They dumped our bag. It's a fairly small time window involved and, as we know they left Pickering in the Fiesta, it's a safe bet they dumped the bike somewhere around here. Hit the cameras and find it for me."

"Righto, we're on it. When you do get back, we've had some luck with the other stuff as well. Call you when we have something."

Cooper wondered what else they had discovered, but it could wait for now. Finding the bike was a clear priority. He thought about contacting Amy but decided to wait until they had more information, also wanting to stay ahead of the police in the search for the culprits. Obviously, Wade was in custody and still the number one suspect, but it was all a little too pat for his liking and, even if he was responsible, there may be others involved.

After what seemed like forever but was in reality only forty minutes, Mark rang back.

"We've got it."

"Well done. Andy's listening in."

"Right, we found a light-coloured trials bike turning off the main road and heading down to Levisham shortly after 10am. It had what looked like some sort of bag on the rear carrier. Didn't look like there was much in it. Around 10.30am, it was back on the main road and this time the bag was full. Rider was wearing dark clothing if it helps. We've been able to get a reg. number and it looked as if there was some sort of design on the petrol tank."

"Good work. Were you able to track it?"

"Oh yes, indeed we did, and I think you'll like this bit. We picked it up in Pickering centre just near the Co-op store. It turned into a small side street, where we lost visuals. Ten minutes later, the blue Fiesta came out of that same street."

"That's great. We'll go for a look."

Mark couldn't keep the amusement out of his voice. "You'll like this bit, Coops. When we backtracked, we identified the car driving into the street and the motorbike driving out, clearly to collect the cash. However, we had a bit more of a search round and who should we come across but our old friend Richard Wade walking by. In fact, he walked past you while you were in the Co-op car park with Ross. By the way, he was wearing dark clothing."

Cooper smiled ruefully. "I'm glad it's amused you. We'll see if we can find the bike if, in the meantime, you carry on with the other searches."

"No probs, boss. It's looking good. One last thing before you go. I bet you'll never guess who sold the motorcycle."

"I don't suppose it was our friendly neighbourhood car dealer Charlie Newton, was it?"

"Coops, you're just no fun these days."

Following the directions given by Mark, the two men were soon in the street where they hoped to find the motorcycle. There were very few houses and they were instantly drawn to the garages at the end of the street, with number four notable for the small patch of slightly damp oil in front of the door and what appeared to be a new padlock securing the garage.

Helpfully, there was an estate agent's sign advertising garages to let which quickly led them to the letting agent, Adam Walker, who was singularly unimpressed when they entered his office as he was preparing to lock up. Identification cards were quickly flashed, which he had no chance of examining, but it must have worked as he cooperated fully. Maybe he didn't care, or more likely he had been busy all day and just wanted to get home to his family.

The file for the rental of garage number four was quickly produced, and neither Cooper nor Andy was surprised to see a copy of the driving licence in the name of James Adamson but bearing a photo of Richard Wade. He was able to confirm his dealings with Mr Adamson had been on the Tuesday of the previous week and, yes, he was using a motorcycle. The frustrated estate agent was asked to wait whilst they made contact with colleagues who, they were sure, would be there shortly.

Cooper went outside whilst Andy chatted to Walker. Again, he was undecided whether or not to contact Amy Clark but decided he must. He had considered picking the lock on the garage to confirm the motorbike's presence but realised it could taint evidence and, in any event, would not really take them very far forward.

She answered the phone immediately, and to say she was angry when he updated her on his afternoon's work was something of an understatement. She went so far as to threaten his arrest for obstructing police in the execution of their duty. He really was beginning to like her. Cooper let her blow off steam before she eventually told him that some of her officers would be there within the hour and to keep Adam Walker there until they arrived. She cut the connection before he could respond.

The officers were there within record time, allowing Cooper and Andy to depart discreetly. They would have liked to remain but, realising they were not all that welcome, decided discretion was the better part of valour. It would have been nice to find out if the bike was there, but it almost certainly was and they would be able to confirm it later.

On the way to rejoin the rest of his team, Cooper's first thought was that it was time to update Sir John Ross on their progress so far. Did he even know that Wade was in custody?

Once again, he was plagued with doubts about the evidence mounting against Wade. He couldn't rid himself of the thought that whilst this job had been meticulously planned and carried out with ruthless efficiency, far too many clues and items of evidence had been left behind. It surely couldn't just be carelessness, so did that mean it was deliberate? Was Wade being set up, and, if so, why would anyone go to so much trouble? Cooper hated being led by the nose, but being taken for a fool was even worse.

FORTY-FOUR

En route back to Leeds, Cooper rang Mark whilst Andy drove.

"Right, Mark, what have you got for me?"

"You won't believe it, Coops. Tony got into the PNC, checked the Mondeo and got a hit. It was stopped leaving Pickering by a North Yorkshire Pc and, according to the information on the system, was driven by James Adamson. At least that was the driving licence he produced."

"When was this?"

"Tuesday of last week."

"From what we have just learnt, that was the day he turned up in Pickering with the motorbike, so it looks as if he has had help. We'll pick you up shortly and pay our friend Charlie a visit. I don't feel that he has been entirely truthful with us, do you?"

"A second-hand car dealer not being helpful, surely not. One last thing. That address on the driving licence does exist, but it's an empty house."

Less than an hour later, all four men arrived at Bargain Motors, relieved to see it was still open despite it being late on a Saturday afternoon. It saved them having to visit Charlie's home address, which had recently been acquired by Mark and Tony using their mysterious ways.

Once again, Cooper and Andy went into the office, leaving the other two in the car covertly monitoring the conversation and ready to offer assistance in the remote chance that it was needed. It would be a brave man indeed that took on Cooper and Andy, even with the support of some of the mechanics.

After a very good day, Charlie was busily totting up the accounts, enjoying a large whisky, when the two men entered. Expecting it to be a customer, the welcoming smile was instantly wiped from his face when he saw who it was. This time, he didn't make any attempt at bravado, instead waiting meekly for them to speak. Cooper took a seat in front of Charlie's desk, whilst Andy stood to one side, staring intently at the car dealer.

"Hello, Charlie. Your replies to my questions over the next few minutes will determine exactly what happens to you and your business, something your boss may not be happy about. Understand?"

Charlie could only nod.

"I said do you understand?"

"Yes, of course."

Cooper never raised his voice, but facing the man's intense gaze and latent air of menace was enough to make Charlie agree to anything just to escape their presence. He was frightened.

"Good. Why didn't you tell us that you had sold a motorbike to the man you know as James Adamson?"

"I forgot."

"Charlie, I do hope you are not going to piss me off any more than I already am."

"Honestly, I just didn't think it was important."

"I want copies of the paperwork. Did he pay cash for the bike as well?"

"Yes."

"Did you not question why someone would pay several thousand pounds in cash for two cars and a bike?"

"Not my business. If I don't know, I can't tell, can I?"

"Why did this man come to you?"

"I was recommended."

"Who by?"

"I can't tell you that. They'll kill me if I involve them. Do what you like, but I'm not going to tell you."

Sensing the man's fear and realising it was a waste of time carrying on, Cooper changed tack. "How did he get the bike?"

"He picked it up from here."

"What about the Mondeo?"

"Some of my men delivered it to Adamson."

"When and where?"

After scrabbling about in the paperwork, Charlie replied, "He wanted it taking to Pickering, so that's what we did on Tuesday last week."

Cooper looked to Andy, who almost imperceptibly shook his head, indicating that he didn't have any questions.

"All right, Charlie, that'll do for now. I do hope I don't have to come back here, and so should you. Is there anything else you want to tell me?"

"No, honest, that's everything."

After a very audible sigh, Cooper directed his steely gaze at Charlie, who looked away and started to lick his very dry lips. What next?

"What about the false number plates?"

"I had nothing to do with that. He asked if I knew anyone who makes plates, so I sent him to the bloke round the corner who does mine. I wasn't involved in that."

Believing him simply because there was no reason to lie about it, Cooper stood and, after obtaining Tom Muscat's details, he and Andy headed towards the door with a final remark.

"Well, thanks for your help, Mr Newton. I do hope for your sake we don't meet again."

Back at the car, he was quickly informed that, as soon as they left, the car dealer had been on the phone again to Jimmy and Mr Harris, merely reporting their visit. There wasn't much doubt in their minds as to who recommended Adamson to Charlie Newton. What was their involvement in all this?

Not bothering to visit the number plate maker – the police could do that – they returned to the house.

Once there, Cooper visited Sir John Ross in his study. He appeared to have shrivelled to a mere husk of a man, a shadow of the confident self-made millionaire he had been. The thought of losing his daughter on top of his wife's death was too much for him to contemplate.

Quickly updating him on the enquiries they had carried out so far and explaining that he was working closely with the police, Cooper told the man his team would be moving out of his house the next day.

"Why? Are you giving up?"

"We don't need to be here any longer as I don't expect any further contact from the kidnappers. We have not given up, nor will we unless you instruct us to stop."

"No. Please carry on, and remember if I don't get Mary back, I want these men dead."

"Got it, John, no worries. We'll be nearby in a motel so we can move freely and operate without disturbing you."

He lapsed into silence, barely acknowledging Cooper as he left the room.

Cooper was getting tired but, before he could rest, he needed to contact Amy Clark. As ever, she answered her phone very quickly.

He updated her on the visit to Charlie Newton, informing her of the way the bike and Mondeo both got to Pickering. He also told her about Muscat, although he didn't expect it to take them any further. For her part, Amy seemed to have gotten over her annoyance, for the moment at least, and appeared to be getting used to their unusual working relationship.

She didn't have a lot to tell him but did mention that a PNC check had revealed that a police officer had stopped Adamson in the Mondeo leaving Pickering the previous week. When shown a copy of Adamson's driving licence, Pc Johnson had readily confirmed that he had been the driver of the car. She actually laughed when the officer admitted to the members of her team who questioned him that he had only stopped the car because he was bored and it was something to do. How many times had it happened that officers carrying out routine duties gained useful, often vital, evidence in major inquiries? So yet more to establish Richard Wade's involvement.

Happy that he didn't have to tell her of his prior knowledge of Pc Johnson's actions, he asked her what was next.

Briefly, it was a further interview with Wade, checking the safe deposit box on Monday and further examination of the phone they had seized. They were continuing in their attempts to pin down the location where the kidnapper made their calls. Lastly, they were considering a search for Mary, but, unfortunately, the search advisors had insufficient information for them to pinpoint a likely search area.

Cooper really didn't like trying to give her advice but suggested that as a lot of money had been spent on vehicles, it might be worth checking Wade's bank accounts. All goodwill vanished once more as she replied acerbically.

"Well, thank you, Mr Cooper. Why on earth didn't we think of that?"

She cut him off before he got the chance to tell Amy that they were moving out of Sir John's house and where they would be. Never mind.

Thinking about their conversation, it was obvious that Clark was not telling him everything they were doing. Clearly, enquiries had to be made about where the false driving licence came from, not to mention where the Fiesta and Mondeo were now. Maybe they were relying on Wade to tell them. Good luck with that.

FORTY-FIVE

Amy Clark's team were having a tough time.

Much of their day had been frustrating, most of it spent following Cooper and his men around, duplicating their enquiries even though it was necessary. Those men would never agree to appear in court, and the only way to make sure any evidence obtained was admissible in a court of law was to record it in statement form by police officers. It was simply unavoidable.

They had recovered the motorcycle from the garage in Pickering, but it didn't help much other than to connect James Adamson, hopefully, to the cash drop-off point. Forensic examinations were continuing to positively connect the bike to that scene. The bike was also linked to Charlie Newton and Bargain Motors.

Both the estate agent who leased the garage and Charlie Newton had produced photocopies of the James Adamson driving licence, bearing Richard Wade's photo, linking the former police officer to both transactions.

Newton had also been able to confirm that he had been paid over £17,000 in total for the two cars and the motorcycle. However, because it was the weekend, they were unable to carry out any enquiries at banks into Wade's finances. It was the same situation with the safe deposit box.

The amount of time Wade had already spent in custody was becoming a critical issue, adding to Amy's problems. Sometime in the early hours of Sunday morning, they would either have to charge Wade or release him, unless they could get a Superintendent to authorise an extension of his time in custody.

The need to interview him further was becoming a priority.

However, all Clark's problems paled into insignificance whilst two questions remained unanswered. Where was Mary Ross? Was she still alive?

As usual, she also had to deal with pressure from the Chief Officer's corridor, anxious for a speedy resolution to their enquiries. At least her boss, Adrian Gregson, was doing his best to keep them off her back and well away from the team's offices.

It was now almost 7pm and, having been in conference with DI Ben Connor, she was ready for the next briefing.

All the team were present and listened intently, many taking notes, as Connor outlined the current position and the problems they faced in establishing Wade's involvement. On the plus side were the videos from the club and photocopies of the false driving licence, which they had so far not recovered, and they still had to establish beyond all doubt that it was fake and where it was from. Of course, Wade's pitiful alibi, which was, in truth, no alibi at all, helped them no end. Pc Simon Johnson's identification of Wade as the man he stopped in the Mondeo leaving Pickering was invaluable, as it linked Wade to the day the bike was placed in the garage and when the car was delivered.

Downsides were the lack of eye witnesses, although they were working on staff from the club, and so far nothing from his mobile phone.

Things got considerably better when one of the officers who, to the annoyance of everyone else, had been on the phone throughout the briefing concluded his call and immediately raised his hand to attract attention.

When given the nod by Connor, the officer brought the room to a standstill as he spoke.

"That was the *Mail on Sunday* offices. They have just confirmed that no one has ever heard of a journalist called Sophie Young, and they have definitely not commissioned anyone to do a feature that would involve Richard Wade. In short, his alibi is complete nonsense."

Both Clark and Connor nodded, with the start of smiles flicking across their faces. Things suddenly seemed better. With the collapse of his alibi, Richard Wade was in a much more precarious position with many questions still to answer.

Connor spoke again. "TT, Karen, are you ready for the next interview?"

Trace spoke first. "We are, but first we need to add that last bit of info to the plan while we wait for Ken Wilkinson to come in."

Clark stepped forward. "Just a couple of other things then. As you know, I have several enquiries running where I am in overall supervision, so I am passing the day-today management of this job to DI Conner. I will of course retain overall responsibility. Secondly, apart from TT and Karen, I want the rest of you to go home, see your families and get some rest. Back for a 9am briefing tomorrow. This inquiry is a long way from over. Goodnight to you all and thank you for your efforts so far."

Back in her office, Clark spoke to Ben Connor.

"Ben, I'm going home, it's been a long twenty-four hours. Are you okay with where we are?"

"Yeah, boss, no problem."

"I don't know what you think, but I'm leaning towards charging Wade later tonight and keeping him in custody for court on Monday morning, where we can apply for a remand to prison. Any thoughts?"

"Because it's the weekend, I don't know if we are going to come up with any game- changing new evidence, so extending custody comes into play. We can of course apply for extensions to his custody at court, but I prefer your suggestion. If you agree, I can make initial contact with the CPS to see what they think so far and what else they need from us to make a decision."

"Good plan, Ben. We can't charge him without authorisation from the Crown Prosecution Service, so we might as well get them involved as soon as we can. If you need me, don't hesitate to give me a ring."

Connor briefed Ds Trace and Dc Lee on his discussion with Amy Clark prior to them going to the custody suite for their meeting with Ken Wilkinson. They updated the solicitor on the state of the inquiry and the evidence they planned to put to his client, making no reference to the possibility of charging Wade later that night.

Thirty minutes later, Wilkinson indicated that he was ready for the interview to go ahead.

Karen Lee kicked things of by cautioning a tired-looking Wade, before reminding him that he was in custody on suspicion of kidnapping Mary Ross.

Wilkinson immediately interjected. "My client has indicated that he will not be answering any of your questions."

Lee smiled at Wade before speaking. "It is of course your right not to answer any of the questions we put to you, but I am sure you will understand that we will ask them nevertheless."

For the next forty minutes, the officers put their questions to Richard Wade. Once more, they covered the videos that they believed showed him taking an unsteady Mary Ross from Fat Harry's nightclub before placing her in the blue Ford Fiesta. He did not answer.

He made no attempt to explain why a driving licence bearing his photograph and the name James Adamson had been used to verify his identity when purchasing two cars and a motorcycle from Bargain Motors. He remained silent when the same question was put to him concerning the rental of the garage in Pickering where the motorcycle he purchased was found. That the estate agent was also able to confirm the man claiming to be Adamson had put the bike in the garage also elicited no response.

Wade maintained his silence, apart from brief whispered conversations with his solicitor.

He refused to respond when asked where he had got the cash to pay for the vehicles.

They informed him that staff at Bargain Motors had

confirmed delivery of the Mondeo to a man in Pickering who they believed to be Adamson. They revealed that, when leaving Pickering that same day, the car had been stopped by a police officer who said the driver was a man by the name of Adamson, who had produced the same false driving licence as proof of his identity. The officer was also able to confirm that the photograph on the licence was actually of Richard Wade. It prompted a further conversation with Wilkinson. However, Wade still declined to answer, although he was beginning to look more anxious.

When asked where the driving licence was and where he had got it from, Wade merely shook his head. It was put to him that it was obviously a fake, but he again declined to answer. When pressed, he again refused to offer any explanation as to why his photograph would appear on a licence bearing the name James Adamson. He gave no response when questioned about the letter found at his home, and addressed to him, from the safe deposit box company.

When asked what the box contained, he just returned a blank stare.

He was finally questioned about his alibi where he claimed to have spent all his time with the reporter Sophie Young. Wade could contain himself no longer and, with a return to his usual bombastic manner, shouted at the officers.

"That's right and if you cretins knew what you were doing, you would have found her by now. She won't have forgotten me."

Trace stepped in. "If I remember correctly, you told

us she had been commissioned to write an article for the *Mail on Sunday*. Is that right?"

"Bloody right it is."

Wilkinson tried his best to shut his client up. "Richard, as we agreed, please do not answer any more questions."

Trace came back quickly. "Mr Wade, would it surprise you to know that the newspaper have never heard of Sophie Young, nor have they asked anyone to write the type of article you described?"

A clearly surprised Wade offered no reply.

Karen Lee took a turn. "So where were you, Richard, when you claimed to be with this mystery woman?"

He refused to answer. Likewise, when asked again about the blue car that picked him up, or to explain why he could not name the restaurant or give the address where he had been with this woman. Where was the photo of her on his phone?

Karen Lee, looking up from her notes, said, "Mr Wade, you don't need us to tell you that you are in a lot of trouble. In any event, I'm sure Mr Wilkinson has already made it clear exactly what a difficult situation you face. Please help us and yourself. Tell us where Mary Ross is."

"I have no idea. I'm totally innocent of all these allegations."

"Is Mary dead, Richard?"

"How the hell would I know?"

"What have you done with the money?"

"That's it. I'm not answering any more of your stupid questions. Maybe you should put more effort into trying to find the real kidnapper instead of wasting time trying to frame me."

The officers persisted with their questions about Mary, but a clearly shaken Wade gave no further answers.

They tried finally to establish if he could account for where he was when the sale of the vehicles took place or when the garage in Pickering was rented. Again, he made no reply.

They eventually gave up after having put the allegations to him and given him ample opportunity to counter the evidence against him.

The interview was terminated and he was returned to his cell.

TT spoke to Ken Wilkinson. "We will now confer with our senior officers and possibly the CPS. Once a decision has been made as to the way forward, we will, of course, contact you, unless you want to wait here. Clearly, the nature of the offence we are investigating means your client is not an obvious candidate for bail, which does not preclude you from making representations to the Custody Officer."

"Are you considering a charge?"

"I'm afraid that's not a decision for me."

"Okay, I'll be at home. Please let me know what is decided."

The solicitor left the building, and the two officers returned to the office to meet with DI Connor.

Once updated on how the interview had gone and bearing in mind his earlier conversation with Amy Clark, the decision was an obvious one for Connor. He instructed Ted Trace to telephone the CPS, who were expecting a call, to request a charging decision, emphasising the need to stress the serious nature of the offence and that the girl was still missing, possibly dead. He knew the experienced

Detective Sergeant would lay out the evidence in a precise and logical manner, making clear to them Wade's refusal to cooperate and lack of a credible alibi.

Trace was back fifteen minutes later with the, not totally unexpected, news that the decision had been passed to higher authority. It was not a surprise considering the serious nature of the offence, the history of the suspect and the fact that the victim's father was a well-known local businessman.

All the officers were slightly taken aback when a Senior Crown Prosecutor rang back a few minutes later and, after a couple of questions for clarification, authorised a charge of kidnapping against Richard Wade.

They would not have been surprised at the rapidity of the decision had they known that the CPS were fully aware of the events so far. Even Cooper had people he reported to, and his updates had been passed along to the relevant people. That is not to say they expected the request to charge Wade that evening, but they were prepared for it at some stage. However, it must be stressed that a charge would not have been authorised unless it was genuinely believed that there was enough evidence to justify it.

Richard Wade was taken to the custody suite and charged with kidnapping Mary Ross at 11pm that night, to which he replied in a loud and almost incoherent voice, "I'm innocent. You bastards are trying to get your own back on me. I haven't done anything."

Ken Wilkinson spoke to his client over the phone, explaining that, as he probably already knew, making representations to the Custody Officer for bail would be futile, before adding one final comment.

"Richard, in view of the serious nature of this offence, it is more than likely that an application will be made at court for you to be remanded in custody. Do you understand?"

"You've got to get me out. You know what will happen to me in prison. I'm innocent, for God's sake."

Richard Wade was duly informed by the Custody Officer that bail would not be granted, and he would be kept in custody to appear in court on the Monday morning. A completely beaten and sobbing man was returned to his cell, where a close watch would be kept to prevent any harm befalling him, either self-inflicted or otherwise.

FORTY-SIX

Miles Kingston spent Saturday in the apartment in an effort to remain out of sight. He knew the police would be active and was worried that Wade, who was surely under arrest by now, may lead them here. However, for some strange reason, he trusted Natasha and if she said Wade would not be able to find his way here, then that was good enough for him. She was a professional, after all, which thought caused him to smile at the double meaning, considering her profession.

He'd had pizza delivered and, despite his best endeavours, had not managed to leave the booze alone. He was not yet drunk, though.

Shortly before 10.30pm, one of his remaining phones rang. It could only be Karl. He really didn't need this but reluctantly answered.

"Karl."

"Hi, Miles, how are you doing?"

"Good, thanks."

"How did things go?"

"Great. I'm rich and Wade should be under arrest by now."

"So the plan worked as we hoped?"

"Smooth as silk, Karl, smooth as silk."

"Good. So if they charge him, as they must, I can expect to see him here sometime next week. No bail for kidnappers."

Miles could hear the pleasure in his voice, more like excitement really. He didn't want to know what was planned for Wade; he never had.

"I haven't got long. The screws will be coming round soon. What about the girl?"

"Yeah, you were right. I couldn't have left her on her own at the farm for that long while I went to Pickering and then to the airport. Besides, what would I have used for transport? No, it just wouldn't have worked."

"So what did you do?"

"You know what I did."

"Has she been found yet?"

"Don't know. Haven't heard anything."

"Miles, what about Harris? Any trouble?"

"No, all good. He wasn't bothered once he got his money back."

"Did you enjoy killing her?"

"Of course not. What do you think I am?"

As he told the lie, Miles absently stroked his recently shaved upper lip. He hoped removing the moustache would make him look less like Wade, and intended to grow his hair longer to complete the transformation.

Smithson chuckled down the phone. "All right, Miles, I believe you, thousands wouldn't. I hope I don't see you again, because if I do, it means you're back in here."

The phone clicked off.

That was it, another burner phone to be disposed of when he went out.

He finished his drink and, before he went to bed, decided it was time to contact the estate agent, Jean. He fancied some female company. He somewhat belatedly remembered that he did not have her contact details and would need to go to her office on Monday. Even though the job was done, it was still proving difficult to keep all the balls in the air at once. Some juggler!

It was also time to decide what happened next, when to leave.

FORTY-SEVEN

By 10am, Ds Lily Croft and Dc Joe Morrell were back at the clinic to meet Brenda Thomas and her solicitor, Alex Watson. They had visited the clinic every couple of days in an attempt to build a rapport with the woman, ensuring that she could be certain her welfare was uppermost in their minds.

The transformation after seventeen days of treatment was quite remarkable. Brenda was clear-eyed, had put on some weight and was much more confident in her dealings with the officers. Whilst the owner of the clinic, a doctor who specialised in drugs therapy, happily agreed to her being interviewed, he did stress that she had still some way to go in her treatment and so should be handled carefully.

Although Brenda had long been prepared for this day, Lily Croft wanted to ensure that she fully understood what was going to happen.

"Okay, Brenda, I just want to confirm what is happening today. We are taking you to the TARIAN building where we can interview you on video. Because it is Sunday, and minimum staff are on duty, we will be able to do things as quietly as possible. As I have already explained to you, our conversations will not be under caution even though we are discussing criminal offences you may have been involved in. That is why Mr Watson will be present, to protect your interests. None of this means you will be prosecuted in these particular circumstances, particularly as you appear to have been forced, against your will, into cooperating with these other people. Is that all clear?"

"Yes, I understand, thank you."

"Good. Are you ready to collect your evidence?"

"Yes, I am. We need to go to my mother's house."

On their arrival, the woman threw her arms around her daughter, expressing delight at how well she looked. Morrell assisted Brenda in recovering a large cardboard box from the spare bedroom of the house. At first glance, it appeared to be full of a considerable number of carefully organised files and documents.

The officers placed the box in their car, careful not to interfere with the contents, which Brenda had assured them were in chronological order. It was clear that she had used her experience as a senior DVLA administrator to organise the paperwork.

They were met at the TARIAN headquarters by both Detective Superintendent Williams and Detective Inspector Davies, both of whom shook an embarrassed Brenda by the hand, thanking her for her assistance.

She was taken to a large room which had been set up with a video camera operated by a civilian technician. In anticipation of the receipt of Brenda's evidence, another two Dc's were present to list each item, formally numbering and recording them for evidential purposes, ready for their eventual production in court. Croft and Morrell, having completely gained Brenda's trust, would carry out the interview in the presence of Alex Watson.

A smiling Lily Croft sat on one side of a large table, with Joe Morrell facing Brenda and her solicitor.

"Are you ready, Brenda?"

Having already had some coaching in what to expect, she answered in a strong, clear voice. "Yes."

"As you have already been told, it is our intention to treat you as a cooperating witness. Mr Watson has requested that you be granted immunity from prosecution in return for your evidence. The granting of a written 'immunity notice' is a somewhat unusual procedure in the UK, so unusual that neither we nor any of our senior officers have ever seen such a document, which, I believe, is more far-reaching than Mr Watson realised. Immunity from prosecution is only granted in serious organised crime cases, and only on the authority of the Director of Public Prosecutions with the knowledge of the Attorney General. It must specify the offences for which immunity is granted, in your case, the production of fraudulent driving licences and your involvement in drugs offences. When previously interviewed under caution, you admitted committing those offences on a large scale while employed at the Driver and Vehicle Licensing Agency. However, you have indicated a willingness to furnish evidence against the men who, you claim, forced you to do this, and against other people involved in the supply of controlled drugs. The granting of an 'immunity notice' is contingent on you being prepared to appear in court as a witness against any persons charged with offences based on the information you give and that no further, more serious, offences you may have committed are disclosed. Mr Watson has studied the document and I believe he is happy with its contents. Do you understand all I have said?"

"Yes, I do."

"I need to make a further couple of points so that you fully understand the situation you find yourself in. Because we are dealing with what are described as serious organised crime groups, you should be in no doubt just how dangerous these men are. You need to be aware that they will not hesitate to kill anyone who crosses them, which places you in considerable danger. This means that we may need to relocate you when this is all over. Do you agree to go ahead, knowing what I have just told you?"

She nodded before adding in a firm voice, "Mr Watson has explained everything. These people are evil and I will do all I can to stop them doing this to anyone else."

On receiving a nod from her solicitor, Brenda signed the document, which he then witnessed. Once it was numbered and recorded, the signed 'immunity notice' became their first exhibit. A copy was given to the solicitor.

"If you're ready, we'll begin. It will be a long day so should you require a break at any time, please say so."

Brenda looked Lily in the eye as she replied. "I am more than ready. These people have ruined my life and I want it back."

So, with a soon-to-be-revealed story that would shock hardened officers with its telling, Operation Dingo began in earnest.

It took Brenda a total of seven hours to tell her story,

introducing her carefully organised documents and explaining their relevance to each situation, before they were recorded and numbered as exhibits by the two Detective Constables.

By the end of the interview, everyone present was tired, especially Brenda Thomas, who, despite her resolve, had become more embarrassed as the previous two years of her life were revealed to those listening. She was certain that everybody would see her in a different light now; sure that sympathy would be in short supply. Hadn't she brought this on herself after all?

As Brenda stood, Lily Croft came round the table and, without a word, threw her arms around the woman. Within seconds, both the vulnerable woman and the hardened detective were crying.

Joe Morrell said, "Well done, Brenda. That was incredibly brave. Thank you, this will help us get those bastards and hopefully prevent them from doing this to anyone else."

Morrell drove her back to the clinic for a well-earned rest and something to eat. Meanwhile, Croft rang DI Davies at home, quickly briefing him on the interview, without going into detail.

"Is it as good as we expected, Lily?"

"It's so much better than that, but I've got to tell you it's a hard watch. It's scarcely believable what these people have done to her. The poor woman has lost everything; money, friends, job and, most of all, her self-respect."

"Will she make a good witness?"

"I think so, but if we can play the video in court, I can tell you there won't be a dry eye in the place."

"Right, Lily, go home and get some rest. We're briefing the whole team at 9am tomorrow, so we can decide the way we move this job forward. I'll want you and Joe to summarise the story as I don't propose to show the tape to everyone. There's no need at this stage, and we will only refer to her as witness Bravo for now."

"Are you worried about leaks?"

"Not really, but it's happened before so why take a chance?"

When Joe returned, both he and Lily hit the pub for a much-needed and very welcome drink or two.

FORTY-EIGHT

Monday was set to be a very busy day for many people in both Wales and West Yorkshire as Operation Dingo kicked into action and enquiries into the kidnap of Mary Ross intensified. For one man, it would continue to be a tale of seemingly unending horror.

Cooper and his associates had spent all of Sunday at their new base in the motel endlessly studying videos from the various cameras along the route from Pickering to Leeds, both from the Friday drop and from previous days. Whilst their objective had been to find where the Fiesta and the Mondeo had gone, they had discovered so much more.

To be totally honest, Cooper had not spent much time working at the screens as he didn't really have the necessary skills for the technical work. His area of expertise was somewhat different, perhaps best described as the more physical aspects of their job. He had spent most of the day in deep discussion with Andy, trying to plan for the various situations they expected to face over the coming days. Other than that, his job was to ensure that the technicians, Mark and Tony, were kept fed and watered.

Having moved into the two motel rooms, they would need to take their laptops and phones with them whenever they went out. It would be a nuisance, but the alternative would be to leave at least one of his men there at all times to protect their specialist equipment, which could leave them shorthanded. It wasn't the best, but it would have to do.

In view of their findings from the cameras, it was going to be necessary to speak to Amy Clark again, but he wanted to wait until the afternoon when, hopefully, they had got Wade's safe deposit box open.

As the TARIAN briefing was about to begin in Swansea, a thoroughly cowed Richard Wade was being transported to the Magistrates' Court.

Detective Superintendent Dai Williams was the first to address the assembled men and women who would work on Operation Dingo, most of whom were police officers but some were civilians with specialist skills.

"Some of you may be aware that Lily and Joe have been looking into suspected fraudulent licences being issued at the DVLA. Thanks to the work of these two officers, it has now been established that over 200 such licences have been created and distributed. It is clearly the work of organised criminal gangs with potentially serious repercussions. I don't need to tell you that they could be used to facilitate people trafficking and any number of crimes where a fake identity needs to be established. We have a witness prepared to give evidence in court whose identity is known to only a small number of people. To ensure that remains the case, the witness will henceforth only be referred to as Bravo to ensure, primarily, their safety but also a successful outcome. Lily will now give you a brief update of the conversations with Bravo before we allocate tasks to you individually. Already, I can tell you that I think we will spend some time travelling up and down the country on this job."

As he sat down, Lily Croft rose to her feet. Although she knew all those present, some very well, she was nervous. This could be a big moment in her career, possibly leading to greater things.

"I cannot hide the fact that Bravo is female as would have soon become clear once you hear her story. I can tell you this woman has been used, abused, intimidated and assaulted several times, both physically and sexually. It is a horrifying story, illustrating how truly evil these men and, in some cases, women are and how important it is that we put a stop to their activities."

The two speakers had certainly gained the attention of the assembled group, who listened intently as Lily outlined Bravo's story to a shocked and silent audience. Beginning with the squash injury and her developing dependence on OxyContin to deal with the pain, she quickly moved on to the illegal supply of the drug by Dr Parker and Dr Reynolds. When they were informed that she was forced to pay both men with sexual favours, there were some muttered comments from the group and many heads shaken in disbelief.

She held her hand up for quiet, explaining that the story would only get worse. She next told them how, when the doctors withdrew supplies, Bravo was referred to the dealer

Marco who demanded cash and when she could no longer pay beat her. Finding out that she worked at the DVLA, he saw a business opportunity and involved other criminals. She was forced to create the fraudulent licences by these men, who soon increased their demands which, initially, she was unable to meet. Once again, she was beaten and her OxyContin supply withdrawn, forcing her into the hands of a street dealer who prostituted her to pay for drugs.

By now completely under the control of these organised criminals, she made over 200 licences, greatly aided by a lack of control at the DVLA, especially during lockdown. She would often meet people at hotels to carry out the transactions, making her particularly vulnerable to intimidation and assault. In the last few weeks, she had been physically attacked by one particular man who humiliated her before forcing her to have oral sex with him.

The assembled officers had heard many similar stories over the years, but none quite as bad as this, especially as it involved a previously innocent, hard-working woman who had been used and manipulated in such a brutal fashion.

Lily wrapped her part of the briefing up. "Unfortunately for these people, Bravo had risen to a senior position at the DVLA, entirely by her own efforts, and is certainly no fool. She is not your usual addled drug addict and was fully aware that at some stage her actions would be discovered. That being the case, she gathered evidence along the way, keeping copies and photos of every driving licence she made, photos of her own injuries and, vitally, samples from those men who forced sex on her. Everything is dated with locations and items supplied. It is now our job to follow this evidence and to bring these people down."

Ds Croft sat down as DI Davies, who would manage the investigation on a day-to-day basis, told them all to have a break before he allocated the various lines of enquiry to individual officers.

Once they returned, individual officers were assigned different tasks with the exhibit officers providing the information and evidence they needed. Particular attention was to be paid to the two doctors and Marco, whilst others would try to identify what was described as a huge man who was instrumental in organising the supply of licences.

Croft and Morrell would focus on the man who had raped Bravo in the hotel room by forcing her into oral sex. Obviously, they had photos of him from the three licences he had obtained but didn't know his real name. However, Bravo indicated the photo on the licence for Peter Webb was how he looked when she had dealings with him. There was also potential DNA from the tissue she had preserved in a plastic bag which would hopefully confirm who he was. An expedited DNA result could be obtained from the forensic laboratory if a premium was paid, but it was not considered necessary in this case. It was usually of benefit in reducing the time and man hours spent investigating an offence but, in this instance, it was not considered worth paying extra to have the samples fast tracked for analysis as this was clearly going to be a protracted inquiry anyway, which would need to take its own course. The same clearly applied to the condom Bravo had recovered from Dr Reynolds. There was much to do.

On the jobs-to-do list was a full forensic examination of the hotel room where Bravo had been attacked. Unfortunately, it proved to be a fruitless exercise as, despite the best efforts of the team, no useful evidence had been recovered due to the room having been cleaned and serviced so many times in the intervening period. The video system had also been recorded over, and none of the staff remembered either the man or the woman.

A number of civilian support staff were tasked with entering details of all the fraudulent licences onto the Police National Computer, emphasising that where they came to the notice of police officers, no action was to be taken other than notifying the Operation Dingo incident room. In addition, they sought instances where they had already come to police notice.

As Operation Dingo was fully swinging into action, Richard Wade appeared in the Magistrates' Court represented by his solicitor, Ken Wilkinson. In normal times, Wade's appearance would have been a media sensation, but an arrangement had been made with the press to maintain a news blackout whilst Mary Ross was still missing.

For some reason, Wade had believed he had a chance of being granted bail, a forlorn hope in view of the serious nature of the charge against him and the ongoing police enquiries. He was remanded in custody to Armley Prison pending an appearance at the Crown Court.

As he was led from the dock, Wade's plaintive cry of "I haven't done anything" was ignored.

Having been informed of the outcome of Wade's court appearance, Amy Clark was quietly pleased with the way things were proceeding, except for the obvious exception of the still-missing girl. Her good mood didn't last when she saw an incoming call from Cooper on her mobile.

"Hello."

"Amy, I need to see you. We've uncovered some stuff that may be very useful to you."

"What is it?"

"It's much easier if we meet."

"Okay. Same place, 2pm."

"Have you got into the safe deposit box yet?"

"Just getting the court order now."

"You do remember that if there is any money, I may be able to identify it for you?"

"See you soon."

Cooper admitted to Andy, who had been listening, that it was not the warmest conversation he had ever had.

When Clark arrived at the café, Cooper was waiting at the same corner table with his pot of tea. He politely stood as she joined him at the table.

She spoke first. "What have you got for me?"

He badly wanted to ask about the safe deposit box but decided that he might need to generate some goodwill first.

"I know your people will be on this, but this might give them a head start. My tech guys spent all day yesterday looking at videos from the street cameras in an attempt to find the blue Fiesta and the grey Mondeo. Long story short, they managed to follow the Fiesta to the mid-stay car park at Leeds Bradford Airport. Wade can be clearly seen to get out of the car with a heavy holdall which he took to the one and only Mondeo a few rows away. He messed about in the boot before heading into the airport terminal with a red suitcase which he took into the public toilets. He never came out."

"I can tell from your smug expression that there's more. Go on."

"We checked everyone who came out of the toilets in the half-hour after Wade went in, finding one man who we were unable to identify as having entered the toilets. Conclusion, Wade changed his appearance and clothing. The second man was dressed in holiday-style clothing with a black suitcase. Best guess is that he had the black case inside the red one and that it had the ransom money in it. We tracked him to the bus for Leeds city centre, which is as far as we got. Hope this helps."

He passed over a number of photographs showing the vehicles and Wade, all timestamped.

"We would have got there, you know."

"Yes, I do, but glad to help. So what about the safe deposit box?"

"We got the order and opened the box earlier. Their systems clearly showed Wade as the user of the box, with his last visit being on the day of the cash drop. We found £5,000 in fifty-pound notes."

"That ties in with him getting the bus to the city centre. That just leaves £395,000 to find. I wonder where that is."

"If you think that you are able to identify the money, you will have to come to the station. If I had brought it here, I would have been breaking all the rules and especially the chain of evidence."

"Okay, let's go."

As they left the café, Cooper gave a barely visible hand

signal to Andy, who had once more recorded everything, to stay where he was.

Cooper was given a pair of disposable gloves prior to examining the one hundred banknotes recovered from Wade's safe deposit box. After ten minutes, he confidently pronounced that they were from the ransom money. The only other person present in the interview room was Amy Clark, who, after a speculative look, nodded in his direction.

"Go on then, tell me how."

"Forty-two of these polymer notes are forgeries. Half of all the fifties in the ransom were forgeries. It was the only way we could have any way of identifying the money without disobeying Sir John's instructions. Believe you me, it took some arranging."

"How can you identify them so positively?"

He took two of the notes, placing them in front of her.

"This is a genuine note. If you look at the picture of the Queen, she is wearing a necklace with three beads on the left side of her neck. The forged note only has two beads. The forgeries were seized as part of a huge operation involving a foreign power who wanted to destabilise our currency, but, as you can see, they made a fairly basic error. It is believed their thinking was that while the new notes were harder to forge, it was probably easier to slip them in under cover of the newly issued notes. It was similar to something we tried to do to Germany during the Second World War."

"Well, Cooper, I've got to say, you must know some very interesting people."

He made no comment.

Having recovered the money, Clark showed him from the building with one last remark.

"Stay in touch."

Cooper smiled, assuming they were once more on friendly terms, for now at least.

Returning to her office, Amy quickly arranged to meet with Adrian Gregson and Ben, when she informed both men of her meeting with Cooper. They were somewhat surprised, with Gregson expressing doubts as to how they would be able to use the evidence of the forged notes in court. Especially as Cooper would not appear as a witness. Maybe they could use someone from a bank, he speculated.

Connor was clearly annoyed, expressing his irritation at having to follow the lead from these men, who, as far as he was concerned, were unaccountable and unofficial. He didn't seem to grasp that they could only act the way they did with official sanction. No matter; it was what it was.

They discussed the seizure of the two cars from the airport car park and the necessary forensic examination which would follow; another task for Connor. They would also need to attempt to find the abandoned case, something which would eventually prove fruitless.

The three officers discussed further options in the search for Mary Ross without developing any new ideas or plans before the meeting broke up.

Having waited all day in the cellblock at the Magistrates' Court, a fearful Richard Wade was finally loaded into the minute compartment in the transport vehicle for his short trip to Armley Prison. Just about six weeks since Miles Kingston had been released from the same place, Wade heard the exact sound that his nemesis had heard. The loud clang as the prison gates were closed behind him, the difference being that Wade was to be confined behind those high walls, not walking to freedom. When was his nightmare going to end?

FORTY-NINE

Miles Kingston thought it was a huge joke to meet his date in the same restaurant where Natasha had first ensnared Wade in their web of deceit, plus it was close to the apartment should his plans for later come to fruition. It was bang on 7.30pm when she walked into the Al Dente restaurant wearing a low-cut and ridiculously short black dress with very high heels, which showed off her excellent legs to great advantage. As she got closer, he could see she had made some effort with her carefully arranged blonde hair and skilfully applied make-up, which covered some of the small wrinkles on her face. All in all, she was more than acceptable, having emphasised her best assets.

He hadn't expected this much when, still posing as Peter Webb, he had rung her at the estate agent's office earlier that morning to arrange the date. His hopes and expectations soared for later.

"Jean, it's great to see you, especially looking so lovely."

He took a chance leaning forward to kiss her on the cheek, and was more than pleased when she did not resist his advances.

"Not looking too bad yourself, Peter. What happened to the moustache?"

"Oh, it was itching a bit, that's all. So it had to go, at least for a while."

As they sat, a waiter appeared with the previously ordered bottle of red wine and two menus.

"I hope you like Italian food, Jean. I've not been here before but it was highly recommended by a friend of mine. She said the food is excellent."

"I love Italian food. It's my favourite, Peter. I hope it's as good as your friend said. It certainly looks the part."

As they had their first glass of the wine, they ordered their starters and main course from the extensive menu. The food was soon served and was indeed excellent.

By the time they were halfway down the second bottle of wine, they were having a wonderful time, with Peter telling his risqué jokes and her responding with hilarious stories about her customers.

Brandies soon followed, with her declining a dessert, making the usual comment about having to watch her figure. He, of course, responded in the traditional manner by telling her that he had no problem watching her figure himself. Somewhat merry, she smiled happily at the compliment, placing her hand over his.

Miles couldn't believe how easy it was.

"Jean, would you like to have a nightcap at my apartment? It's just round the corner."

Slightly slurring her words, she answered, "Have you forgotten I rented the apartment to you? I know where it is, and a nightcap sounds like a lovely idea to me."

Quickly paying the bill, he took her arm as they left

the restaurant. Once outside, he stopped and took the opportunity to kiss her full on the lips without resistance from the slightly unsteady woman. His luck was in.

Within minutes, they were seated close together on the sofa with a drink each and his arm around her shoulders. A heavy petting session soon followed, with Jean's dress almost disappearing to reveal even more of her shapely legs.

Not a man to hang about, especially when he thought he was onto a winner, he put his hand on her leg, sliding it further up her thigh as they breathlessly kissed. To say he was surprised when he felt a hand on his, halting further progress, was something of an understatement. Not a man to be denied, Miles attempted to continue his efforts, believing she was just playing hard to get. When she pulled back from their kissing and pushed him away, he realised she was not messing about and really did want him to stop.

Reluctantly controlling his emotions and rising anger, he stood up.

"What's the matter, Jean? I thought you liked me."

"I do, Peter, I like you a lot, but it's just a bit soon for me. I hope you understand."

All was not lost. "Sorry, Jean, if I was going too quickly for you. It's just that I really do fancy you. Look, let's have another drink and I'll get a taxi to take you home. How's that?"

As she tried to straighten her clothing, Jean smiled nervously but remained confident in her ability to keep her amorous date at bay as she had done so many times before. "That sounds good."

"Gin okay?"

She nodded. "I just need the loo first."

As she disappeared to the toilet, Kingston poured her a gin and tonic, adding the special ingredient left behind in the bedroom drawer by Natasha. Having seen how the Rohypnol had worked on Mary Ross, he had no doubts that he would soon be in bed with the reluctant estate agent. He didn't see any problem really; it was clear to him that she wanted it but was playing hard to get. Did you see the dress she was nearly wearing, for Christ's sake? All he was doing was helping her out. Besides, he'd spent a bloody fortune on her tonight. She owed him.

Jean woke from a deep sleep filled with strange dreams, or was it nightmares? Opening her eyes with some difficulty, she saw a smiling Peter Webb standing over her whilst he shook her shoulder vigorously. What was he doing here?

"Come on, you slapper, you've had your fun. It's time for you to be leaving."

Realising that she was naked in a strange bed, with no recollection of how she got there, Jean could only stare at him. She was so thirsty it was hard for her to speak anyway.

He pulled the covers from her in an attempt to hasten her removal.

"Come on, for fuck's sake. I've got things to do."

Ineffectually trying to cover herself with her hands, she managed to blurt out, "Did we? Did we... you know... last night?"

"We certainly did. It was great and you really enjoyed it, but you do scream an awful lot, don't you?"

She reluctantly sat up, pulling a sheet in front of her in

an attempt to hide her embarrassment. "I need a shower first, please."

"Sorry, Jean, you've only got time for the toilet. You're late for work anyway."

Totally lost, all she could do was nod dumbly. She stood up, almost falling down when she bent over to pick her clothes up from the floor before staggering towards the bathroom. As she got to the bedroom door, he pulled the sheet from her grasp before slapping her so hard across her already sore bottom that she gasped in pain.

"Just thought I'd have a final look, and I know how much you like being spanked."

Miles Kingston was clearly not a man interested in long-term relationships.

Minutes later, after using the toilet, the still-confused woman found herself in the corridor outside the apartment, not exactly dressed for the day, particularly as her knickers were in her handbag. She had no idea how they had been ripped. Staggering down the stairs and onto the pavement, she was mortified when she saw her appearance in a shop window, sure that everyone would know what she had been doing, even if she didn't.

Beginning to feel lots of aches and pains, Jean used her mobile to ring a taxi, managing to keep control until she was behind her own front door, when she broke down into almost uncontrollable tears.

FIFTY

Miles Kingston didn't know what to do next, really wishing he could speak to Karl Smithson for some much-needed advice. He had no one else to turn to. He had no family, apart from the witch who called herself his mother, whilst his own nature and criminal lifestyle meant he had no close friends. Certainly, there was nobody he could trust.

Deep down, Miles knew that he should have left Leeds already, probably the country even, but for some reason was reluctant to do so. He had the money to go wherever he wanted, so why not? Fully aware that the police would be hard at it, especially once the girl's body was found, he would have to make the move soon or risk arrest. It would have to be this week or probably never. It did cross his mind to question if he really wanted to leave and if he had the balls to start over in a foreign country.

Had he known how the net was beginning to close, the kidnapper would have already been on his way to Hull for the ferry to Europe. Instead, he went back to bed.

In South Wales, the Organised Crime Unit were

making considerable progress. Details of all the fraudulent driving licences had now been entered onto the Police National Computer with some pleasing results. Firstly, at least two of the men using the licences had been deported as a direct result of their criminal activities. Others had come to police notice, but because the licences were issued by the DVLA and, on the face of it, legal, no action had been triggered.

However, the biggest and most exciting breakthrough so far had been in discovering that the man using the licence in the name of Richard Wade was in custody charged with kidnapping by West Yorkshire Police.

Another entry showed that James Adamson had been stopped by a police officer in North Yorkshire. That meant that two of the three licences obtained by the animal responsible for raping witness Bravo had come to police notice.

As the licences were processed, it had quickly become apparent that there was a very strong Yorkshire connection as over forty of the licences had addresses in that area of the country. Unsurprisingly, none of the names were of anyone with prior criminal convictions, although some had since managed to be convicted of offences, usually of a fairly minor nature, though.

There was perhaps another, although flimsy, connection to Yorkshire. The huge man who threatened Bravo had spoken with what was described as a northern accent.

Several licences were also for women, most of whom seemed to have Eastern European-sounding names, raising thoughts of potential people trafficking. A great deal more work would be needed to establish if these licences had been used for other purposes, perhaps to open bank accounts or obtain passports. That would necessitate another line of enquiry with the Passport Office, checking for matches between passports issued and the licences in the last two years.

The inquiry was snowballing, perhaps beyond TARIAN's ability to cope with it, raising the possibility that it may become a countrywide investigation managed and run by the National Crime Agency. In the meantime, they would plough on, with visiting their sister unit in Leeds a priority. The man using the name James Adamson was their number one target, both because of what he had done to Bravo but also because he was a potential lead to those behind the whole driving licence scam.

The two doctors identified by Bravo had already been arrested by separate teams, who had found sizable amounts of OxyContin in the homes and offices of both men. Interviews were imminent. There was a limit to what the team could manage, so both Marco and the street dealer had been passed to the Drug Squad to deal with. They were keeping observations with a view to firming up evidence against the men and identifying the best time to strike. Marco, of course, was undoubtedly a key witness against the men at the centre of this criminal enterprise.

Clark and Connor had their own breakthrough to consider, although they were far from sure what it meant and if it helped or hindered their case.

The result of Wade's phone analysis was in. The technicians had found nothing of great evidential value in the case they were building against the former policeman, but potentially information that could help him.

Firstly, they had managed to find the picture of a stunningly attractive blonde woman, perhaps the one Wade had insisted he was with at the time the kidnap was taking place. Several calls were identified as having taken place about the time Wade had claimed that he was in contact with the woman. They had managed to identify what was believed to be her number. Richard Wade's phone had not been used from the Wednesday evening until Friday late afternoon, remaining static in Leeds city centre during that time, which would tend to support his account. Nothing else of value was found.

The officers were somewhat confused. Did it mean Wade was telling the truth when he claimed to have been with the woman whom he believed to be a reporter, or was it just an elaborate alibi? It was not a total surprise that his phone had not been used as the kidnappers were known to have used burner phones, but why was it left in Leeds?

That raised two more actions for the inquiry team. Find the apartment Wade claimed to have stayed in, but where to start? They had not had much success so far. Next, trace the phone and hopefully identify the blonde woman.

At something of a loss and desperate for anything to give the inquiry a boost, Clark reluctantly made a call to Cooper, who was more than a little surprised to see that she was ringing him. Perhaps they were working together after all.

She quickly updated him on the information about Wade's phone but was forced to admit there was little else going on at their end. The forensic examination of the two cars recovered at the airport had yielded nothing of great value, only a few smudged unidentifiable fingerprints. It looked as if the interiors of both vehicles had been wiped down. They had, however, found the cloned number plates in the boot of the Fiesta, confirming that it was the one used to transport Mary Ross. The Mondeo still had cloned plates on, with the real ones in its boot. They were desperately attempting to find where the cars had been prior to being dumped at the airport, hopeful that it would help to find Mary but with little success so far.

After thanking her, he passed on his own news.

The phone manufactures had been in touch, having managed to identify where two of the phones had been sold. The good news was that both shops had CCTV systems, but the bad news was that quality was crap. They had managed to get pictures of what they believed to be the same man, buying both phones. However, the pictures were so poor that, even after being enhanced by Mark, a positive ID was impossible and certainly would be of no use in court. They were not confident that they would get any more information about the other phones. It was looking like a dead end.

One possibly significant piece of information was that one of the burners was about as little as you could buy, being small enough to conceal in the palm of your hand or, perhaps, internally. Cooper observed that he really didn't know why anyone would need such a tiny phone unless they needed to conceal it for some reason.

Having carried out numerous prison enquiries, Amy told Cooper that, in her experience, they were often smuggled into prison for use by the inmates, who could more easily hide such small phones. She admitted that she had no idea what it meant, but perhaps it was something to bear in mind.

After admitting that you learnt something new every day, he promised to drop the pictures off at the station, before ending the call.

They both needed something to spark the inquiry into life.

FIFTY-ONE

Kingston woke early. At first, he was confused as to where he was, but the smell of decay and the gloominess told him that he was back in his old flat. So he had come full circle, but at least he was a lot richer and about to leave the country. Or was he? Miles was still not really sure why he hadn't left already.

He knew he'd done the right thing in abandoning the posh apartment the night before, having suddenly realised that the stupid slapper might decide to involve the police after their busy night. He didn't really think she would but decided to play safe. He hoped this would be a safe bolthole for no more than a couple of days. He just needed to stay away from his mother.

He might have thought differently if he knew that Jean Cook was in a Police Station at that very moment making a report of what had happened to her.

Two officers were facing the nervous woman across the interview-room table, trying to put her at her ease.

The female officer spoke first. "Okay, Jean, I understand you want to report a rape. Is that correct?"

"Yes, it is, but I'm not sure what happened or if it is even rape. I'm not sure now."

"Why don't you tell us the story and we'll take it from there. Just take your time."

She nodded. "I went on a date with a man on Monday night. We went to a nice Italian restaurant and had a really good time. He seemed so nice."

"Where did you meet this man?"

"At work. I'm an estate agent."

"So tell us what happened."

"This is where it gets very difficult for me. We were getting on great, so I went back to his apartment with him. It wasn't far away. He made some drinks and we sat on the sofa together. We were kissing and everything was good, I was enjoying it. I think he got the wrong idea, though. Maybe I shouldn't have worn such a short dress."

The other officer stepped in. "Look, Jean, whatever happened, it's not your fault. So please tell us what he did."

"He put his hand on my leg and started to work his way under my dress. I pushed his hand away, but he tried again. Just for a second, he looked really angry when I stopped him the second time, then he said we should have another drink before he got me a taxi. It was a gin and tonic he made while I was in the toilet."

The first officer spoke again. "Keep going, all in your own time."

Jean took a deep breath before answering. "This is the problem. I can't remember a single thing until I woke up the next morning in his bed. Or I should say he woke me up, but he had changed, he was really nasty."

"So why do you think you were raped?"

Clearly embarrassed, the woman was reluctant to answer at first, but did so eventually. "Well, I was naked in his bed and I'm very sore down there, if you know what I mean. I'm covered in bruises and I've got some bites on me as well. I've tried to cover it with make-up, but you might be able to see a bruise on my cheek. The other thing is, when I was getting dressed, my knickers were torn. I had to go home without any."

The female officer put her hand on Jean's hand. "Jean, I've got to ask this and it is important. Did you consent to sex with this man at any time?"

"How can I have done? I didn't even know it was happening."

With that, she broke into tears, causing the interview to be temporarily halted.

When they resumed, the officers were delighted with the information that Jean was able to give them, including that she knew where the apartment was as she had actually rented it to her assailant. The scene of any crime was crucial in gathering evidence and establishing the truth of what had happened. They were even happier when she told them that the man was called Peter Webb and that she had a photocopy of his driving licence with a clear picture of him, although she did remember to say he had shaved off his moustache.

Unfortunately, it would transpire that there was no record of this man, certainly not with a criminal history, and the previous address he had provided in Keighley would also prove to be false.

Despite Jean having bathed several times since the offence, she was subjected to a full medical examination on the off-chance that her assailant's DNA could be found. As well as that, photographs were taken of her numerous bruises, some of which appeared to be grip marks on both her upper arms. Her buttocks bore several, what can best be described as, angry red wheals, as if she had been struck with a cane or possibly some flex. She had clear bite marks on both breasts and her inner thigh.

Both the officers, who dealt with this type of offence on a daily basis, were shocked by the severity of some of the injuries sustained by Jean and could only wonder what sort of man they were dealing with. More importantly, why hadn't he come to police notice before?

Later that afternoon, they would go to the apartment in an attempt to arrest Peter Webb, who had of course left. Using the keys provided by his victim, they were able to enter and ensure a full forensic examination was made of the property. Amongst all the evidence they recovered was a green cane of the type used to support pot plants stained with what appeared to be blood. No doubt it was the cause of the injuries to the poor woman's buttocks.

Having been unable to locate him, Peter Webb was circulated on the PNC as wanted for rape.

Constantly updating the PNC on the fraudulent driving licences and the people named thereon, the South Wales team quickly became aware of the West Yorkshire Police interest in Peter Webb. That meant all three of the licences supplied to Bravo's rapist were currently in use in Yorkshire.

Superintendent Williams quickly decided that Croft and Morrell should travel to Leeds the following day, indicating that he would contact someone he knew stationed in the Organised Crime Unit there.

When Williams rang Amy Clark, he told her very little, only that they had a major operation underway which may impact on her own ongoing enquiries. Busy as she was, Amy was intrigued and readily agreed to meet his officers.

FIFTY-TWO

Wednesday was proving to be a very busy day for everyone.

Cooper's men waited patiently as he spent fifteen minutes on the phone with someone from the Bank of England before he was able to tell them what it was about.

"Well I never. Right, boys, it looks as if the trick with the forged notes has come up trumps again. A fairly large amount has been paid into a local bank not too far from here. We need to go and have a look."

Andy spoke up. "Look, Coops, we've known you long enough to know that, judging by the smile on your face, they told you something else."

"Well, would you believe some of the money was paid in by our good friend Charlie Newton and some by the bookkeeper for a company called Harris Holdings. Now where have we heard the name Harris before?"

The laughing group packed up and headed off for the bank, glad to finally get a positive lead to follow up.

An hour later, Cooper and Andy once more entered Charlie's office, having confirmed he had paid in over a thousand pounds to the bank, 600 of which was in forged notes. He was not pleased to see them.

This time, Andy led. "Charlie, this is the third time we've had to come here and, I've got to tell you, we're getting pissed off. We expect quick honest answers to the questions we are about to ask you, and if not, we may become even more annoyed. Do you understand?"

Completely cowed by the calm, threatening manner these men displayed, he could only nod.

"You paid some money into the bank late on Friday afternoon. Where did you get it?"

Relaxing after such an easy question, he replied confidently. "Takings, of course."

The car dealer never really saw Andy move but certainly felt the pain of the blow to his mouth as blood splashed onto his shirt front.

"Shall we try again? Where did the money come from?"

Charlie might be frightened of Harris and Jimmy, but the immediate threat was in front of him. He had to survive this before he could begin to worry about them.

"George gave me the money and told me to pay it in."

"That's better. So who is George?"

" He's the bookkeeper."

"Who does he work for?"

"Mr Harris."

"Would that be Harris Holdings?"

"Yes."

"Last question. Where do Harris and George hang out?"

"At the betting shop."

Cooper stepped in. "All right, Charlie, I'm glad we managed to sort this without any further unpleasantness. I really do hope, for your sake, we don't have to come back. We will, though, if we find out you've made any more phone calls when we leave. Goodbye."

Back at the car, the other two men confirmed that, on this occasion, no phone calls had been made. Time to talk to Harris.

Cooper walked into the betting shop alone, although he was wearing a concealed microphone enabling his three associates to hear everything whilst they waited outside. The room was empty apart from a scruffy man standing behind the counter who was, as usual, engrossed in his newspaper. He completely ignored the new customer.

"Tell Mr Harris I'd like to speak to him, please."

"Don't know no one called Harris."

"Listen, dickhead, I suggest you get on the phone and tell Mr Harris that Charlie Newton sent me."

The man picked up the phone and had a short muffled conversation with someone.

Minutes later, a very large man with a face like thunder entered the shop from a door at the back of the premises. He was very tall, very wide and looked a right handful. This must be the Jimmy he had heard so much about. He looked around the room, beckoned Cooper over and indicated that he should go into a short corridor revealed by the now open door. As he entered the corridor, he was not surprised to feel a hand on his back pushing him against the wall, where he was rapidly and expertly patted down. Cooper went with it, deciding that you needed to pick your fights carefully, and this was definitely not the time, nor was such a confined space the best place to challenge the immensely strong man. Needless to say, nothing was found as, expecting something like this, he had taken the precaution of leaving his automatic with Andy.

Jimmy pointed to an office at the end of the corridor where Miles Kingston had been such a frequent visitor. Once inside, he saw Frank Harris for the first time, sitting behind his desk. As Kingston had discovered, he looked anything but a gangster, more like a provincial bank manager.

Harris went through his usual routine. "Take your clothes off."

"Now why would I do that?"

Harris looked surprised to be disobeyed and furthermore to be questioned. "I don't talk to anyone I don't know until I make sure they're not wired. I like my conversations to stay private."

Cooper couldn't help smiling, which seemed to irritate Harris even more. "Well, that's all sorted then. Of course I'm wearing a wire. So no need for a search."

Relaxed but ready, Cooper expected a reaction and was not disappointed. He saw a slight twitch of the man's eyebrow and heard the creak of a floorboard behind him. Having positioned himself where he could see a reflection of Jimmy in the glass of a picture on the wall behind Harris, he moved rapidly.

Stepping slightly to his left, Cooper spun round quickly on the balls of his feet before driving the point of his right elbow into the monster's nose as hard as he could. Jimmy stopped dead as the crack of the cartilage in his nose breaking sounded loudly across the room. He stood still, clearly surprised and confused, with copious amounts of blood and snot running down his front, unable to see because of the tears in his eyes. He did not go down.

Cooper had used his elbow as it concentrated all the energy of the assault in one small area, causing maximum damage. It always amazed him that people risked breaking the delicate bones in their hand by punching the hard bone of the face and head. Stupid.

With a complete lack of compassion, he closed once more on Jimmy, this time clenching his right fist but with the knuckle of the middle finger protruding slightly to once more focus the impact on one small point. Putting as much power as he could into the blow, he punched the helpless man in the left side of his throat. The pain was instant as his neck jerked to one side, causing possible cervical damage; however, far more dangerous was the immediate swelling to his windpipe, making his difficulty breathing even worse. Still he did not go down.

Cooper, who was wearing heavy work boots, had had enough by now. Moving forward once more, he stamped just as hard as he could with his full weight behind it on the outside of Jimmy's left knee, forcing the joint to bend inwards at an impossible angle. Accompanied by some more loud cracks and cries of pain, the leg gave way completely, rendering it incapable of bearing Jimmy's weight. He fell to the floor like a felled oak tree, unable to move and probably unable to ever walk again without assistance, so severe were his injuries.

The trouble with Jimmy was that for many years he had relied on his size and strength to intimidate people and, where that failed, to overpower them. Whilst Cooper was a muscular and athletic six feet one tall, he was still dwarfed by Jimmy, fooling the thug into believing it would be situation normal. He had never come across anyone as well trained, competent and totally ruthless as Cooper so was unable to recognise the threat he posed. Bad mistake.

Having seen a suspicious bulge in his jacket earlier, Cooper bent over and removed an automatic pistol from the now stricken minder's pocket. He quickly ejected the magazine and the cartridge from the chamber before dropping all the items into a wastepaper bin.

Turning to face Harris once more, he was not surprised to see that he was holding a handgun pointed in his general direction. A completely unruffled Cooper took the seat in front of the desk.

The stunned crime boss could not believe what he had seen this man do in the previous few seconds, because that was all it had taken for him to dispatch his enforcer without appearing to break sweat.

Cooper shook his head ruefully. "There was no need for any of that, was there? All I wanted to do was talk and now you have lost Jimmy. By the way, you might want to get him an ambulance. I don't think he's getting up anytime soon, do you? You can put the gun down as well."

"Why should I?"

"Well, if you shoot me, then you're not going to find out why I'm here. However, it would be in your own interests as the people listening to us are just across the road and, believe me, you really do not want to meet them. I can tell you they think I'm a bit of a pussy and not really tough enough for this business, but they, trust me, certainly are."

Recognising the implied threat in Cooper's words, Harris, without further comment, put the weapon into the top drawer of his desk, knowing if things went wrong he'd never get it out again in time.

He picked the phone up quickly, dialling a number. "Charlie, get round here with some of your boys and something to carry Jimmy out on. He's had an accident. Then you'll need a vehicle to take the useless piece of shit to our doctor friend."

Minutes later, Charlie and his crew arrived to load Jimmy onto an old door before carrying him out with some difficulty and not too carefully. All were amazed at the state of him and his agonised cries, but no one commented as they averted their gaze from Harris and his visitor. The truth was that none of them felt much sympathy for Jimmy, all of them having felt his wrath at some time or other.

"So what is it you want?"

"Well, firstly, I'm here to tell you that you've got quite a big problem."

"So what would that be?"

"Would you be surprised if I was to tell you that a lot of the money paid into the bank on Friday by Charlie and your bookkeeper was forged? I don't suppose you'd be very happy that it's now forfeit either."

"Of course I'm bloody surprised. You don't think I'd be stupid enough to pay forged money into a bank if I knew, do you? I suppose you know how that happened."

Cooper nodded, wondering how much to tell this man. He reasoned that if you wanted to get something, then you had to give something.

"Yeah, it was me. I arranged to have the forged notes used as part of the ransom for the return of a kidnapped girl so we could hope to track the money. Well, it worked a treat. The question now is how did it get into your hands?"

Harris controlled his temper as he got on the phone once more, instructing George to bring some of the £50 notes.

"So you're to blame then?"

"Only indirectly. Are you involved in the kidnap?"

"Are you fucking kidding?"

A very nervous George entered the room, bringing several samples of the notes. Cooper spread them out on the desk, showing them the difference between the genuine and the forged notes.

"Considering how the money came to be in your possession, I think you need to give me all the fifty-pound notes, forged or not, don't you, Mr Harris?"

Getting angrier by the second, Harris instructed the hapless George to gather all the money he had received on the previous Friday, accompanied by a warning that he would deal with the man later. He was not only down the fifty grand of his own money which he had advanced to Miles Kingston but he had also lost the expected fifty grand profit. Somebody had to take the blame.

"So what now?"

"Well, I suppose the big question is if you weren't involved in the kidnap, where did you get the money from?"

"You know I can't tell you that, not now anyway. I need to speak to some people first."

"Do you know a man called James Adamson?"

Harris answered truthfully for once. "Never heard of him."

"Okay, fair enough. I think you are angry enough to want revenge on whoever brought this shit down on you. The police don't know about you yet, but they could, of course, become involved."

"I've got the message. Give me a phone number and I'll be in touch."

As Cooper wrote down his name and the phone number, he had some final words for Harris.

"Mr Harris, I mentioned revenge earlier. I understand you might want to seek revenge against me and my associates, but I must caution you against such thoughts. You might possibly win, but only at a huge cost. Trust me; it would not be worth it. Lastly, I think you should know that the girl was kidnapped over a week ago and, despite the ransom having been paid, she has still not been returned. I'm sure you can draw your own conclusions. I should also tell you that my employer has given me very explicit instructions on how to deal with the kidnappers should she have come to any harm. I believe that includes anyone involved, no matter to how limited a degree."

Harris, whilst seething inwardly, tried to remain calm in the presence of this man, at the same time considering what he would do to Kingston and Smithson when he got hold of them. They had to pay, both for the money they had cost him and the shit they had got him into. Frank Harris could not afford to be taken for a fool by anyone; he had a reputation to maintain. For fuck's sake, what had possessed the two idiots to get involved in the kidnap, and probably murder, of a young girl? What really bothered him, though, was the people he had to explain this cock-up to, so soon after having to inform them that their valuable source at the DVLA had been lost. They were not going to be happy. Having the stink of failure on you was not good in his line of business.

Finally, he nodded in acceptance to Cooper, who had been waiting patiently.

Taking the bag of fifty-pound notes with him, he left the office without further comment, returning to the three men waiting in the car, immediately asking them if the bug he'd fixed under the gangster's desk was working ok.

Tony replied. "Yeah, he's just finished kicking the shit out of that poor bastard George, and now he's on the phone talking to somebody called Alteo. Another name, Roel, has been mentioned, and so have you."

"Make sure we get a tape of this phone call. As usual, edit me out of it. Let's hope he doesn't find the bug."

Andy was unable to resist temptation. "Coops, I was really surprised it took you three goes to put Jimmy down. Maybe you're losing your touch or you are a pussy after all."

The rest of the crew, including Cooper, burst into laughter, even more loudly when he replied.

"Yeah, well, you lot better not bank on it."

When they counted the money later, it totalled £95,000, including that recovered from the bank. There were a sufficient number of genuine notes for Cooper to keep their fee. The rest would be returned to Ross, with the forgeries being returned to the B of E.

The amount handed over by Harris certainly raised eyebrows in Cooper's team as they questioned exactly what service he had provided to earn such an amount.

FIFTY-THREE

Miles Kingston was fed up of being stuck in this stinking flat, not being able to go out or to get himself some female company. He still couldn't stop fantasising about Natasha and had been sorely tempted to contact her. Realising that would be too risky, he had finally made up his mind that it was time to leave, fearing the net was beginning to close. First, he had to get his money and passport from the safe deposit box.

On top of everything else, he still worried that, eventually, Frank Harris would find out that he had been played for a fool, certain he would be far from happy and that swift retribution would follow.

It was getting late, but he decided there was time for one more drink before bed. He had not managed to take a sip from the glass when a phone started ringing. Believing he had disposed of all the burner phones, he was somewhat confused when he became aware that the noise was coming from his haversack. He was even more perplexed when he saw it was Karl Smithson ringing.

Reluctantly answering the phone, he heard that familiar voice.

"Hello, Miles, I thought you weren't going to answer."

"I did think about it."

"Funny man. You know you can't ignore me, Miles. I know too much."

"I know you played me along just to get back at Richard Wade, so now I've got to run before the police or Harris get to me. I'm going tomorrow."

Maintaining a reasonable tone, Smithson answered. "Don't be stupid, Miles, you knew what you were getting into. Yeah, I got what I wanted, but don't forget you got a lot of money out of the deal. Anyway, you can't go tomorrow, I need a favour."

"Fuck off."

"Stop pissing about, I haven't got much time. One word from me in the right ear and you'll never get out of the country, certainly not in one piece. I want you to see our friend that bent screw Collier on Saturday morning at the same place as before and bung him a grand, five hundred quid for services rendered and the rest so he can buy some stuff for me. I've got people to pay."

"Come on, Karl, I can't wait that long. Once they find the girl's body, they'll soon make the connection to me. It's only Wednesday now. I can't risk another three days."

"Miles, you owe me and this is the final payment."

Knowing his co-conspirator well, Kingston was sure that he would carry out his threat without a moment's hesitation. Why hadn't he gone already?

"All right, Karl, I'll do it, but remember, if I get caught, the police just might find out you were involved."

"Please don't threaten me, Miles. I don't like it. I've got thirty years left to do inside, so it's not much of a threat, is it?"

"Okay, I'll do what you want. What exactly did he do that's worth five hundred quid?"

"That's the good bit. He got himself an overtime shift on the remand wing where our friend Wade is currently residing. All he did was go missing while a couple of lads had a chat with that bastard."

"So what happened?"

"They were supposed to be cleaning, but they got into his cell and the old pool ball in the sock did the rest. They slashed him up a bit as well."

"Is he dead?"

"No, he's in the prison hospital, but he's not bad enough to go to hospital on the outside. I don't want him dead yet, I'm going to have some fun with him first. It was just a taste of what's to come."

"Jesus, Karl, remind me not to cross you."

"Just do as I ask and we're all square."

With that, he ended the call.

A despairing Kingston cursed himself, firstly because he hadn't got rid of the burner phone as he had intended and secondly for not having got out before now. He poured himself another large drink, having rapidly gulped the first one down during the worrying conversation with Karl. He might not be leaving yet, and on top of that, he now had to risk going out to get some more cash.

He was starting to see his future life not on a sunny beach somewhere but in a place of high walls and steel doors.

FIFTY-FOUR

Detective Superintendent Clark had certainly had better Thursday mornings.

First was a call from Armley to tell her that Wade was in the prison hospital, having suffered a fairly severe beating. So far, they did not know who was responsible, and although they were making enquiries, it was not expected that the offenders would be identified. At this stage, she had no reason to believe Wade had been attacked for any other reason than that he was a former police officer.

Next was a meeting with Ben Connor and Gregson for an update on the Mary Ross kidnap. Basically, they had hit a brick wall and were getting nowhere. They had made no progress in identifying the blonde woman on Wade's phone or any of the numbers on it. They had been reduced to using the cameras covering the city centre to trace the movements of both the Mondeo and the Fiesta, which appeared to show Wade shopping at various places. One minor success was a sighting of the blue Fiesta heading in the direction of the village where Wade lived. Unfortunately, due to a shortage of cameras, it could not be proved the car had actually gone to his address. Did that mean it was the blue car that picked Wade up on the night of the kidnap? They had, so far, been unable to establish that the vehicle had returned to the city, but were working on it.

Once again, the three officers speculated as to whether Wade had acted alone or with an accomplice. They had no doubt he was responsible for kidnapping Mary Ross, with or without help. At this stage, it appeared they were going to struggle until Mary was found, alive or dead. They all agreed that they needed a miracle if they were to progress this case, and, as pressure was coming from above, it needed to be sooner rather than later.

Even Cooper, when he rang, had nothing to report, having decided to keep his meeting with Harris and Jimmy quiet, which in turn meant he could not tell her about the recovered ransom money.

To round off her morning, Amy called Sir John Ross with an update on their progress, or lack of it. As always, he was very subdued but remained gracious, thanking her for the update and the efforts of her team. Unintentionally, he made her feel even worse.

At 1pm, the miracle Clark yearned for walked into her office in the form of Ds Lily Croft and Dc Joe Morrell. She welcomed them warmly and, after introductions all round, they sat at her conference table making small talk until the coffee order was delivered.

"Let's get started if you're ready. Dai Williams tells me you have some information to help with our current enquiries, and God knows we need it."

Croft smiled a little nervously. "We hope it will, ma'am, but there may be a lot more to it than that."

She was intrigued as to what could be considered more than a kidnap and possible murder inquiry.

"Let me get someone else in here."

Following a brief phone call, Ben Connor entered the room minutes later and a further round of introductions took place.

"Okay, when you're ready, Lily."

"I assume that you know the South Wales Regional Organised Crime Unit is known as TARIAN, so if you don't mind, for ease, that's how I will refer to us."

Confused by the name, Connor asked an obvious question. "I'm sorry, why TARIAN?"

"It means shield in Welsh, a name that I believe speaks for itself, so I am sure you can understand why we have adopted it."

As Connor nodded his understanding, Croft continued. "Recently, we unearthed a major breach of security at the DVLA where we have identified an employee who produced in excess of 200 fraudulent driving licences. I must stress this woman is a victim, who has been treated appallingly by ruthless men from organised crime groups. At the moment, we are feeling our way forward carefully, but we believe there may be international connections. We have called this inquiry Operation Dingo, with our witness identified only as Bravo for her protection."

A clearly impatient Connor butted in. "It sounds as if you've got a lot on, but where do we come in?"

Morrell took his turn. "One of the first things that became apparent, even though we haven't been on this for long, was a strong Yorkshire connection, and we believe it's even possible that the whole operation is being run from this area. For instance, over forty of the driving licences have been produced with addresses in Yorkshire. We also know you have a man by the name of Richard Wade remanded in custody on a charge of kidnapping and have circulated another man by the name of Peter Webb as wanted for a rape. We believe the same man is responsible for raping our witness Bravo."

Clark stepped in. "Shit, I don't like the way this is going. I don't know anything about this Webb bloke or a rape inquiry, so, if you don't mind, let's take a break while we get somebody in here who does."

Half an hour later, they resumed the meeting, having been joined by Ds Helen Riley, who was supervising the ongoing rape inquiry. Once she had been brought up to speed, the story continued.

Ds Riley confirmed that Peter Webb was being sought in connection with the rape of an estate agent in the apartment she had rented to him, but so far he had not been traced, nor did he appear to have a criminal record. Having brought the file with her, she triumphantly placed the driving licence photo on the table at the same time, describing him as a nasty bastard who, it was believed, may have used a date rape drug before being extremely violent towards the victim.

A grim Joe Morrell took the same photo from his own file, placing it next to the one on the table before explaining that the licence was fraudulent and had been created by Bravo. He then placed photocopies of Richard Wade's driving licence and the licence in the name of James Adamson bearing a photo of Richard Wade next to the others on the table. He told them that all three fraudulent licences had been produced at the same time by Bravo at the behest of the man known only as Webb. He went on to tell them what this man had done to Bravo and exactly what a dangerous man they believed him to be.

Clark and Connor looked at each other, both with stunned expressions and sinking feelings, whilst they wondered why this man had these driving licences. Just to put the icing on the cake, Morrell remembered to add that a man had been stopped near Pickering who produced the James Adamson licence as proof of his identity.

Clark looked at him. "Yes, we know about that. The Adamson driving licence has been used as proof of identity when buying vehicles, including the grey Mondeo he was driving when stopped."

A thoughtful Clark picked up all the photos, studying them carefully. "The question for me is why has this man had three driving licences made, none of which appear to bear his real name?"

No one replied.

Clark turned to Connor. "Did we recover Wade's driving licence?"

"I believe so, ma'am, because he used it when buying the cars from Bargain Motors, or so we believed."

"My worry now is that maybe someone is trying to set Wade up. If so, why? If that's the case, we've fallen for it hook, line and sinker. We have to find out one way or another, and quickly. Dear God, was he actually telling the truth?"

DI Connor spoke up. "Don't forget that Pc Johnson, who did the stop and check of the Mondeo, has confirmed that Wade was the driver using the Adamson licence,

362

so perhaps it's more a case of conspiracy than of Wade being innocent. Clearly, it wasn't him who obtained the fraudulent driving licences, so maybe if we find that licence and Bravo's rapist, it will help identify exactly who else is involved. Surely with the evidence we have, it's impossible for Wade not to be involved."

"We need to find out and quickly, Ben. This is getting more confusing by the minute."

Keen to make what he considered to be a telling contribution that he hoped would put the blame firmly on someone else, a scowling Connor responded. "If only that idiot Johnson had had the sense to check the driver out properly, we may already have had him in custody, preventing a kidnap and a rape. If nothing else, he should have at least seized the fraudulent licence. Bloody useless uniforms!"

Sitting back, with a smug expression on his face, Connor was satisfied that he had deflected any future blame onto the wholly innocent Pc Johnson.

Instantly recognising the Detective Inspector as a 'Teflon man', one who was always able to make sure that nothing stuck to him, Dc Morrell couldn't stop himself from defending the maligned Pc Johnson, a man he had of course never met.

"Sorry, sir, but I think I should point out that these licences, while fraudulent, are not something created by some backstreet forger. They are in fact real licences produced at the DVLA but with false names and photographs. You would have to know they bore false details to identify them as fraudulent, so, to all intents and purposes, they are real licences. I don't believe that officer could have done more than he did, and at that time he certainly had no grounds to seize it."

Clark quickly raised her hand to prevent a clearly annoyed Connor from responding, at the same time suggesting they should move on.

Croft threw a warning glance in her colleague's direction, before sliding another photograph across the table. "Sorry, I almost forgot this picture. It was taken on a doorbell camera at Bravo's home. It's a bit grainy but if you know this man, it may be clear enough to recognise him. He speaks with what is described as a northern accent and appears to have been the man who intimidated the woman into producing the licences in such a large volume. We also believe he may have been responsible for supplying some drugs."

After one glance, Clark spoke quietly. "Oh shit! That's Jimmy Scoular. I'd recognise that evil bastard anywhere."

A surprised but pleased Croft responded. "Sorry, who exactly is Jimmy Scoular?"

"He's the minder-cum-enforcer for the local Mr Big round here, Frank Harris. This is getting complicated. As a matter of interest, why did you say TARIAN's inquiry may have international connections?"

"Many of the names on the licences are what appear to be foreign names, and at least two people in possession of fraudulent licences have been arrested for criminal offences and later deported. We believe the spectre of human trafficking and drug dealing may be raising its head."

"That fits with what we already know about Harris. He is believed to be connected to other organised criminal gangs, but we've never got anywhere near him."

Amy Clark turned to Helen Riley. "How far have you got with your enquiries?"

"Well, as you know, we've circulated Webb and are awaiting the forensic results from the apartment in the hope we'll get his real name. Enquiries at the block where the apartment is have got us nowhere other than, I suppose, somebody mentioning he had a grey car in the underground car park. We did think we had struck lucky with the security system in the apartment block, but it turned out the cameras hadn't been working for weeks."

It was all starting to tie up together.

"Right. Get on to the forensic people to organise an expedited examination of all the samples from the apartment. I will authorise the additional costs. Emphasise the urgency, I want them over the weekend if possible. If you'll go and do that now, please, Helen, and not a word to anyone about what you have heard today."

Once she had left, DI Connor spoke. "Ma'am, I'm sure you remember that Bargain Motors is run by Charlie Newton, but it's actually owned by Frank Harris. Buying and selling cars is a good way for him to launder money."

So they were beginning to identify the links between the suspects and the crimes they had committed. However, they still needed to establish exactly who had done what and why.

All four officers still present at the meeting agreed that Peter Webb was central to everything and was the key to unlocking so many of their problems. He was connected to both rapes, to Richard Wade, maybe even to Frank Harris, and was possibly an accomplice in the kidnap of

Mary Ross. Finding him may lead to them finding the still-missing girl.

Before leaving, Lily Croft summed up the situation for the Yorkshire officers.

"Our witness has been supplied with OxyContin by two doctors, both of whom demanded sexual favours in return. She was then passed to a drug dealer who took most of her money before he latched onto the driving licence scheme as a way for her to pay for supplies. This is where Jimmy became involved, demanding further licences from her, and when she objected, her drug supply was cut off. They passed her to a street dealer who prostituted her to pay for drugs. After that lesson, she made more of what they demanded, sometimes meeting customers in hotels. Often, payment was made in drugs and money. We believe Jimmy Scoular was probably supplying the referrals to Bravo, the drugs to the doctors and the dealers while collecting cash. Which of course leads us back to Frank Harris and whoever his associates may be. As you can see, this is evolving into something massive, especially now we add your offences to the mix."

The TARIAN officers returned to Wales, having gained important information, made useful contacts and ensured close cooperation would be maintained. They had agreed that the Leeds kidnap and rape enquiries would progress as normal, but that no moves would be made against anyone else until a coordinated large-scale operation could be mounted against all those involved. At least they had saved some money by not seeking an expedited examination of Kingston's semen left on the tissue so carefully collected by Brenda. Clark's team were going to pay for that, which meant he would be identified soon with the results, no doubt matching theirs when eventually received from the laboratory.

On the drive home, Lily Croft couldn't help thinking, with considerable regret, that had they carried out the semen examination sooner, their unnamed suspect may already have been in custody, saving Jean Cook from her ordeal at his hands. Hindsight was a truly wonderful thing. She returned to Wales even more determined, if that was possible, to put the evil bugger behind bars as quickly as possible.

Once everyone had left, Clark went to see her boss, Adrian Gregson, updating him on the afternoon's events. He was not a happy bunny, telling her to get it sorted and to be bloody quick about it.

"Amy, this is turning into a right shitshow, and, if we don't sort it now, when it hits the fan we'll all end up covered in it."

Making no reply, she left his office.

FIFTY-FIVE

Other than not being able to get a job anywhere else, Robert Grundy didn't really know why he had opted to become an estate agent. He supposed that was the same reason why he kept doing it, even though he hated the job and was pretty useless at it.

Take today. He had barely got sat down before his boss started on about the farmhouse let, demanding to know when the next instalment of the rent was going to be paid. Having failed to get a response from James Adamson on either his mobile number or the farm's landline, he was told, in no uncertain terms, to get up there and find out what was going on.

It was a hot day. He was sweating, stuck in traffic and generally fed up with his lot. He reasoned that it couldn't get much worse and at least he was out of the office, away from his boss. Unfortunately for him, Robert Grundy would soon find out that things were about to get much, much worse than he could ever have imagined.

The first thing he noticed as he finally pulled into the farmyard was that there was no car parked there. Heaving himself from the driver's seat, Robert approached the front door and saw there was some sort of black material across the front window of the house. He supposed it was for privacy whilst Adamson was writing his book, bit odd, though. He was not surprised there was no response to his knocking.

Having no choice, he reluctantly took the spare keys from his pocket and nervously unlocked the door. As he opened the door, he started to announce his presence when his shout was choked off as a dreadful smell from inside hit him. Almost gagging, he took a step back, gulping in some fresh air. What an earth had James Adamson been doing? Surely that smell wasn't from cooking, although he guessed it could be from food gone off.

Holding a handkerchief across his mouth, Grundy tried again, walking hesitantly along the short hall before opening the door to what he remembered was a downstairs bedroom. As he did so, the smell seemed to get even worse, undoubtedly made so by the window being covered up, which also ensured the room was almost totally dark.

Reaching for the wall switch, he turned on the ceiling light to reveal the most horrifying sight of his life when he saw what was clearly the body of a young girl on a bed. A fundamentally decent man – he was unable to explain later how he managed to do it – Robert approached the bed believing the girl might need some help. He never got anywhere near, before he realised that she was dead and that the smell was emanating from her decomposing body. Before he turned to run from the room, he noticed what looked like a chain attached to her wrist.

He'd seen these scenes on television true crime

reconstructions and had never been able to understand how the flies got in, but they did, and this room was no exception as they buzzed angrily around the girl's body.

On reaching fresh air, Robert Grundy was promptly and understandably sick.

He knew what he had to do. He was opening the car door before remembering that it was no good getting his phone when there would be no signal. He thought about using the landline in the house, but nothing on earth was going to get him back in there.

He quickly drove down the lane to the main road, turning left back towards Leeds, stopping at the first lay-by he came to. Ironically, it was the very same spot from where Miles Kingston had sent his first message to Sir John Ross, using Mary's phone. Grundy managed to make the 999 call to the police, reporting what he had seen and telling them where he was now. Within minutes, when he heard the first sirens, he was getting out of his car to meet them.

Having led the first two police cars to the farmhouse, Robert waited outside in his car as two officers entered the building. Fully aware that it was a crime scene, neither officer went any further than the bedroom door, looking in to confirm the presence of a human body. Having done so, they left as quickly as they could, anxious to get back into the fresh air, before the Sergeant used his radio to pass a number of messages to the control room. He confirmed the suspicious death of what appeared to be a female and the exact location, requesting the presence of CID and scenes of crime officers.

The Pc stood guard at the door whilst the Sergeant did

a full circuit of the building. Satisfied that the house was secure, he returned to the front where he tried to calm the agitated estate agent, asking why he had come to the property in the first place.

Whilst other staff were contacting the required personnel, the Control Room Inspector, who, because of their position, was aware of the kidnap inquiry, rang Amy Clark to inform her of the discovery.

"Ma'am, it's the Force Duty Officer. I'm sorry to tell you we have a confirmed report of what appears to be the body of a young girl. Officers at the scene say that she appears to be chained up. The scene is being preserved and SOCO are on their way."

"Oh shit! There may be an explosive device in the building so pull everyone back to a distance of at least one hundred yards immediately. Can you arrange for the bomb disposal people to attend, and please make sure no one else enters the building until it is declared safe. I'll get my team together and we will attend immediately. I stress no one goes in without my authority."

The call was ended by the other officer with a final frosty comment. "That would have been nice to know sooner. We could have lost some officers today."

Clark realised she had made a serious error by not having previously made sure the Duty Officer was aware of this possibility, only being able to put it down to the secrecy surrounding kidnap inquiries. Still, it was a bad mistake which could have had serious repercussions.

Having been given the location, Amy updated C/Supt. Gregson before gathering several officers, including DI Connor, and heading off to take charge of the crime scene.

It was four hours before the scene was declared safe to enter. An imitation explosive device consisting of a dog collar with plastic boxes and wires affixed had been found, matching that which the girl had round her neck on the first ransom text.

Shortly after the bomb disposal team had left, Amy and Connor, wearing full protective equipment, entered the bedroom. Despite their masks, the smell was almost unbearable as was the heat and presence of the swarms of flies. They were able to say, after only a brief glance, that it was almost certainly the body of Mary Ross, noting the chain shackling her to the wall by her wrist just as had been seen on the kidnapper's photo. They did not linger.

The SOCO team went in to begin a preliminary examination of the scene, leaving the body alone until the pathologist had attended. With Connor in charge, Clark left, knowing she was the one who had to deliver the news to John Ross, not something she was looking forward to. Still, that was why she was paid the big bucks.

Once she was able to get a signal, Amy Clark rang Cooper.

"We've found Mary."

"I know. I'll meet you outside Sir John's."

Not bothering to ask the mysterious man how he knew about the body or that she was heading to see the girl's father, she broke the connection. Logically, his men were probably monitoring police radios, and it was usual for the senior investigating officer to inform families of these sort of developments personally. At least she hoped it was as simple as that; otherwise, it would mean he had sources within her force, something she didn't want to think about.

She may have been much less sanguine about things had she realised that Cooper's specialist companions had the ability to track her phone's movements and were, in fact, doing that now.

The police officer was not surprised to see that Cooper was waiting outside the house; she was getting used to him being ahead of her. They went to the door together, where they were admitted by a tired-looking housekeeper, Mrs Richardson. She took them to Sir John's study, where the grey-faced man was unable to hide his apprehension at their joint arrival.

Amy did not mess about; her experience being that bad news was bad news no matter how you delivered it.

"Sir John, I'm sorry to bring you the worst possible news. We have found the body of a young girl, and, although no formal identification has yet taken place, I'm sure it's your daughter. I'm very sorry."

The millionaire businessman slumped into his chair with tears running down his face. He had everything that money could buy, and yet he was now a man who had nothing.

"How did she die?"

"I'm sorry but we don't know yet. I will try to get an answer for you as quickly as we can. You should be aware that the press will be on to this fairly quickly, and, because of your history, it will generate a great deal of interest. I am arranging for a Family Liaison Officer to be with you for a while. The FLO will keep you up to date with what is happening and help you deal with the press and anything else you may need."

"Thank you. If it's all right with you, I'd like to speak with Mr Cooper alone, please."

Somewhat surprised, Clark nodded and left the two men alone.

"Mr Cooper, did we do anything wrong?"

"I don't think so, John. My feeling is that Mary was probably murdered before we even handed over the cash."

"In that case, I definitely want you to carry out the instructions I gave you previously. Are you still okay with that?"

"Absolutely, John, we already have things underway."

"Will the police be a problem?"

"I don't think so. We have access to sources who will not deal with them, so, in terms of information, we are some way ahead of them."

"What about this man Wade they have in jail?"

"John, there's something not right about that, and I'm far from certain that he is actually involved. I hope to get confirmation in the next couple of days. I will keep you informed, but it may well be that you won't see me again. I'm sure you understand that once the job is done, we will need to make ourselves scarce."

"Thank you for everything, Mr Cooper."

He stood, reaching out to shake hands with Cooper, who promptly turned and left the room, leaving the grieving father to his memories.

Amy was waiting for him outside. "What the hell was that about?"

Cooper had to think quickly. "First, he wanted to know if he would get the ransom money back and then he terminated my employment."

"Really? Well, he may get it back, who knows? I can't say I'll be sorry to see the back of you, though. Maybe you aren't quite the hotshots you thought you were, and things may well have turned out differently if you had involved the police sooner. Goodbye."

She returned to her car and drove off without a backward glance. He had intended to broach the subject of Harris and his man Jimmy but was glad he hadn't bothered. Her disdain for him was obvious, and clearly they were not working together anymore. On reflection, he probably would have found it difficult to explain how he had established their connection and even more so if he tried to explain Jimmy's little accident.

Cooper sat in his own car reflecting on how nice it was to be popular; he really must try it one day. Time to get moving. Whoever they were looking for would soon learn that the girl had been found and, if they weren't already, would be on their toes pretty damn quick.

In an attempt to get moving, he rang Harris.

"Who's this?"

"Cooper."

"How the fuck did you get my number?"

"Does it matter? You've got bigger problems than worrying about that shit. The girl's dead."

"So why are you ringing me?"

"Come on, Frank, you know why. Who did you get the money from?"

"I still have to speak to someone. I'll let you know tomorrow morning. Okay?"

"Don't let me down, Frank, or things could get nasty."

On his way back to the motel, Cooper was acutely aware of just how tight time was becoming, and if he didn't get there before the police, carrying out Sir John's instructions would prove difficult; not impossible but much more difficult. Whilst he didn't underestimate the police, he knew they were constrained by rules that he did not have to abide by. That was his advantage and he fully intended to use it.

Meanwhile, the police were doing what they do, carefully gathering evidence, in the first instance to identify the offenders and then to mount a successful prosecution. That started with a close examination of the farmhouse by the scenes of crime officers, who, following the pathologist's attendance and removal of Mary's body, were able to carry out their work.

The preliminary findings were that Mary had been manually strangled and had probably been dead for over a week. Both opinions would later be confirmed by the autopsy and examination of the insect life inhabiting the girl's body by a forensic entomologist. Briefly, that would be done by identifying the development stage of the bugs recovered from the body and by knowing how long it took to reach that level from when the eggs were first laid.

With that knowledge, combined with the details of the cash drop and subsequent movements of the offender, it was concluded that the girl had probably died within no more than two days of the kidnapping.

Having authorised the extra cash for expedited examination, numerous items were recovered from the scene and sent to the laboratory where, hopefully, fingerprints and DNA would be identified. Some documents had been found, including tickets for admission to the car park at Leeds Bradford Airport, where Wade had been seen on camera to leave the Mondeo and Fiesta.

Some receipts would also show Wade had shopped for some of the items found in the farmhouse, including the mock explosive device that had been around Mary's neck.

Earlier in the day, Robert Grundy had taken investigating officers to the estate agent's, where he was able to produce the tenancy agreement with a photocopy of the driving licence in the name of James Adamson but the photograph of Richard Wade. Everyone remembered that was the driving licence produced to police by the man driving the grey Mondeo near Pickering.

Now Mary had been found, Clark needed to decide how soon to interview Richard Wade further because, of course, he was now the main suspect for her murder. On the face of it, the weight of evidence against Wade was almost insurmountable. She couldn't remember a case where so much evidence had existed against one suspect, especially where it appeared that so much careful planning had taken place beforehand. It was unbelievable that a former police officer, even one as poor as Wade had been, could have been so stupid. The connection between the evidence unearthed by TARIAN and the offences in West Yorkshire was, at this stage, unfathomable. It was hoped the forensic evidence from both the farmhouse and the rape scene would identify the connection, if any existed, and especially enlighten them as to who Peter Webb was and how Wade fitted in.

She couldn't help but remember Cooper's suspicion that it was all too easy.

Whilst the police worked long into the night, the man in question and his team made sure of a good night's sleep, in anticipation of a busy weekend.

FIFTY-SIX

When the early-morning phone call woke Frank Harris, he knew instantly who it was. After all, very few people had his home number. He answered it immediately, trying to sound confident.

"Frank Harris."

"Good morning, Harris. This is Alteo."

"I've been expecting you."

"Quite so. Since you rang me yesterday, I have spoken to Roel at home and I should tell you that he is not impressed with what is happening in Yorkshire, or with you."

"Everything is under control."

"That is not how it appears to us, Harris. In the last few weeks, you have lost the money you used to support this idiot Kingston and somehow lost our source at the DVLA. That alone could cost us a great deal of money. If the police are involved, many of our people will be in danger of arrest and worse. It is not good."

"My information is that she is not talking to the police, so we should be okay."

"If only it were so. Our information is different. We need to cauterise this wound as soon as possible, which will be your job when we find her."

"Yes, I can do that, Alteo."

"Can we be sure of that? By the way, how is Jimmy?"

"Not good. He won't be any use to us in the future."

"Another serious error of judgement on your part, it would seem, Harris."

"I've told you I can sort it."

"Who are these men you wish to tell about Kingston?"

"I don't know who they are, but they are seriously scary bastards. I do know they're not the police."

"Roel has authorised you to give them Kingston and this other man. No more mistakes. You may be getting visits from the police, especially now the girl has been found murdered. Be ready. Remember, we will be watching closely."

The phone clicked off.

Harris was sweating profusely as he wondered why he had ever let himself become involved with these Albanian thugs. He had always thought of himself as ruthless, but these people took it to a whole new level. How the hell did they know the girl was dead? He'd only heard it himself yesterday.

Needing to move, and move quickly, Harris rang Cooper, arranging to meet him in his office at ten that morning. As he showered and dressed, he worried that this whole thing was beginning to spin out of control and all because of that pair of pricks Smithson and Kingston, not that the Albanians would see it that way.

Bang on time, Cooper entered the betting shop and

was promptly shown through to the inner sanctum without the need for any searches. They were partners now, or a better description might be uneasy bedfellows drawn together by necessity. Before taking a seat in front of the desk, Cooper lifted his top to show that he was not wearing a wire whilst he waited patiently for Harris to make the first move.

He slid a large brown envelope across the desk. "In there, you'll find a picture of a lowlife by the name of Miles Kingston and a second picture of him in disguise as someone I don't know. I understand he wanted the pictures in order to obtain driving licences. I've included the only address I've got for him. He's the man who paid me in funny money."

"Why did he pay you?"

"Because I advanced him the money to finance the job, but I didn't know it was a kidnapping or he would never have got my backing."

"That was a bit remiss of you, Frank. Anything else?"

"Yes. He planned this job with a man called Karl Smithson, who's currently in prison for murdering a police officer."

"What's his interest?"

"No idea."

"Thank you. Hopefully, we won't need to meet again."

With that, Cooper returned to the car where Mark confirmed that everything had been successfully recorded by the bug they had previously planted. He instructed him to make a tape of the conversation as soon as they got back to the motel. Harris had been really careless, almost like he was not paying attention. Perhaps he had other things on his mind, which raised the question of whom Harris had needed to speak to before he could give them the information. Even more reason for Cooper to be careful. They may be very good at what they did, but it was as well to remember that there were some very nasty people out there.

Taking the photos from the envelope, he saw a clear image of the man who, unknown to Cooper, was using the name Peter Webb. The second one was clearly of Richard Wade, which matched that on the James Adamson driving licence. The team started to realise what was happening and how the kidnap had probably been carried out by Kingston masquerading as Wade. The disguise was more than good enough to fool most people.

There followed a debate between the four men as to whether the police, specifically Amy Clark, should be told of their discoveries. They concluded that the only benefit would be to get the falsely accused Richard Wade released from prison, and it would probably make it harder for them to carry out their instructions from Sir John Ross. They decided to wait.

As it was the only address they had, all four men drove to Miles Kingston's flat, hoping it was still his address and that he was still there. They had only been there for half an hour when an instantly recognisable Kingston walked along the street and into the house. They saw that he was minus the moustache he was sporting in the photo, but there was no doubt it was him.

Cooper couldn't understand why the idiot hadn't done a runner already, but there was no accounting for these people. He obviously had no idea that Miles had been to his safe deposit box before going to give a grand to

Collier as instructed by his ex-friend Karl Smithson, with a further important call to make later.

"Right, this is the plan. We can't risk doing anything here, at least not yet. Andy, you and Tony stay here to keep an eye on our man in case he runs. We'll go back to the hotel so Mark can do the tape while I find us another car. We'll be back to relieve you later unless you call us in the meantime. I'm pretty sure the police won't have anything together before Monday, so we've got a small window of opportunity to finish this. Everyone happy?"

Receiving three nods, he and Mark left on foot.

Cooper was absolutely right. The police were treading water whilst they waited for the forensic results, which were unlikely to arrive before Monday. In the meantime, it would be a case of trying to reconstruct the story of the kidnap and murder, establishing as accurate a timeline of events as possible. They still did not know the connection between Webb, Adamson and Wade except that the latter two appeared to be one and the same person. Hopefully, all would soon become clear.

The store receipts found at the farm did open up another line of enquiry, with officers visiting the various premises named on them. One from B&Q related to the chain and some other items found in the house, and, as it was timed and dated, they could view the relevant video tapes. Sure enough, they showed Richard Wade purchasing the items for which he could be seen paying in cash.

Significantly, in a pet shop, the man they still believed to be Richard Wade was seen purchasing a dog collar, once again paying in cash. Video tapes in other outlets repeated the same story.

FIFTY-SEVEN

Cooper and Andy returned at 9pm in a nondescript hire car. Rejoining the other two, Cooper was quickly updated on the day's events.

"He went out again, Coops. We did the usual, me on foot and Tony took the car. As it turned out, it was a good thing we did. Kingston had a large holdall with him and went straight to a car hire place. He came out in that red Nissan parked over there. Silly bugger never looked round once. This is where it gets really interesting."

"I know you're enjoying yourself, Andy, but is there any chance you could speed things up?"

Smiling broadly, Andy continued. "Yeah. He drove to a safe deposit box company and went in with the holdall. He was out after about fifteen minutes and the holdall was obviously a lot heavier than when he went in. If you ask me, it's probably the ransom money and he's going to run."

"Anything else?"

Tony chipped in. "Nothing he's done, boss, but we managed to put a tracker on the car, so we should have no trouble following him."

"Good job. I think you're right, especially since the discovery of the girl's body has hit the news. He must have heard it, so it's odds-on he's going to go. The big question is when and where? You must be right about the money as well. He would hardly leave it behind, would he?"

Cooper and Mark took the night shift, keeping observations on Kingston's flat, whilst the other two returned to the motel to catch up on some much-needed sleep. You never knew about these things; it could go on for days, even weeks, but that seemed highly unlikely in this case.

At 6am on the Sunday, after an uneventful night, Andy and Tony returned to relieve the two men. Long used to such surveillance operations, the two of them had taken it in turns to catnap but, nevertheless, returned to the motel for a rest. Cooper had told them all that he fully expected something to happen today so would be back before 1pm unless they contacted him sooner. He also told them that he would be emptying the motel rooms and paying the bill, hoping today would be their final day on this job. He did not intend to return if he could help it.

Cooper's men were not the only ones waiting for something to happen. The police had more or less carried out all the enquiries they could and were now stuck waiting for the forensic results. Nothing new had come from TARIAN, who were now pushing for their own results from analysis of the tissue used by Brenda following Kingston's assault on her. They were hopeful that it would give them the true identity of the man they knew as Webb, but also prove the truth of her account as it was expected the tissue would contain not only the man's DNA from his semen but Brenda's as well from her saliva.

Everyone was waiting for something, but not Miles Kingston, who had been listening intently to the radio and television reports of the girl's murder. He had decided that it was long past time for him to make good his escape, wishing he had done so much sooner. If it hadn't been for his obligation to that prick Smithson, he would probably have been sunning himself in Spain by now.

No sooner had Cooper and Mark returned than the murderer came out, carrying his heavy-looking holdall and haversack, both of which he put on the back seat of the Nissan car. Driving off, he was followed by the team, who confirmed that their tracker was working properly, enabling them to stay well behind their target. If they got too close, even he might notice them, especially if it turned out to be a long journey.

It wasn't long before they found themselves on the M62 motorway heading east to God knows where. They soon found out, however, when they drove into the outskirts of Hull, where Miles pulled onto a garage forecourt. By now on a dual carriageway, as they approached the city, Kingston's followers continued down the road where they waited in a lay-by for him to resume his journey.

What he wanted to go to Hull for was something none of the team could answer, reasoning there was not a lot there and certainly nothing if you travelled further east. Perhaps a boat from the east coast, but that seemed a little fanciful even if he had the contacts to arrange it.

Miles was an angry man determined to get back at some of the people who he considered to have manipulated him, not to mention causing him to delay his escape. Ever since he had found the last unused burner phone in his haversack, Miles had been considering whether it was worth putting it to what he believed was good use. To hell with it, why not?

Before he changed his mind, Miles quickly called the number he had entered into the phone before leaving his flat.

"Armley Prison. How can I help you?"

"I want to pass on some information about one of your officers."

"I'll transfer you now."

Another voice came on. "Senior Officer Quigley. Who is this, please?"

He remembered Quigley, a right hard bastard.

"I'm not telling you that, but if you're interested, I've got some information for you."

Having heard such allegations many times before, Quigley was never sure which he hated more, the time-wasters or those who really had something to tell him, so it was with a heavy sigh that he responded.

"All right, what do you want to tell me?"

"You've got a bent screw working there. He's probably bringing some stuff in on his next shift and you might want to check him out. He's called PO Collier."

"How do you know this?"

"Because I'm the one who pays him the money."

A little more interested now, Quigley had a further question. "So who is he bringing stuff, as you call it, in for?"

"Karl Smithson."

"Is that all?"

"You could check Smithson's cell for a phone."

"Okay. Thank you, I'll look into it."

"Last thing. Smithson paid Collier five hundred quid to go for a walk when Richard Wade got a seeing-to."

Before Quigley could say anything else, Kingston rang off.

So much for honour amongst thieves, but he didn't care. As far as he was concerned, a bent screw deserved to be grassed, and as for Karl, it was about time he found out that he wasn't the big man he thought he was. Miles was having the last laugh and would soon be sat on a beach somewhere with a good-looking woman at his side. That amused him even more as a woman was something Smithson would never have again.

Feeling very pleased with himself, he went into the garage shop where he bought some sandwiches and a bottle of Coke. Back outside, he unwrapped the sandwiches, dropping the cellophane in a nearby bin, dumping the burner there at the same time.

Neither Cooper nor his men had been able to see what Kingston had been doing in the car so were totally ignorant of his telephone call, not that they would have been bothered anyway.

The journey continued into Hull city centre where Kingston parked in a car park and walked away, dropping the keys in a waste bin as he did so. He was carrying the holdall and his ever-present haversack. Some of Cooper's team were about to deploy on foot when they saw he was heading for a nearby taxi rank, where he waited in line behind a couple of other people. He gave every appearance of being the most relaxed man in the world as he casually smoked a cigarette whilst waiting for a cab. After a short wait, one arrived, collected Kingston and drove off towards the east of the city.

Having been debating for some time what on earth Kingston could want in Hull, the pursuing team had their answer when they started to see the signs for the ferry terminal. Cursing themselves as fools for not realising what he was up to, Cooper had to think rapidly.

"Mark, get on the computer and book three tickets for today's sailing. That must be where he's heading."

Passports were not a problem; they always carried some, which were seldom, if ever, in their real names.

He then rang Andy in the other car, telling him what he had done and that he would join him and Tony in their car for boarding the ferry. They would need the car to get home from the other side. Mark would return the hire car so as not to attract any unwanted questions about why it was abandoned at the ferry terminal.

His final instruction was that Tony should follow Kingston into the ferry terminal building and stick to him like glue, hoping to hear details of his booking, specifically his cabin number. If that failed, they would need to find him on the ship, following him closely until they located his accommodation.

It took only minutes for the team's online bookings to be made, allowing Cooper to join Andy inside the terminal without delay. Still some way from boarding time, the place wasn't very busy, so the men had a clear view of Kingston, with Tony stood immediately behind him at the desk. Once he had finished, Tony took Kingston's place at the desk, asking some meaningless questions to explain his presence, before returning to his comrades.

"Deck 10. I've got the number. It's at the stern of the boat. He didn't have a booking so it looks as if you were right, boss. The discovery of the body has spooked him."

"Looks that way. We're all on 10 as well. Andy and me have got a shared cabin and we'll board with the car. Tony, you go on as a foot passenger and stay well away from us during the voyage. Hopefully, if things have gone to plan, we'll pick you up in Holland and the three of us will drive to Calais so we can catch the ferry back to Dover. If it doesn't, we won't have any option but to stick with the scumbag wherever he goes. So here's the plan."

Cooper first reminded them of the presence of CCTV cameras on the ferry, for which he had prepared some countermeasures, but they would unavoidably identify them as having been on the ship, if not exactly what they got up to. He outlined his simple plan to, once and for all, deal with Miles Kingston, without being caught. The others raised no objections, and, after Tony had taken his overnight bag and some other equipment from the car, they split up.

The three men trusted each other implicitly, having carried out a number of similar operations over many years. The whole team had complete confidence in Cooper because of his inspirational leadership and calm manner, particularly when under pressure, along with his careful and detailed planning, which was usually followed by the successful execution of their plans. Additionally, he was always prepared to take on board the views of others. However, they all knew that no plan was perfect, so an ability to adapt in changing circumstances was paramount.

FIFTY-EIGHT

Miles was feeling pretty good. He had nearly £300,000 in his bag, having recovered it from Peter Webb's safe deposit box along with his own passport. It was good to be Miles Kingston again and not have to think who he was supposed to be all the time.

He couldn't help marvelling at his own genius, completely overlooking the death of one young woman and the vicious assaults on several others. He certainly wasn't the least bit concerned about what happened to his erstwhile friend, Smithson, and that pig Collier.

Well remembering his conversations with the very scary Harris, he delighted in having shown them all that he was a man of some ability, certainly not one to be underestimated. He had successfully carried out what that smug twat had called a very complicated plan and he'd done so without receiving that metaphorical punch in the mouth.

However, Kingston believed his greatest achievement was to escape the attentions of the police, not to mention Harris and Jimmy, in such a clever way. Who was going to think of a ferry from Hull to Europe? It truly was genius, or so he thought, completely overlooking the fact that his passport details would be on record as a passenger on the ship.

When boarding later that evening, Miles would do so with a spring in his step, looking forward to his new life in the sun. He may not have been quite so happy if he had not been so totally oblivious to the presence of his travelling companions.

FIFTY-NINE

Whilst waiting to board, Cooper was pleased to see Kingston outside the terminal building smoking, simplifying his plans greatly. The second time he went out, Andy, who smoked occasionally, was sent to join him.

"All right, mate, can I cadge a light off you, please?"

With a smile, Kingston passed his disposable lighter over.

Having lit his cigarette and taken a deep drag, Andy smiled appreciatively. "Thanks, mate. Have you been on the ferry before?"

"Yeah, I have."

"Are there plenty of places you can go to smoke?"

"Plenty. Which deck are you on?"

"I think it's 10. Does that sound right?"

Kingston nodded. "I'm on 10 as well. There's a place at the back end of the ship, a bit of open deck. There's others further up, but that's a good spot. For some reason, it doesn't get too busy."

"Thanks for that, I might see you later then. I'm Andy, by the way."

Kingston shook Andy's outstretched hand, introducing himself as Miles. "Might see you on that smoking deck then, Miles. It's nice to have some company, my mate doesn't smoke."

With that, he returned to sit with Cooper, who couldn't resist a comment. "Looks like you've made a new friend. Hope you're not going to be sharing a cabin with him."

Both men laughed, but without much humour.

Andy managed to share one more smoke break with Kingston prior to boarding, hopefully building a rapport with the man, who maintained a tight hold on his bags at all times. Probably no one else would notice. Most people were doing the same, not wanting to lose their luggage.

Later that evening, by now in the North Sea, Andy approached Kingston in the bar on deck 9.

"Miles, is it? I'm just going up to deck 10 for a smoke. I know it's a bit of a trek, but like you said, it's okay up there. Do you feel like coming?"

Not a little fed up with his own company, Kingston readily agreed. There were only two people on the deck and after a desultory conversation and a couple of cigarettes each, the two men were warming to each other.

"Miles, my mate's on about an early night and, as far as I'm concerned, the boring bastard can fuck off as soon as he likes. Do you fancy a drink when he's gone?"

"Suits me. Catch you later."

Back in the bar, Andy quickly updated Cooper, who smiled grimly. "Good. I'll put Tony on standby. I had a word with him while you were out there and he tells me it's going to be a piece of piss."

Twenty minutes later, Cooper stood up, making a great

show of stretching and yawning before leaving the bar. Andy immediately joined Kingston, ordering whiskies for both of them. The time was now approaching 11.30 and the bar was beginning to thin out.

Andy looked round carefully before speaking. "Miles, you look like a man who might be a little bit more adventurous than my mate. I've got a bit of gear if you're interested, but we'll have to make sure there's nobody else on the deck with us. How does that sound to you?"

"All right by me, Andy, definitely. I like a bit of weed now and then. Now?"

Andy nodded, standing up whilst pretending to be a little unsteady on his feet. Cooper, who had positioned himself in a dark corner near to the bar, called Tony at once.

"Do it now."

Tony immediately activated whatever electronic device it was that he had with him, instantly causing the ship's entire CCTV camera system to be closed down.

"Coops, everything is on the fritz. I'll get on with my side of things."

Cooper had taken a chance in shutting all the ship's cameras down without knowing if there was anyone already on the smoking deck, but he didn't want them recording Andy heading along deck 9 before going up the stairs with Kingston, nor him following them for that matter.

Silently following the two men, he went onto the exposed deck where he saw Miles and Andy standing near to the starboard rail looking out to sea as they silently smoked. The only other man on the deck threw his cigarette end over the side before leaving, passing Cooper, who averted his face as he did so.

Time was now of the essence. Kingston must have heard something as Cooper, abandoning any attempt at silence, ran up behind the two men. It was far, far too late for the heartless criminal as Andy reacted instantly with a massive punch to his stomach. Bending over in pain and gasping for breath, Miles Kingston was unable to resist as the two men picked him up, one on either side, and, unceremoniously, dropped him over the ship's rail into the cold North Sea.

As he hit the water, Miles was unable to understand what was happening. Already struggling to breathe from the punch, the cold water drove what little breath he had left from his lungs. Not a good swimmer at the best of times, he had nowhere to go now, lasting only a few minutes as he despairingly looked for some sign of help from the ship. Unable to shout, he could only watch in horror as the ship continued on its journey, leaving him buffeting in its wake.

He died by violence, just as he had lived. Was it justice? Who knows, but he wasn't going to hurt anyone ever again. In Mafia parlance, Miles Kingston was now sleeping with the fish.

Back in their own cabin, Cooper contacted Tony.

"We're all done, what about you?"

"The cabin lock was easy. I've got the money and his other bag. I'm back in my own cabin now."

"Switch everything back on then. See you in the morning."

Cooper, who had minimal knowledge of electronics,

never ceased to be amazed at what Tony and Mark could do with all their little gizmos.

The ferry docked on time at 8.30am the following day and, having eaten a hearty breakfast, the three men linked up and set off on the four-hour drive to Calais, stopping only once to put Kingston's backpack in a rubbish bin. It was true to say that none of them appeared to be burdened by a troubled conscience; in fact, a better description of them would be that they were in rare good humour. Their only regret being that they had failed to save Mary Ross, something they knew had been beyond their control, accepting that she was already dead before the cash drop and having been instructed not to try to trace the girl by her father. It was best described as a post-operational high.

Having boarded the Dover ferry without a hitch, Cooper made a phone call.

"Ross speaking."

"Sir John, it's Cooper. We have completed your instructions to the letter. We have recovered nearly all of the money, which will be back in your bank account shortly, minus our fee and some small expenses."

"You can keep all the money. It's a job well done as far as I am concerned. How many were involved?"

"Just one. Thank you for the offer, but we agreed the fee and that's what we'll take. You won't see us again. Goodbye."

He ended the call before Ross could ask any more questions. He thought it unwise to mention to the man that Karl Smithson had planned the whole thing from his prison cell. Whilst they would have been able to finish the job, even in prison, what was the point? Locked up for a very long time, Smithson's miserable existence would only have been relieved by death. Let him suffer as he considered another failure. There was also no need to mention the forged banknotes, which had proved so instrumental in them tracing Kingston. He was sure the Bank of England would be happy to get the vast majority of the notes back, having worried about the potential damage to the British economy. Cooper had never believed that £100,000 worth of forged notes could cause too much damage but put it down to the nervous nellies at the bank panicking over nothing. Anyway, he assumed that they would be happy now it was sorted.

SIXTY

After a disappointing weekend, with little or no progress, Detective Superintendent Amy Clark sincerely hoped the meeting scheduled for 1pm this Monday would re-energise the inquiry. The results from the forensic samples sent to the laboratory were in and being scrutinised by her team, who would all be present at the meeting. It was clear the inquiry was stalled, in need of a new direction and, above all else, requiring new evidence to prove or disprove the involvement of their suspects. She had scanned the reports herself and was confident they would help to move things forward, but grey areas remained.

On entering the briefing room at exactly 1pm, she saw the top table, for want of a better expression, was full and included her deputy DI Ben Connor, Ds Ted Trace, Dc Karen Lee and Ds Helen Riley. She was a little surprised, although she probably ought not to be, to see her boss, Detective Chief Superintendent Adrian Gregson, sitting off to one side of the room, complete with a notepad and pen.

She stood before the assembled group.

"You are probably all aware that we now have the results from the analysis of the forensic samples recovered at the scenes where Mary's body was found and where Jean Cook was raped. As you know, we are fairly sure that these two offences are linked, although we don't yet know how. In addition, we strongly believe there are connections to enquiries currently being undertaken into serious offences by our colleagues in South Wales. There are many confusing aspects to this investigation which, hopefully, by the end of the day will become much clearer. At the moment, Richard Wade is on remand in Armley for the kidnap of Mary Ross, so it is essential that we establish beyond doubt his guilt or otherwise as quickly as possible. He has yet to be spoken to regarding the girl's murder, which is obviously a priority. We will discuss, as a group, the findings, hoping to untangle the mass of contradictory evidence we have at the moment. Remember, everyone here has an input, so don't be afraid to speak up. DI Connor will start us off. Over to you, please, Ben."

Connor rose to his feet, enjoying, perhaps a little too much, being the centre of attention. This was his chance to shine in front of Gregson.

"Having studied the forensic reports, we are very hopeful that they are going to help us to clarify some of the evidence we have already gathered to prove Richard Wade's involvement in these offences. I don't intend to go through all that again, only where it directly links with the new scientific evidence we have received. I'll start with the farm crime scene. We are already satisfied that the girl was murdered there and that she died fairly soon after the kidnap. We had already established that Wade had used the alias James Adamson, supported by a fraudulent driving licence, to rent the property, but we have so far been unable to prove beyond all doubt that he had been inside. We can now do that. Although there was evidence of an attempted clean-up, a glass and some cigarette ends were found in the bedroom where Mary's body was discovered. Wade's DNA has been recovered from both items, with his fingerprints being found on the glass. Unfortunately, nothing was found establishing his physical contact with Mary. Any questions so far?"

A young Detective Constable raised his hand. "Isn't it a little odd that a former police officer, who had cleaned up the scene, could be so stupid as to leave those clearly visible items behind? Not forgetting of course that he had left a bag of receipts and car park tickets as well. It looks beyond careless, to be honest."

Clark stood up. "If I may answer this, Ben. Those are good points and we are not ignoring them, but you should remember that Wade left the job ten years ago and was not a very good policeman even then. You are all experienced enough to know that no matter how clever criminals think they are, it is always their mistakes that allow us to catch them."

Connor resumed. "There is nothing else of real relevance relating to the farmhouse at the moment, so let's turn to the apartment where Jean Cook was raped. Most of you have not been party to the information we had that made us think there was a link between the two crimes. We believe we now have that link, but things are still far from clear. DNA from four people who have recently been in the apartment, the first of whom is our victim, Jean, has been recovered. Happily, there is plenty of evidence to support her account. We then have DNA from a man called Miles Kingston, who Jean has identified as the man who rented the apartment and attacked her. However, he was using the name Peter Webb and, would you believe, had a fraudulent driving licence to prove his name and former address. It turns out that Kingston is the self-same person who purchased three licences from a DVLA worker in Swansea before raping her. South Wales have just informed us of their own forensic results, which they also received today. The third person is something of a surprise to us as we have no idea why Richard Wade would have been there. It is something we urgently need to speak to him about. Our final DNA sample is from a woman by the name of Lesley Nickolay who, it transpires, is a high-end prostitute from down south. Is everyone still with me? If it's okay, I think now would be a good moment to have a smoke break for those that need it and coffee for the rest of us. There is more to tell you."

Whilst having a quick drink with the two senior officers, Connor was pleased when Gregson complimented him on the briefing, telling him that he believed a confusing story was being explained about as clearly as it could be, although he did liken it to a cheap detective novel.

Buoyed by Gregson's remarks, Connor resumed the briefing. "Right, this is where, hopefully, we can establish some of the links I spoke about earlier, but in all honesty we still do not understand them all. The South Wales Regional Organised Crime Unit, or TARIAN as they prefer, has a major inquiry running into the production of several hundred fraudulent driving licences which, they believe, are being used by organised crime groups. There is evidence of widespread drug dealing and possibly people trafficking, which is why this information must not be divulged in any circumstances. Many of the fraudulent licences have addresses in the Yorkshire area and Jimmy Scoular has been identified as the man delivering drugs to Wales, as well as giving instructions to a victim pressurised into making the licences. I am sure you have worked out that if Scoular is involved, then Frank Harris will be as well. Jimmy doesn't take a leak without the okay from Harris. It turns out that the three licences purchased by our rapist Kingston were a copy of Richard Wade's own licence, one in the name of James Adamson bearing Wade's picture and finally Peter Webb's with Kingston's picture on it. Clearly a link between Wade and Kingston, although we do not know exactly how, but we have to consider the possibility that Wade has not acted alone. Of course, most of the ransom money is still to be recovered. Perhaps Kingston has it. Looking at the photos of our prostitute, she is, without doubt, a very attractive lady, but, more to the point, it is her picture on Wade's phone, who he identified as the woman he claims to have spent time with during the kidnap. Suddenly his alibi may not be as ridiculous as we thought, but she certainly is not a journalist. So we have some links that help us, but others that might be described as muddying the waters. The tart has been arrested at her home in Essex and should be here fairly soon. I've no doubt she has had a fairly frightening journey, doing a hundred plus mph in the patrol car we sent for her. I'm hoping she will give us the information we need to finally understand what this is all about."

As he sat down, the officers all started talking at once, speculating about the information they had just been given and advancing various theories, each one more fantastic than those previous.

Another officer stood waiting for the hubbub to die down before speaking.

"One of our actions today was to follow up with that bent car dealer, Charlie Nugent, about the cars and motorcycle he claimed to have sold to Wade. He looked to have had a smack in the mouth and was unusually helpful. In fact, he changed his story completely. He now says that he was instructed by Scoular to sort the vehicles out and to tell anyone who asked that they had been sold to Richard Wade. He now says that's not true, but he didn't know the man who collected them, only his first name, Miles. It was this man who provided Wade's driving licence to copy for his records. No doubt it's this Kingston bastard, but we should be able to confirm that later with some photos."

Completely taken aback, Connor almost lost it. "Why are you only telling us this now?"

"We were late getting back because we got a statement from Nugent before he changed his mind, and as the meeting had already started, I never had the chance. Neither did I realise how significant it was until I heard the briefing."

Clark stepped forward. "Do you know what changed his mind?"

"He was pretty cagey but it would seem he had a visit from some people who scared him more than Jimmy, who, by the way, got pretty banged up by one of these men, and, according to what Nugent has heard, Harris will need a new minder. Apparently, Jimmy is probably going to need a wheelchair for the rest of his life."

There were gasps of amazement from some of the other detectives who had dealt with Jimmy Scoular in the past and were fully aware of what sort of man he was and exactly what he was capable of.

Looking at the officer, Clark had a sinking feeling in her stomach, knowing full well who Nugent was talking about. She looked at the officer, hardly daring to ask but knowing she must.

"Nugent works for Harris and I'm sure he wouldn't dare to cross him, Jimmy or no Jimmy. There are plenty of other thugs available, so what else did he say?"

"Well, ma'am, it was a bit odd. He sort of dropped it into the conversation that he didn't think Harris would mind, almost like he'd been given permission to talk to us, but he didn't know who these men were. Oh, there's one thing more, he gave us the name of a number plate maker he recommended to Miles, something I'll follow up later if that's okay with you, ma'am."

Thanking the officer, Clark closed the briefing, informing everyone that they would be further updated once Nickolay had been questioned.

All she could think was that they may have the wrong man in prison, wondering if he had been set up, but how and why? She was clearly not the only one thinking that, judging by the scowl on Connor's face and Gregson's thunderous expression as he said, "Amy, my office now, please."

Shit! This was going to be a difficult conversation, not one she was looking forward to at all.

"Amy, I want you to enlighten me as to how this has all become such a mess. Is Wade involved or not?"

"Sir, the simple answer is I don't know. It looks like he may have been set up, but I've no idea why and I find it hard to believe anyone would go to such trouble. If that is the case, then the amount of planning and preparation is massive. On top of all that, we have videos that seem to show Wade abducting the girl and further evidence linking him to the vehicles. I simply don't know how someone could impersonate him so well if that is the case. My only thought is that possibly Kingston and Wade are working together."

"If Wade is not involved, we need to find out quickly and get him out of prison as soon as possible. We already know the man's in danger. So what's your plan?"

Clark noticed that it was to be her plan, meaning success would, no doubt, be shared, but failure would belong to her alone. She remembered the adage that 'success has many fathers whilst failure is an orphan'. How true.

"Obviously, we need to find Kingston pretty damn quick. I'll get Ben on it straight away. How involved he is in this, we don't know, but he is definitely wanted for the two rapes and God knows what else. Nickolay will be here soon and she should help clear things up for us, possibly even confirming Wade's alibi, ridiculous as that sounds."

"Okay, but time is not our friend. The press are getting very interested and so are those on the Chief Officer corridor. Last thing, Amy, those men who visited the car dealer and dealt with Jimmy Scoular so viciously, are they your mysterious friends hired by Ross?"

"Trust me, sir, I intend to find out."

Her next meeting was to be with Ben Connor, who was an extremely unhappy man. His dreams of glory were disappearing before his eyes, and he certainly didn't want to be associated with a major cock-up or, even worse, a huge miscarriage of justice. Amy Clark had no doubts whom he was blaming for the position they found themselves in.

Connor was unable to resist the temptation to remind Amy that he had warned her of the inherent dangers in working with Cooper and his team. Brushing his comments aside, she informed him that he needed to get a dedicated team onto finding Miles Kingston, with particular attention paid to his background and previous associates.

Finally, she told him that when the lady from Essex arrived, he was to be the lead interviewer along with a female detective. He was happy to do that, sensing a chance to display his own brilliance as the man who unlocked the intricacies of this major case. Not as bright as he thought, Connor didn't realise that Clark was associating him totally with whatever the outcome of the investigation was. If they failed, then he would go down with the ship as well as her. She was fed up with his sniping and refusal to take responsibility or display any initiative. It was safety first all the time with him. All she wanted was his loyalty.

Time was moving on and she was knackered; her head was spinning whilst she tried to unravel this puzzle. She freely admitted to herself that she had no time for Richard Wade; in fact, she actively disliked him as an arrogant coward who had been violent towards women. However, she already felt responsible for the assault on him in prison, so if he turned out to be innocent and incarcerated because of her, she had no idea how she might feel.

Clark had reached her office door, intending to visit her team to rally the troops as best she could, when her phone rang. Answering it without checking who was calling, she was surprised to hear a familiar voice.

"Hello, Amy, how are things?"

"What the fuck do you want, Cooper, or whatever your name is?"

"I'm calling to help if you will allow me to."

"Go on then."

"I suspect by now you may be looking for a man called Miles Kingston and if not you should be."

Exasperated beyond belief by the man's confidence and self-belief, she snapped back. "Yes, we are. It's about time you realised that we are not totally useless. We did manage before you showed up, and I'm sure we'll continue to manage when you leave."

Cooper replied with those measured tones that so annoyed Clark. "I just wanted to let you know not to waste your time looking for him. He's been dealt with."

"What do you mean dealt with?"

"I think you know. Anyway, he won't be causing any more problems."

"Cooper, you can't just ring me up to say you've murdered someone."

"I don't believe I said that, but never mind. I'm also sending you a tape recording which is no good evidentially but may be useful for intelligence purposes. On it, Frank Harris is having a telephone conversation

407

with a man called Alteo, and a second named Roel is also mentioned. I believe both those names may be Albanian. The interesting thing is he sounds as if he is reporting to his boss and asking for permission to talk to me."

"How did you get that?"

"I'm sure you can guess. Anyway, you should also know that Frank Harris financed the kidnap."

"How do you know that?"

"He told me, of course."

"What the hell have you got us all into?"

"Just trying to help."

"I suppose it was you that spoke to Charlie Newton and put Jimmy in hospital."

"What can I say? He really shouldn't have tried to search me."

"I think we should meet."

"I don't. My job is finished and you won't see me again. Goodbye and good luck, Amy."

The call ended.

Cooper had agonised long and hard as to whether he should also let Amy have the tape where Harris admitted financing the job, but had decided against it. It would have raised too many questions about why he had not given her the names of the perpetrators and the photographs Harris had given him.

Now what was she supposed to do? Did she take his word and terminate the enquiries? But how would that look and how did she explain it? The alternative was to waste a lot of time and money looking for someone she knew would never be found. He might have thought he was helping, but all he had done was to give her a massive dilemma.

All thoughts of rallying her team disappeared as she stared at the wall, trying to decide what to do. The only firm conclusion she came to was that there was no way she could tell Gregson, and especially not that backstabber Connor.

SIXTY-ONE

Devoid of make-up and dishevelled after her early-morning arrest and harrowing journey, Lesley Nickolay was still attractive enough to turn heads as she was booked into custody shortly after 5pm. She made no comment when told that her detention was being authorised on suspicion of conspiracy to kidnap and murder. Neither offence was a surprise, having already been told the same on her arrest at home. One benefit of the car journey back to Leeds was the time it afforded her to consider the position she was in and to try to work out all the angles. Going to prison was to be avoided at all costs. Having been before, and definitely not liking it, she would do whatever was needed to prevent serving more time.

The woman declined a solicitor, well aware that if things got too tricky she could ask for one at any time, which would mean the police had to stop interviewing her. The reason was simple: she wanted, needed, a deal, and, in her experience, solicitors usually just got in the way.

Donovan and his colleague began the interview at 6.30pm, after Nickolay had been given some food and a drink. By 8pm, the officers were back in the briefing room ready to tell everything they had learnt from her. The only person missing was Gregson, who had gone home. Maybe he was trying to distance himself from what he considered to be a total shambles.

Ben Connor was very pleased with himself as he summarised the interview, believing that he had scored a major success. He began by simply saying that Nickolay had admitted everything without hesitation but offered an explanation for her involvement, accompanied by an offer to give evidence in court if necessary. Briefly, her account was that she had been hired by a man in Leeds, known only to her as Miles, to keep another man out of the way for a couple of days. When asked if she would recognise Miles again, her response was that she had his photo on her phone, it having been sent by Jimmy. She admitted her working name was Natasha and that was how Kingston knew her. She was not sure if she knew his surname. When reminded of the serious nature of the offences, Nickolay told them Miles had only told her he wanted the man out of the way whilst he did a job, claiming she would have run a mile had she known what he was really up to.

She confirmed that, as instructed, she had pretended to be a reporter by the name of Sophie Young, arranging to meet the man she later learnt was Richard Wade in an Italian restaurant before taking him to an apartment where he was well entertained for two days. Everyone in the room knew exactly what was meant when talking of entertaining him. Connor seemed to relish pointing out that this covered the period from the night of the kidnap to the following Friday afternoon.

Nickolay revealed that she was paid £10,000 for her services. It was put to her that it was a lot of money, so she must have realised the planned job had to have been something serious. Her response, and this is where the tears had started, was that she'd had no choice. When Jimmy tells you to do something, you do it or pay the consequences, and, in any event, she had to pay half of the money to Frank Harris as his commission for providing her with work. She claimed to be scared to death of both men. That was basically it, other than that her offer to give evidence was conditional on her not being prosecuted.

A shaken Amy Clark looked at Connor, seeing the triumph in his eyes.

"Ben, do you believe what she is telling us?"

"I do. Occasionally, her guard slipped and it was obvious what a hard-hearted bitch she is, but I believe she's telling the truth. Just as Wade did, she told us about the Italian restaurant and the apartment, none of which she would know unless it happened. By the way, I forgot to mention that Miles dropped Wade off at the restaurant in a blue car."

"Well done, Ben. Unbelievably, it's looking like Wade's ridiculous-seeming alibi may be true, and it would also explain why Wade's phone was static in the city centre for that period of time. More links are becoming evident, including the blue car, the apartment and of course Frank Harris and Jimmy Scoular. We need to redouble our efforts to get hold of Miles Kingston as soon as possible, and, in the meantime, I'll speak to the CPS and the prison about what to do with Wade."

Connor couldn't resist putting Amy on the spot one

more time. "What are we going to do with Nickolay, ma'am?"

"Nothing for now. She is obviously involved, but it may be better to use her as a witness. That's a question for the CPS. Update the Custody Sergeant that we're still making enquiries and we would like to keep her in custody overnight. The usual reasons; serious nature of offences, likely to abscond, criminal associations. I'm sure you'll manage. Anything else?"

One of the detectives spoke up. "Are we forgetting Wade's fingerprints and DNA found at the farmhouse?"

"No, we're not, but we have wondered how careless it was to leave a glass and cigarette ends where they could be found so easily. My only thought is that if this is a put-up job, then these items are portable and could be brought from elsewhere, although I have to confess I don't know how. Obviously, we need to bear them in mind, but, in view of all the contradictory evidence, I don't believe it's enough to keep Wade locked up. We can always arrest him again if new evidence comes to light."

That ended yet another briefing, with most of the team heading home or to the pub.

Feeling guilty about exhorting her officers to redouble their efforts to find the man she already knew would never be found, Amy contacted the CPS. The conclusion being that Wade would need to be taken before magistrates in the morning for his immediate release from custody to be granted.

Next, she rang the prison duty governor.

"Hello, this is Detective Superintendent Clark. You have a man on remand by the name of Richard Wade who we now believe may be innocent. We intend to take him before magistrates in the morning, but, in the meantime, I think it may be a good idea if you were to put him in isolation for his own protection."

"Oh dear, Superintendent, I fear you are a little too late. On his release from the hospital wing, Wade was attacked again, this time with knives. He is currently in an NHS hospital under guard."

Barely believing things had become such a mess so quickly, she asked the obvious. "How is he?"

"The last report was that his condition is serious but not life-threatening. He has been slashed quite severely about the face and neck, but the worst is that he has lost an eye."

"Okay. I'll be in touch in the morning."

For the first time in many years, Amy Clark felt like crying. Much as she disliked Richard Wade, no man should have to suffer as he had, and much of it was down to her. She wouldn't have been human if she wasn't also anxious about her own career, sure there would be an investigation which would result in the need for a scapegoat. Looking back, everything was clear, and it would be easy to identify failings in the investigation headed by her. Nagging at her mind, though, was the question of who had gone to so much trouble to set Wade up so completely, willing to sacrifice an innocent girl in the process, and why. From the little background information she had gleaned on Kingston, it appeared to be way beyond his capabilities.

SIXTY-TWO

Monday was proving to be a difficult day for many people, not the least of whom was PO Collier who, when arriving for his night shift, was met by SO Quigley and a deputy governor in the locker room.

Collier's uniform colleague, whom he had known for many years, wore a grim expression as he spoke.

"Just a routine check, Brian. As you know, most of the illegal stuff in here is brought in by officers, so the use of random searches is one way of discouraging anybody from doing so."

"What if I refuse?"

"I don't understand why you would do that, but, anyway, you know that we have the power to carry out searches."

Panicking and not thinking at all clearly, Collier could only nod his consent.

Quigley put on a pair of latex gloves for the search and minutes later several packets of pills and white powder were spread on the table along with a quantity of cash, all of which had been found concealed in Collier's clothing. He was immediately informed that this was now a police matter and they would be contacted at once. The contraband was put into evidence bags.

In a desperate bid to save himself, Collier pleaded with both men. "Look, it doesn't have to come to that. I'll tell you everything I know. Please just don't get the police."

The deputy governor looked at him with an expression completely devoid of any sign of sympathy, before replying in a voice dripping with scorn.

"You know the rules, and, unfortunately for you, we follow them to the letter. The police will be here shortly and you will be expected to cooperate with them. It's the only way to help yourself."

Collier was escorted to an office to await their arrival, wondering how he would ever survive on the other side in prison.

To the prison staff, speed was of the essence as it was essential that they discovered who was the intended recipient of the smuggled goods and if they had received similar items previously before word got out about Collier's arrest. They needed to search that cell or cells as soon as they could.

By 6am, they had the information they needed.

Karl Smithson was rudely awakened only minutes later by a hastily assembled team of prison officers. His cell door was thrown back, crashing against the wall as the group ran in, quickly securing the groggy prisoner. Knowing what they were looking for, the officers soon found the mobile phone hidden in the back of his television, plus a small supply of pills in a drawer wrapped in one of his socks.

He had been in prison long enough to know that it was impossible to conceal anything from a proper search. The trick was to keep stuff out of sight and definitely not to do anything which might invite such a search. So why had the burglars, as the prisoners called them, decided to do his cell at this time of a morning?

Informed he would be seeing the governor later that day, Smithson was left to think about the possible consequences for him, complacently deciding that as these things were common in prisons there was little likelihood of being returned to a maximum security establishment. He went back to sleep.

SIXTY-THREE

When she appeared in the Magistrates' Court that Tuesday morning to explain why Richard Wade should be released from custody, pending further enquiries, Amy Clark had no idea how that day's events would prove pivotal to her investigation.

She had to listen to some scathing criticism of the police from Wade's solicitor, Ken Wilkinson, who made absolutely sure that both the magistrates and press were fully aware of the attacks on his client, making great play of the severity of his injuries. The CPS solicitor had little to say, quite content to let the police shoulder all the blame.

Somewhat despondent, Clark returned to the station at a loss as to what to do next, but that problem was quickly resolved by Connor, who was waiting eagerly for her return.

"How did court go, ma'am?"

Only half joking, she replied, "I should have let you go, it was a bit bloody."

"Well, this might cheer you up. Last night, a prison officer at Armley was arrested for smuggling stuff in for prisoners. He poured his heart out and, would you believe, he owed Frank Harris for quite hefty gambling debts."

"Well, I can't say I'm surprised, it happens all the time. What has it got to do with us?"

"The go-between who supplied the officer was a certain Miles Kingston. When the officer dealing did a PNC check, he saw that Kingston was wanted by us so came to see me."

"What was he smuggling?"

"Drugs and money, it appears. The interesting thing is that it's not that long since he was released from Armley himself."

"Go on, Ben, I can see you're dying to tell me something else."

"Yes, indeed, ma'am. The prison officer, a fella called Collier, gave up the name of the prisoner who was to get the contraband, so his cell was turned over this morning and they found a mobile phone and some drugs. The thing is, you know him very well."

"Okay, I can't wait."

"Karl Smithson."

"Oh, dear God. He's the only man who hates Richard Wade more than me, and he's not that keen on Sir John Ross either."

"I'm afraid it gets worse, ma'am. Kingston shared a cell with Smithson for eighteen months. It seems likely to me that they must have planned this between them. They certainly had plenty of time."

"It certainly looks that way, Ben. Kingston got a lot of money out of it, while Smithson got his revenge against Wade, who he blames for all his troubles. Smithson always claimed the original kidnap would never have happened if John Ross hadn't sacked him from his factory job. Total nonsense, of course, but by arranging the kidnapping of Mary Ross, he also got back at the man. I wonder if the murder was all part of the plan at the beginning."

"So what next?"

"Unless you've got any better ideas, I think we should check the phone found in the cell to see if there is anything of use on it, although I'm not hopeful. The other thing is to look at the videos and photographs of Wade. Our whole reasoning for charging Richard Wade is based on the fact that he has been caught on numerous videos carrying out different tasks during preparation and the commission of the crime. He has also been seen by a number of witnesses, mainly estate agents but including a police officer, who all identified him. That was why we so readily dismissed his alibi, which now appears to be true. Incredible though it may sound, I can only believe someone, probably Kingston, was impersonating him. What do you think?"

"I think you must be right. You can do wonders with make-up these days, I suppose, but I'm going to take some convincing. I'll get our people on it at once."

"Good. One last thing. Release Nickolay on bail. I've spoken to the CPS and we agree that there isn't enough evidence to charge her with conspiracy, and the chances of a successful prosecution if we did are slim. So unless any new evidence comes to light, we may as well use her as a witness."

"I suppose we could always ask Frank Harris."

"Funny man, but we could go and talk to Karl Smithson."

Once Connor had left her office, Clark considered the wisdom of talking to Smithson, concluding that as he had always liked to brag about how clever he was, it was possible that he would do so again. It was worth a try.

In a crime such as the kidnap of Mary Ross, establishing an offender's motive was always an important part of the prosecution case. She had never been satisfied that Wade did it for the money and was unable to think of another reason for him to do it. Now, if indeed Smithson and Kingston had conspired together to commit the crime, motives were much more clear. Money for Kingston and revenge for Smithson. Had he actually planned all this to get Wade into prison where he could arrange for him to be assaulted, or was he seriously intending that the man was convicted and given a long prison term?

Much later, the two detectives sat across a table from Smithson.

"Hello, Amy, it's always a pleasure to see you. It's been so long."

"Cut the crap, Karl. I think you know why we're here."

He laughed out loud. "If it's about the phone, it's not mine. The screws planted it."

"Will it prove you've been speaking to Miles?"

"Miles who?"

The interview continued in much the same vein, the prisoner sparring with the officers, giving evasive answers and generally having a good time. Accepting the futility of wasting any more time with him, Clark called for the prison officers to return him to his cell. As he was being led from the room, Smithson turned for a parting shot.

"Don't leave it so long next time, Amy. By the way,

have you ever noticed how, in the right light, Miles looks an awful lot like that idiot Wade?"

"So, Ben, I think he's just told us that a closer look at those videos and photos may not be such a waste of time."

Smithson could be heard laughing as he walked along the corridor.

SIXTY-FOUR

Amy Clark loved her job, and was good at it, but the current inquiry had been a total bastard and, as she privately admitted, had not been her finest hour. That was why she was a little anxious as she made her way to Gregson's office the following morning, fairly certain it wasn't for a pat on the back.

She was proved right as her boss summarised the inquiry so far, with special emphasis on the failings. He questioned why some obvious clues had been missed, suggesting it was perfectly clear that someone could have been impersonating Wade.

Looking at a stony-faced Gregson, Amy realised it was going to be worse than she thought, at the same time thinking it might be obvious now but she didn't remember him mentioning it before.

Gregson continued to outline faults, all of which were of course easy to see with all the clarity that hindsight afforded them. He never blushed as he stated that had they organised a better search, the girl may have been found sooner, ignoring the fact that the pathologist believed she was already dead when the police became involved.

In a never-ending list of faults, he was very unhappy that they hadn't verified Wade's alibi sooner, without actually telling Amy how that should have been done. Her boss was clearly not prepared to take any responsibility as he went on, suggesting that the money in the safe deposit box and the letter at Wade's home was clearly a set-up, which should have been obvious.

Knowing full well how this worked, Amy remained silent, waiting for him to reach his most serious criticism and, judging by what had been said so far, it was sure to be something she wouldn't like.

"Amy, I think it's obvious that this inquiry has not gone as well as we might have hoped, and, as the person in command, you must bear the responsibility for that. You may be able to explain those failings, but there is no way I can accept your collusion with that man Cooper."

"Well, sir, he had information and we needed it, so I felt it best to talk to him. Don't forget he had a head start on us and did save us some time by sharing with us."

"Did he share everything?"

"How can I answer that with any certainty? Probably not, I would think."

"You should know that DI Connor has been to see me, expressing his concerns about working with this man. He also tells me that he warned you of the obvious dangers in doing so. Is that correct?"

"I think it's fair to say he was uncomfortable. However, I should remind you that you were also aware of my meetings with Cooper."

Totally ignoring her last comment, the hammer blow fell. "I've got to say that your actions may well have compromised this investigation and led to criticism of the force. There is sure to be an investigation. With that in mind, I have been instructed to remove you from leadership of the investigation."

"I see, sir, and who will take over?"

"Acting Detective Chief Inspector Connor."

So the disloyal, scheming bastard had got his way. He would be planning to take the credit for a successful conclusion to the case with most of the facts already established, no doubt guaranteeing his promotion. Knowing that Connor would ultimately fail to find their main suspect, Miles Kingston, gave her a massive, if uncomfortable, feeling of satisfaction, making her grateful for Cooper's final contact.

If he noticed her smirk, Gregson chose to ignore it.

"So what happens to me?"

"Two choices. Either you can retire, but you are perhaps a little young for that, or a uniform post in the Personnel Branch. I'm afraid you've seriously blotted your copybook, Amy. I did my best for you, but the Chief Constable is adamant, I'm afraid."

With heavy sarcasm, she replied, "Oh, I'm sure you did. I expect you will be staying in your present position."

Not waiting for an answer, she left his office, slamming the door behind her. Ultimately, Amy had no choice but to take the job if she wanted to continue working for a few more years, enabling her to retire on a full pension. She tried to tell herself that working office hours, with weekends off, would be a welcome relief from the long and stressful hours she had worked for years in CID.

So Gregson was right; it had turned into a total shitshow and she was buried so deep in effluent that she would be lucky if she ever saw sunlight again.

Back in her office, Amy rang Dai Williams at TARIAN, using her personal mobile phone. Having previously listened to the tape Cooper sent her, she passed on the information it contained relating to the involvement of Frank Harris and the possible Albanian connection. She confirmed that it could not be verified but was believed to be from a trusted source who would not be prepared to be a witness. Nevertheless, she hoped it would be useful intelligence for their forthcoming operations.

Superintendent Clark's final act before leaving the office was to contact the Governor of Armley Prison, whom she quickly updated on their suspicions about the conspiracy between Smithson and Kingston. She confirmed that he was unlikely to be charged with any offences in connection with the kidnap and murder at this stage but emphasised she was convinced of his guilt.

Considering the offences he had committed whilst in Armley, the Governor, armed with this new information, had no hesitation in contacting the Home Office. That night, a kicking and screaming Smithson was taken by prison van to a maximum security prison. It did not help his mood when one of the guards told him that the Isle of Wight was lovely at that time of year.

It would seem lots of people were on the move, whether they wanted it or not.

Some months later, it would be with some satisfaction

that, in her role as Head of Personnel, she was the officer who signed off on Ben Connor's transfer to a small station as a uniformed Inspector. It appeared she was not the only one who would get no further promotion.

SIXTY-FIVE

Several weeks later, Lily Croft met with Brenda Thomas in the safe house she had been living in since her discharge from the clinic. This calm, confident woman was hardly recognisable as the crushed and beaten one whom she had first met when arresting her at the DVLA.

The purpose of the visit was to provide updates on the criminal proceedings so far. Brenda had already been informed that the two doctors, Parker and Reynolds, had both been charged with illegally supplying controlled drugs and had received suspended sentences when they appeared at court. However, she was now able to tell the woman that both men had received a much greater punishment by being permanently struck off the medical register by the General Medical Council, meaning they would never be allowed to practise medicine in the United Kingdom again. So the men who should have protected her had received their just desserts for so callously using Brenda to satisfy their own sexual needs and, when tired of her, delivering her into the hands of drug dealers and worse.

Less good news was that the man who had raped and humiliated her in the hotel room had still not been apprehended despite having been identified as Miles Kingston from DNA recovered on the tissue she saved.

Lily was able to finish by telling her that Marco and the street dealer had also been arrested, with their organisations being broken up and both men receiving custodial sentences.

Brenda was very happy with the outcome, believing that Kingston would take his turn before the courts soon enough. She would not previously have considered herself a vengeful woman, but Brenda couldn't conceal her delight when told that Jimmy had met someone more ruthless than himself and was completely incapacitated. Served the evil bully right.

Brenda questioned when the enquiries into the fraudulent licences would be concluded, meaning she could return to something resembling a normal life. She was told soon but was reminded that they were dealing with large organised crime groups who would look to exact retribution on her once she had given evidence in court. She would not be able to remain in Swansea and would need to be moved to a new location with, ironically in view of what the case involved, a new identity.

Believing that she was largely responsible for all the problems she had brought upon herself, Brenda was more than willing to appear as a witness in court. She saw it as her route to redemption.

SIXTY-SIX

The brothers Roel and Alteo were not educated men but they were highly organised, cunning, hardworking and, most of all, totally ruthless. They would not allow anyone or anything to obstruct what they saw as their business. They may have considered themselves as businessmen, but anyone who knew of their existence would have viewed them as the leaders of a powerful international organised crime group.

Having been the major beneficiaries of Brenda's illegal sideline at the DVLA, the brothers were not happy when she disappeared and, more to the point, with the end of the fraudulent licence supply line. Having brought many of their countrymen and women into the country illegally, the driving licences helped provide them with false identities. This had allowed them to expand their operations in drugs, prostitution and people trafficking, generating huge amounts of money which they often used to bribe local officials. With the assistance of those people, they were able to start buying property, including hotels. They thought it immensely funny that the UK Government was paying them money to house asylum claimants who had already paid the brothers to bring them across the Channel to England.

The two men were above all pragmatists. Their sources, of which there were many, had been unable to tell them what had happened to Brenda, some believing that she had simply run away. Roel, still in Albania, decided that they could not take the risk that the police had her.

In consultation with Alteo, who was running the UK business, he decided they must close down as much of their operation as they could, returning some of their senior staff to Albania, beyond the reach of the British police. It was doubtful they knew their identities, but, in any event, it was better to play safe. Some smaller fry were left to keep things running, having been assured they would be taken care of should they be arrested and imprisoned or deported.

Their view was that it was simply business and common sense. If they took a chance that nothing would happen, and it did, their operations could be set back years. Why take the risk? They expected to be back in full operation within six to twelve months, even sooner if the police remained ignorant of the majority of their many businesses, both the seemingly legitimate and the outright illegal.

The properties were all protected by having British men and women fronting them, so the revenue stream would continue, even if it was temporarily reduced.

After months of intelligence-gathering work, TARIAN, in conjunction with a number of other forces and anti-crime groups, launched Operation Dingo, their nationwide assault on criminal gangs. They were elated with the successful outcomes as numerous arrests were made – including over forty Albanian illegal immigrants – several major drug rings in cities across the UK were shut down and a number of trafficked women were saved from the hell of enforced prostitution. The only slightly odd thing was that all those who were charged with offences pleaded guilty at the earliest opportunity. Most received moderate sentences and, on completion or partway through the sentence, were deported.

So Brenda Thomas was not required to give evidence in court; however, the information she had given was instrumental in ensuring the police had managed to strike some blows against organised crime, if not quite as damaging as they believed it to be. Brenda thoroughly deserved her indemnity from prosecution and a chance at a happy life.

Roel watched the press conferences with amusement as any number of senior police officers and politicians queued up to give them, trumpeting the success of the police operations and making exaggerated claims of the damage done to organised crime. Within a month, the excitement had died down and his people started to return to the UK, with another source of false ID's already established at the Passport Office. This was how business worked, recognising problems and minimising the damage to your organisation by taking sensible precautions. In fact, the brothers anticipated, no, demanded, an increase in productivity as staff returned from their enforced holidays at their expense.

Unfortunately for Harris, the clear connection to

Yorkshire from the number of fraudulent licences with addresses in the area together with Brenda's identification of Jimmy ensured that his West Yorkshire operation was particularly hard hit. Jimmy had been identified as the source of the illegal drugs by both doctors, although not by Marco and the other dealer. They knew better. However, although everyone knew who Jimmy worked for, there was insufficient evidence to charge Harris with any offences.

The information from Cooper had been a boost to the investigation, confirming they were looking in the right direction, particularly in terms of the foreign nationals. At least they had the first names of the men suspected to be running the whole network. Enquiries would continue.

Unfortunately, the law of unintended consequences came into play. Not all the fraudulent licences had been supplied to Albanians, the greater number having been used by British criminal gangs. Totally unprepared, not being party to the knowledge that Roel and Alteo had, they were hit very hard by the police, who virtually destroyed some of their organisations, leaving many gaps in the market ready for exploitation. Nature abhors a vacuum of any sort and the brothers were quick to step in, taking over the drugs operations immediately, with everything else soon to follow.

So the massive blow the police had dealt to organised crime across the country, which they considered a great success, had unwittingly helped to create a larger, more fearsome and dangerous organised crime group.

Now in her new role, Amy Clark, of course, had no

official involvement in Operation Dingo, watching from afar, applauding its apparent success.

Some good had come from it all, she hoped. The cooperation between her team and the TARIAN officers had helped in clearing up several crimes. They knew that Miles Kingston had kidnapped and murdered Mary Ross with the assistance of Karl Smithson. The killer was still listed as wanted, but she knew he would never be arrested, not something she could share with her colleagues. Although it went against all her beliefs, Amy was not sorry that he had been 'dealt with', as Cooper put it. Despite everything, she had liked him and wondered what wrong he was attempting to right at the moment.

So, in her mind, they had reached a satisfactory conclusion clearing the rape of Jean Cook and the woman in Wales that she only knew as Bravo. She just wished they could have charged Smithson with something, but, despite everyone being convinced that he was involved, there was simply not enough evidence to have a realistic chance of convicting him. At least he was back in maximum security with all the restrictions that entailed.

Clark was glad that she had quietly been to see Jean Cook in an unofficial capacity. Whilst talking to her in a pub, she made it very clear to the woman that she need not fear the return of Miles Kingston. Jean was an intelligent woman, picking up quickly on Amy's references to his disappearance and the information she had gleaned from a reliable source that he would never be seen again. The relief she saw on her face was worth the risk Clark had taken.

Her only regret was that she was unable to give the

same information to Witness Bravo, who had suffered so horribly at Kingston's hands in Wales. How could she? She didn't know her name. Telling the TARIAN officers was not an option. She couldn't risk exposing herself by revealing her knowledge of a probable murder, particularly as she knew who was responsible.

Maybe she could tell Dai Williams at some stage in the future, confident that he would take a more pragmatic view. Justice was justice, after all, no matter what form it took. Still, it would be a risk, probably not one worth taking. Something to think about.

SIXTY-SEVEN

Frank Harris really didn't like driving, much preferring to relax in the back seat whilst someone else chauffeured him about. That had been one of the unfortunate Jimmy's many jobs, and, in the weeks since he was injured, Harris had not yet found a replacement. Not for one minute did it occur to him to wonder how his former minder was.

He had been totally preoccupied dealing with the fallout from the massive police operation, which had resulted in most of his activities being so badly disrupted that they were either temporarily closed down or, in some cases, permanently. He was fed up with the pressure from the Albanian thugs and their constant attempts to insert their men into what he saw as his personal fiefdom. Of course, he knew that wasn't true, fervently wishing he had never got involved with the foreign madmen.

Nearing his home outside of Leeds, he was surprised to see a temporary traffic light that hadn't been there in the morning. What the hell were they digging up now? As usual, there was no sign of anyone actually doing any

436

work. Forced to stop as, just his luck, the light changed to red as he approached it.

Cursing as he drummed his fingers impatiently on the steering wheel, Frank Harris was surprised to see a large motorcycle pull alongside him. He took little notice, convinced they were just trying to steal a march on him by racing ahead once the light changed to green. He wasn't the least bit bothered as he stared fixedly at the traffic light, willing it to change so he could get away from the infernal racket of the bike engine.

If he had been paying more attention, he may have seen the motorcycle pillion passenger pull a small automatic machine pistol from inside his jacket and point it at Frank's car window.

Harris never heard the weapon being fired or felt the bullets that killed him instantly. The stolen motorcycle roared off, being found later in a ditch several miles down the road along with the discarded weapon and a remote control to operate the traffic light. The presumption being that the two men had been picked up by car and driven rapidly from the area and, with their job done, probably from the country.

It would later be discovered that a total of ten shots had been fired, all of which had hit him, with four entering his head.

Roel, if he had thought about it, would have realised that his business was like any other legitimate one, or even the police for that matter. There was the Chief at the top and, beneath them, a pyramid of middle managers who ran operations on a day-to-day basis, and, just like the police, if anything went wrong, someone had to pay a price. Of course, a replacement was needed as well.

In the case of the police, Amy Clark was the one to pay that price, although she was finding the regular hours and stress-free job not nearly as bad as she had thought it would be. The beneficiary of her demise, although not for long, had been Ben Donovan.

Obviously, in Roel's judgement, Harris was the one to be sacrificed and, unfortunately for him, the Albanians did not deal in transfers, preferring more permanent solutions. The added benefit being that other employees received a clear signal that failure would not be tolerated and became aware of the consequences for them should it happen. The one promoted, to the surprise of many, was Charlie Newton. Unknown to Harris, or anyone else, Newton had always been Roel and Alteo's man, reporting to them regularly. However, he would be given some Albanian assistants to make sure there were no further slip-ups.

One could only wonder why Newton hadn't told the Albanians about Cooper and his men, perhaps not wanting to reveal how easily they had dealt with him. Or, more intriguingly, had the two brothers known all along and been happy to let things take their course, hoping others would oust Frank Harris for them? Even they couldn't have foreseen the true scale of the events which would unfold.

Business was business and a necessary skill was to take advantage of opportunities when they presented themselves, which, with total ruthlessness, Roel and Alteo certainly had. The new kids on the block had taken charge.